A MAP OF THE EDGE

A MAP OF THE EDGE

THE ISAAK COLLECTION

DAVID T. ISAAK

A Map of the Edge

Copyright© 2023 David T. Isaak and Pamela L. Blake
All rights reserved

The characters and events portrayed in this book are fictitious. Any similarity to real persons, living or dead, is coincidental and not intended by the author.

No part of this book may be reproduced, or stored in a retrieval system, or transmitted in any form or by any means, electronic, mechanical, photocopying, recording, or otherwise, without the express written permission of the publisher and copyright owner. Brief quotations may be used for reviews or for articles or promotions.

Published by Utamatzi Inc.
Huntington Beach, CA 92646
www.utamatzi.com

Professionally edited by Shavonne Clarke
Cover design and art by Jeff Brown Graphics

ISBN 978-1-958840-04-7 (Hardback)
ISBN 978-1-958840-05-4 (Paperback)
ISBN 978-1-958840-06-1 (Electronic)
ISBN 978-1-958840-07-8 (Audio)

*Dedicated to David's dear, life-long friend,
Peter, and the love of Peter's life, Virginia, now
a dear friend as well*

The road of excess leads to the palace of wisdom.

—William Blake

The Marriage of Heaven and Hell

INTRODUCTION TO THE ISAAK COLLECTION

My husband, David Isaak, and I first met in January of 1969, in ninth grade world history class. When I saw him walk into class, I immediately decided we needed to be the best of friends. He had similar feelings. Our first date was to an Iron Butterfly concert in February of that same year.

David and I were together for over fifty years, ever since that first concert, and I thought we'd have lots more time together. That was not to be. He was only sixty-seven when he died—he turned sixty-seven laying in a hospital bed after a massive stroke. He died three weeks later, and did not come home to me. However, he left behind a treasure: five glorious novels. I won't judge you if you feel like I may be biased. I am. His novels *are* great, though. Here is what the editor of David's novels, and fellow author, Shavonne Clarke, says about the second of the novels, **A Map of the Edge**:

> "*A Map of the Edge* is an ornate, technicolor gem of a novel. Isaak navigates the terrain of adolescence and trauma amidst a dreamscape of 1970s music and sex and drugs that feels both immediate and wistful.

The emotional landscape of this novel—as with all great stories—becomes more textured in the months and years after reading. Layers become clearer, and new ones appear. This feels right; there is a sense of this story existing in a liminal space that we can only see in retrospect: right on the edge of things, where our growth into adulthood is perilous and headlong and vivid beyond imagination."

—Shavonne Clarke, editor of *The Isaak Collection*

My mission in life now is to ensure that this literary treasure is David's legacy. We did not have children, but David encapsulated some of his fine mind in the form of these thought-provoking, amusing, diverse, passionate stories.

These five books form **The Isaak Collection**. In addition to the penetrating and sometimes dark coming-of-age story, ***A Map of the Edge***, the collection includes: ***Tomorrowville*** (dystopian future-fiction), ***Things Unseen*** (a murder mystery with metaphysical underpinnings), ***Earthly Vessels*** (magical realism, with the forces of light and dark battling on Earth), and ***Smite the Waters*** (a political thriller with a twist).

Here, in David's writing, you can hear the voice of a man who is now silent, but whose words will live on—reaching across time. Words that speak loudly of David's passions, of his sense of social justice, and of his appreciation for other humans and the complex relationships we have with one another. Please join him—and me—as he continues his journey.

Thank you.

David's wife, Pamela Blake
Huntington Beach, CA
July 2022

1 | CITRUS TREES IN SERRIED RANKS

I remember her at the breakfast table on that last morning, spooning out our scrambled eggs, the left side of her face bruised from jaw to ear. If the mark hadn't been so obvious, maybe everything would have been different—but how could she go to the supermarket with a purpling palm-print for everyone to see?

Of course, it wasn't the first time Dad had hit Mom, but in the see-no-evil, hear-no-evil world of Southern California in the mid-sixties, they'd always kept it hidden: mostly behind the bedroom door, and always below the neck. Everyone, even she, could pretend nothing had happened; just no swimsuits or sundresses for a while.

Perhaps she would have stayed if I'd done something, or at least tried to do something. Sure, I was only eleven, but I knew he was hurting her, and I felt gutless and guilty that morning as I sat at the silent breakfast table, my nose in a book.

So at some level it felt like justice when she vanished, taking my brother Michael, aged six, and my baby sister Becky, but leaving me behind with Dad.

It was years before I understood the real reason I was abandoned, though it was literally staring me in the face.

"He's acting out," the school counselor said about my behavior in the months after Mom left. "He's just expressing frustration at his sense of abandonment."

"This misbehavior—the shoplifting, the fights, the truancy, the vandalism—these are all attempts to seek punishment," the County psychologist said two years later, addressing a group of school administrators as though I wasn't in the room. "Just as in a divorce, the child blames himself for the loss of a parent. Rick blames himself for his mother leaving the family."

She was wrong. I didn't blame myself, I blamed Dad.

By 1969, when I turned fifteen, the two of us had discarded any pretense of trying to get along. I'd let my hair grow long, despite Dad's constant threats to cut it by force, but even Samson-haired and stoned most of the time, I was far from being a hippie. No, my idols were the local Chicano street punks.

We lived in Redlands, California, but Dad's egg ranch had been over in Highland…until it went bankrupt. His new job might have been the only thing that saved us from murdering each other. A former competitor, Andrews Egg Ranches, hired him on to run their swing shift up in Yucaipa, 5 p.m. to midnight, supervising the cleanup crews and the packing houses. As soon as the plant closed, he'd speed to the bar to get in an hour and forty minutes of drinking before they closed at 2 a.m. At most, our schedules only overlapped for an hour or two a day; at best, we didn't see each other at all.

I'd fool around after school—on the days when I bothered to go there at all—until he left for work around four in the afternoon. If the truck was still in the driveway, I'd take a walk or hide in a neighboring yard until it was gone.

A few days after my fifteenth birthday, it happened.

I waited next door in the Turners' yard, shielded by their camellias, and watched his Ford pickup back out of the drive and angle hard into the road. As always, he revved the engine in neutral between shifting from reverse to first.

After the truck disappeared down the street I went into the house and took a shower. I dried off, wrapped the towel around my waist, and stepped into the hallway.

I didn't see him standing there until he grabbed me by the hair from my left side. He pulled so hard I nearly fell over.

As I fought to keep my balance, he jammed a hand up close to my scalp and I heard, and felt, the unique scrinching sound of hair being cut.

I pushed hard at his chest and he staggered back. He stood there, breathing hard, kitchen shears in one hand and a footlong hank of damp hair in the other.

"You *fucker*," I said, more amazed than angry.

"Come on," he said, as if we were going somewhere. He stepped toward me.

I ran for my bedroom, stumbling as the towel on my waist fell around my ankles. I slammed the door behind me so hard it bounced back open, hit the wall, and nearly shut itself again. My fingers patted the left side of my head: a big patch of damp stubble. "Fuck!" I brought my hand away, and it was covered with blood. "*You sonofabitch!*" I shouted, so loud my voice cracked.

He pushed open the door with the toe of his workboot. "Hair's comin' off. Today."

It had been years since I'd played baseball, but my Louisville Slugger still leaned in the corner, and I picked it up, smearing the handle red. "I'll kill you," I said, and was surprised to find I was crying.

He took a step into the room. "Put it down." Another step. "We can do it like this, or you can put on some clothes and we can go to a barbershop. Your choice."

My voice trembled. "Get out of here." The tears on my face began to drop onto my chest and roll down, and I remembered I was naked.

"It's *my* house, and I'm your father. Now come on." One more step into the room.

"You're not my father," I said, and hefted the bat over my shoulder. "You're some kinda goddamn freak."

He stopped and exhaled through his nose, a controlled little sound, as if a doctor had probed a tender spot. "Oh," he said, "I'm your father, all right." He almost smiled. "In fact, you're my only son."

I stared.

He looked down at the shears in his hand as if they were some alien artifact, then looked up at me again. "Why do you think she left you here?"

I swallowed, tried to speak, and had to swallow again. "Not true..." I said.

"Oh, it's true." His mouth smiled now, a joyless upturning of the lips. He opened his mouth to say something more, and then simply shrugged.

He turned and shambled from the room. From the hallway his retreating voice said, "Take a long look in the mirror, kid. It's you and me."

I let the bat fall to the floor to join what he'd dropped there: kitchen shears and a handful of my hair.

After his truck drove away I stumbled to the bathroom. My scalp wound was only a nick, but the bloodflow was spectacular. It took forever to stanch the bleeding.

The bright-pink Band-Aid—how can they call that color *flesh*?—sat at the center of a three-inch circle of short, uneven hair, high on the left side of my head. I tried tossing strands of my remaining hair over the naked spot, but my hair was still damp, and there was no way to assess the damage until it dried.

Finally, reluctantly, I studied myself in the mirror. Recalled Mike's face, Becky's fat little baby face. I had a despairing intuition that my old man had been telling the truth.

How long had he known?

The bathroom counter and sink were streaked with blood, crimson marbling the Harvest Gold tiles and the white of the porcelain. Fuck him, he could clean it up himself.

After I pulled on jeans and a tee-shirt I grabbed a book and sat out on the front steps. Up and down the block the first cars were arriving home from work. It felt good to be outside of the goddamn single-family stucco jail; plus, I didn't want to be trapped in there if he decided to ditch work and come back for round two.

I looked down the street to the end of our block of little cottages, to where the orange groves started up, and I had a vision of myself as from above, there on the front steps, surrounded by a sea of oranges.

Redlands, I'm told, was once a piece of paradise. The Redlands Colony was founded by eastern real estate developers in the 1890s, and promoted as God's country, a place in the sun where gentleman farmers could buy a hundred acres, hire an overseer, and devote their days to the arts and literature.

The setting was spectacular. Sixty miles inland from the farming communities of Los Angeles, Redlands sat on a high, red-dirt plateau. The San Bernardino Mountains soared up in a giant ridge to the north, ten to eleven thousand feet high, and then, by some freak of geology, wrapped themselves southward to form embracing arms. Clear, clean air—from the mountains you could see Catalina—and three-hundred-forty days of sunshine a year.

Cinderella in sackcloth, waiting for the night of the ball.

The fairy godmother was oranges.

Hard now to understand that oranges in America once bespoke luxury and wealth. Today every Safeway or Kroger has a bin heaped high with them, any time of year. Oranges are sold by the pound and the bag, marketed like potatoes.

Once an orange was something you got at Christmas if you'd been very, very good.

Each of the groves had its gingerbread Victorian mansion, the curlicued porches open to the breeze like astonished mouths, shocked to find themselves flanked by palms.

By the time I was born, in the 1950s, Redlands had passed through the Norma Jean phase, had exhausted the Marilyn period, and was strictly Sunset Boulevard: faded beauty with delusions of grandeur. Stately Victorians stood here and there, but my side of town was filled with squat bungalows and cottages. Our house sat on the last street where all the faces were white. On the next street over, a third of the faces were dark and Hispanic, and by the time you'd moved three blocks that direction—where most of my friends lived—everyone was "Mexican." Some of the Hispanic families were pure Spaniards who'd been there since the days of Rancho Lugonia; most of the rest had been in California for generations. As my father pointed out with disdain, many of them *couldn't even speak Mexican.*

Half of the original groves were gone, but the city was still hemmed in by miles of orange trees, Navels for eating, Valencias for juicing. Unfenced and unguarded—who'd bother to steal oranges?—the groves were where we grew up, where we played army, where we had our first cigarettes, our first booze, our first everythings.

A mature orange tree is shaped like an igloo, a dome of glossy green stretched over a hollow. Push through the curtain of leaves and you're hidden in a private space about eight feet in diameter. Seen from the crow's nest of one of the windmachines—the tower-mounted propellers that kept frost from settling during the rare winter freeze—the groves were a massive army encampment, rows of shiny tents settled in for a long siege against the mountains.

※

I needed to talk to someone, but not to any of my friends. In my crowd, part of being a man, which I urgently wanted to be, meant playing tough about things connected to your parents. If your dad beat the hell out of you, it was okay to explain the bruises, dismissively; but it wasn't okay to let your friends know that your parents had made you change your hair or your dress or your behavior, and the worst thing of all was to let on that your parents had made you cry.

Growing up, Ronny Turner next door had been one of my best friends. We'd gone in different directions, the way kids do around puberty, but Mrs. Turner still liked me. After Mom left, Mrs. Turner made a point of talking to me whenever she got the chance, listening patiently to my invective about Dad.

Halfway across the Turners' lawn I hesitated, remembering Amanda. Amanda Turner was seventeen, one of my hopeless wet dreams, utterly beyond reach. But even if I knew there was no chance, not in this lifetime, I wasn't sure I was willing to let her see me like this, red-eyed from crying and with a spazzy gap in my hair.

The need for sympathy won out. I knocked on the door. Nothing. I rang the doorbell, waited, then hammered with my fist. In the backyard their terrier, Rookie, started up a ruckus, but no sounds came from inside.

I scuffed my way back to our steps, sat down, and opened up the copy of *No Exit* I'd left there. Maybe because it was a play rather than a novel I couldn't get lost in it.

It was time for a little artificial courage. I had a good private supply of booze. When Dad got home from the bars around 3 a.m., he'd pull out a bottle and keep drinking. Whether he managed to stumble off to bed or simply passed out on the couch made no difference—he'd never remember how much of the bottle was left when he stopped for the night. I was free to drain off the bulk of what remained, sometimes adding back a little water to disguise the extent of my thievery. In the crawlspace beneath the house I assembled a pretty respectable liquor cabinet.

Screw him, though. I went back into our house, opened one of Dad's bottles of Jim Beam straight out of the freezer, and poured myself an ultra-strong whiskey and Coke in a massive souvenir beer stein. I left the bottle on the kitchen counter, uncapped, and went back out to the front steps.

A third of the way through the drink, I finally assimilated what had just happened. For four years I'd been asking why Mom left me behind. Well, now I knew: because, unlike my siblings, I was my father's child. I almost laughed. The way I felt about him, how could I blame her? I'd leave me too.

Even if I found her, she probably wouldn't want me. It didn't matter. I'd just split—run away to the Bay Area, or a commune in Oregon. I was tall for my age, and most people thought I was older than fifteen…

Up the street, a real motorhead car came around the corner, a blue Duster with red racing stripes, the rear jacked up like a stinkbug's butt over double-wide smoothie tires. The *Sgt. Pepper's* part of me grimaced as it *blum-blummed* its way in my direction, but the street-punk part of me stirred with envy.

It stopped in the middle of the street in front of the Turners' place. I recognized the driver, Jeff Halloran, the older brother of my childhood pal Steve. His hands were wrapped around one of those tiny rubberized steering wheels the drag-racers all used. His knuckles clenched tight as he said something to a passenger hidden behind the glare on the windshield.

The passenger door burst open, and Stacy Slater rolled out of the car and snatched her purse off the seat. "*Don't, and won't!*" she said, and slammed the door. She stomped around the front of the car and over toward the Turners' yard, her miniskirted legs wobbly on high platform shoes. Before she got to the curb, she changed her mind, walked back, and, with great deliberation, kicked the car. She paused for effect, hands on hips, and then headed back toward the sidewalk.

The driver's-side door flung wide and Jeff jumped out. "Hey!" he said. He stood there, scanning the sides of his car for any damage, and then carefully shut the door partway so he could check it, too. Once he'd decided the car was okay—cork soles on the platforms, I suppose—he spoke to Stacy's receding form. "*Stace…*" His voice was surprisingly whiny for a well-known tough.

She was already on the Turners' porch, and answered with an upraised middle finger, not bothering to look back.

Jeff looked from her to his car and back to her, and then gave me a classic *what-the-fuck-you-looking-at* glare until I dropped my gaze. He got back in, revved the engine to wailing-high RPMs, the whole car trembling with aborted forward motion, and then squealed off, leaving rubber on the street and burnt tire drifting in the air.

Far down the block I heard an angry resident yell as the car sped by, and then a faint screech of tires as it rounded a distant corner.

Stacy banged on the Turners' door once more, and then came down their steps holding her bag of a purse by its throat, the shoulder strap dangling near the ground.

I knew Stacy well, though I doubted she knew me. Too old for me, seventeen, gorgeous in a way that hurt, a Size 5 body in a Size 4 epidermis, so that she seemed ready to split right out of her skin. Long, straight black hair down to her butt, too much Swinging London makeup, and the trendiest of trendy clothes.

"They're not home," I called to her, though one might suspect she had already worked this out.

She looked over, noticing me for the first time. "Huh?" she asked, squinting.

"They're gone. I was over there before."

She walked across their lawn. "You know where Amanda is?" she asked from our driveway.

"Nah. I was looking for them all maybe twenty minutes ago." Well, I was looking for *Mom* Turner, but I wasn't under oath.

She came over to the steps. Her mascara had smeared into dark downpointing arrowheads, broken into little channels where the tears had run heaviest. "Do I know you?"

"Umm...maybe."

"Sure. You're that kid that used to hang out with Stevie... Dick Leibnitz, right?"

"Rick." I held up the beer stein. "Want a drink?"

"Yeah, that's right, *Rick*." She reached for the mug, took a swallow, and then blinked as the alcohol content announced itself. "Whoa." She sat down on my right and waggled her hips back, trying to tug down her skirt without using her hands. She dropped her purse and finished the job with her free hand, just covering the crotch of her daiquiri-ice panties. She took another drink, this one a long gulp. "You got bigger."

"Yeah."

"You hang out with Stevie anymore?"

"Not really."

"Good. He's a shit. And his big brother is an even bigger shit."

I listened as she listed Jeff's deep faults and character flaws, nodded thoughtfully in the right places while I studied her smooth legs, made sympathetic sounds when she told me how evil, how Machiavellian Jeff could be, and, whenever she paused in her tirade, passed her the whiskey and Coke for another drink. When I could, in moments when

I was brave enough, I stole glances at her face. Her ruined mascara was endearing, a point of vulnerability that made it seem like we might be from the same planet.

I touched the left side of my head. Now that my hair was dry, it seemed to cover the Band-Aid. We were nearing the bottom of the stein when she said, "You're nice. You're not like other boys, you actually *listen*... Hey, you wanta smoke a joint?"

I'd been feeling pretty proud just to be sitting next to her. Having her ask if I'd get loaded with her left me speechless.

Misunderstanding my silence, she said, "It's not just some ditchweed horseshit, I mean, it's really far out. Been soaked in hashoil."

"Sure. I mean, yeah, great."

She tilted her head back at the door to the house. "Inside?" My eyes widened, and she said, "Out back?"

I sighed. "Maybe. But my dad is Narc of the Century. If he came home..."

"I'm hep. You gotta car?"

I shook my head, trying to be cool despite the fact that, in SoCal terms, she'd just asked, *You gotta penis?* and forced me to admit, *Nope, ain't got one.*

"Huh." She tilted her head toward the end of the street, and I reflected on how sophisticated it was to gesture with an inflection of the head, as if you couldn't be bothered to lift an arm. "Grove, then." She paused. "You got a bottle of Coke or something?" I nodded. "Bring it along."

Halfway up the block she paused and clung to my arm for balance while she pulled off her shoes. She stuffed them into her big shoulderbag, then rolled the bottoms of her feet on the sidewalk and sighed with pleasure. "Fucking giant shoes," she said. "We only wear them for you, you know."

"For me?" I asked. "But I don't care."

"I meant *guys*," she said, and pushed my shoulder for emphasis. "I didn't mean *you*."

I wasn't sure how to take that, but I wanted it to be a compliment, so I decided it was.

Whatever she might think, boys in general didn't care about fashion and would just as soon that girls went naked 'round the clock. X-ray vision, totally wasted on that twit Clark Kent, must be the commonest adolescent male fantasy; well, that, and being the last guy on earth following some vague cataclysm that thankfully spared certain girls. But when I thought about it, I was pretty sure Stacy didn't need to hear any of this.

After we crossed Judson Street and entered the grove she stopped to wiggle her toes in the crumbly red dirt, and then plowed ahead like a real Redlands Girl.

The blossoms had long since fallen and the year's oranges were still green baseballs on the trees, but the scent of citrus was strong in the air. Stacy reached back for my hand and led me on through a half-dozen rows until she spotted a tree she liked.

She parted the branches and, ducking her head, led me inside.

It must have been nearing six o'clock—still sunset outside, but dim and shadowed beneath the dome of the tree. Hard dried leaves crackled underfoot, releasing pungent oils that rose up to tickle our nostrils.

"Shit," she said, "how'm I going to sit down on this stuff in a miniskirt?" She giggled. "Haven't done this in a while."

I pulled my tee-shirt over my head and spread it on the ground. "Here."

I sensed her gaze on my face, but my eyes still hadn't adjusted so her expression was lost in the darkness. She sat down on the shirt, then grasped my hand and pulled me down beside her. "See?" She patted the shirt beneath her. "You *aren't* like other boys, are you?"

I felt exposed, my torso naked to the evening. My skin anticipated insects crawling across it, but I forgot about all that after she torched up the first joint.

The brightness of the lighter flame burned itself into my retinas, and smaller versions of its sunburst continued to crawl across my vision as we smoked, appearing on the right and drifting to the far left where they dashed around the back of my skull to enter from the right again, like actors in some slapstick play.

We didn't talk much at first, and by the end of the second joint I was so stoned I wasn't even sure I could. Marijuana for me is usually soporific, but this stuff was psychedelic. Psychedelic and aphrodisiac, as if I needed one; my hard cock was painfully tangled in my underwear, but I didn't dare try to adjust myself.

Stacy could still talk, though, and did, and the tones of her voice from the shadows beside me were like fingers stroking up and down my spine. She talked about Jeff and about other guys she had known and about how nobody cared about her, not really about *her*, and…

My mind drifted, and then I heard her saying, "But, I liked it, riding around in a car that everybody looked at, and now what am I going to do?—I mean, girls who get their own cars and cherry them out, that's so *pathetic*, and…"

She trailed off and stopped. "God," she said, "listen to me. You must think *I'm* pathetic. Cars. What kind of *car* my boyfriend drives. What kind of fucking car *I* drive."

I heard her breathing shorten and I bit my lip. I'd been so happy, just listening to her go on and on, and now because of something I'd failed to say, God knows what, she was going off the rails.

"I'm sorry," she said, her voice catching a little. "Fuck, you sit here and listen to me and all this shit, you must think I'm so fucking *shallow*, I *am* so fucking shallow, my *life* is so fucking shallow, and…"

No, I wanted to say, being with you is like a walk in Eden, but instead I reached for her in the darkness and wrapped my arms around her shoulders and she crumpled up beside me and she was crying, and something cut loose inside me, my happiness since she'd sat down beside me and my sadness at the fact that it couldn't last, that everything about my life was shit except for this single moment, that this afternoon was all I could really ever hope for, and I felt tears running down my cheeks and I turned away so she wouldn't know and tried to keep my breathing steady but kept my arms around her as she sobbed.

And at last she sat up a little and I felt her fingers on my jaw. I rolled my head farther away but her hand touched my cheek, and, astonished, she whispered, "*You're crying too.*"

I started to deny it, but she used that same hand to pivot my face toward her and then pulled my head down to her hers and kissed me, hard and open-mouthed.

There's a tropical fish I'd seen in *National Geographic* where the female is this big solid animal and the male is this tiny little thing that rides along, clasped onto her, a diminutive passenger. Even though I was bigger than Stacy, that's how she made me feel: she was the center of gravity, and I was plunging toward her, a meteor streaking to destruction across her vast sky.

Annihilation. Did I care?

Nope.

I was stuck there in that kiss as if I had sprouted from her mouth until we fell back onto our sides and she made me move my hand—the one that wasn't pinned beneath her—by guiding it down and clamping it onto the swell of her hip.

After that, I needed no encouragement. I fought to work my fingers up under the rear of her miniskirt, realized at last that it was too tight, and worked the skirt up instead, crumpling it until I could get a good handful of pantied flesh.

Stacy kept her tongue battling against mine, battling and winning, and I'm not sure I would have been able to breathe if she hadn't sometimes exhaled into my mouth, erotic artificial respiration. Her hand slid down my naked belly to my waistband, and she fumbled open the buttons and pushed my pants and underwear down as well as she could.

Her hand groped at my cock and I moaned but realized I wasn't hard anymore.

She pulled her mouth away from mine. "Wow," she said. She lifted her hand away and massaged her fingers back and forth across her thumb, assessing the same sticky stuff that I now felt chilling on my crotch. "When did that happen?"

"When we were kissing, I guess."

"You popped your rocks from *kissing* me?"

"Well…yeah."

"Whoa." She stood up into a crouch under the limbs of the tree, unzipped her skirt, and peeled it and her panties off together. "Then getting you up again should be easy, huh?" She pulled her blouse off, and, with charming awkwardness, struggled her way out of her bra.

I sat up but she pushed me down onto my back with a little shove, and I felt the sharp edges of citrus leaves, like a bed of nails for apprentices. She stood with her legs astride me and said, "Lift up." I lifted my hips, and she pulled my pants and underwear down onto my calves. I let myself down, the leaves poking the length of my body, but she ordered, "Again." When I arched up she positioned my tee-shirt underneath me, and I thought she was being considerate of my naked butt until she knelt down straddling me and I realized her knees were on the fabric to either side of my pelvis.

"Here," she said, "do this for a second…and then we'll take care of you." She pulled my hands up to her breasts and held them there, sitting down on me.

I'd felt breasts before, seven of them, to be precise: Brenda (two), Julie (two), Emma (two), and Carolyn (only the left one, and that only very briefly, the bitch). But numbers eight and nine, beneath my palms just then, made me marvel at mammary diversity: Stacy's were smallish and tight, with hard little raspberries as nipples. Smallish, tight, and so very Stacy.

I felt the heat of her straddling my crotch, and between that and my hands on her breasts I had wood in seconds—not just wood but serious wood: oak, teak, ironwood.

She reached down with her hand and squeezed. "Guess we won't need to take care of you, then."

I was a little disappointed not to be *taken care of*, which sounded promising, but when she fitted me to her and worked herself down onto me, any regrets fled far away.

I don't know how long it took—probably not as long as I remember, and certainly not as long as I wanted—but at one point she sat down hard, laid her chest against mine, and whispered, "Are you getting ready to come?" It had the slightest hint of accusation.

"Maybe…" I admitted.

"Well don't," she said. "Help me first." She rolled a shoulder up against my chin. "Very gentle, just bite me."

I nibbled at her skin, and she said, "No, here." She used her hands to move my face so that my lips touched between her shoulder and her neck, at the muscle or tendon or whatever the hell it is that connects the two. I bit softly, and she made a vague sound, and I took the round, hard cable that runs across there and clenched it lightly between my teeth and squeezed my teeth so that it popped free and she moaned and bore down on me and said, "Yeah, *there...*"

Cool. Even I could do that.

I did it again, and again, and even though she wasn't moving her hips the shudder ran all the way down and clenched at me.

She breathed into my ear, "Keep that up, just that, and I'll let you do *anything*."

Anything I wanted, anything I knew about, we were already doing, so I went back to nibbling her shoulder tendon, and she went back to riding me, and she gasped each time her tendon popped from between my teeth, and I was wondering if I should switch to the other shoulder when finally she sat up, leveraged herself down on me hard, grinding, and my consciousness disappeared into a very small, slick portion of the world.

I came, but I was so excited that it hurt more than it felt good; the physical effect wasn't that different from getting kneed in the balls, leaving me cramped and gasping. But my spirit was so radiant that for a moment I thought I might be glowing.

I'm the only guy I know who lost his virginity on his back, though maybe the others aren't telling.

For the record, I've tried that neck-tendon thing on other women since, and the results have ranged from puzzlement to aggravation.

She kissed me and then lay there on top of me, and I only went half-soft inside her, even though we stayed like that forever. Maybe she even went to sleep. That would have been fine: I'd live under that tree with her, fasting until the green oranges ripened enough to eat.

Eventually she roused herself and kissed me again, to cover that moment where she lifted her hips and I slid out of her. She pressed her palms on my chest to help push herself up onto shaky legs. She bent over and rummaged through her purse until she produced the bottle of Coke we'd brought, and popped the cap with an opener on her keyring. Instead of drinking it, she covered the lip with her thumb, shook it hard a dozen times, and then squatted down and eased herself onto her thumb and the neck of the bottle. Even in the dark I saw her thumb flick out suddenly, and watched the glistening foam erupt through her dark pubic hair.

Then she stood up, knees half-bent and wide, and started dabbing at herself with a napkin, still holding the half-empty bottle in her free hand.

"What…?" I asked.

"No rubber. You don't want me to get pregnant, do you?"

I watched her clean and wipe herself in the darkness under the tree, a few silver spots of moonlight on her skin, and there wasn't a graceless thing she could have done.

She held out the bottle. "Drink?" she asked, joking.

"Hell, yes," I said, and reached for it.

We stumbled out of the grove in the dark, arm in arm, weaving on unsteady legs. It seemed impossible to feel these two things at once—a deep sense of peace coupled with a rising, giddy happiness. My life was set now: I was ready to take a job at the local burger joint and come home every night to Stacy, and, a house, and, well, something.

"You think I'm a slut now?" she asked, quiet, her voice almost bitter.

I tripped, regained my footing. "I don't—" I stammered. "I just…" I stood still and looked into her eyes. "I think you're the most wonderful person I've ever met."

She kissed me. Must have been the right answer.

"Let's not tell anybody about this, though, okay?" she asked.

As we crossed Judson Street, an RPD cruiser pulled away from the curb and then zoomed past us, turning on its lights only after it had gone by.

Stacy's arm tightened on mine.

We walked a few houses down the sidewalk of my block, and then the sound of a well-tuned engine came from behind, headlights throwing our shadows out in front of us.

"I still have my stash," Stacy whispered.

"Give it to me," I said. We walked a few more steps, the car behind us moving at our exact pace. "*Give it to me.*"

She reached into her purse and passed me a baggie.

"I'll come to your house later," I whispered. I stuffed it into my pocket, walked a little farther, then spun about and ran.

Back to the grove. It took a good half-minute before the patrol car responded, and I heard it reverse into an urgent three-point turn, but by then I was across Judson and leaping for the first furrow of the grove.

Maybe we should have played it cool and just kept walking. Who knows? But in the grove, I was uncatchable, eighty acres of endless green domes to hide beneath.

I hid the stash—probably twenty bucks' worth, no mean sum—under a pile of leaves at the base of a windmachine, and then kept moving, mainly to waste time. I spent two hours making sure the heat was off—walking the perimeter of the grove a few rows in, loping out occasionally to peer down the streets. No patrol cars; just the usual light evening traffic, with the occasional low-rider blasting Hendrix into the warm night. When I felt sure they'd written me off, I went back for her baggie. I sauntered out of the grove a quarter-mile east of where I'd entered, and crossed Colton Avenue into a tract of new houses. A hundred acres of oranges had been torn out to make way for them. The lawns were still being seeded and the hiss of sprinklers filled the dark.

It was maybe a mile to Stacy's house—everybody knew where the Slaters lived. I was convinced that she'd be waiting there for me, to thank me for saving her from a bust, and bringing back her stash. I was pretty sure she loved me already, but this would seal it.

When the prowl car came by the first time, I kept to my nonchalant stroll, but the car circled back. I heard the whine of a power window lowering; a flashlight blinded me.

I ran. Into somebody's backyard, trying to toss her stash onto the roof but without time to see where it landed…

Once they had me cuffed in the backseat, they retraced my steps and found the baggie.

I said my people were all runners.

I never said we were good at it.

2 | LIFE IN THE HOLE

The cotton pajamas were a faded blue, bleached to whiteness in spots, as though I'd been dressed in clouds. I didn't yet rate socks or shoes, so as they marched me to my cell the soles of my feet picked up bits of dirt from the chilly floor.

Friends had told me Juvie was stuffed with kids, but my cell turned out to be a single: a mattress on a concrete platform and a lidless toilet. I sat on the bed as indicated, and the counselor said, "It's three in the morning. Intake shower and de-licing at six. Breakfast tray under the door at seven… Barber don't come till day after tomorrow, and you don't go into General Pop till the hair comes off." He looked around the featureless room as if there might be something to see, then added, "Squares of toilet paper over there are a day's ration, so use 'em careful; use 'em up in less'n twenty-four and you're gonna be scraping shit with your fingers and rinsing 'em off in the crapper."

The massive steel door *whoomed* shut and the lights dimmed.

It was like a movie, but the wrong movie. I'd pictured a hallway of open cells, where we could rattle our tin cups against the bars and shout at the guards. This was scarier, silent and barren.

Back at the station the cops had kept at me nearly five hours in total, making sure to give me long periods sitting alone in the room between interrogations. Where had I gotten the stuff? Did Stacy give it to me? Was Stacy's older brother involved? Where was I taking it? Why did I run?

Stacy knew nothing about it, I insisted. I didn't know her family. I'd found the baggie. Yep, just a-layin' there. Lame story, I know, but they couldn't knock holes in something so simple and boneheaded.

They'd made it clear that if I pointed the finger at Stacy, or better yet at her brother Trev, there'd be no charges against me. In return, I'd made it clear that wasn't going to happen. Much as I admire the Bogart persona—*I ain't takin' the fall for any dame, sister*—when the moment of truth arrived, to my surprise I'd found myself mounting the scaffold, declaiming, *'Tis a far, far better thing I do…*

Investigating my cell took all of five minutes. Above the toilet was a small window barred by grillework, the edges of the metal rounded by decades of repainting. Through the window I saw a fenced basketball court, but it looked abandoned, ragweed sprouting through the broken asphalt.

On the bed, a Bible. Enough of my pals had been inside that I knew Bibles were not to be sneered at: the tissue-like pages made great rolling papers. Demand for the Good Book in Juvie was so high the Gideons must have thought mass conversions were taking place.

But I had nothing to roll, and despite my weariness I was still too jittery to sleep. I stank of dried sweat and itched everywhere.

The overhead in the cell was dimmed too much for reading, but I discovered I could sit on the toilet and raise the Bible to an angle where the light from the window just allowed me to make out words.

My arms soon ached, and the massive concrete floor sucked the warmth from my feet. I skimmed through some random *begats*, a few proverbs, and then lost myself in the cadences of *The Song of Solomon* and images of Stacy: *…the joints of thy thighs are like jewels, the work of the hands of a cunning workman…thy navel is like a round goblet, which wanteth not liquor—*

I tossed the book down beside the bed, climbed under the covers, and tugged down my pajama bottoms, reaching for my stiff cock with both hands. Squeezed, stroked, and then brought my right hand up to my mouth to wet my fingers with saliva…

The smell of her was suddenly in my nostrils, my hand sticky with sweat and our half-dried secretions. I licked my fingers, my palm, tasting, and the scent of her engulfed me, revived by the moisture of my tongue. I draped my hand over my nose and mouth, eyes closed, and let my breath fill me with her fragrance until at last I fell asleep, my erection forgotten.

Two counselors rousted me out of bed at six and I stumbled along behind them to the showers. They made me strip and then covered every inch of my skin with white powder from a flexing aluminum can, the metal *whonking* like a tin goose with every squeeze.

"Hold out your hands," the bigger of the two ordered, gesturing with a plastic gallon jug.

"No, stupid, like this," the other one said, cupping upturned hands together.

The big guy filled my hands with viscous rust-red fluid. "Rub it into your hair. Really work it in."

I sploshed the goop onto the crown of my head and began massaging it through my hair. It was acrid. My eyes watered, and I wanted to rub them, but my hands were sopping with the stuff. A blurry glance down was a glimpse of a low-budget horror film, streams of dark red trickling across my white-powdered body.

The icy shower hailstormed onto my skin, but I stepped into the spray without hesitation, eager to rinse the harsh chemicals down the drain.

They had me in clean pajamas and back in my hole before 6:30. The old sheets had been stripped away. Fresh ones were folded on the pillow, but my fingers trembled too hard to make my bed. I curled up under the rough blankets and listened to the doors of the General Population cells opening. Murmurs, grumbles, and laughter came under my door as boys herded to their morning showers. Faces peered through the little window of my cell door. Some of the shorter inmates needed to jump to look inside. A few waved through the glass; quite a few more flipped me off.

I hugged myself, grateful to be in bed, and fell asleep.

"What the *hell* is wrong with you?" a voice demanded, much too close to my ear.

I sat up, dazed.

A flat-faced man stood next to the bed, glaring down. He pointed at the floor to his side. "You know the rules. You eat the damn chow, you push the tray back under the door within fifteen minutes. Your fifteen minutes was up two hours ago."

There was indeed a tray, divided into compartments like a TV dinner: oatmeal, a pile of canned peach slices, and what looked like a diamond of red jello. Jello for breakfast?

"Sorry," I said. "They just put me in here—nobody explained anything."

"Hmph." He rubbed his palms on the thighs of his trousers. I glanced at his face again. Something was badly wrong with it, as if all the bone and cartilage had been removed from his nose, along with the bulk of his cheekbones. His visage was actually concave. I looked down to avoid staring. "Well," he asked, "you want to eat something, then?"

"Not really." He waited. "I'm not hungry."

"You sure?"

"Yeah."

"Thirsty, then?"

I became aware that my tongue was dry. "A drink would be good."

He pointed at the door and my eyes followed his finger. Beneath the window of the cell door a little tray had folded down and inward to form a shelf, a door within the door. Two large paper cups sat there.

I went to the door and drank one down nonstop. I picked up the other and got through it in three long drinks.

"Back on the bed, now," he said. "Sit Indian style."

Baffled, I obeyed.

"Two rules," he said, holding up a fist, "anytime you're on ice. First rule is, never make anybody come into your hole unless you're so sick you're dying." His index finger flicked up. "Lotta guys, they have to come in after your tray, they'll fuck you up good before they leave. Second rule." His middle finger rose. "Any time anybody *does* come in here, you keep your ass on the bed and your feet off the floor. Understand?"

"No," I said. "Why does it matter if my feet are on the floor, and—"

"Hold on, hold on. Didn't ask if you knew why we *got* these rules, I asked if you *understand* what they are. You understand?"

"Sure."

"Good. You just sit there and keep your feet off the floor till I'm gone, then." He bent and lifted the tray, swung the cell door open, and stepped outside. He looked back at me. "Hope they let you out into General Pop soon."

"Wait," I said, "what's your name?"

"Just call me Aaron," he said. He pulled the door shut and locked it. His hand came through and grabbed one paper cup from the shelf, crushing it, and then mashed its twin into the same strong fingers. The fist withdrew with the wadded cups, and the shelf tilted up to become part of my cell door again.

※

I made certain I stayed awake until lunch: a sandwich hiding a slab of unidentifiable meat, mushy green beans, a roll, and two more cups of water on the shelf in the door. I devoured it and then shoved the tray through the high gap under the door.

I drowsed on the bed.

Yells from the hallway awakened me. I ran to the door and looked through the porthole, but the back of someone's head blocked my view. Struggling, grunts, cries of pain, and shouting boys.

The head shifted a few inches, and I could see the fight, or rather the end of the fight. Both of the boys were on their knees by the opposite wall. The bigger of the two had his victim's arm twisted behind his back, and he used this as a lever to smash the other's face into the cinderblock wall. Blood already smeared the point of impact, but it happened again. And again.

The boy blocking my window whooped with delight and jumped away. I peeked up and down the hallway. Maybe two dozen boys, most of them cheering; a few young faces pale with fright but unable to look away. Where the hall opened into the common room two counselors stood with their backs to the scene, arms folded, chatting as if they didn't hear a sound.

They let the boy get his face slammed into the bricks a few more times before they turned. The burly red-headed guard, his cheeks flushed, bellowed, "Okay—what the hell's going on here? Hit your holes, *now!*"

The crowd scattered, leaving the victim on his side. The boy's bloody hands cradled the ruins of his face, but his legs kept moving slowly in alternation, as if taking steps.

A counselor's beefy fist bammed the porthole in front of my nose, and I got the hint that I wasn't supposed to be watching.

I sprawled on the bed and listened to the vague sounds coming under the door: grown male voices, footsteps, and whimpers with a gurgling undertone. Later, mops and buckets, and much later still, a whistle, and the GenPops leaving their holes for the common room.

A loud thump, as if someone had kicked my door. I looked over. A scrap of paper on the floor. I picked it up. A strip torn from the bottom margin of the Bible. In green crayon: *You never saw nothing.*

I wadded it up and threw it in the toilet.

I lay down on the bed again and began to drift, but feared falling asleep and missing my dinner tray. After much pondering, I took my Bible and stood it on edge a few inches in from the door.

The *whump* of the book falling woke me from a troubled sleep. Sure enough, my dinner tray.

When a counselor came through later with a clipboard, asking about the fight in the hallway, I testified that I indeed never saw nothing.

I read the Old Testament until lights out and then shed my pajama bottoms and climbed between the sheets.

Many boys—maybe the majority of them—jerk off to visions of movie stars, swimsuit models, or centerfolds, but good fantasy for me involved girls I knew. Well, *knew* is too strong a word, but girls from my town, girls I had met, or at least seen—living, breathing people.

Within those parameters, though, I was utterly faithless. I'd switch partners in mid-fantasy, even in mid-stroke. Women have an inkling of what goes on in the cramped little porn theaters of the male mind, and tend to resent it, as if it's a conscious assault. With some guys, maybe it is. Me, I always felt helpless. An inner vision of one girl would seduce me back into my brainstem, only to leave me at the mercy of some other, unexpected girl—often a girl I didn't even like—who'd leap from the shadows and seize the dream for a while, often passing me to someone else before I finally got off. During orgasm, girls riffled before my inner eye like a pack of cards, their crowd of faces blurring.

But Woman gave way to Stacy. She'd made appearances in my fantasies before, a member of a large ensemble cast, but now the intimate memory of her hijacked the whole show, leaving her alone under the spotlight. I couldn't have summoned up the face of another girl if I'd tried, and as to bodies—well, hers was the only one I knew, and my fantasies couldn't improve on it.

When you're fifteen and in love and locked in a room with nothing to do, your masturbatory capabilities are heroic. Six times? Eight? Each time I shot my depleting supply of DNA onto the sheets, each time I released my sore cock with a sigh, each time I settled back and closed my eyes for sleep, Stacy would climb atop me, exhale her sweet breath into my nostrils, and we'd be off again. Every new session took longer—to be expected—but they also became more intense, vivid as fever dreams, until at last she flung me down on my mattress, wrung out and pumped dry, and vanished to wherever a succubus spends her time off.

After breakfast the next day I stared at the walls and mooned over Stacy, imagining what she might be doing right then. Just setting off for school, probably. Her friends, the popular, hip crowd, would gather around her as she walked onto the quad, but she'd be strangely self-possessed and quiet, hardly able to smile, as she wondered where I was, what I was enduring. Or maybe she was at home, having taken to her bed, claiming she was too sick for school…

Nah. Even my unrestrained imagination, which had already bedded half the girls in town, even that bold contriver couldn't make Stacy pine away for me. But I was deeply, morally certain she was thinking of me, that her mind was turning toward me at odd moments, making life in my absence feel hollow, and so I moved from her plight to imagining my arrival back in town.

Keys in the door interrupted me, and I barely had the presence of mind to pull my feet up onto the mattress.

"How you keepin'?" Aaron asked from the doorway. "Haircut day."

"I've decided not to get it cut."

He peered at me. "You sure you want to start this, boy? It's gonna mean heartache."

I exhaled heavily. "Yeah. No haircut. It's a free country."

Aaron snorted through his flat nose. "Pretty funny comin' from a kid sitting in a cell." He chewed on the inside of his mouth, began to say something further, but finally just stepped outside and pulled the door shut.

The next visitor was the red-haired counselor. He filled the doorway, no obvious emotion in his eyes, but his cheeks were flushed again, as if someone slapped him only moments before. "What's this about no haircut?"

"Don't want to get one, that's all."

"You don't get your hair cut, you don't go into General Population."

I remembered the scene in the hallway the day before. "I'm in no hurry to get there."

He came into the cell far enough to push the door nearly closed behind him. "You little cunt," he said, in a quiet voice. "We could come in and hold you down and just do it. Maybe cut your pretty face up accidentally at the same time." The flush on his cheeks spilled over his jawline and reddened his neck. "But I'd rather just watch. You want to stay in here? You want to live in your pajamas? *Good for you.* A week on ice, you'll do anything to be let out." He let the words hang for a long time before he reached one arm behind him, his eyes roaming over me, and tugged open the door.

The boredom of isolation was a blessing compared to living with the teen thugs I saw through my porthole. I didn't have a library but I had the Bible; I had my memories of Stacy. And, though faces peered through the window in my cell door from time to time, I had comparative privacy. I'd always spent a lot of time alone; after Mom disappeared, the house was usually empty. Even when I started hanging with my rough, crosstown crowd, I'd still spent hours by myself, wandering the orange groves, or hiking through the desiccated arroyos north of the city.

After a few days, masturbation became a delicate matter; genital skin gets raw yet never calluses over. So what? I had the time to be excruciatingly delicate.

I discovered other things, too. The biblical *begats* are more interesting than you'd think, especially when mumbled under your breath like a mantra: alien and hypnotic, they make you feel like a shaman chanting over the trembling body of one possessed. I learned that, deprived of booze and drugs, a reasonable facsimile of intoxication can be achieved by breathing in and out through the nose, long smooth deep breaths until your whole body begins to shake and quiver. And, if you care, it's nice to know that, with grillework on your cell windows rather than bars, you can climb up there and, moving carefully, like an arthritic spider, rotate yourself around until your butt faces the ceiling and your face seems set to plunge into the toilet, and just hang there…

When the snotty red-headed counselor came back what must have been a week later—it was, once again, haircut day—I was drunk on oxygen, fearless, stupidly arrogant. I could take it, I could hold out until the bureaucracy rolled ahead and let me out. Then I'd run, no, float, no, fly, to Stacy's front porch, my hair and my honor intact, and she'd run to me, elegant and perfectly poised despite those clunky platform shoes, and even though she was my height, I'd hoist her high into the air, and spin her about, everything in slow motion… Even at the time I knew that the imagery was worthy of a shampoo commercial, but it was what I needed to keep me going.

I stayed on ice. It must have been ten days or so (I lost track) before Leo came.

Leo Malheur was tall and coal-black, with a serious, frowning face. Probably no more than twenty, his manner made him seem older. "I'm your probation officer," he said, as a way of opening the conversation.

"I don't—" I began, and then coughed. I'd forgotten how to use my voice. I cleared my throat and began again. "You must be in the wrong place. I don't have a PO." I coughed again, swallowed. "Haven't even had a hearing."

"We had a hearing. Last week. Your father represented you."

"He doesn't—don't I have the right to show up at my own trial?"

"It wasn't a trial, it was a hearing, and the short answer is, no, you don't." He leaned against the wall just inside the doorway. "Not even certain there'll be a trial. Once a juvenile-court judge appoints a temp PO, the prosecutors tend to take their lead from the PO. In your case, me."

I waited for him to continue, but he just stared. I ventured, "And?"

"*And*, most everybody's being cooperative. Your father, the case officers, the judge." He straightened up, glanced at the shoulder of his dark blazer where it had touched the wall, and brushed it off with three quick slaps. "Everybody but you."

"But—" I began.

Leo held one long finger to his lips and shushed me. "Listen. There's three basic things could happen here. One, we could ask that you be placed in a foster home. Fat chance; they want sweet little babies, not wiseassed teenagers. Two, I could recommend the court send you to YA in Chino to do actual time. Three, I can recommend you be released back into your father's custody under long-term probation." He dropped down into a cowboy squat, heels off the floor, one elbow on the highest knee. "Now here's what I want you to understand: There's no further trials, no further hearings, no nothin', until I file a recommendation brief on you. You're in limbo, boy. Adult laws don't apply in here. I can let you sit here in those blue PJs till you're old enough to get drafted, and never file a goddamn thing."

"It's not fair," I whispered.

"Things ain't. Point is"—he grunted as he stood—"point is, it's how things work. You want me to get you out of here, I want some signs of cooperation. I want you out in Gen Pop, getting along and making nice with everybody, before I stand in front of a judge and claim you've seen the error of your ways. And the first step is, the hair comes off."

"I won't do it," I said.

He shrugged. "Then I guess I won't be back to see you." He moved as if to leave.

"Please," I said, "it's all I've got."

He stopped and looked at me as if I were a bad piece of abstract art, trying to figure out my intent, but not much liking what he saw on the surface. "If that's true," he said at last, "then you're the most pathetic fucker I've ever met." He looked down at the floor and took a long breath. "You think it over. When I hear from the counselors that you've had a haircut, we'll talk."

He leaned out into the hall and yelled, "Hey!" Summoning someone with keys to lock me back up, I suppose.

He considered me while he waited. "A couple of your teachers tell me you're smart, like to read. That true—you like to read?"

I nodded, staring at the floor.

"You ever read anything by Kafka?"

I frowned and looked up. "Sure. Like the thing where the man wakes up and finds out he's turned into a huge insect."

"Yeah. That's the guy. He once said something like this: *In the battle between you and the world, back the world*. He was right." We both listened as footsteps came down the hall toward my cell, the jangle of keys echoing in the corridor. He spoke low and urgent as the guard came closer. "We're all fragile, kid. Don't give 'em an excuse to break you."

Over the next few hours, I raged, fumed, and, hiding my face in the blankets, I wept. I hated them all, the whole corrupt adult world, with their exercises of petty power, their ignorant barbarian urge to smash anything new or strange, their need to force all of creation onto bended knee.

Most of all, I hated them because they had won.

What point in dreaming hour after hour of Stacy if she'd be married and gone by the time I got out? And, I realized shakily, I was starting to lose my mind. People can make you crazy if they won't leave you alone, but if they ever decide genuinely to leave you alone, really alone—well, that's when the true madness starts.

I waited until I saw Aaron passing in the hall, and got his attention by hammering on the door. He came over to my window, a concerned look on his distorted face. "You okay, boy?" he asked, his voice faint through the door.

"I want to get my hair cut," I said. He cupped his hand to his ear, and I pointed at my head. "Hair cut!" I shouted.

3 | SHAKING HANDS WITH A DEAD GUY

Ah, the problem of timing.

The barber, it turned out, came to our ward only once a week, on a day determined by an exquisitely complex schedule. "Shoulda spoke up two days ago," the red-headed counselor said. "You missed the boat."

"So I'm stuck in here until he comes again?" I asked. A sense of injustice colored my voice.

"Can't let you out in Gen Pop like that. A shame, too—we need your cell." The tip of his tongue rolled back and forth under his lower lip. "Lemme think about it. Maybe we can work something out." I wanted to be optimistic, but his manner worried me; he seemed oddly pleased.

Aaron came during afternoon Hole Time, the daily settling-down period between the excitement of Commons, when the GenPops were allowed to socialize and play games, and the orderly assembly required to march out of the unit to dinner. Everyone—except those of us on ice—lazed in their cells with the doors open to the hallway, a few of the bolder ones whispering loudly across the hall, chatting to friends in other holes.

Aaron led me to a cell about five doors down and gestured with a sweeping hand for me to enter.

It was a double, a raised platform with mattresses against either wall, but a third mattress had been laid in the middle of the floor to turn it into a triple.

There were already three boys in there. To the left, a wiry, mean-looking guy about my age sprawled on his bed, reading a comic book. On the bed opposite, two frightened kids, one black, one white, sat with their backs against the wall, knees drawn up in front of them. They couldn't have been more than twelve years old, if that.

The guy on the bed rolled into a sitting position. "Aaron," he said, his voice whiny, "we already *have* three guys in here!"

"Turn it down, Eric." Aaron's hand touched my shoulder, urging me in. "He'll be outta here by dinner. We're making some rearrangements."

I stood stupidly in the entryway to the cell. Unwelcomed by the occupants and unable to decide on etiquette, I sat down atop the head of the mattress on the floor.

"You're that guy who wouldn't let 'em cut his hair, right? I'm Eric."

"Rick." I glanced over at the two youngsters still frozen in place, and they just stared.

"Ignore them," Eric said. "Transfers from the Pussy Ward."

I raised my eyebrows to signal incomprehension, and Eric gladly explained that the Pussy Ward was an entire section of Juvenile Hall reserved for children who'd been taken away from their parents for their own protection; kids who had been molested, or beaten, or simply abandoned, were stuffed into cells until the County found foster homes…or, more often, gave them back to their parents after promises of better behavior. But every part of Juvie was overflowing, and the Pussy Ward was already running four to a hole, so they'd started taking the more mature kids, meaning ten and older, and putting them into cells in the other wards. "It's been like Christmas for the queers around here," Eric said. "Like having candy delivered to your door. But I ain't a homo, so it's fucking obnoxious." Eric glared across the room at them. "Listening to them crying at night and shit… Hey, maybe they'll move them out, and let you stay here… Hey, Hardin!" he shouted at the hallway.

A passing counselor wheeled about and came to our doorway. "*Mister* Hardin, Decker."

"Mister Hardin. Sorry. Was wondering, since you're moving people, maybe Rick could stay here and the two pussies could move to where he's going?"

Hardin shook his head, a big grin widening across his face. "Your pal there ain't going into Gen Pop, you know, not until the barber comes. But since he's been such a good boy, and volunteered to get his little trim, we're putting him in with somebody else who's not allowed in Gen Pop, just for company. After he showers and gets new jams, he's gonna be rooming with Carley." He rubbed his nose with the back of his hand and added, "And stop bitchin' about who we bunk you with, we been good to you. Closest you're gonna come to tail until you're eighteen—chances are, you're headed to YA, and then you'll *be* tail."

Eric waited until Hardin walked away before he muttered, "Fuckin' homo." Then he looked at me as if seeing me for the first time, and stretched out his open hand. I shook it, and he said, "Wow, cool."

"What?"

"Never shook hands with a dead guy before."

Behind his hornrims, Todd Carley, the most feared inmate in Ward Four, had the face of an overgrown toddler. He was broadshouldered and massively muscled, but he would have won no bodybuilding competitions; his hips and waist were broad too, and his swollen muscles were padded with a thick layer of pink fat.

Eric had been happy to fill me in on Carley before they moved me to my new hole. A well-known tough in San Bernardino, Carley was in this time for pulling a guy's eye out during a fight. "Didn't just gouge it out," Eric told me, "gouged it out and, when it was hanging there by the nerves or something, he pulled and just snapped it off. Threw it away, off onto the street."

Carley's latest stunt was the reason he was out of Gen Pop. According to ward scuttlebutt, they'd moved someone from the Pussy

Ward in with Carley. He'd complained twice to the counselors, claiming that the kid's wailing had kept him awake. After a few days, he came up with his own solution. "After lights out last night, he stretched the kid out on the bed," Eric confided in a low voice, "and put one knee down to hold the kid's arms over his head and put his other knee on the kid's legs and then pulled the kid's pajamas down and then sat there with a book of matches, burning the kid. Burning his dick, I mean, and his balls, and everything..." Eric had glanced up at the two kids in the room with us as if to suggest to them that maybe Carley'd had the right idea.

My new roomie. He studied me from his seat on the opposite bed, a petulant look on his chubby face. "You're that guy. The guy who wouldn't cut his hair."

Didn't seem to be much point in denying it, as the evidence still cascaded over my shoulders. "Yep."

"Good for you." He tried to reach around and scratch a place on his back. When he found he couldn't reach, he settled for rubbing his back on the wall. "Suppose you think that makes you tough, huh?"

"Not particularly. Just didn't want a haircut."

"You don't like short hair?"

"Don't want to have it myself."

"How about my hair? You like my hair?" He shifted his shoulders and leaned forward a little.

I shrugged.

"You have a problem with my hair?" he asked.

I took a deep breath. "I don't have any problems with anybody. Except my PO. And my dad. And, oh, yeah, that fuckhead counselor with the red hair."

Carley breathed in and his nostrils flared. "*Bradfield*," he intoned, like a necromancer working with a foul name of power, "*Brad*field. *Randy* Bradfield. Lives on Avenue J. Gonna get a visit from me. When I get out. Him and his daughter both. A daughter. Can you figure it? Fuckin' queer's got a daughter. He's got every mop-duty kissy in here sucking his dick. Suckin' his dick. So they can stay up late. Watch TV... How's he get a daughter?" He frowned. "Adopt?"

Carley's puzzlement seemed genuine, but I had no intention of trying to explain bisexuality to him. I shrugged again.

"*Brad*field probly put you in here. Huh? Way of fucking with you?"

I made the universal *who knows?* palms-up gesture.

"You heard about me, then?"

"A little."

Carley's fat face smiled, and he shifted his bulk forward enough to put his feet on the floor. "You scared of me?"

I thought about this for a moment before I answered. "Sure."

He dropped his voice and stage-whispered, "You oughta be. You must be wondering. After my last roomie."

I did my best to not react, and after a moment he laughed. "Sorry, man. I'm just tryin' to fuck with you. Anyhow, they tossed the place good." He pantomimed unfolding a matchbook and striking a light. "No more matches." He hitched himself onto the bed so his back was against the wall again and gave himself a big hug. "You must be wondering, though. What kinda freak. What kinda freak they put you in with."

I raised my eyebrows, letting him pursue it if he wanted.

"Sounds fucked up, huh? Burning some kid's weenie." He hunched down, confiding. "It's a *plan*." He rubbed his hands up and down opposite arms, as if trying to warm himself. "Seems freaky, right? *Crazy*. That's the plan. They decide I'm nuts, it's outta here. No YA, no Chino. Over to Ward B. County Hospital. And when they decide you're okay again—*you're out*."

"Maybe," I said. "Risky, though. Like *One Flew Over the Cuckoo's Nest*."

"What the fuck's that supposed to mean?" He went from self-satisfied to annoyed in two seconds, and in two seconds more he was on his feet, fists clenched. "What the fuck you mean?"

"Nothing," I said, "just the book, just like in the book, that's all."

"What fucking book?"

"*One Flew Over the Cuckoo's Nest.* It's a book." I searched his eyes, and found them still suspicious. "A novel." Even worse. "A story."

"About what?"

"About this guy, he's in prison, and he decides to pretend he's crazy to get moved to a mental ward instead. Randle McMurphy."

"Huh. What's he in for?"

Initially I planned to just give him the gist of the tale, the one-paragraph version, as a caution against his scheme, but every time I mentioned a new character or event he wanted details: Why was Chief in there? Where was he from, how did he grow up, what were his parents like? What did Nurse Ratched do when she wasn't at the hospital? Did she ever go out to dinner? Get laid?

I soon discovered two things: First, that the writer had only hinted at the lives of most of his characters, and that the reader's mind had automatically connected the dots; and, second, that I didn't remember the details of the story as well as I had believed.

My final revelation was most important of all, to wit: within the compact world the novelist had created, you could make up an infinity of side stories; and, as soon as I realized that this was what Todd Carley needed, I did it. I wasn't sure at first that I had the ability, but as soon as I dedicated myself to the telling, two archetypes welled up and possessed me. At the start, I was the storyteller beside an ancient campfire, recounting the trials of our ancestors, and by the end, when Carley had relaxed onto his bunk, staring upward at the movie I was putting into his mind, I became the mother lulling her child to sleep.

No sweet dreams for Todd Carley, though. After midnight, I awoke to sounds of wordless protest. He lay on his back and struggled with the sheet as if it had him pinned. He whimpered, but "—chair—" was the only word I could make out.

I sat up. "Todd?" I waited. He made a pained noise in his throat, and I swung my legs out of bed and winced as my feet hit the cold cement. When I leaned over him he seemed to be asleep, but tears glistened on his cheeks in the dim light. "Todd?" I asked, a little louder.

His eyes opened and he squinted up at me in fear. "What?" He gasped for breath. "What?"

"You must have been having a nightmare. You were crying."

He bolted upright and out of the bed, caught me by the shoulders, and hurled me back onto my mattress. He landed on top of me, pinned my arms under his knees, and leaned forward, his nearsighted eyes searching mine. "Wasn't crying," he whispered, "wasn't goddamn crying." His hands trembled on either side of my face, open-palmed, but his fingers curled in a little as if longing for action. "Take it back."

Take it back? I hadn't heard that since the third grade, and a small, suicidal part of me wanted to laugh, but fear won out easily. "I take it back, Todd. I take it back."

"Wasn't crying."

"You weren't crying. You weren't crying." I tried to ignore how close those hands were to my eyes. I swallowed. "Todd, I'm your friend. I'm on your side, remember?"

He stared at me as if he'd never seen me before, and then, to my relief, something human woke behind those suspicious eyes. He pushed himself off of me, driving the wind from my chest in the process, and shambled back to his own bed. He slumped down with his shoulders against the wall, his bare feet on the cold floor. After a long silence, he said, "Tell me more about McMurphy, Rick."

I'd already reeled out my version of *Cuckoo's Nest* for three hours before we'd bedded down, and now I had to come up with an additional hour before he settled back to sleep. I awoke to the breakfast tray exhausted.

Carley wanted more, right then.

"I can't, Todd," I said. "You have to give me some time to remember. I can only remember so much."

"Why?" he asked, suspicious. "Don't you know the story?"

"Sure. But"—I lied, suddenly inspired—"it's a really long book."

That had the desired effect. I could tell that Carley was intimidated by books, and in his mind it stood to reason that trying to remember a *really long* book would be arduous. We agreed on ground rules—time for me to think undisturbed during the day, and no more than a couple of hours of story each evening.

So began my brief career as Scheherazade.

In my feeble hands, McMurphy became even more of a trickster. He arranged for the hijacking of a truckload of pizzas for the ward; he supervised the digging of a tunnel, so the inmates who were in on the deal could spend occasional evenings in town; and, when the evil shrink and his family went on a month's vacation, Randle rented out the man's house, at cut rates, to members of a motorcycle gang. Nurse Ratched developed a tawdry sex life. Chief started standing up for himself.

In short, I wrecked Kesey's beautiful, economical story, and wrecked it in increasingly implausible ways, transforming it from a lean tragedy to a mental-ward version of *Hogan's Heroes*. But it kept Carley entranced and sedated; he asked endless questions, but they were never challenges—just requests for *more*, more of everything.

The strange thing was, County Hospital was probably where Carley actually belonged. Stories kept him entranced, and the promise of a story to come would keep him on good behavior. But at odd moments I'd find him staring, head tilted to the side, his face slack, the human part of his mind apparently taking a vacation, while his pupils dilated and contracted, as if what he watched alternately aroused and repulsed him.

After four days, the barber showed up.

Two of the counselors led me out of Spaceship Carley, each guiding me by an elbow, and into the common room. I was wobbly on my feet, and only then realized how weak I had become.

Maybe twenty guys were waiting to get chopped, but the counselors took me to the front of the line and sat me down in a metal folding chair. As my pajama-clad butt touched the metal, there was applause and a number of whoops. I'd been away from people for so long that the noises were uninterpretable; I couldn't tell if I was being lauded or jeered at. A little of both, maybe.

The barber was just some guy, could have been a grocer, could have sold insurance. No insignia of the profession, no white jacket, just a pair of scissors in the pocket of his plaid shirt, and an electric razor dangling from his hand.

"Leave the part, will you?" I asked. My natural part was on the left, and creating a reliable furrow down the center had taken years of careful husbandry.

"Whatcha say, kid?"

"Just asked if you'd leave the part. Took me forever to train it."

"Yeah, we'll leave it…"

He left it, sure enough, but that's about all he left. He shaved me nearly bald, but down the center of my head a two-inch-wide strip of hair still sprouted on either side of the part, a finger's length of hair all along it flopping to the sides like a limp, undersized Mohawk.

The Common echoed with laughter as the counselors took me back to my hole.

When the door locked behind me, Carley giggled. "You look like a cunt."

I've never liked that word, *cunt*, an ignorant, abusive, grunting sort of a word. And *vagina*—sword-sheath—is too clinical, too military, too Roman. *Pussy* is better, warm and cute, but still doesn't come close. I can't propose a better term for the Holy of Holies, but being called a cunt in my present mood wiped away my sense of self-preservation, and I sat down hard on my mattress and said, "Just fuck off, Todd."

My words hung there in the cell, with big danger arrows pointing at them. I waited for him to hammer me to a pulp, not really caring.

His voice was contrite. "Sorry, man. Didn't mean anything." He seemed sincerely worried about offending me. "But, you know"—he giggled again—"that *is* what it looks like."

I ran my fingers down the center of my part, front to rear, and fell back on the mattress, smiling in spite of myself. Just great. Cunt-head Rides Again.

I sulked until late afternoon, when, true to his promise, Leo reappeared. Carley and I both snapped our legs up off the floor when we heard the key in the door. Leo looked at Carley with disapproval, then gestured for me to come. "Let's take a walk."

It was Hole Time, so the ward was filled with the quiet buzz of conversation from open-doored cells, but Leo and I were alone in the common room. We paced a wide circle, the ping-pong table at its center. The windows of the room were translucent, with hexagonal wire netting embedded in the glass, like an up-market chicken coop.

"You're out of here tomorrow," Leo said.

I paced next to him, my hands clasped behind my back. "I guess."

"Your father came up with a proposal that the juvenile court accepted, and I signed off on it. Otherwise, it probably would have been YA. Not that your record's that bad, but there's rumors of behavior that never got you busted, from teachers, and—"

"And my dad."

"Yeah."

We continued our long circuit, absorbed as two monks walking a meditation path.

"He's a prick," I observed, after a long silence.

Leo paced beside me, considering this proposition, and finally said, "True." We walked a while more, and Leo added, "A racist prick, in fact."

I glanced up at Leo.

He grinned. "I'll deny I ever said that. But you gotta understand: He wants to destroy you. And, you go off to CYA, he wins, wins big time. You just gotta hang on, man, hang on till you're eighteen."

"It's three years."

"It is."

"You don't know what it's like."

He stopped and turned to face me. "Listen, Rick. You don't know shit." He locked eyes with me. "Don't tell me what I do and don't know."

He held my gaze until I had to look down.

We resumed our slow pacing.

"So what's the plan?" I asked.

"The plan is, tomorrow, you're released into your father's custody."

"And…?"

"And, that's all I'm supposed to tell you."

"C'mon, Mister Malheur—what's happening?"

"What's happening is that you're being released into the custody of your father. That's all I can tell you. That's all you need to know."

"Oh, for God's sake—"

He pivoted and grabbed me, one big hand on each of my shoulders. "You listen careful. You want to get even? You want to show 'em all?"

I nodded, swallowed.

"Then do this: just survive. Stop reacting. Live to grow up and then walk away from 'em all."

"I—I don't know if I can. Three years…"

He let loose of my shoulders, and I had to scurry a few steps to catch up as he resumed pacing.

"Stay alive, stay free. Stick around, and come back and dance on the graves of those sonsabitches." Leo looked down at me, his eyes hooded. "That's what kept me breathing till I was eighteen."

<hr />

When the moment of truth came, I couldn't do it. I couldn't lobotomize Randle McMurphy.

At the time, I told myself that Todd Carley wouldn't be able to handle it, and I think that was probably true. But I'm not sure I could have handled it either, not then, and I've often since reflected with amazement on the fact that Kesey himself was able to do it. Oh, artistically it was the right thing to do, the perfect thing to do. But still.

In the Rick version, expurgated yet expanded, McMurphy realizes what is afoot and goes back to prison rather than lose his volition, rather than run the risk of having his frontal cortex severed.

Carley lay silent in the dark for such a long time after I finished that I wondered if he'd fallen asleep. "Rick? What happens to Chief?"

"Oh." I'd forgotten the one glimmer of light, Hope at the bottom of Pandora's Box. "He breaks out, gets away, goes back to where he's from. He's okay then."

Carley pondered. "And McMurphy? What happens to him?"

"I don't know, Todd. That's where the story ends."

I myself was nearly asleep when Carley added, "I hope McMurphy's okay."

I did too. But I knew he wasn't.

<hr />

Before the counselors came to process my release, Todd Carley stood and shook my hand. "You're cool," he said. He didn't release my hand, and, engulfed in his meaty grip my palm began to sweat. "I'll look you up on the outside." He made a movement that might have been an aborted attempt at a hug, but instead released my hand and slumped down onto his mattress.

I was touched, but fervently hoped he'd never look me up.

After weeks in pajamas my street clothes were alien things, heavy, rough, and redolent of another world. Bending over to pull up my trousers I caught the scent of citrus on the denim, and, fainter, a whiff of Stacy rising from my unwashed boxers.

Dad waited outside the front gate, leaning against the door of his pickup. He looked at me with something that seemed like satisfaction, but didn't say a word as I circled around to the passenger side and climbed in.

Once we were headed east on Interstate 10 out of San Bernardino, he spoke. "It's a whole new ball game now, pal." Even though we were in fourth gear, he kept his right hand on the knob of the gearshift. "You're on probation. Piss me off, step out of line, and all I have to do is call your PO and you're back inside. Incorrigibility. Ever hear of that? It's a crime."

He waited for me to respond. I didn't. "So here's the story," he continued. "You finish out this school year—not much left—you keep your nose clean for the summer, and next September you'll start at the military academy in New Mexico."

"Oh, for chrissakes!"

"You watch your mouth. It's going to cost me a mint sending you there, but it's the only thing that can straighten you out." He floored the accelerator to roar around a car towing a U-Haul. "It's my fault, how you've turned out, I guess. I was too easy on you. Too damn generous to everybody. Well, that stops today. You got it?"

I leaned against the passenger-side door, weak from confinement and sick at heart. I considered pulling the door open and heaving myself onto the freeway.

"I asked," he repeated, "if you got it."

"I got it."

"'Cause if you got any problems with it, we turn right around. You can spend the next three years in YA, or put yourself up for foster care." He snorted. "They'd be lining up to adopt you, I bet. Yeah, you're just a real damn prize."

My face against the window glass, I watched the broken white line speed by.

"So," he asked, "all that okay with you? Any problems?"

"No," I whispered.

"Speak up."

"No. No problems."

We sat silent as the freeway carried us above the rooftops of Redlands. We passed the Orange Street offramp, and the University Street offramp, both logical ways of going to our house. When we passed the Ford Street exit and started up the steepish grade out of Redlands, I finally asked, "Where are we going?"

"You're going to be costing me so damn much money, I put the house up for sale and moved us. Andrews Ranch has a few houses they rent to supervisors. Cheaper. And get you away from those dumb spic friends of yours." He smiled, savoring this last victory. "We live in Yucaipa now."

4 | MEDIEVAL TIMES

Yucaipa sat only ten miles east of Redlands, but it might as well have been in another state. Ten miles apart, but their high-school teams didn't even play in the same league; Redlands reached west, toward LA, while Yucaipa looked east, to the forgotten towns of Banning, Beaumont, and Coachella. If Redlands was a prosperous, civic-minded New England town, Southern-California style, then Yucaipa was California's answer to Faulkner, inbred and isolated.

The Crafton Hills, brush-covered and dry, separated the two towns—though, strictly speaking, Yucaipa wasn't a *town* at all, but rather an *unincorporated area*, a haven for those who didn't care for zoning restrictions. If you wanted to keep goats and roosters in your backyard, if your idea of bliss was having five cars up on blocks on your lawn, if you wanted to escape from city property taxes that paid for useless improvements like sidewalks…well, then, Yucaipa was your little piece of paradise.

There was a time when Yucaipa—a Native American name meaning Green Valley—had aspirations. The location was scenic enough: a high mesa that butted against the steep slopes of Grayback on the east, wrapped by hills on the north and west, and walled in by crumbly mounded badlands on the south.

Early real-estate developers had tried to create a land rush, sponsoring free tours from LA, via train to the Redlands station, and by car from there. Yucaipa Boulevard ran from the Dunlap flatlands and suddenly climbed up onto the mesa, and speculators paid to have "The Boulevard" lined with tall, fast-growing eucalyptus, a multimile corridor leading to lots staked out and ready for subdivision. But the money never seemed to flow uphill from Redlands, and when the County decided to widen the road they tore out the trees, and Yucaipa Boulevard became a broad four-lane strip of cheerless asphalt, baking in the sun.

Some entrepreneurs tried to reshape Yucaipa into an upscale retirement community. Despite expensive advertisements, however, wealthy retirees persisted in wintering in Palm Springs and summering in Santa Barbara, and the planners lowered their sights. Rest homes and senior mobile villages—that is, trailer parks—sprang up here and there across the valley.

Once the speculators realized that their dreams of an elegant, profitable community had evaporated, they began to offload their holdings any way they could. In the Depression years, Okie immigrants could pick up title to a plot in Yucaipa on a pay-as-you-go basis, living in tents and tarps until they could cobble together shacks.

The big change came in the late 1940s, when egg ranches, backed by government loan programs, were scouring the Southland for cheap, semi-rural land within striking distance of the swelling urban markets. Giant chicken ranches weren't welcome in most communities: they were eyesores, they stank, and they bred infinite armies of fat bluebottle flies. But Yucaipa—well, no zoning controls, no real planning, and, hell, half the residents had chickens in their yards anyway.

Our new home, courtesy of Andrews Egg Ranches, was down in the middle of Dunlap Acres, the flood plain below the mesa. Once every decade or so, heavy rains brought floods roaring down from the lofty mountains, but by the time the waters had churned their way through the montane gorges they were more like horizontal mudslides, and they lost their force completely as they passed through Dunlap, layering the streets, the yards, and the insides of houses from two to four feet deep in silty mud. Many of the cottages and bungalows displayed a two-tone effect, the paint applied too thin to cover the stains of the last high mudflow. The Yucaipa mesa, perched above Dunlap Acres, had sheer sides where eons of repetitive floods had carved high banks, yet everyone seemed surprised when what had been going on for thousands of years happened yet again. Rather than discouraging development, the cheaper land down on the floodplain was the first to be filled with houses—some of them respectable Old California bungalows, but many of them little more than shacks.

Our house was decent, even fancy by local standards, a two-bedroom stucco affair with wood floors and central heating. The grounds were leafy—two Chinese elms flanked the drive, and an ancient pepper tree sat in the center of the front lawn like a lumpy frowning troll. Trees are the key to telling Old California from New California: traditional houses are shaded on all sides by trees, while new tract homes sit naked beneath the sun, counting on air conditioning to keep the occupants alive.

"I gotta go to work," Dad said. "Don't get any wise ideas about hustling down to Redlands to see your friends. I'm going to call later on, and make sure you're around."

"I have to stay in the house?"

"No. But if I call two different times and you aren't here, well..."

He started for the door, but paused. "Find that razor and trim your hair. You look like a twat."

Another gynecological euphemism I didn't care for, but I took his point.

An hour of searching later, I found the razor. Mom had bought it in a fit of economy, planning to become the family barber, but after the first few attempts there emerged a quiet consensus that the savings weren't justified by the costs.

Hefting it in my hand, I wondered about her. What had she wanted, and did she have it now? I resented her for leaving me, yet she had become a vital pinpoint of hope in my life. You could start again. You could disappear and become someone else, shed your past like a snake and emerge glistening into the sun, all of your old scars abandoned with the skin you'd outgrown.

I trimmed my hair. It didn't look good when I was finished, and, trying to even out my mistakes, I nearly shaved my head, but being bald was better than that humiliating horizontal stripe. Bald could even be cool, I told myself, look at Yul Brynner.

I looked like I'd been discharged from a cancer ward.

I almost called Stacy. I got as far as getting Information on the line, asking for the Slaters on Palm Avenue, when I froze. I wasn't ready yet.

I knew we'd had something special, I knew that she was thinking about me…but I didn't know for sure anymore. Knowing for sure and just knowing are miles apart, and my certainty had fled the day they chopped my hair. Like Samson, I'd once had the strength of many; that night, I no longer had the strength of even one.

A phone call was out. I had to see her, face to face, or better yet, skin to skin, and that would have to wait—for a weekend, when I could hitch down there, and for a day, a day I longed for, when my confidence would be as buoyant as the day I took the baggie from her hand.

My things were still in boxes, stuffed into the little bedroom out back. I started unpacking, but it felt pointless. I lay down on the bare mattress of my bed and realized I needed to sleep.

But before I did, I set the alarm for 6 a.m., early enough to get me to my first day at Yucaipa High School.

No sight nor sound nor scent of girls in weeks, and now there were a dozen. Most of them had affected hip attire, but, as always in any class, a couple looked as if their mother had dressed them. Though tempted to despise everyone hailing from this third-rate cowtown, I had to admit that some of the girls were rather attractive—not Stacy, but still…

Any looks of admiration or interest I cast were most pointedly not returned.

The new kid. Bad enough being the new kid, the new kid at the end of a school year; I had to be the new kid with the refugee haircut.

I first saw him in Earl Ubelovsky's fifth-period Algebra class.

At first I didn't pay him much attention. I was busy trying to pretend to listen to Ubelovsky's lecture on the quadratic theorem while checking out the girls. The guy was hard to overlook, though: a pink-and-orange jacket of upholstery brocade, tight blue trousers with huge cuffed bellbottoms. A storm of black hair, medium-long, each lock a dark wave that curled out, crashed down against his skull, and then flung high once more.

It wasn't his looks that kept my attention, though, but rather the fact that he held his algebra book up with both hands, a paperback opened inside it. Readers worldwide constitute a secret fraternity, and here was a special member of our club, a clandestine reader, an outlaw.

I strained to see the title.

He sensed my gaze and looked over. His eyes were black as his hair; and though his complexion was pale a dark undertone lurked there, as though his skin were a fabric stretched taut around a shadow.

He winked, and went back to his book.

Down in front, one of the girls I had been favoring with covert glances raised her hand.

"Melissa?"

She sat up straighter and tossed her flouncy hair, tangling it on a huge hoop earring. "Mr. Ubelovsky, I still don't understand why there's two solutions to a quadratic equation."

Ubelovsky shook his heavy Slavic head. "Why is the sky blue? Because it is, that's why."

Melissa looked dissatisfied and slumped down in her seat.

Another girl, one of the dressed-by-Mom contingent, shot her hand in the air. "Linda?" Ubelovsky asked.

"But there *aren't* always two solutions to a quadratic equation. Sometimes there's only one."

"No. There's always two. It's just that, sometimes the two of them are the same one."

Clear as mud. Worried glances were exchanged all over the room.

"But," the teacher continued, "I know where this sudden interest in math theory comes from. You're all just trying to delay the quiz."

Universal groans.

The quizzes passed back from hand to hand, two stapled pages with purplish lettering. I inhaled the brain-swelling odors of fresh mimeo fluid as I handed the stack over my shoulder.

The counselor had warned me that I "might be a little behind," since, because of scheduling problems, I was being tossed into a class for sophomores and juniors; and he encouraged me to "just tread water" for the remaining two weeks of the semester. I didn't tread water. I flailed, drowning. On half of the questions I didn't know where to begin, and on the other half I was less than confident of my approaches. The top of the student desk was so uneven from years of students carving into the surface that my writing wobbled and twice my pencil plunged through the paper.

While the rest of the class strove diligently with the test, I examined the desktop, running my fingers across the grooved word as if reading Braille. Scarred with initials, words, geometric figures, hearts, and a few items that couldn't have been intended as anything but excavations, each stab at immortality recorded there helping to obliterate an earlier inscription, until nothing at all came through clearly, as if two decades of students shouted for attention at once. There was a profound lesson there, I supposed. Either that, or I was deeply bored.

When the bell rang, we passed our papers forward. As I left the class, the kid with the brocade jacket was at the front desk, asking Ubelovsky, "Can I have an extra of the test? I'd just like to work some of the problems when I have a little more time."

Yucaipa High School didn't have hallways. The classrooms were in long rectangular buildings, and these were loosely tied together by covered walkways that ran past open areas surrounded by low concrete walls. The architect must have envisioned the spaces as gardens. What they were in practice were large squares covered with mounds of English ivy, ivy that sent its tendrils crawling over whatever rubbish happened to fall there. There must have been a hundred layers of artifacts held in that ivy matrix, a treasurehouse for future archaeologists—if they could work their way past the thousands of black widow spiders that lived within.

I sat down on the concrete wall and opened *The Plague*. My school day was over, but many of the other students had one more class, and I watched them scurry along. To my left the guy in the brocade jacket paced along deliberately. Using his math book like a clipboard he scribbled in ballpoint pen.

"Hey, dipshit!" a voice called from my right. I knew the words had to be directed at me, but I ignored it and tried to find my place in the book. "Hey!" The voice was closer. "Hey, *you*, fucker, what do I have to do, kick you in the head?"

I looked up. The speaker stood ten feet away, hands on hips to either side of a massive beltbuckle. Down the breezeway three of his friends leaned against the lockers, watching. He stepped closer. "My friends want to know where you got the haircut. Are you, like, just back from 'Nam? Want to show us how you can kill a guy with a single blow?" Guffaws from one of the watchers.

The guy in the brocade jacket walked into the space between us, still scribbling, and sat down next to me. I saw that he was working on a copy of the algebra test. "Ignore him," he said under his breath. "Just talk to me."

"Hard test, huh?" I asked.

"Hmm? Oh, no, not really… Hang on a second." He flipped to the second page.

"Hey, Linc," my tormentor said, "I'm *talkin'* to that guy."

"No you aren't, Glennie," he answered, without looking up from his work, "*I'm* talking to this guy. You're just being a jerk."

"Hey…" Glennie said, searching for words. "Hey, fuck you, Linc." He stomped right up in front of us and glowered down. He had a pinched, shit-kicker's face, and the muscles twitched in his rangy forearms. "You think I can't kick your ass, too?"

Linc sat the test down beside him, carefully pinning it under his textbook, and slipped his pen into a pocket of his brocade jacket. He stood up, but instead of squaring off, he looked up and down the breezeway. He whistled, waved to someone, and then sat down again.

"Oh, sendin' for your mom?" Glennie said, his tone now less self-assured. "Can't take me on yourself?"

"That's right." He positioned the book on his knees, clicked his pen, and went back to working problems.

"You're afraid to fight me, aren't you?" A crowd had started to gather. "Come on, be a man, you little hippie." Glennie was close enough now that he could have slugged either of us.

Linc looked up. "You know, the first time I got laid, I realized that being a guy was about something else." A couple of the bystanders chuckled. "You should try it some time."

"Yeah, dickless." Someone stepped in close beside us, and I had to crane my neck back to see him, a big guy with a blond beard. "But if you're into fighting, hey, I can help you out there."

"Piss off, Rob," Glennie said. "This isn't your problem."

"That's right. It's your problem, and you should take it somewhere else."

"I'm not afraid of you."

From there it progressed in the usual fashion, with escalating threats, a few sharp shoves, and friends elbowing in to pull the two of them apart and arrange a meeting off-campus.

The crowd dispersed, Rob and Glennie shouting a few last threats over their shoulders. Only when we were left alone did I realize that Linc had gone back to working his math problems.

He folded the test in half, inserted it in his math text, slammed the book shut. "There," he said.

"Thanks, man," I said. "That guy was coming for me for no reason."

"No big deal."

"What's the story with the extra copy of the test?"

"Oh, I always hand in the wrong answers on the test. But every so often I get a copy and work it for real, just to make sure I can. What's the story with your hair?"

"Juvie."

"Appalling. What for?"

A moment of truth. What cool people called marijuana varied from place to place and month to month. When the media caught up with a term, it was quickly abandoned by those in the know—until, that is, it became so standard in speeches by the uncool that it could be used sardonically. The really hip scanned the pages of pamphlets for outdated words that clueless bureaucrats informed even-more-clueless parents was current marijuana jargon: reefers, boo, tea, pot, grass, Mary Jane, M, 13…and damned if their pronouncements didn't become self-fulfilling, as we seized on their "insider" jargon and made it our own, loving its lameness. I decided to be conservative. "Weed,"

I said, but then, in case that was outdated, added the note of exotica: "Soaked in hashoil."

"How much?"

"Maybe twenty joints."

"Huh. I try not to carry more than I can eat."

"It was complicated… Wait a minute, are you saying you deliberately blew the test?"

"Indubitably."

"I don't get it."

"Ubelovsky is a shithead. He's an *Ag* teacher, for the luvva Buddha, and they have him teaching two math sections. 'Why is the sky blue?' The guy causes damage." He ran fingers through his hair as if adjusting it, and it immediately flopped back into its own wild pattern. "No way am I going to perform for him, and let him think he's some kind of decent teacher. No way."

"I don't get it. You're deliberately messing up your own grade… what does that prove?"

"Nothing, to most people. Lots to me. Here…" He opened the book, handed me the test. "Check it out tomorrow. You good at math? I'm Lincoln Ellard, by the by. You want to smoke a joint?"

I hesitated, unsure of what to respond to first. "Uhhh…Rick Leibnitz, and sure, I'd love to. And I'm not very good at math."

"Name like Leibnitz, you ought to be dazzling." He saw my incomprehension. "*Leib*nitz? *New*ton? *Cal*culus?" He shrugged and gave up. "C'mon. Let's stroll down to the park."

The mesa of Yucaipa proper was bisected by a great arroyo, but its upper reaches had been tamed; huge concrete pipes had been buried to carry the waters when they came, and the sharp edges of the wash had been bulldozed into long slopes. The Park—also known as Seventh Street Park, and Yucaipa Valley Park—sat on a long south-facing slope just below the high school. A corridor of taller deciduous trees ran along the top edge of the slope, but the trees farther down were conifers of an intermediate age—trees just tall enough that you could sit crosslegged beneath their branches and be hidden from prying eyes.

A popular site, made even more popular by the adjacency of the high school.

For the school authorities, the Park was something they didn't have to worry about. For the police, it was just too damn much trouble: the parking lot was at the bottom of the slope, and by the time a San Bernardino County sheriff could haul his ass up a couple hundred yards of steep grass, whatever might be happening would have stopped, moved, or been hidden.

So it was that Linc and I could scoot under the low branches of a Colorado blue spruce and torch up while school was still in session.

As we smoked I filled him in on how I came from Redlands to Yucaipa, trying to find some way to make myself sound a romantic figure rather than a loser. When I trailed off, we sat in silence for a while. I exhaled smoke into the still air and leaned back on my open palms, last year's conifer needles like bamboo mats beneath my hands. "So what," I asked, "were you reading in class?"

Lincoln finished his inhale, swallowed it, and talking from his mouth alone so as to minimize smoke loss, said, "Zlazny…"

"Huh?"

He fumbled at a pocket of his jacket, still holding his breath, and tossed me a dark paperback.

Roger Zelazny's *Lord of Light*. A black cover with mandala-like flames forming Hindu figures. Science fiction?

He passed me the last of the joint and blew out a lungful of smoke. "Zelazny. Read it twice already. Want to borrow it?"

I sat up to take the roach. "Don't read sci-fi or fantasy." I drew the last hot breath down my throat.

"Oh? And what *do* you read? Only the later Joyce, perhaps? Sherlock Holmes? David Copper-fucking-field?"

This struck me as funny and I blew out perfectly decent smoke laughing. "Don't you mean David-fucking-Copperfield?"

"No, no. The Copper-fucking-fields, the Copper-fucking-fields of Burfordshire, a noble, notable hyphenated family. How'd you get to be such a snob?"

"There's nothing wrong with reading good literature."

"No, what's wrong is *missing* good literature because you've got your head stuffed up your ass." He said this so matter-of-factly that I wasn't even offended. I was about to continue the debate when he shouted, "Lissa! Hey!"

Melissa from Algebra was passing with two friends, about ten yards away. and all three bent down and peered to see who was shouting. Melissa, her straight blond hair hanging down as she leaned forward, was dressed in a blouse, miniskirt, and knee-high boots. She smiled when she saw Lincoln.

He gestured for them to join us, and they all crouched down and duckwalked under the blue-needled branches—more of a problem for Melissa than the other two, one of whom wore a long peasant skirt, the other of whom was sheathed in an electric-blue bodysuit with a zipper that ran from neck to pubic bone.

"By the way," Lincoln said to Melissa, who attempted to maneuver from her hunch to a seated position despite the impediments of a short skirt and high-heeled boots, "it's because of short wavelengths."

"What?" She waggled down onto the bed of needles and tugged down her skirt, keeping her knees pressed together.

"What Ubelovsky asked when you asked why there's two solutions to a quadratic: *Why is the sky blue?* It's blue because blue light has such short wavelengths that it gets scattered all over the sky by air molecules. Of course, what the moron meant is that there's no answer—but there is an answer."

"Is there an answer to *my* question, then?"

"Several. But the easiest way to think of it is like this: There's a squared term in the quadratic, right? Well, what's the square root of four?"

"Two."

"But what do you get if you square *minus* two?"

"Four— Oh, I get it. Why didn't he just say so?"

Linc shrugged. The other two girls were looking bored at this exchange, so he began introducing, pointing to us one by one. "This is Rick Leibnitz, descendant of Newton's famous rival, and probably heir to some damn German principality or another. But, at the moment, he's a kid with a price on his boyish head, having only recently been kicked out of Juvenile Hall. Melissa Terrill—you know her from class…Randi Mayfield"—this the brunette in the peasant skirt, slim but buxom—"and JenBen," the latter the bobbed-haired blond girl in the bodysuit.

"JenBen?" I asked.

"She is known by many names," Randi intoned, casting her voice low in a mock-archaic tone. "Bennifer. Jenny-bean, Jenny-belly. Jennifer Benedict: JenBen."

Lincoln snapped the tip of a wooden kitchen match with his thumbnail, gestured with the flame as if he had performed an act of prestidigitation, and lit another joint. He puffed it to get it started and immediately passed it to Melissa. She toked, coughed, toked again, and passed it to Randi. Before it got to JenBen, Lincoln fired up another and handed it to Melissa.

When the joint got to me I drew in the heady smoke and tried to pass it to Linc, but he waved it off and pointed back in the direction from whence it had come. I passed it back to JenBen, who hit it hard, who then passed it to Randi, with the result that Randi ended up with a smoking joint in either hand. She laughed and shrugged, her wonderful breasts lifting as she did so, and put both of the joints to her lips and drew on them with one breath, a novel gesture that I found vaguely obscene. She passed the joints to Melissa and Jenny, crossing her arms to ensure they continued traveling in the right direction.

When the joints were done we sat in a friendly, speechless circle, the fumes of the weed clearing from our noses to be replaced, with marvelous stealth, by the resinous scent of pine.

"Where were you before?" JenBen asked. "I mean, before here and before Juvie."

"Redlands."

"Oh, Sonny Sunkist."

Randi leaned in to the circle a little. "Another exile arrives in Siberia. Swell fucking town, huh?" There was something elegant about her, rarefied, her long face like that of an expensive purebred canine.

"It's okay," I said, and the lameness of it echoed in my ears.

"She can afford to be snide," Linc said, "she's a senior. Off to college next year."

"Wow. To where? To study what?"

"To UC Santa Cruz," she said, "and I'm sure you don't really want to hear about it." She sniffed at the air, and the image of her as a beautiful dog was reinforced.

"No, I do, I'm interested."

Linc pointed at the copy of Camus laying by my side. "He's actually sort of a literary snob, this guy. Probably headed to read the Classics"—he exaggerated it into *Clossics*—"at Oxford or somewhere."

Randi raised her eyebrows, not sure if she was being teased. "Well, I don't really want to talk about it," she said, and then proceeded into a ten-minute, stoned monologue about trying to choose a major and the problem of deciding what to do with one's life. I listened with only a small part of my mind, the rest of me watching her. As she warmed to her subject, however, she locked eyes with me, preventing my gaze from traveling farther south than her long, exquisite nose.

I'd have sat there gladly all day, but she interrupted herself with an embarrassed laugh. "Jesus, listen to me. I don't usually go on like that."

JenBen threw an arm around Randi's shoulder and hugged up against her. "Sure you do, hon, every time you get loaded."

A commotion upslope. Melissa fell back onto her elbows and arched her neck to see—an unwise maneuver in such a short skirt, but her glossy paisley panties were up to the challenge of public display. "Rob Motiff," she said, "oh, and Glennie, too… I think they're gonna do it!"

Randi sighed, but joined Melissa and JenBen as they scrambled onto their knees and edged their way out from under the tree. They stood up holding each other's arms in a woozy trio, seemingly ready to topple backwards down the slope, and then headed toward the gathering crowd.

Linc raised his eyebrows, twisted his mouth, shrugged, and turned his palms up—made every gesture of indifference known—and, with a grunt, rolled onto his knees. "May as well…" he said. "It's sort of our fight, I guess."

The fight was already well underway by the time we got there. Rob Motiff was a big blond, broad-shouldered and narrow-hipped like a movie cowboy. Glennie pulled on the James Dean side of the fence, wiry, dark, and loose-limbed.

Both had drawn blood already: Rob's nose bled onto his shirt, and Glennie had a cut above his eye that made him shake his head to keep his vision clear.

They stood apart for a moment and then closed again, pounding at each other.

I was used to the Mexican style of fighting—lightning-fast, precise, and vicious, like dueling with rapiers. Back in Redlands, when a fight happened at a party, it was usually over too quick to gather much of a crowd—by the time people knew something was going on, someone was already on the ground clutching at an injury: throat, face, testicles. When the fights were serious, it all happened too fast to follow; somewhere in the whirlwind of jabs a razor would come out and one guy would slice the other one's belly. The nose-tickling smell of blood always came first, but often it was followed by the stench of an opened intestine.

The Yucaipa style of fighting was more medieval. If the pachucos down in Redlands were fencing masters, the Yucaipa crowd seemed to be more like armored knights: a slow, labored hammering away, trying to win by sheer force rather than dexterity.

It was brutal and yet boring, like watching male moose crash into one another.

Wake me up when the mating starts.

Rob landed a hard blow on Glennie's face, and the crowd shrieked as a spray of crimson droplets landed on them. Girls brushed at their blouses and backed away; boys pushed in closer.

Glennie was still game, but blinded by his own blood, and he stumbled at Rob, swinging his fists where he expected his opponent might be. Rob hit him hard, a real piledriver, and knocked him down.

Then he kicked him. Stomped him. Booted him, in the head, in the gut, in the crotch, until Glennie hugged himself and rolled onto his stomach, trying to hide his vital parts. This of course only earned him a bootheel in the kidney, and then, as a finale, Rob kicked one of Glennie's arms from beneath him and put his boot down on Glennie's exposed fingers and started crushing them into the grass.

This at last brought a scream of pain, and Rob relented long enough to ask, "You give?"

"Yes!" Glennie's other hand clutched at Rob's ankle, trying to spare his fingers.

"Then kiss the ground I walk on. Kiss it." Rob leaned again, and Glennie screamed, and then kissed the ground, over and over, still fighting to lift the boot from his fingers.

Rob lifted his foot, and Glennie rolled into the fetal position, clutching his injured hand, his face glossy with mingled tears and blood. Rob started to walk away, paused, and then turned to deliver one last vicious kick to the midsection.

Rob marched down the hill toward the parking lot, and I watched the crowd dissolve, most of them following him.

I felt a little sick, and the look on the faces of some of the girls as they trailed after him made me even sicker.

A few guys knelt around Glennie, trying to sit him up. Aside from that, Linc was the only one left. "You need a ride home?" he asked.

"You have a car?" I'd figured he was my age. "How long have you been driving?"

"Three months. Legally, at any rate."

We started back up toward the school, walking in silence for a moment.

"What an evil fucker," I said.

"Rob? Nah. He's like most of them, except bigger."

"But he was—" I groped for the words to express what was so wrong, and found that I didn't really understand how I felt. I'd seen more damage done before, without this sickening feeling. But this was too close to torture…

"Cruel at the end," Linc said, "cruel and deliberately humiliating. Is that what's bugging you?"

"I guess." I glanced back. They had stood Glennie onto his feet and were helping him limp away. The grass glistened red where he had lain.

"Well. Consider the fact that Glennie would have done just about the same thing if he had won. And remember how he was messing with you for no reason."

"Not the point." I was really stoned, and what I had just seen gnawed at me.

"Agreed. My point is, it isn't that Rob's a bad guy. He's like most of them, or like most of them would like to be. They're all just unevolved. Monkeys, fighting for dominance."

"Yeah, but he's King Monkey." I frowned, thinking hard. "And that's kind of a test, isn't it?"

Lincoln just said, "Hmm," and sat down on the grass.

I joined him. "Glennie looked pretty fucked up didn't he?"

"Probably end up in the hospital, yeah." He lay back and looked up at the sky. "You ever know anybody who got raped?"

I started to say no, then changed my mind. "I don't know."

"Good answer. Only that or *yes* make sense." He was silent for a moment. "The funny thing is, if you're a woman, and you get raped, even if it's nothing more than two minutes of forcible in-and-out, it's supposed to be this lifelong trauma, something you'll probably never get over. And maybe it is, I don't know. But, guys—well, they can get beat almost to death, in front of a crowd, and they're just supposed to pick themselves up and get on with things. It's somehow character-building. And not only does the guy get his face smashed in and ribs cracked and who knows what else, but afterwards nobody's even sympathetic. He's a Loser, a Beaten Guy, not worthy of wasting sympathy on." He laughed, and gestured at the world in general. "Nobody cares. The schools, the police, the parents: nobody cares. Everybody buys it. Boys will be boys. Part of growing up. And then people wonder why the world is so twisted."

I wrapped my arms around my knees and thought. All the violence and rage in me—how would it play if I were King Monkey? I didn't like the answers much.

"It'll all change, though," Linc said. "We're headed for a new world."

"Sure. What're you gonna do with people like Rob? Send 'em to Sunday school? Give 'em some kind of a pill?"

Lincoln sat up. "There *is* a pill, you know."

I made a rude sound. "Yeah, right."

"You ever drop acid?"

"LSD? No. Done lots of drugs, but everybody says it just kind of makes you weird. Hippies and college professors, right?"

"*Everybody* is full of shit about almost everything. Try it before you decide."

I shrugged. "Okay, you got some? Let's do it."

He laughed, a sound of genuine surprise and amusement. "We need time, man, the stuff is slow. We need twelve, fifteen hours, not an afternoon. Howabout Saturday?"

"Yeah…yeah, I can do it. No, wait…" I'd planned to hitch down to Redlands to see Stacy on Saturday. I paused and reflected that during the last hour she hadn't risen up in my mind's eye. A vacation from my obsession, yet it felt like I had lost something. I needed to see her again. "Sunday?" I asked. "Could we do Sunday instead?"

"Even better." He jabbed my arm. "Pack your head. We're going on a trip."

5 | THE POULTRY POOL

I stared at Lincoln's extra copy of the test as Ubelovsky wrote the workings and answers on the chalkboard. Every answer Ellard had given was correct, though his way of arriving at them didn't always match the teacher's. My own test had a big red *53* circled at the top. Better than half, but just barely.

The test that Lincoln now held in his hands displayed a large *38*, along with a red-pencil scrawl: *Keep trying, you've improving*. He saw me squinting at the comment and gave me a cheery smile.

I'd weaseled on our weekend plans. When I'd arrived home the previous night, there was a note from Dad: Company picnic Saturday at noon to six. You <u>will</u> come and be clean sober and decent. These are the people who put food on our table your mouth.

I needed to see Stacy, needed it and feared it. It bothered me that she hadn't tried to get in touch with me when I was in Juvie. Or had she? Probably people on ice didn't get mail…

I called Juvenile Hall, and, after being passed around by the evening staff, I found someone who assured me that I was wrong—if mail had come for me and been withheld, it would have been handed to me upon my release. No, there couldn't have been a mistake…

I had to get there on Sunday. I had to.

Linc was decent about it, though he teased me about cold feet, and dragged me down to the Park to toke up and meet new people.

The Andrews' picnic wasn't for the entire staff, only supervisors and office workers, but with families along the crowd must have totaled at least a hundred guests, maybe twice that.

Fortunately, the Andrews residence could handle it. I'd never been in a house with even two bathrooms before; over the course of the day, I counted six, and there may have been more hiding. A sprawling ranch-style house perched on a ridge, as far from his fly-ridden egg farms as possible, the most astonishing feature was the backyard: a patio the size of a baseball diamond, and the famous pools.

Everyone had heard about the swimming pools, but I'd never quite believed in them. The smaller of the two, a kid's wading pool, was a perfect egg. The adult pool, a huge affair, formed the outline of a chicken.

Or so they said. Down at ground level, it was really impossible to tell: chicken, crab, road-kill? I didn't see the point—a joke where the punchline always had to be explained.

Dad marched me over to meet Mal Andrews, the big boss himself, a rawboned man of about sixty, who eyed me suspiciously before shaking hands. I imagined that Dad had explained how much trouble I was, slanting his story vertical in the process.

Mrs. Andrews was a very different matter. She stood near the buffet, supervising the caterers, dressed in a thin shift. She spun when Dad said, "Sue?" and she gave the two of us a smile like the coil on an electric stove, blank at first and then moving from dull red to orange-hot.

She reached out her hands and captured one of mine and one of his, and Dad and I stood there as two points of an uncomfortable, incomplete triangle while she welcomed us—she'd heard so much about me, was so pleased I was living up there now…

Her shift turned out to be a beach cover-up, open in the front, showing nothing but a red bikini beneath. This was Mrs. Andrews? She couldn't have been more than twenty-five, and she was luscious. I used my incessant nodding to look up and down as she babbled. Her lipstick was a perfect match to her bikini.

"And I'm sure you brought your swimsuit," she said, "it's going to be so hot this afternoon—but maybe you'd like something to eat right now. We're serving up twice, a lunch now, and then a dinner at five…" I think she noticed me noticing her, because she suddenly switched to, "And, I bet you'd like to meet my daughter, Leslie…" She stood on tiptoe and peered through the crowd. "She's probably over by the fence, sunning, even though she ought to be up and entertaining our guests. But I'm sure you two would have lots to talk about…but you probably want some lunch first?" She smelled of perfume and salt.

"I'd just as soon swim first, Mrs. Andrews."

"Call me Sue."

"You call her Mrs. Andrews," Dad said.

She rolled her eyes, and I made my escape. I'd have lots to talk about with her daughter Leslie? Leslie would be, what, maybe eleven at the oldest? Sue Andrews had been nice to me, and was crotch-stirringly attractive; but she dismissed me as if I were a child, and I was wounded.

Not so wounded as to avoid a hard-on. I went to the bathhouse and pulled on my swimsuit, chlorine in my nostrils and tepid water on the concrete underfoot, and then fought to tuck myself down my right leg so I wouldn't show.

The water in the giant faux chicken was perfect. I dove, swam its length underwater, and surfaced with air exploding from my lungs. The sunlight refracted through the shattered water and bounced off the white pool plaster, almost blinding. I did laps, back and forth, sometimes diving and frog-kicking my way near the bottom, eyes open to the blurry world, and it occurred to me that heaven, if such a thing existed, might be like that, luminous from all directions and yet without heat, a cool supportive fluid bathing you every moment.

I swam myself to exhaustion and hauled out onto the tile coping. I could feel my eyes reddening from the chemicals in the water. Others— mostly my age or younger—were starting to get in the water; I'd set a trend. Many of the teens climbed into what would have been the chicken's comb and beak, where a shallow shelf let them sit chest-deep.

A great opportunity to go over and introduce myself, but I couldn't do it. Too many new people in a whole new town. Pale and skinny from my time in lockup, topped off with a degrading haircut,

I knew I wouldn't elicit, *Who's that mysterious new stranger?* but rather, *Who's the dork?*

I went over to the grassy area along the back fence and lay on a web-back recliner, letting the sun beat against my closed eyelids.

A little noise of surprise from the foot of the recliner. A teenaged girl stood there, an open hardback copy of *The French Lieutenant's Woman* in one hand, a sandwich in the other. She'd obviously walked right to that spot before looking up from the pages.

"Sorry," I said, "did I take your place?" I rolled off the recliner and into a seated position on the grass. She protested in monosyllables, but I ignored them. As an afterthought, I pulled my towel off the recliner.

"I don't need to lay *there*," she said, "I was coming back and just wasn't paying attention."

"Lay back down," I urged. "I'm fine. No sweat."

She chewed on the inside of her mouth. She wore a flower-print bikini over a darkly tanned body. Sunglasses hid her eyes, but from the shoulder-length black hair I guessed they would be brown.

She made a moue of annoyed indifference, and spun around, sat, and finally leaned back, all without use of her hands.

"I'm Rick."

She took a bite of her sandwich.

"Is it good?" I asked. "The book, I mean."

"*I* like it."

She made as if to start reading, but I persisted. "I like Fowles a lot."

She flipped open a flap of the dust jacket to mark her place, and pushed her sunglasses up onto her head. The eyes were blue. "If you tell me *The Collector* is your favorite book, I think I'll go sit somewhere else."

"I don't know what my favorite book is, but that's certainly not it. I liked it okay, but I loved *The Magus*. Though I don't read Greek, so I missed a couple of things."

She laughed. "Yeah, they don't teach much Greek out here in the sticks."

"So, one of your parents works for the ranch?"

"You could say that. I'm Leslie Andrews. Mal Andrews is my dad."

"Oh." That explained how she could afford hardback books. "Sue—uh, your mom, mentioned you."

"My *step*mother. So I don't imagine she mentioned anything nice."

"Just said she thought we'd have lots to talk about."

"Oh really? Well, if my stepmonster said that, she must not think very highly of you... Why are you here today, anyway?"

"My dad works for yours. Jack Leibnitz."

"Oh, you're the Leibnitz kid—the one that's always in trouble. But I thought you were supposed to be a hippie or something."

Swimsuits are revealing anatomically, but they take away many of the clues we use to tell what kind of person we're looking at. Was Leslie a cheerleader? A hippie chick? A Bad Girl? She seemed smart, and was more physically developed than I, but that was all I knew for certain.

I took a deep breath and gave her a quick synopsis: got busted, went to Juvie, ended up in Yucaipa. I didn't mention that military school was a mere three months in my future.

"Wow. What a drag... You want a drink?"

"I can get them."

"No. I mean a *real* drink. Whatever you like. They keep a bar inside that could drown Los Angeles."

I told her I'd have whatever she had, and I got to watch her walk off, which made me tingle. In the last week I'd already been unfaithful to Stacy in my mind a thousand times, with a dozen different girls. I felt ashamed, but my body—and my subconscious mind, I guess—felt no guilt at all. A few hours with Stacy, though, and my fidelity would be restored; of that, I was morally certain.

Leslie came back with two vodka-tonics. She held out her glass to clink. "To Yucaipa, may we soon escape it."

I raised my eyebrows.

"I thought," she said, "I'd be going to college in the fall. UC Santa Cruz."

"You're a senior?"

"A junior. But I applied for early admission. And I thought they were going to take me. But for earlies they do interviews of the relatives, and the school decided that my 'emotional maturity' wasn't advanced enough to go to college yet. It was Susan, I'm sure of it. She doesn't want me here, but she'd rather have me here and unhappy than somewhere else and having a good time."

I nodded. "So what happened to your mother? I mean, if that isn't too personal."

"My dad divorced her when he decided he needed fresh meat."

"And he got custody?"

"No. I lived with my mom for about six years, down in San Diego. But she married this real creep, and the minute I got tits he was just all over me—nothing you could really prove, you know, just sort of spying on me, and 'accidentally' walking in on me when I was dressing. Touching me whenever he could. Ick. So I told Mom, and she told me to stop being so provocative, which I wasn't being except for the physical fact of hitting puberty, and we started fighting about it, and I said that it boiled down to one of us going, either him or me, and…" An acid smile. "You see where I've lived the last three years, so you know the story. At least Susan doesn't grope me; she just doesn't like the competition."

"For your dad?"

"For anything. She thinks she owns all the men in the world, that they're all supposed to cluster around her fat ass, the way the lives of the workerboy ants in a colony revolve around the queen."

Sue Andrews most definitely did not have a fat ass, and the worker ants in a colony are all female, but I foresaw no gain from pointing out either fact. "I'm sorry," I said.

"Yeah. Well, at least it won't be long. Just another year. Then no more Susan, no more Yucaipa. You, too, Rick—get out of here as fast as you can. This town is a wasteland… Hell, this town isn't even a town."

I agreed, secretly; but staying there in Chickenville seemed preferable to a military academy. Teenage boys surrounded by nothing but other teenage boys. What kind of pervert came up with that idea, anyway?

Late Sunday afternoon, Linc and I parked his used Impala in front of my former Redlands home.

A *For Sale* sign was planted in the center of the new-mown lawn. We walked across the sweet-smelling grass to the side of the house, and I pushed open the little door that led to the crawlspace.

My bottles were still all there, in glorious profusion.

We loaded them into the car trunk, filling it. "You're sure you can keep these somewhere?" I asked.

"No sweat, ace. Plenty of space at my place."

Then he drove me crosstown to Palm Avenue, and dropped me off three blocks from the Slater house.

"You sure you don't want me to hang around? What if she's not here?"

"She'll be here." I was stubbornly convinced of this, for no real reason.

"Okay. Your decision. Just remember—you could have dropped some L with me and spent the afternoon listening to the Choir Eternal instead of what you're doing."

"Fuck you, Ellard."

"Noted. I'm going home to put your liquor cabinet away."

He pulled a U-turn, slow, careful. He'd explained it to me. Drive under the speed limit. Drive a low-profile car. Obey all traffic laws. Not because you're a Boy Scout: Don't draw attention to yourself on the road. Never confuse your car with your cock. *Driving is a privilege, not a right*, and that fact is the thin wedge the authorities hammer on to invade your privacy.

None of my Redlands friends thought like that. I didn't think like that…but I saw his point.

The Slater Place. Stacy's house. A three-storied fantasy Victorian, with wood-shingle onion domes topping the whole at the left and right corners. I studied it from the sidewalk on the opposite side of the street. The estate wasn't lucid; confused as to place and time, grandmotherly gingerbread filigree ornamented St. Petersburg minarets, the whole surrounded by date palms.

Just go over and ring the doorbell. Just do it.

I couldn't. I walked up and down the block, unwilling to cross the street. I played out fantasies—Stacy rushing into my arms. I played out catastrophes—Stacy coming out of the house clinging to Jeff Halloran's arm. No, wait, she'd been sent away to live with a great-aunt in Rhode Island; no, wait, she'd died in a tragic car accident; no, wait, she was alive and well, but refused to speak to me…

I kept the animal pacing up for an hour, until an elderly man came out of a nearby house and stared at me, fists on hips.

Circle the block instead, then. Round this way, stop before the old man's lawn, double back…

I was in a state of despair when a car pulled into the Slaters' drive.

Stacy climbed out of the passenger side.

She was everything I'd remembered: slim, vital, refulgent with sexuality. She waved, and watched the car back out.

A girl. A girl had dropped her off.

Stacy headed up the walk to her porch, and I was into the street without thinking. A car swerved around me, honking. She turned and stared.

"Stacy," I shouted, as if she might bolt.

She looked at me without recognition as I ran across the lawn to stand in front of her, panting from the run and from a sudden terror that leaked from my bones.

She frowned. "Rick?" she asked.

I nodded, found I couldn't breathe, swallowed. "Yeah."

"They caught you."

I nodded again. I stood with my arms at my sides, willing her to rush into my embrace, unable to reach out myself.

"We should have played it cool," she said, "just kept walking."

"I—" I began. *I got busted for you*, I wanted to say, *for you*.

She saw something in my eyes. "Let's go out back." She reached for my hand and led me around the side of the house, and we'd gone several yards before I realized she was touching me again, what I'd dreamt of, her actual flesh against mine, and I squeezed her hand and she squeezed back, but tentatively, or so I imagined, and I tried to give myself up to the happiness of being with her again, but couldn't.

There was a remnant of an orange grove behind her house, with a few trees removed in the center to make room for a gazebo. We sat there, holding hands, but with several inches, several miles, between us, staring at our feet.

I sensed her gaze on me and lifted my face. "Your hair," she said. "It was so beautiful."

I couldn't look at her.

"Are you mad at me?" she asked.

No, I wanted to say, you're what kept me alive…

"I love you," I said.

She sighed and looked down, shaking her head. "Rick…"

"I *do*."

She took her hand from mine and interwove her fingers in her lap. "It was wrong of me to take you to the grove that afternoon. I should—"

"How can you say that? It was—it was the best thing that ever happened in my whole life. I—"

"But it was a mistake. We shouldn't have done it."

"Why?" My voice developed a whiny edge that I despised, but I couldn't control it. "Didn't you like it?"

She took my hand in both of hers and looked at my face. "I loved it. It was really fun. And I'll remember it forever. But now look at us."

"What? What do you mean? I'm back now, and—"

"Rick." She squeezed her hands hard around mine. "Listen. It was just supposed to be fun, that's all. I'm *graduating* in a couple of weeks. I'm eighteen in a month."

"Doesn't matter," I said, and turned my face away, squeezing my eyes shut. "Doesn't matter how old we are."

"It does. I'm grown up. I may even enroll over at Valley College. Do you know how crazy that is, a college girl with a tenth-grade boyfriend? It isn't even legal."

I turned and pulled her to me and kissed her hard, and she let my tongue inside her mouth and kissed back, but then gently, firmly, unwrapped my arms from around her and pushed me away. Her lips stayed on mine until the last moment.

"Don't you want me? Didn't—didn't you feel anything?"

She breathed in and out, her inhales deep, her exhales shaky. "It isn't that. Sure, I'd love to ball you again, but—"

"Then *do*. But it isn't just the sex—"

"I know it isn't just the sex. That's the problem." She seized her index finger in her opposite fist and twisted her hand back and forth as she talked. "Rick…I think I'm getting married."

"You think?" I was suddenly groggy, my mind fumbling for something to say that would change it, some point of purchase. "Why? To who? Can't you just—can't we have some time? If you let me show you how—"

"Rick, Rick, honey…don't you see that it doesn't make any sense, you and me? And there's lots of other girls, girls your age…"

"Don't *say* that," I said, my voice trembling. "There's nobody like you." I wiped the back of my hand across my eyes and it came away wet. "Stacy, *please*…please, I'll do anything you want…"

"Now do you see why it was wrong? Now you think you're in love with me—"

"I *am* in love with you."

"Just because you've been inside me doesn't mean you know me, Rick. You're in love with your idea of me."

"I know you." I sniffled. "I know you better than you know you. You don't even know who you are."

"Oh, God." She raked her fingers back through her hair. "See? God, I feel terrible."

"Don't. Just tell me what I need to do. Just—"

She stopped me by putting her fingertips on my lips. "Shhh. Leave it. Please, for me, just leave it alone. Let me remember our time in the grove, not remember you hating me."

"I don't hate you! I *love* you!" With that I burst into real sobs and covered my face with my hands.

Stacy gathered me in her arms and I curled down, reaching around her and sobbing with my face against her chest. "Oh, Rick… Oh, honey, honey…I'm so sorry…"

She rocked me and I sobbed, not only for the loss of her, but for all the losses in my life, and now for the loss of all hope.

"Honey, honey…" She just kept rocking, petting my ruined hair.

When I calmed enough to speak clearly, I said, muffled by her breasts, "It isn't the end. I'll always, always want you. You'll change your mind."

Rock, rock. "No, honey," she whispered. Rock, rock. "*You'll* change *your* mind, honey. *You* will."

I was silent after that, her blouse wet against my face, the smell of her seeping through the fabric. From overhead, the cawing of crows, calling out to gather the flock together as they headed to their evening roosts.

That night was the first time in years that I cut myself. Stranded on the Ford Street onramp trying to hitch a ride back to Yucaipa, I slumped down and sat with my back against the post of the *Freeway Entrance* sign.

I started by tossing the pebbles and bottlecaps in easy reach—not real throws, just weak flicks that landed them a few yards away. When I picked up the triangle of brown beer-bottle glass, I used it to trace a big *S* on the inside of my left forearm. I dragged the tip of the glass in the same pattern again and again, leaving a pink track of irritated flesh behind at first, until finally little dots of blood appeared. I watched them well up into a string of dark beads, and then I began dragging the glass along the pattern again.

I'd pause in my engraving whenever the long stoplight changed, and hold up my thumb, the glass clutched safely inside my palm. Then back to carving again. I never cut hard or deep on any pass, but the cumulative effect turned gory, the blood trickling onto the dust by my side, the red gone blackish under the dim streetlight.

It took me by surprise when a car finally stopped. I jumped up and started to run, then realized I was dripping blood everywhere. I held my forearm against the front of my shirt, pressing hard on my diaphragm.

I pulled open the door and jumped in; no need to ask where he was going, as there were no offramps until Yucaipa.

The driver, a guy in his thirties with long, razor-cut sideburns, stared at the blood on my shirt. "You need to go to the ER? Is it your stomach?"

"No. Arm. Just keeping the blood off your upholstery."

He considered, and then looked over his shoulder as he pulled out onto the ramp.

"You fall or something?"

"No."

"Jesus. Did somebody do it to you? You want to report it to the police?"

"It wasn't her fault." I rocked slowly forward and back, recreating Stacy's rhythm from the gazebo. Rock, rock, rock. "It was an accident."

6 | A LADDER OF PINK BAND-AIDS

Without Stacy to dream of, all the light went out of me, and the week that followed was grim. I wandered through my classes, mute and glassy-eyed; went down to the Park each day to smoke with Lincoln; took the long walk home each afternoon, refusing rides, and lay on my bed. For the first time in my life I was too apathetic to read.

My numbness obliterated my self-consciousness. Focused on the growing darkness inside, I didn't care what the other kids thought about me, and this seemed to make me more attractive. By any objective standard, my social circumstances improved. Girls at school went out of their way to say hello to me: Melissa, Randi, JenBen, even Leslie Andrews. Through Lincoln's little smoking circle I met dozens of new people. Linc seemed to know everyone.

When he dropped through the school for our first biweekly review, Leo, my PO, noticed. "Your attitude's changed," he said. "A lot of the hostility seems gone."

Sure. Death of hope does that to you. Military school, Chino. Who cares?

People stared at the ladder of pink Band-Aids that cross-hatched the inside of my left forearm, but no one asked about it.

Over that week, I gradually added a matching set of Band-Aids to my right forearm. Not initials, not anything, really; just a slow aimless absentminded slicing at my skin. As the hieroglyphics emerged, I wondered if, when I finished, they might spell something; if perhaps, as in the Kafka story, the name of my crime was being cut into my flesh.

Lincoln stood stalwart through my depression. When we were alone, he spouted forth theories, plausible and preposterous by turn, about life, women, music, books, the War, the future. At first I thought he simply liked to hear himself talk, which indeed he did, but I came to understand that he was filling in the silences. Refusing to accept my inner collapse, he was doing the work of friendship for both of us. He even tolerated my apathy about our postponed acid trip. "It'll happen," he said, "when it needs to."

The final week of school did nothing to buoy my spirits. For summer vacation, I was expected to get a job and save some money to fund part of the cost of military school (reminiscent of those military dictatorships where your family must pay for the bullets the firing squad uses on you). At least I had a reprieve from the most likely avenue of employment; to my father's disgust, Andrews Egg Ranches was unionized, and the union rules precluded hiring workers under sixteen, even for summer jobs.

In that last week of school, the daily patterns vanished. Some classes expanded so finals could be given; others, where term papers were due, stopped meeting altogether.

On Wednesday, I was finished by noon. Lincoln was off in a physics final.

I walked home in the mounting heat, a Band-Aid peeled back so I could worry at a scab with my fingernail. I toyed with the idea of suicide, but who would it be for? My dad would just point to it as evidence of what a jerk I was; and my mom would probably never hear about it. Stacy would probably feel guilty, but I'd never wanted to make her feel bad; on the contrary.

American legends die hard. There's always a new place, right? You can head for virgin land and homestead, or join the Navy, run away with the circus…

Not possible anymore. Not at fifteen, in any case. Until you're sixteen, you can run, but you can't make a living.

The shade of the pepper tree in our front yard felt like cool water after the midday sun. Clusters of peppercorns, a preposterous pink like cake sprinkles, crunched under my feet as I crossed to our front door.

I heard a noise as soon as the key turned in the lock. There were no lights on inside, and my eyes were still adjusted to the outdoors.

Two figures scrambled upright on the sofa.

My dad, naked to the waist.

Sue Andrews in her panties.

They stared. Mrs. Andrews' eyes were wide with fear, her fingers clutching at the sofa to either side of her knees. Then her face relaxed with relief, and her arms crossed to cover her breasts. Her eyes darted as she searched for some plausible form of *this isn't what it looks like*, but no words came.

Dad's face changed from ludicrous surprise to a hard squint. "You son-of-a-*bitch*," he said, and on the last word launched himself at me.

Too stunned to move, I was easy prey. He grabbed me by the throat and slammed me against the doorframe, then hoisted me until I stood tiptoe, choking. "You little fuck," he said, "what are you trying to pull? What are you trying to do to me?"

"Jack!" Sue shouted.

"What are you doing here?" He slapped me across the face. His fingers were sticky. "Middle of the fucking day…"

Sue grabbed his arm. "Stop it! It's not his fault!"

He shrugged her off so hard she stumbled back. He released my throat, pulled back, and punched me with his fist, smashing the left side of both mouth and nose. The force sent me sprawling onto the front walk.

I smelled Sue Andrews smeared on my face where he'd slapped me, and then the musk of her disappeared beneath the more insistent smell of blood.

He started through the doorway but Sue jerked him back by his arm. He whirled on her and raised his hand, open-palmed. She grabbed his wrist.

They stood in profile just inside the door, him heaving with anger. "*Don't you ever raise your hand to me,*" she whispered.

Even as I struggled to my feet, I kept my eyes on her. My God, what a centerfold body.

He lowered his hand.

She covered herself with her arms and turned to me. "Go somewhere. Don't say anything. *Please.*"

"Say anything to anybody, you're dead!" Dad yelled at my retreating back. "You'll be in YA so fast you won't know what happened. *Got that, pal?*"

Sue said something sharp but quiet, and the door slammed.

There were no sidewalks down in Dunlap, hence no curbs. When I came to a low cinderblock wall I sat down. The mouth wasn't bad, but the nose wouldn't stop bleeding. I pulled off my shoe and put it back on barefoot, using the sock to stanch the blood.

If Sue Andrews wanted to have an affair, she could have picked from whole battalions of willing men. What the hell would lead her to settle on my dad?

Go somewhere, she'd commanded. Where did she think I was welcome?

I'd have to call Lincoln Ellard, I supposed.

I wandered down the street pressing the sock to the side of my face. Something felt wrong about this, bleeding in the blaze of the afternoon sun.

I realized I had no idea where Linc lived. Probably up near the Andrews clan. Always so neatly turned out, such weird, slick clothes: his family had to have money.

At the little grocery store I kneed the door to the phone booth, folding it inward. I opened the phone book and wedged the spine of the hard protective cover between my hip and the wall. With my free hand I paged to the *Es*. Only one Ellard in Yucaipa, *M. Ellard*, on *32323 Indiana.*

Less than five blocks away.

I'd walked Indiana Street before but never paid attention; just another Dunlap neighborhood, leafy in parts, baking under the sun in others. Mostly houses and cottages of varying sizes and states of disrepair, but a few businesses too: One rusty quonset hut declared, *Welding—Antiques—Bait*.

I passed a run-down nursery, wooden posts supporting a quarter-acre of sunscreen netting. The street numbers left a gap; the next was 32525.

Street addresses in Yucaipa are unpredictable; there are unexplained holes, counterbalanced by extras stuffed in as afterthoughts, resulting in street numbers like 9402½B. They always get them in order, though, which meant I had passed the Ellard residence. Probably the wrong Ellard anyway; Lincoln's folks were probably unlisted despite the extra cost.

Green Mansions Nursery. On one whitewashed post, brass numerals: 32323.

A nursery. It couldn't be right, but I stepped through what passed for a doorway in the screens.

A rush of humidity, almost liquid in density, and, in my one working nostril, a swelling odor of planting medium, the smell of life: rot and growth and manure all entwined.

Two Mexican-American workers went about their business without even looking at me.

I ventured farther in. Centered in the sunscreened area was a wraparound counter and a cash register, and, as I approached, a woman rose into view.

"Gracious!" she said. Despite her speech, she had to be under thirty, tall and big-boned, with straight blond hair that managed to be unfashionable.

"Lincoln Ellard live around here?" I asked, my words slurred by the pressure I kept on my nose.

"You a friend of Linc's?"

"Yeah. Need to clean up."

She locked the register and came around the counter. "You sure do." She put one arm around my shoulders and steered me toward the back of the nursery. "I'm Martha." I almost asked if she were Lincoln's mom, but she added, "I'm Linc's sister."

Linc's house was a two-bedroom cottage that had been built with floorboards laid directly on the ground, not unheard of in the early days of Yucaipa building. In the dry climate, it might be decades or more before they gave way, usually to termites; and when that day came, why, all you had to do was pull them up and lay down new slats—redwood or cedar if you were feeling rich.

Martha got me cleaned up in the tiny bathroom. I wadded enough toilet paper up my nose to stop the blood for a while. "We'll give you a little lie-down in Linc's room until he gets home then."

She led me to what seemed to be the back door and opened it.

Linc's bedroom had once been a back porch, the former screens walled in with tongue-and-groove siding. A makeshift closet held his shirts and jackets in ordered rows; pants, boxer shorts, and socks were folded on shelves. Dozens of others were shelves laden with books, some of them so near the slanted ceiling you'd need a chair to get to them, and all of them were adjusted so their spines stood even, a bulwark of words.

Martha sat beside me on the bed as I lay with my head tilted back, snuffling coagulated snot and blood down my throat, waiting for the body's microscopic beavers to dam the flood.

"What happened to you, hon?"

"My dad beat me up."

"Whatever for?"

"Walked in on him and a woman."

"In the bedroom?"

"No. In the living room. I didn't know they were there."

"Now, that's their problem, ain't it? What you should do, you should report him."

I snorted, then realized it was a bad idea to exhale so hard. "Nah. That's the problem, you see? He reports *me* for something: I go to jail. I report *him* for something: I still go to jail."

She chewed her lip. "Ain't right, though, is it? I mean, you may need to swat a kid a few times. But I don't hold with beating on children."

It seemed as if there were something I could do, steps I could take, authorities I could contact, if only I were wiser. I riffled through possible solutions, and came up with nothing; nothing, at any rate, that didn't put me into state custody.

Sounds from the living room brought me out of a doze. "I know somebody came in," a woman's voice accused, "crept in, when they thought I was sleepin'. I heard 'im, all quiet and voices in the back room."

The door stood ajar. I heard Linc's voice and Martha's start up together, trying to calm the woman.

I opened the door and all three of them looked my way. "See, Momma, it's just Linc's friend, Rick."

The woman on the sofa must have been in her sixties, improbably old for Lincoln's mother. Her gray hair was pulled back into such a tight ponytail that it smoothed the wrinkles on her forehead to tiny creases. Her bulging eyes studied me with fear and suspicion. "Not comin' around from Delia's? Not one of them from the Church?"

"No, Mom," Linc said. "He's just a friend from school."

She held the belt of her housedress in her lap, wrapping it round one fist by rotating the other, then unrolling it again. "Maybe so. But I know they been coming around here…"

Martha sat down next to Momma and draped an arm across her shoulders. "I'll keep a good lookout for 'em, then." She looked up at Linc and tilted her head toward me and the back porch. Linc waved me back into his room and followed.

As he shut the door he said, "She gets…confused." I sat down on the bed. "What the hell happened to you? Wait, let's get a drink first. Your booze, after all."

The other door in his room led to the backyard. A refrigerator sat humming against the rear wall of the house; when he opened it, there were all of my bottles, along with stacked six-packs of soft drinks.

We left the door open to the outside in hopes of an afternoon breeze, and sat on the floor with our backs against the bed, drinking rum and Coke. I told him everything—not my thoughts and feelings, of course, but all of the events—Mom's vanishing act, Dad's apparent psychosis, the details about my PO, the imminent threat of military school, Stacy and her desertion. Flies gathered in the room as I talked, the fat flies of early summer, and Linc eyed them with distaste as he listened.

When I got to the description of what had happened that afternoon he stopped me, waving his open palms in the air like a mime with a hyperactivity disorder. "Whoa, whoa, hold it. He's balling Mrs. Andrews…like, the egg guy's wife?"

I nodded.

"Far fucking out. The Lord hath delivered him into your hands. Mission complete. Problem solved."

"Not really."

Linc hunched forward in excitement, leaning his elbows on his crossed legs. "Just tell him unless he backs off, you'll blab it all over town. You're in the driver's seat now."

I began shaking my head in the negative even before he finished. "You don't understand. One word to my PO, I'm bounced back. Then it's YA until I'm eighteen, or, if I'm really lucky, a year in Juvie followed by some foster home with twenty kids where they sing psalms eight hours a day." I sighed. "I might just as well off myself."

Linc blew out an exasperated breath. "I know you haven't got it easy. But do you have to be such a pussy about it?"

"You don't know what it's like."

"Yeah? Look around you. Think this has been paradise?" He waved at his whole universe. "But you know what? I got it fucking *made* compared to a lot of kids in the slums. And I *got it made*, compared to most kids in other countries. And, if you look at human history, *I got it made*, compared to almost everybody that ever lived."

He waited for me to respond. I just looked back at him, so he continued. "You could be a fucking serf slopping hogs on your lord's estate in medieval Russia. You could be a sex slave in the Mideast today—they have them, boys and girls both. You could be chained to your oar in a Roman galley. You could be in Auschwitz. You could be born without legs. You could be born retarded. You've been blessed, God knows why, so stop being such a fucking whiner."

"You're probably right," I said, though this was a purely intellectual concession. Emotionally, I doubted that anyone had ever suffered as I had.

"*Probably* isn't a factor here. Face it: you're not at the pinnacle of ease and knowledge and comfort in all of human existence to date, but you can *see* the pinnacle from here. Walking distance."

"You got it all figured out, I guess."

"No. But I've sure got more of it figured out than you do."

I stopped wallowing in self-pity long enough to realize that he was certainly right about that part. I knew nothing. "So what do I do now?"

"Stay here tonight. Don't go home, not tonight, not tomorrow… We'll figure out some place for you to stay from tomorrow; I mean, you could stay here, but Momma…"

"Yeah. But my dad'll probably call my PO and report me."

"Hah. He and Sue Andrews will be shivering the whole time, wondering where you are and what you've said to who…excuse me, *to whom*."

"You don't understand him. He's vindictive. He'll hurt himself so long as it hurts somebody else more."

"Yes. But you can bet that Sue Andrews feels differently. And if she gets divorced for adultery, she probably doesn't get left with much." He grinned, a wide, malevolent smile. "So, let the lady do some of your work for you. We've got other stuff to take care of."

"Like?"

He produced a ball of crumbly beige hash from his shirt pocket. "Blonde Lebanese." He checked his wristwatch. "It's after five. Come on, I'll show you the nursery." Braced on the heel of one palm, he pushed into a standing position and offered me his hand. "Ever hear plants grow?"

❦

Sleeping on the Ellards' living room couch was like a fever dream. While I was talking to Lincoln, most of my fears about tomorrow had fled like an experienced guerilla army, leaving behind nothing but smoldering campfires; but once I was alone in the dark they infiltrated the borders of my stoned consciousness, determined to overthrow the shaky government of my mind. The nursery outside had a powerful floodlight in the parking lot, and the harsh light punched its way around every curtain, making the surrounding shadows even darker; lines of light cut around the edges of the door, as though someone were slicing through the wall with a blowtorch.

At least twice Mrs. Ellard came out of her room to peer at me. I fell into a confused recurring dream of my mother disappearing into a bank of fog, but it wasn't my mother anymore, it was Stacy, and I tried to get up to follow her but Todd Carley had me pinned down, my blue government pajamas down around my knees, and a lit match hovered over my groin and I smelled my pubic hair singeing. He leaned down close, eyes huge behind those horn-rim glasses, and his breath came hot on my face as he demanded, "But how does the story end, Rick, *what happens* to all of them?" My eyes opened.

Mrs. Ellard's face was only inches from mine, her eyes searching my features for signs of I knew not what. I didn't move. The odors of her night-breath settled on me, mouth smells in a halo of lilac and talcum powder. At last she nodded, straightened up, and shuffled back to her bedroom.

Morning woke me to sounds from the kitchen. I groaned and held my head. Martha leaned around the corner. "Breakfast!" she sang, as if she were a regular part of my morning routine.

She jerked her head back. When I stumbled to the kitchen she and Linc were side by side at the narrow stove. As far as I could glimpse between their jostling figures, she was working two pans at once, scrambling eggs in one and frying bacon in another, while Lincoln grilled pancakes in a heavy skillet. "Move your scrawny ass," she said, and bumped her bottom into him. Taller and bulky enough to pick him up if she'd cared to, her hip took him in the low ribs and knocked him sideways.

"Hey." He flipped the pan and caught the pancake like a pro. "Keep that up and you'll get the ones that land on the floor." He looked over his shoulder at me. "Sit down, grab a spot."

The style of the kitchen table was already old in the sixties, legs of curved stainless-steel pipes supporting a chipped laminated top of some miracle material. The surface had once been white but had yellowed, like real ivory, and the gold sunburst-and-stars patterns looked like the crazing on a cracked glass windshield.

Linc and Martha continued screwing around as they cooked, and I felt as if I'd slipped into an alternate universe, one where Norman Rockwell had gone White Trash. Crazy Mom in the back bedroom; me, Linc's homeless friend, his face bruised, violating the terms of his probation in innumerable ways; and the siblings, who must have had different fathers, playing bumper cars with their butts as they cooked... Well, shorten my tie and call me Jimmy Stewart, 'cause *It's a Wonderful Life*!

Cynicism retreated fast when Linc slapped down a plate in front of me. I looked in astonishment at a stack of hot pancakes, a pile of scrambled eggs, and a whole hog's-worth of bacon, what seemed like more breakfast than I normally ate in a month. He came back a moment later with silverware and a huge glass of orange juice.

My throat was dry and I took a huge gulp, and then followed it with a smaller swallow, savoring it the second time around. "Fresh," I gasped.

Linc sat down with his own plate and juice. "Oranges're free," he said, gesturing with a thumb over his shoulder toward the rear of the property. He slid a giant bottle of syrup across the tabletop. "Eat."

Eating the first few bites only got my juices going. Ravenous would be an understatement. The eggs were heavenly, fried in butter, scrambled up with onions, chives, and chopped peppers, just hot enough to make the insipid sweetness of the syrupy pancakes seem luscious.

Martha returned, having taken a tray to Momma's room, and brought her own plate to the table. I gestured at the eggs, my mouth full of food, and made sounds of appreciation in my throat. "Like your eggs like that, hon?" she asked.

"She cooks almost everything Mexican style," Lincoln said. "Figure her daddy must have been a wetback."

"Yeah?" She forked pancake into her mouth. "Why am I the blondie, then? You're the one who looks like a reject from a mariachi band."

"*Re*ject? I'm the frontman, Numero Uno."

"Yep. Reeky Ricardo." Martha turned to me. "You don't need to eat so fast, we're not gonna take it away from you."

"But he *does* need to eat so fast." We both looked at Lincoln. "State comprehensives? Didn't you say yours started first period?"

"Oh shit." I stood up, knocking the chair back with the rear of my knees.

"Don't say that word when I'm eating," Martha said, her voice mild. "Puts me off my feed."

"Don't panic," Linc said. "I'll give you a ride, we've got time. But when you finish up you'll need to get showered, borrow some of my clothes, wash your hair and take a piss or whatever—"

"That word either," Martha said, "specially when I'm drinking orange juice."

※

It was one of those fill-in-the-bubble exams. Do NOT make any marks outside the bubble. ERASE all incorrect marks COMPLETELY. The times I'd taken these before, every few years, these warnings and the twisted, panicked energy in the room had made me so nervous I could hardly pay attention to the questions.

That day it was different. I did my level best, considering each question, marking the answer if I knew it, guessing between the only logical possibilities when I didn't. Out of four or five options, I realized, usually at least one is preposterous, and another is a trick. Throw those out, and it's a multiple-choice test with only two or three answers... and I didn't even care if I chose the right one.

An easy test. I finished every section early and put my pencil down on the desk. Mrs. Cathcart, the proctor for our section, glared at me—you aren't really trying, are you?—but I spent my time looking around the room. Melissa sat a couple of rows in front of me, yanking on her hair with her left hand while her right worked the problems. Instead of her usual miniskirt, she wore a white peasant skirt, and her panty line was clear underneath it. With enough study, I even worked out their color—pink—and located the square imprint of the fabric-care tag just at that point where the swell of her ass arched out from the small of her back.

At the end of the third section, basic math, I slouched sideways and looked out the window, afraid that if I stared at Melissa any more...well, just pretty sure I shouldn't stare at Melissa anymore. Girls don't have problems like that, and they seem weirdly unaware of what's happening with the boys around them.

Leslie Andrews sat by the window. A flock of sparrows fluttered by outside the glass, no more than a foot from her head, but she worked away, unaware of the world rushing past.

Mrs. Cathcart cleared her throat and squinted at me. The other students took this as a sign that she was getting ready to call time soon, and redoubled their efforts, moving their pencils in tiny little capsule shapes on the IBM punch cards.

Beautiful, sexy, smart, not necessarily in that order, Leslie was out of my league. After Stacy I knew better than to obsess over these goddesses who were practically in college. As long as I was going to long for the unattainable, why not a movie star, or Miss February, or some other airbrush queen? Why long for someone close enough to hurt you?

But Leslie and I seemed to have something in common now, though I couldn't figure out a good way to bring it up. *So, have you noticed that my father is balling your mom? Oh, sorry, your stepmother...?* Whether she'd noticed or not, it was bound to get her attention, but I couldn't figure out how to hopscotch my way to the next square: *Well, then, just for symmetry's sake, howsabout we—?*

Three more sessions of *STOP!* The word was framed in a hexagonal border, the authorities assuming that Californians would recognize the shapes of road signs even if we couldn't read. *Put down your pencil. DO NOT go on to the next section until instructed to do so!*

When it was over, after three hours, we wandered out into the June sun, at eleven in the morning already a hammer falling from the sky. Linc's bellbottoms and shirt were both short on me, and I realized that I was considerably taller than him, a fact that had never registered before. "Check the pockets," he'd added that morning, before he drove off to park, and when I did I found three tight-rolled joints and a pack of matches.

I leaned on the wall outside the door. Everyone else seemed obliterated by the exam. Melissa slumped past me, unseeing, taking her *Delicate—Hand-Wash Only* panty tag somewhere else.

Me, I felt pretty good, considering that Stacy had stomped my heart flat, that I couldn't go home, that I'd probably end up in YA any day, and to top it off had the previous night's sleep interrupted twice by a crazy woman. I was free, for the moment at least, free with a triplet of joints in my shirt pocket.

Leslie's eyes were only the bluer for being bloodshot. She tossed her black hair and looked as if she'd expected me—expected me, and was wearied by the prospect. "How was the test?"

I shrugged. "Okay."

"What happened to your face?"

"My dad beat me up. You want to go down to the Park and torch a few joints?"

She stared at me for so long that all my what-a-dipshit bells were clanging, until she said, "Sure."

Her pants fit her like sleek fur, and I kept glancing down as we walked around the back of the school. She noticed me watching the roll of her hips and, misinterpreting my stare, said, "Pants days during finals."

"Ah." The rules. No pants for girls except on the extraordinary "snow days;" no snow on the ground, then, no matter how cold, the girls could stand there at the bus stop with their legs turning blotchy blue. Miniskirts no more than four inches above the knees—a problem readily managed by partly unzipping the skirt and tugging it down before the monitors got there with the yardsticks. No *OAB*, "overaffectionate behavior," as if there could be such a thing, which basically meant "no dry-humping on campus."

No wet-humping, either, I guess. Way too affectionate.

The dual purpose of our schools: educate, and stamp out affection.

"I'd been hoping to find you before the semester ended anyway," she said.

"Oh?" I asked. "Why's that?"

We crossed the concrete curb that separated the school from the Park.

"If you're hoping that I haven't been able to get you out of my mind since the day I met you, then you're a retard."

I've been called worse.

She selected a spruce, ducked down under it, and I followed.

The book of matches in the shirt pocket read *Libra* on one side. On the other, it announced:

> Libra loves peace
> Libra loves love
> A kind of harmonious
> Sort of a dove.

I decided not to share these immortal lines with Leslie.

I torched up a joint, drew on it, and passed it. She took her time, unshouldered her big purse, and then sucked down smoke as if she did it every day, widening and narrowing her lips to get the right mix of air to cool her throat and yet maximize the flow of dope to her lungs. Freaky and erotic, the precision of her motions, the actions of a girl who knew what she wanted and took it. It reminded me of Stacy somehow, and my throat tightened.

"Hey," Leslie grunted, holding in her hit. She was holding the joint out to me. She exhaled. "You going weird on me?"

"Sorry. Just thinking about—something." I took the joint and hit it hard.

She dug into her purse. "Here." She groped, brow furrowed, as if she were up to her shoulder in a drainpipe. "Here." *The French Lieutenant's Woman.* "I finished it. Thought you might want it. Unless you already bought it."

Already bought it. Right. My resources would allow me two local phone calls and a Coke at a burger stand, as long as I didn't go for a large.

What the hell was wrong with me? A beautiful girl bothers to remember that you like Fowles, brings the book, carries it around all day. "Wow." Nice repartee. "I mean, great, I really—" I hit on the joint again and passed it to her. "Thanks. I was really looking forward to it. What did you think?"

She had her lungs full of smoke and waved her hand to signal she wasn't ready to speak. She took her time, and then lay back on the ground before she exhaled a cloud of dope. "I think I liked it. But the end...well, let me know what *you* think."

She was so substantial laying there, a presence vast and much more centered than I. Older, it's true, seventeen compared to my fifteen, but it was more than that. I must have weighed more than her, but I felt skinny and weak and awkward. When women hit puberty a power descends on them, like a gravity field, while boys are still these wobbly-kneed wimps, running alongside and goosing each other on the butts. They say that men have all the power, but it's the boys who have to prove themselves, by being smarter or faster or meaner or crazier or somethinger... Maybe the biologists have it right. Women are the fount, the stuff itself, and boys...well, many are called but few are chosen.

I might have been on the verge, the stoned, what-have-I got-to-lose verge, of trying to explain something like this to Leslie, but a voice said, "If you're just letting that burn, then give me a toke."

Lincoln. Who else? He dropped into a crosslegged position under the low roof of the tree, and a pretty waif of a girl followed, hugging onto his arm after she sat.

"Lincoln Ellard," Leslie said, without sitting up. She reached and took the joint from my hand. "And all grown up." She pulled on it hard without abandoning her lip-carbureting skills, and then passed it to him.

"Slumming, Leslie?" he asked. "The irresistible animal magnetism of us po' boys finally get to you?"

"In your dreams," she said.

"Mmm-hmm," he agreed, sucking on the joint.

He introduced me to Lisby, who smiled lazily in greeting, the side of her face pressed to his shoulder.

"An industrious morning," he said to me, "my day's labors done even before I go sit and fill in the bubbles. I've got you a place to live."

"He doesn't have a place to live?" Leslie asked, still on her back, looking up through the branches of the tree.

Linc raised his eyebrows at me. I shook my head, letting him know I hadn't told her about her stepmother. "Sure, he has a place to live. But his current roomie seems to like busting up his face."

"The County has a nice cell for me to live in, too, which is where I'm going to end up when my PO finds out I haven't been going home at night." I flicked the cherry off the roach. "Maybe you guys can send me books. Last time I had nothing but the Bible for weeks on end."

Leslie rolled a little in my direction and the heft of her bra-less breasts shifted beneath her blouse. Funny how a little thing like that can clench at the base of your spine. "A cell with nothing but the Bible," she said. "Like being a monk."

"No girls around, either," Linc said. "A society of celibates. Or homosexuals."

"Is that true, the thing about guys in jail?" Leslie asked. "I mean, did you…?"

"No," I said, "not really."

Lincoln laughed. "You think he'd tell you if he'd been balling guys?"

"Maybe. He reads a lot. Knows it's common as dirt."

Lisby, dropping her silence for the first time, made a sound of disgust. "I think it's creepy."

Leslie sat up and stretched. "What's creepy about it? What do they do to each other that they don't do with girls? Is it creepy when they do it to us?"

Lisby thought about it. "I think that too much boy stuff or too much girl stuff all in one place is creepy, period. And having them locked up and in bed together…man, that's way too much boy stuff in way too small of a space."

"The Bible says it's an abomination," I said. "Of course, the Bible also says, 'Round not the corners of thy head, nor mar thy beard'… another abomination."

Leslie smiled. "We must be pretty abominable, then. I don't see a corner on a single head here."

"'For all have sinned,'" Linc said, "'and fall short of the glory of God.' Or maybe your head doesn't get corners until you're old enough to vote."

"So where am I going to be crashing?" I asked.

"Giles Richards and his parents are going away for a few weeks…"

"Oh Christ," Leslie said. "Pompous letterman jackass jock…"

"I'm not saying he should date the guy, Leslie. It's just a place to stay. And not even in the house—there's a trailer out back." He looked over at me. "Cool with you?"

I imagined that the authorities would be coming after me soon enough, and where I spent my time until then was less important than spending it well, swallowing as much as I could of all the things I was going to miss out on. I was headed to YA or military school; only a matter of when. I opened my hands, palms up. "Great."

"You're welcome to stay with us instead if you want," he added, "if you don't mind Momma coming out every few minutes to see if you're a space alien. Or maybe Martha'd let you sleep with her." He was amused by this, the idea that anyone would want to sleep with his huge, dowdy sister.

I would have crawled into bed with Martha if she'd so much as winked at me. She was much older than me, and she'd never be on the cover of a magazine; but she was kind and strong, and I sensed an earthy core to her that it would be a delight to uncover.

Stacy had insisted that I was different from other boys. Maybe. If so, one of the big differences is that I *like* women, really like them. Individually, collectively, and as some sort of neo-Platonic abstraction—hey, they're just a great idea.

I'd gotten so distracted by the concept of climbing into bed with Linc's big sister that I'd glazed over; I actually thought of telling him that I'd rather stay at his place, until I realized this was nothing more than his little joke—and my little fantasy. "Yeah, trailer, whatever," I said. "That's great. You're a cool guy, Linc."

"If he were as cool as he thinks he is," Leslie said, "he wouldn't be stuck out here in the sticks."

"I like it here," he said, "and the edge is where everything happens. Ask any chemist. Ask any historian."

"They're talking about the edge of somewhere," she said. "This place is the edge of nowhere."

7 | TRAILER PARK OF THE GODS

For the third time that night, my middle finger edged the crotch of her panties to the side and tickled its way into her, and I kissed her harder so the increase in passion could allow her to pretend, for a few moments, that it wasn't happening. So perfect: velutinous flesh retreated and then clasped around my finger. From her little shudders and moans into my mouth, I knew she wanted it as much as I. Well, almost.

And, for the third time that night, JenBen writhed her hips away from me, abandoning my wet fingertip. "I can't," she gasped, yet again.

"Can't what?" I asked, panting for breath.

She pulled herself onto her arms and backed herself to lean against the wall. "Can we talk?" Breathless, she fanned herself with her hand. It wasn't just the heat of passion; June settled heavy on the Southland that year, and despite the open windows, the trailer sweltered.

"Sure." I hoisted myself up and looked at her. Both of us glistened with sweat. Her breasts were the merest suggestion, sudden nipples erupting from the smooth expanse of her chest.

Self-conscious at my gaze, she covered them with an arm.

"Can't I even look?" I asked.

She giggled, stoned and drunk. "Okay. Here." She dropped her arm to the mattress and let her knees fall open and allowed me to see her, sweaty white flesh interrupted only by a pair of electric-blue panties. "Happy?"

I pulled myself back to lean against the wall beside her. "Very."

"Drink?" She pointed past my head.

I seized the big rum and Coke from the shelf and took a gulp before I passed it to her.

The room we were in was all bed, a wall-to-wall mattress raised three feet from the floor. If you stood on your knees, your hair brushed the ceiling. When Linc said *trailer*, he'd meant it literally; this was no mobile home, but a short silver capsule that, in the days before its tires went flat, was designed to be towed behind a car. The six-by-six space we were in was half of the total; a wall and door separated it from the couch and table that formed the so-called living room.

Linc and Lisby were on the other side of that door, quiet now; they'd been fucking loud and hard, in two sessions, a background score for our sweaty groping, their sounds emphasizing what we wanted but weren't doing.

I undermined the purpose of our time-out by running my fingertips across her breasts. She made a sound of pleasure, but when I let my palm stray down across her belly she pushed my hand away.

I kissed her on the neck, and tried biting the tendon in her shoulder, ever-so-gently popping it from between my teeth.

"Don't...that's *weird*."

I sat up. "Sorry."

"I've never done it before," she said. "Gone all the way, I mean." She took a long drink. "They think I have, Melissa and Randi, they think I do it as much as they do, but I haven't ever."

"We don't have to," I said. "I'm having fun."

"Are you?" she asked, peering at me in the dim light. "This is enough?"

"Oh God yes," I said, and slid my hand across her nipples again. She pinned it on a breast with her free hand.

"You don't need to do it?"

"I've only ever done it once, and that was great, but we can just mess around. I'd lay here and mess around with you *forever*." My hand escaped and slid down between her legs, keeping chastely to the outside of her panties. I kissed her to preempt any protests, and massaged the wet crotch of her underwear.

She pushed my shoulder away with an upraised elbow and I realized that she was still holding the drink, gimballing it on high so as not to spill it. I took it from her, put it back on the shelf, and made to kiss her again, but she stopped me with a hand on my cheek. "There's other things we can do, you know," she whispered, "but I've got to trust you."

"Whatever you want."

"You've got to promise me." Her breath was short and urgent against my face. "Promise me we won't do it, no matter what. Can you promise me?"

"Promise what?"

"Promise that we won't go all the way."

"I promise. I promise."

She hesitated, said, "I'm trusting you," and then pulled my mouth to hers, kissing me hard as if there was nothing else in the world, sucking at my tongue with the focus of a hungry baby at the nipple.

The change in her was immediate, fully committed. No longer squirming away or fending me off, she hauled me to her like a fisherman with a full net. When I worked the tip of my finger around the edge of her underwear this time she shoved my hand away, still kissing me, and rolled her panties down, wriggling her legs and kicking them off.

Then she took my hand in hers and clamped my palm to her wetness.

I had to break off our kiss to gasp, and then it was her turn to gasp back when I slid my finger into her, but this time she let her legs open wider and said, "Yeah, do that…"

There are moments so unified, so flawless, so entire of themselves, that you will them with all your being to go on forever.

God Almighty could have designed me to live only in that minute or so, letting my finger probe her, listening to her sounds, feeling her pelvis push back at me, but JenBen stopped in the middle of a kiss and pulled my hand away. I groaned in protest, but she rolled onto her knees, tugged down my boxers, and wrapped her lips around me.

Paralyzed with pleasure, I couldn't even breathe, and irrelevantly I realized that Lincoln's tirade on his back porch had been the truth—I was blessed, compared to almost everyone in human history, undeservedly, rapturously blessed, young and healthy and safe and free, at least for the moment, and Jenny Benedict had my cock in her mouth and was sucking at it like there was nothing in life she'd rather do.

She stopped to pull off my boxers, then arranged me so I lay flat on the bed. "You don't have to if you're not into it," she said, "but you can do me too, if you want."

"Love to," I answered, unclear on what she meant, happy to go along with it.

When she straddled my face I understood.

Now *that* was wonderful. Ten minutes before, I had been forbidden to venture a finger into her; now she was open and pressed right into my face. I licked and sucked and rubbed my face up and down, inexpert but enthusiastic, and whatever I was doing had the right effect, because her mouth and her hand redoubled their efforts and I exploded, and she swallowed, once...

On my second spurt, she gagged—such an ugly word, but from where I lay, a glorious event. Her stomach muscles clenched in a long flow that reached right down into her pelvis, extruding her labia into a wondrous kiss against my mouth, and as my third pulse came it happened again: a rolling wave from her throat to her crotch to my tongue.

It's in the moments when they're doing something undignified that women overwhelm you with their elegance.

When boys do something undignified, we just look dopey.

She lay her face down on my hip, her hand still clutching my cock, and let her pelvis sink down harder on my mouth. I kept licking, my hands pulling the balloons of her ass down as if she might float away from my lips.

"You're still hard," she said.

"Mmm," I agreed. Numb, but still hard.

"Put me on my back," she said, "it's easier for me."

It wasn't a question of *putting* Jenny anywhere; so far she'd called all the shots. Maybe she thought my ego wanted the illusion of control; maybe she was turned on herself by the illusion that she wasn't in control. She rolled onto her back and I laid on my stomach with my face between her legs, my own legs bent, the tops of my feet touching the laminated fake-pine wall.

Linc and Lisby had started up again out in the living room, and their noises came through the open windows to either side of the bed, in perfect stereo. In the pause as I lowered my face to JenBen again, we heard Lisby, quiet and urgent, say, *"No, not like that… No, go ahead…"*

After that, Jenny may have been listening, but I was near-deaf, her thighs around my ears.

In this position she could steer me, and did so, moving my head around to direct my tongue where she wanted it, pulling when she wanted more force. My cock was still stiff beneath me, and as JenBen got more excited, sensation returned, and I found myself grinding my hips against the mattress as she ground hers against my face.

Her legs were wide and high, and her fingers had a tight grip on the back of my head. She pulled my face up so our gazes met across the rising and falling plain of her torso. Her half-lidded eyes showed pupils dilated to tunnels. She whispered, "Do it…" I hesitated. "Do it now, I want this to be my first time…"

I tilted my head down and went back to tonguing her, working that hard nub at the vertex of her labia, and she groaned with frustration. She jerked my head up and pulled on my ears with both hands, trying to drag me onto her. *"Please,"* she whispered. "C'mon, just *fuck me*."

I pushed her hands away. Was this some kind of crazy test? "No," I said, panting, "*trust*, remember?" Wondering why I didn't just do as she ordered, I went back to work.

"*Goddammit!*" She slapped the mattress.

I reached up beneath my chin and slid my middle finger into her and she gave a deeply affirmative groan and reached for my head again, curling her torso into a ball, clasping opposite elbows around the back of my skull and tugging hard. I waggled my head side to side as fast as I could, tongue smashed between her pubic mound and my lower lip, and I moved my finger slowly, contrasting with the frantic rhythm of my head, until, as gently as I could, I added the tip of my index finger.

Tight, but just the right thing to do.

Birds don't necessarily hear better than we do, but scientists have discovered that they hear *faster*. What to us sounds like a single note or call in fact contains elaborate variations, a huge amount of information packed into a short space of time.

As I eased my fingers into her, JenBen gave a bird cry, the most complex sound ever heard—surprise, pleasure, alarm, guilt, joy, panic, puzzlement, desire, revulsion, greed, hunger, a whole spectrum of human reactions packed into one little rising gasp that ended in a question mark.

I felt the tension in her body, all-too-ready to say *stop*.

Only the briefest of question marks, though, because she rolled herself tighter around me, and though I couldn't move my head I did what I could with my tongue, and she only let me run my fingers in and out three times, knuckle-deep, before she shuddered and gripped me with her whole strength, smashing my nose against her pubic bone.

Her inner flesh moving around my fingers, clenching and crawling, did me in, too; pushed down hard against the mattress I had my own orgasm; but it was a remote, paltry thing, theoretical, too much of my mind roving through JenBen.

She made a sound then, a sound that made me think for a moment I had somehow harmed her; but afterward she released my head and uncurled her body, relaxing. I lifted my face and breathed. She let her legs down to the mattress, then paused, lifted one leg and reached down under it to my wrist, urging my fingers out of her.

I dragged myself up and lay beside her. "Thank you," she said, and hugged herself up next to me; but a moment later, realizing how hot it was, she rolled back to the side and sprawled out, exposing as much skin to the air as possible. "That was so good... Being able to just *go*, without worrying about, you know..."

"Thank *you*."

Suddenly concerned, she nodded in the direction of my groin. "Oh, I forgot, do you need me to...?"

"No. Took care of itself." She seemed puzzled by this information, so I rolled over and kissed her. I let my hand stray across her little breasts, nipples gone soft in our sweaty aftermath, then slid it down her wet belly to caress her pubic mound. The moment I touched her there her whole body jerked as if I'd rapped on a sore tooth, and she pushed my hand away.

"No no no no," she said, "no more. All used up." Then, in the voice that girls use to tell boys what ought to be obvious about the female body, she said, "You can't touch it after something like that, not for a while." She frowned. "You sure you don't need—?"

"No, no. I just like touching you. I don't know how you keep your hands off yourself."

She giggled. "It's different when it's your own body. I mean, how do you keep your hands off *your*self?"

"I don't."

"Oh. An honest boy. As long as we're telling the truth, I don't either. But I don't…reach inside, you know, I only touch my…well, when you get off that way, it's really really sensitive for a while. So, hands off." She paused, then added, "Plus, I have to pee."

So did I. The noises from the other side of the door had quieted somewhat, but a little sound from Lisby made it clear they weren't done out there yet.

We exchanged a look. Though we were already on rather intimate terms with Linc and Lisby, having listened to them balling for the past three hours (and Lisby was both vocal and explicit), it didn't seem right to open the door on them, even if it were only to get out of the trailer.

I removed the rusty thrust-pins holding the screen in the window. That screen must have been original factory-issue, and its fabric was now fragile as a spider's web; I tore a corner as I worked it free. The bottom edge of the window was only a foot above the mattress, so it was a simple matter to leverage myself through the opening, feet first and face down, and lower myself to the ground. I waited there naked, my feet in the powdery June dust, as JenBen followed, and I wrapped my arms around her beautiful butt and let her slide down my chest until she touched the earth.

We sighed a grateful duet as the dry air evaporated the sweat from our skin.

The only illumination came from streetlights far away, filtered through trees; but the yellowish soil showed bright enough to show the path across the field to the McFaddens' back porch. We crossed to it hand-in-hand, foxtails brushing our calves: strange and wonderful to be naked out of doors in the middle of a town, yet isolated, as if we wandered through some damaged, cut-rate Eden.

I opened the screen door on the back porch and flipped on the light, one of those yellow bug lights. A step up, through the kitchen, and a right in the hallway to the bathroom. I started to follow JenBen in, but she lightly pushed my chest with an *are-you-crazy* look, and closed the door between us.

Funny where people decide to draw the lines on intimacy.

I wandered back outside and pissed on what the McFaddens must have fancied was their back lawn, a square where the brown weeds of the field had been mowed flat.

I'd spent the previous night on Lincoln's couch once more, managing to feign sleep through most of Momma's visits, and early this afternoon Giles had given me, after some debate, the key to his family's house. "You can't go in the house, just the trailer," he'd said at first. A burly senior, veins bulging on his forearms, his worried tone was at odds with his macho looks.

"Come on," Linc said, "there's no toilet in the trailer."

"Yeah." Giles chewed his lip. "Okay. You can go inside, but just the bathroom. And the back porch, you can use the refrigerator out there. But please, please, guys, no parties in the house…Dad'd kill me."

Lincoln clapped him on the shoulder. "You're a good dude, Giles."

Giles had brightened. "Yeah. Any time, Linc, any time." He frowned as he worked the key off his keyring, and then studied me with concern. "Don't fuck anything up, okay?"

"I'll vouch for him," Linc said, and it was settled. "Have a good time in Idaho."

"Utah."

"Ah. Of course. Have a good time in Utah, then."

Forty-eight hours ago I'd been settling down on Linc's couch, having been punched out of the doorway of my so-called home; now I had a place of my own, at least for the next three weeks.

Beyond three weeks? I'd probably be locked up again before the problem arose. Why worry?

The screen door creaked and Jenny reached her arms around me from behind and hugged me. "Would it be okay to take a shower?"

"Sure."

"Wanna join me?"

I did indeed.

Cool water. A chance to look at her in the light. Soaping each other.

"I sort of have a boyfriend, you know," she said.

I didn't know what I was supposed to say, so I lathered her nipples again. Breasts: they get so dirty in the course of a day.

"Brad's like, away at college this year. Well, not right now, right now he's got some summer job in Oregon."

I decided her ass hadn't been attended to, so I soaped it up too, and she gave a little squeak as I ran the bar of soap up and down between her cheeks. "So he doesn't mind," I asked, keeping my tone casual, "that you're, um, hanging out with other guys?"

"Well I'm not, you know, going all the way with anybody. I haven't with him, either…" She put her hands on my hips and wheeled us around in tiny little steps so she could get under the spray. "Is that a problem?"

I wasn't quite sure what she meant. "You mean, for me?" She nodded. "Why would I have a problem?" There had been a time, not long before, that this sudden announcement might have hurt; but, by crushing my heart flat, Stacy had given me an unexpected, unrequested gift: the power to not fall in love with every girl I touched.

"I don't know, I just…well, I didn't want for us to get too involved." She ducked her head under the shower-spray, massaging her scalp, and emerged sputtering. "It's just, I like you, but there's Brad—"

I wondered what Brad would think of us in the shower together, and why he must have been dead-set on marrying a virgin in the first place, and what the hell JenBen saw in such an obvious lunatic, but then dismissed it as none of my business; for all I knew, Brad might be banging half the coeds in Oregon with Jenny's blessings. "I like you a lot," I said, and stroked her face, "but if this is what we have, well…it's plenty for me."

"So, if we see other people and stuff, it's okay…?"

It was okay.

My cock came back to life as we toweled off, and I turned away, afraid I'd somehow spoil things. Down, boy.

Think about something else—math, or changing a tire, or plumbing, no, wait, not plumbing, too wet, all those orifices and pipes and…

Think about violation of probation.

On the way outside, JenBen paused to flip off the porch light, and then said, "Don't tell anybody the truth, okay?"

"About what?"

"You know...that we didn't really *do* it."

Over the years I've had women suggest that we should pretend to the world that we hadn't fucked when in fact we had. JenBen was the only one who ever asked me to pretend that we had when in fact we hadn't.

Fine with me.

The McFadden place must have been a farm once, five acres in the center of a Yucaipa neighborhood, its perimeter ringed with sad eucalyptus. The cottage, a three-bedroom clapboard structure, sat close to the street, whitewashed wagonwheels half buried to either side of a gravel driveway. Out back, things had collapsed: chicken coops, pigeon roosts, the remains of a corral and stable, the dry wood silvered from years of relentless sun, the structures all listing to the side or bowing down in the middle. I'd had little time to explore earlier, since, at Linc's invitation, JenBen had arrived with Lisby to have an inaugural party.

The trailer sat beneath a lone chinaberry tree, the space in front of its door trampled into a permanent half-moon of dust. A ragtag assortment of lawn furniture surrounded a charcoal pit and grille, and as JenBen and I found our way back through the dark we saw Linc laying on one of the webbed lounges, Lisby snuggled up beside him with a leg thrown across his hips. "Thought you guys were remarkably quiet in there," he said.

I was glad they were done at last, eliminating the need for me to climb back through the trailer window to retrieve our clothes.

Lisby's petite body turned out to be more voluptuous than I'd imagined, especially on her side with one hip tossed high, and I felt my cock start to jerk upright again.

All in a moment I saw one of the reasons society dictated the wearing of clothes. Imagined dialogue from JenBen: *"Jesus, you've been with me all night, and now you're getting a hard-on from looking at her?"* And my imagined, *"Yeah, but, I've been trying to keep from getting hard again all through our shower, and I was doing a pretty good job, and making a point of not looking at you, but I've never seen Lisby naked before, and—"*

Clothes protect us from unwanted sincerity. Especially us boys.

Without unclamping herself from Linc's side, Lisby used her free arm to pull a tee-shirt from a pile of clothes and drape it over herself. If she thought this was somehow less arousing, she was dead wrong, but JenBen diverted all eyes by lifting her arms high above her head and stretching, groaning as she did so, rising onto her tiptoes to reach an extra few inches into the night sky.

My penis snapped to full attention, and I sat down in the nearest chair and leaned forward, pressing my forearm down to bury Mr. Happy between my thighs.

"God, it feels so good out here tonight," Jenny said.

Lincoln smiled at me. It seemed he knew everything I was experiencing. More, it seemed that he divined what was in all of our heads just then, that he knew, and was pleased and amused by it. His eyes drifted down to my covered groin, and his smile widened before he looked back to Jenny, where she still stretched, glorying in the night.

My breasts are too small, my butt's too big, my *this* is too *that*, an unending litany I've heard from women over the years, but that night JenBen stood there, knowing we were both watching, that even Lisby was casting covert glances, she stood there flatchested and wide-hipped and she stretched and rolled her skeleton under that sheath of skin and muscle and looked over her shoulder at me and every molecule of her body said, *This is Jenny Benedict, and aren't you lucky to see me, aren't you blessed just to be near me?*

Yes, and yes again. My virgin goddess.

Well, semi-virgin.

It's hard to appear debonair and sophisticated when you're naked and trying to conceal your erection. I wanted to punch my hard-on right in its defiant, one-track nose, and find a way to do so without attracting attention.

JenBen sashayed to the door of the trailer, so pointedly paying no attention to us that it was clear she felt our eyes on her.

When she came back, still nude, she tossed my clothes into my lap. She'd brought her own clothes, too, but draped them on the arm of the lawn chair beside me before sitting down there, still loving the night air on her skin.

Now that my jeans were in a wad over my crotch, I could relax enough to enjoy it too; balmy air, distant noises, the trembly dry California breeze. Directly above, the sky glittered with stars, but to the west, beyond the hills, the ochre air of Los Angeles glowered, sixty miles distant.

The four of us sat silent for a long time until JenBen looked at her watch and discovered it was nearly one in the morning. After that, a flurry of activity: Lisby trying to hide herself as she dressed, me hunched forward and pulling on pants over my persistent hardness, JenBen and Lincoln dressing with slow and deliberate motions, neither of them embarrassed nor eager to part with the caresses of the feeble wind.

We walked out to the driveway together, me stepping delicately as the sharp gravel poked at the soles of my feet. We paused by the side of Jenny's yellow VW bug. Lisby wound herself around Linc for a goodnight kiss, and JenBen and I followed suit, though with less desperation. She rubbed her pelvis against my obvious erection. "Do this again some time?" she whispered.

"*Any* time."

Linc and I waved as the VW crunched down the drive. "Nice night," he said. We turned and headed back toward the trailer. "Did you get there?"

"Where?"

He snorted. "Did you unite in cosmic bliss? Come together as one, make the beast with two backs, have profound and mutual carnal knowledge, each of the other? Did you get your dick wet?"

I felt the dust covering my bare feet as we walked. "Yeah."

"Well, don't overwhelm me with details. I've just always wondered about her, JenBen…is she as great in bed as she pretends?"

"Better," I said, with total honesty. "And what's it to you? Sounded like you were having plenty of fun with Lisby." After the brightness of the streetlights out by the driveway, I had trouble seeing the path, and stumbled off into the weeds.

"Lisby…" He sighed. "Great sex, but she's…"

When he showed no signs of concluding this thought, I asked, "She's...?"

"Clingy. Wants to, I don't know, be skin-to-skin with you every living moment."

Didn't seem so bad to me, but what did I know?

We arrived back at the trailer. He elaborated. "It's like she doesn't want a life of her own. She's a throwback to the fifties or something."

I sat down in one of the chairs. "She's really sexy."

He remained standing, hands on hips. "Granted. Point received, noted, registered. There's more to life than just hot sex."

"Sure. Taxes, air pollution...balloon animals..."

"Screw you, Rick. And if she turns you on, have at her, if she'll let you. I'm not the jealous type, and she's not my 'girlfriend,' though she'd tell you different. Sharing her with you'd be a relief." He leaned his head back and looked up at the Milky Way. "She drags me down, man."

"Gee, what a bummer."

He laughed, and then dropped to one knee beside my chair, both his hands on my arm. "I'm going to tell you a secret," he said. A far-off streetlight put diamonds in his black eyes. His face still wore a sardonic smile, but his voice was all seriousness, as if half of him wanted to disavow the earnestness of its twin. "*You live in an animal.*" He paused, breathing with intent. "You live in an animal, you need to be kind to that animal, but the animal isn't you. Let it play and eat and fuck and sleep and shit and whatever else it needs, *but don't forget who you are.*"

He squeezed his hands tight on my arm and then, as if embarrassed, stood with his hands clasped behind him and looked at the wicked light kindled over the LA basin.

I waited. "But suppose I don't know who I am?" I asked, at last.

His stormy head of hair shook against the glow of the sky, and I realized he was laughing. "That *is* the problem, isn't it?" He turned back to me. "The road home, the path back. Well, lucky for all of us, there's some shortcuts. You should get some sleep. You've got a big day tomorrow."

"I do?"

"Saturday. Did you have plans?"

"None."

"Then, I repeat: You've got a big day tomorrow. I'll see you in the morning." And with that he headed off into the dark.

Inside the trailer I flicked on the light. The coffee table in what passed for a living room had been upended to make room for the sofa cushions to be spread on the floor.

Thumbtacked to the door of the so-called bedroom was a note reading *Grocery Money*, with a twenty-dollar bill tacked beneath it.

Why the universe was suddenly so generous, in the persons of Linc and JenBen, I had no idea.

I stripped off my pants, and lay on the mattress. I was getting hard again, smelling Jenny on the bed, remembering her in the shower, recalling her and Lisby outside under the stars, but I just lay there, not touching myself, a single wall lamp burning, and my mind followed the electricity out through the wall, down the long orange extension cord to the house, up through the wires and down the wooden Southern-California-Edison creosote-laden poles, through the transformer substation, up into the high steel towers that stalked across the countryside, down to a turbine spinning between giant magnets in some far-off powerplant, on to the oil-fired furnace that drove the steam, back into the oil itself, through the pipelines and into the ground and back through time to the swampy vegetation that had been crushed to produce it all, and I saw the long, tenuous branch of history from which I hung suspended, my life, my unlikely life, supported by chance and technology and eons of time, and for a moment—just a passing moment—I forgot all about my cock.

8 | SAN FRANCISCO DOESN'T NEED US

I watched the bright grass in the park tremble and slither, and tried not to let my mounting anxiety show on my face. An hour into it, LSD was nothing like what I'd anticipated—no dancing fairies, no paisley skies, just a subtle shift in outward appearances and a profound uneasiness in my gut. "It looks like the whole Park is tilted," I said to Linc.

He laughed. "The whole Park *is* tilted. Why do you think we had to walk uphill to get where we're sitting?"

Noon, and already it was sweltering, even beneath the shade of a spruce. Linc seemed relaxed, but I caught, or thought I caught, darting glances of concern. Did I look as confused as I felt? "I mean, too tilted, more tilted than reality."

"You're just noticing how things really are. Just sit back and take it in."

Easy to say. Between smoking dope every day and having painfully exciting, strictly bounded sex with JenBen the night before, I'd forgotten my real situation. Kicked out of the house, squatting in a trailer, headed for military school or more likely back to Juvenile Hall. No money. No family. No Stacy. I was, as Linc put it, noticing how things really were, and they weren't good.

I lay back on the soft ground under the tree and stared up through the branches. So many branches, so many needles on every branch, just so much of everything…

Tension twisted my shoulders, clenched at my stomach. "I feel, well, kind of nervous. Maybe a little nauseated."

"Normal. It'll pass...but, sit up, and we'll hurry it along."

I heaved myself up from the ground, and it felt like my perception lagged far behind my body's motion, light and sensation pouring in as I moved, and continuing to pour in even after I was upright. "Whoa."

Linc had unscrewed the barrel of a ballpoint pen, and was busily fashioning a small bell from a piece of aluminum foil. I stared, captivated by his focus and dexterity. What he ended up with looked like a Hershey's Kiss, and he twisted the open end, where the candy would have that little paper tag, around the pen barrel. From somewhere he produced a safety pin, opened it, and pricked little holes in what would have been the base of the Kiss. "Traveler's pipe. Zero paraphernalia if the cops stop us."

He pulled a sticky cube of Moroccan hash from a pocket, thumbnailed off a corner of the green block, and set it at the center of the network of holes.

"I think I'm a lot more stoned than you are," I said.

"Nah. I'm just used to it. I could drive now if I had to. Though I sure as hell wouldn't *want* to. Trust me, you get used to it." He flicked a lighter and touched it down, sucked in a long hit.

When he offered it to me I waved it away. "Too loaded already."

"Try it," he said, in that strained voice used only when trying to hold smoke in the lungs, "you'll feel better."

I took the makeshift pipe, my full attention on not wobbling it, not tipping off its glowing cargo. I sucked the powerful smoke down and held it. Held it longer than seemed possible.

When I exhaled, it was as if a giant spotlight had been aimed at the entire Park. The ground, the grass, the trees, even the playground equipment at the bottom of the hill, all of it lit into aggressive brightness, and undulating waves passed through all that I saw. Far off I heard a lawnmower start up, and beyond it, miles away, the steady roar of cars on Interstate 10, and then layered atop that the voices of little children at the bottom of the slope, screaming with glee as they chased in the circles of some impromptu game. The sounds began to quaver, as if synchronizing with the waves that moved through the ground. "It's all *breathing*," I whispered.

Linc took the pipe, examined the ash with a critical eye, and then blew the foil clean with a puff of breath. "Yeah. A hit of hash when you're coming on, and it's *Welcome to Oz*." He set about reloading, and I marveled at his physical competence; I wasn't sure I could have undone a button on my shirt. "It does all breathe at some level, you know." He sucked in a long hit and passed the pipe to me, precious smoke coiling wasted into the air.

I tried to take it without thinking about the motions, just let the brainstem take over. It seemed to work; I got a long hit, and the ember on the tinfoil barely smoldered when I finished my inhale.

Through a smoky exhale, Linc said, "You ever hear of the de Broglie equation?"

I shook my head, unsure even of the word.

"You know about wave-particle duality?" My eyes must have gone round in confusion, because he clarified: "You know, how sometimes light is a wave, and sometimes it's a hard little particle? So it diffracts and bends like a wave, but other times it bounces, like it's a tiny ball?"

I nodded and let the smoke out of my lungs, and once again watched the world get more colorful and more rhythmic. My tension slipped away. Now it felt like the waves were moving through me.

"De Broglie was a physicist who said, suppose it isn't only light that has that duality. What if all particles have wavelengths? And he proved it. Atoms have wavelengths, and the electrons and protons and neutrons inside the atoms have wavelengths. It all relates to their speed and mass, but they don't travel straight; they move in these sinusoidal lines, like waves."

"Wow." Was he telling me this just to mess with my mind? It was strange and seemed deep, but why tell me this when I was already so overwhelmed?

"Wait. That's not my point. You just had to understand that bit first. The thing is, de Broglie found that all things have wavelengths, related to their speed and velocity. So when you fire a rocket into orbit, it actually follows a sinusoidal wave—one that is really long, and doesn't have much amplitude, because a rocket is so heavy. When a pitcher throws a baseball, it actually goes up and down, side-to-side, with a certain periodicity."

"Really?" I frowned. "Why can't we see it?"

"We can't see the hands on clocks move either, can we?" He took the pipe from my hand where it dangled uselessly. "But think about this: The Earth itself has a wavelength, because it's hurtling through space, and we're all moving with it, all vibrating up and down at the same speed. And when we drive in a car, we lay another wavelength on top of that basic one, a little vibrating pattern riding up and down the great big curve we're all on."

Something tickled at the back of my mind. "Harmony of the Spheres." A Greek thing, wasn't it, relating to the movement of the planets and the idea of a plucked string?

"Exactly. So it really does all move. It really does all breathe."

"Is that what I'm seeing?"

"Who knows? The thing to remember is that everything's tied together in a way we usually don't see. The idea that we're separate is an illusion. We're part of the planet, and part of all the plants growing around us, and I'm in you and you're in me—"

I laughed, stoned and loving it. "Isn't that a line in 'I Am The Walrus?'"

He laughed too. "Close, close indeed. And it's exactly what Lennon was talking about."

Downslope a car pulled into the parking lot, a tape deck wafting the intricate guitar traceries of "Black Mountain Side" through open windows. The rumble of the engine and the music stopped as one.

I leaned back on the heels of my hands. My whole body trembled with something near to delight. I didn't want to do anything but be there. I didn't need to talk, to read something, to worry, to impress anyone, just breathe.

Just breathe.

I closed my eyes and watched the sun come red through my eyelids, darker through the dendritic branches of the tiny veins, veins that divided apart and then divided again and again, down to the finest capillaries, the blood cells edging through single files in tiny pulses…

"Linc!" A male voice shouted from downslope. "Dude!"

I opened my eyes. Two figures strode up the grassy slope, one waving. Something familiar about them…

Rob Motiff, the vicious fighter I'd watched on my first day in the Park, and Don Briscoe.

I knew Don because we both had Leo Malheur as our probation officer, but that was about all we had in common. Don had been busted for breaking into an auto parts store; whenever he saw me, he asked, *Seen the nigger lately?* or some variation. *Coon, jigaboo, pickaninny, swamp guinea*…his normally monosyllabic vocabulary expanded to a positive thesaurus when it came to racial epithets.

Great. At least half of the last people in the world I wanted to see.

Rob sat Indian style. "Linc," he said, "just the man we were looking for." He wore a blue tee-shirt a size too small, a pack of cigarettes rolled into the sleeve.

Don got down onto one knee, leaning on the other one, and acknowledged me with a nod.

"We're trying to score some weed," Rob said, "and it's dry, dry, dry. Then I saw you, and I told Donnie, hey, man, if anybody knows, it'd be Linc."

"Don't have any right now," Linc said. His finger rummaged in his shirt pocket. "I can turn you on to this, though. Tide you over." He held out a cube of hash, probably a full gram.

Rob took it. "You're a lifesaver, man." He looked at the lint clinging to the cube with distaste. "Haven't you heard of tinfoil?"

"Yeah. But it makes it hard to eat the shit if they're gonna search you."

Rob chuckled. "You always did worry too much. What do I owe you?"

"Nothing. We help out in tough times, don't we?" Linc held his hand out again, palm up. "These, too." A pair of Blue Flats tabs, identical to the ones we'd taken earlier.

"What're those?" Rob asked.

"Acid."

He snorted. "You never stop trying, do you?"

"You never stop refusing. Try it, Rob. It's free."

"No way, Jose," Rob said, but plucked the pills out of Linc's hand anyway.

"What're you taking those for?" Don asked. "Are we gonna be fuckin' hippies now?"

"The way things are going, I'm not going to turn down dope of any kind. Who knows, maybe we'll cruise up to Big Bear and try them."

"Not me," Don said.

"Just don't try to drive after you take 'em," Linc said. "Give 'em at least eight hours."

"C'mon, man, you've seen me drive when I was so fucked up I could barely see the road."

"That's why I mentioned it."

I watched this whole exchange without putting in a single word. I was still stoned, serenely wiped out, and watching Rob and Don and their macho body postures was an education, as if I were watching some other species from a wildlife blind.

Don looked upslope and said what sounded like, "Crow."

Rob put his fingers in his teeth and whistled, a sound that made me wince.

Thirty yards away, Walt Masello stopped, and the girl hanging on his shoulder lurched to a stop along with him. Cro, for Cro-Magnon.

Rob gestured, and the pair of them came over and stood above us, Walt rock-solid, the blond girl clinging to him unsteadily, her face downcast.

"Rick—you know the Cro?"

I did, but only by having him pointed out. I shook my head.

"Rick Leibnitz, Walt Masello…and, Jilly, is that you under there?"

She looked up, a slow drunken sexy smile spreading her wide mouth. "Hey, Linc."

"What the fuck is *she* on?" Don asked.

"Reds," Caveman answered. "Told her not to do 'em on top of beer. We're heading back to my place."

"You got any weed?" Rob asked.

He didn't. The discussion turned to the Great Grass Famine of 1969, which had finally reached even Southern California. Everyone except me ventured an opinion—the Mafia, the government eradicating Mexican crops, middlemen holding back inventory to drive up prices…

I watched Cro and Jilly. His nickname was deserved—a jutting browridge, sloping forehead, and a thick jaw that looked like it could crack nuts. His forearms were thick and had no taper toward his wrist, hard knuckly fingers seeming to spring directly from his arm. One of these arms reached around Jilly's waist and supported her as she lazed against him.

"What I heard," Cro said, "is that the government is spraying crops with stuff that makes you sick when you smoke it."

"Then why isn't it getting here so we can buy it and get sick?" Rob asked.

Cro shrugged. "Just what I heard."

"My theory," Linc said, "is that the government is really cracking down on marijuana, and nothing else."

Rob frowned. "Why? Isn't weed about the wimpiest dope around?"

"Yeah. And that's why. They'd rather have all the youth in the country really fuck themselves up. You wait. People are going to be doing more downers, more wires. Heroin is going to make a big comeback. And grass itself is going to transform into something way more severe."

"Man, Linc," Cro said, "you really do need a couple of joints. You're getting paranoid."

"Tell me about it a few years from now. And just wait and see. Back before prohibition, Americans mainly drank beer and wine, but in the twenties it all became hard liquor—who wants to run beer across the border at five percent alcohol when you could run ethanol-enriched gin at fifty percent? Ten times as much kick in the same volume. Just wait: Someday the dealers will breed marijuana so strong that a joint'll knock you on your ass."

Cro laughed. "I wish they'd hurry up, then."

"Let's siddown," Jilly urged.

"Yup," Cro said. "Time to go home." He let loose of her waist and swatted her on the butt, much harder than the traditional let's-go pat. Instead of yelping she hummed and snuggled up closer to him. "See you guys, then." He steered her back up the hill.

Don snickered. "He's gonna fuck her brains out, ain't he? I bet she'll pass out."

Rob rolled his eyes. "She balls him all the time already. Why would he want to do her when she's passed out?"

"I would."

He probably would, I thought. There was something repulsive about the way that this particular image turned him on, and he shifted his hips. Normally I wouldn't have noticed, but my quavering, acid-fueled hyperawareness told me he was hiding an erection.

There's a lot of things you'd rather not know about.

There was a lull in the conversation, and Don noticed me watching him. "Seen the jungle-bunny lately?" he asked.

I exhaled loudly through my nostrils. "Why don't you lay off with the racist shit, huh? It's old, it's stupid, and it makes people think you're an idiot."

Don's whole body tightened, and, as though this created pressure that rose into his face, his eyes narrowed to slits. "I could kick your fucking ass, dickface."

"Yeah? What would that prove?" I was so relaxed that the bad energy roiling from him didn't even affect me.

"That I can kick your ass."

Rob laughed. "And *I* can kick *your* ass, Don. And it proves I can kick your ass, but that's about it. And I've seen your PO, and I bet *he* can kick your ass, too."

I could see Don's thoughts as clearly as an ornithologist could see a bird swell its chest or raise the crest on its head. I could beat up Rick, but they probably won't let me. And Rob just sort of threatened me, and I really ought to call him on it, but he'd pulverize me... Don laughed too, dismissing it all as banter, but I could tell he was still seething.

"Can you guys give us a ride?" Linc asked.

Rob looked perplexed. "Sure. But I parked right next to your car..."

"Don't want to drive right now."

"Pussy. Where to?"

"Just down on Oak Glen Road."

Getting to my feet was a mind-expanding experience. Linc elbowed me and winked as we followed Rob and Donnie down to the parking lot. I felt tall, angular, all long loose limbs, and I'm sure if I'd mentioned it that Lincoln would have told me that my perception was correct. Probably was: I'd been growing quickly that year, and now stood tall for my age, maybe three inches higher in the air than last year.

Seated in the back of Rob's jacked-up Malibu, the roar of the engine firing up made my head rattle, but it was soon replaced with "Black Mountain Side" at full volume. We drove down 7th Street to Yucaipa Boulevard and Rob turned left by punching the accelerator and blasting across all four lanes of traffic. As we neared the bottom of the hill, Jimmy Page's guitar started into the machine-gun strum, slam-slam-slam! lead-in to "Communication Breakdown." Rob turned the wheel hard right, shot down Oak Glen Road, and dropped us fifty yards farther on, where the road curved hard east and dipped into a sandy wash. "Here?" Rob shouted over the music.

"Yeah," Linc shouted back, "perfect!"

I struggled out of the car. Rob pulled a wide U-turn, sand windmilling from his tires, and tore off back down the road.

We stood and listened as the blast of music and horsepower disappeared, and then Linc started laughing. It was contagious, and I joined in without even being sure why.

We were still giggling when we crossed the road and headed up the wash in the direction of the sere Crafton Hills. "What's with them, anyway?" I asked, and then burst into giggles again.

Linc tried to control another outburst of giggles, failed, and had to stop and catch his breath. "Just macho assholes," he said, "same as most everybody. Me big monkey, me hit you, impress girl monkey."

"Why do you know them, then?"

"Ah…Rob used to be my best friend."

"What happened?"

"Puberty. Male hormones took his brain hostage."

"That's no crime. I mean, they took over my brain, too."

"Yeah, but not the whole chest-beating scene. And the sad thing is, the guys like us get laid more."

I wasn't so sure of this, since I certainly didn't seem to; but I stayed silent.

"He'll evolve someday," Linc said. "Maybe soon, if he tries one of those little blue pills."

The idea of Rob and Donnie stoned on acid the way that I was at that moment struck me as the most ludicrous thing I'd ever heard, and I laughed so hard I sat down on the sand, wiping tears from my eyes.

Eventually I calmed, and my laughter sounded creepy echoing in the wash and bouncing around in my ears. "Where the hell are we going, anyway?"

"Up into the hills."

"Why?"

"There's cool places there."

I looked at the hills with suspicion. "Looks like a lot of brown to me."

"Trust me."

The path we followed led out of the blinding white sands of the wash and into an orange grove that flanked the hills. One of the few groves left in Yucaipa, it clung to the hillside as if it were a growth that had crawled up from Redlands. Windmachines, and a high density of smudge pots; the fact that we were higher in elevation was apparent, but when we entered the grove I immediately felt at home.

When we reached the upper limit of the grove, Linc led me into a narrowing gap between two high banks, which then channeled us into a slot canyon between the two highest hills.

Inside it was dark and cool, bare cliffs rising a hundred feet on either side of us. The strata showed like they'd been exposed by a surgeon's knife—crumbly dirt, porous white limestone, more amorphous soil, then hard greenish rock. It settled in on me; ages of sediment, heavy, calm, uncaring.

We strayed farther in, and came to the first trees—individual sycamores, white and twisted, like exposed bone. Everything that had passed beneath them for the last two centuries had left a mark, that their curves and maneuvers reflected all the ecstasy and misery that had gone on beneath their spare branches: hungry Indians hiding out in the hills, half-mad Spaniards pursuing and killing the last grizzly bear… and us, stumbling, stoned children wandering away from the crazed slash-and-burn world just a half-mile outside the canyon mouth.

We wandered for what seemed like hours, the acid coming on stronger, before we stopped. Finally Linc gestured for me to sit beside him on a huge boulder. It glittered, the bright mica alternating with bands of dark hornblende. He produced his jury-rigged pipe and fired up a load of hash.

We smoked in silence, getting more stoned, as the walls of the hills leaned in around us. To our left, a tortured sycamore; to our right, a matrix of sun-bleached roots protruding from the ground.

"Tolkienesque, isn't it?" he asked.

"What?" His face was huge, compelling, dominating my whole field of vision, and I had no idea what he was talking about.

"Tolkien? Lord of the Rings?"

The names were familiar, somehow, but unattached to concepts. He could have been talking about religious denominations, brands of toasters, or breeds of dogs. "All that magic and fairies stuff?" I asked, uncertain if I was making sense.

"Yeah, sure." He swept his hand before us, displaying the world. "Are you telling me this *isn't* magic?"

I had no answer to that.

The canyon walls around us bulged and flexed, and my usual mind-chatter was smothered beneath the massy presence of the hills. It was an eon before I spoke again, and my words sounded strange and preposterous in my own ears. "It makes you want to do something…"

Linc came out of his own reverie, blinking at me. "Do something?"

"You know…be something. Not just…I don't know."

"So what's your vision of the future? What do you want to do?"

"I've never thought about the future much. There's always something hanging over me, something bad getting ready to happen." It was true. Only for the brief time I'd been in love with Stacy, before she shut me out, had I dreamed of a day when things would be better. I laughed. "Kind of an awful way to live, huh?"

"No kidding."

"But there's always something. My dad's going to turn me in, or send me off to military school, or my PO's going to pop me for violating probation…"

"Man, you got to think past all that stuff. And I don't mean think *through* it, I mean think past it, set some goals that are way beyond your immediate problems. You'll never get anywhere if you figure you've only got the choices that are right in front of you."

The way he spoke straight up into the air, his eyes covered, it seemed as if he were lecturing to an invisible audience. "Should I be taking notes?" I asked.

"Probably. You have to have a map, man, a map that goes right out to the border of what you can imagine. You can't just head across the valley saying, oh no, look at those mountains, how am I ever going to get over them, isn't it all hopeless? Think about where you want to be, the place you imagine on the other side, and your vision will get you there. If you're just going to stare at the mountains and worry, you may as well just sit down and cry." He ran his fingers through his hair, and it was so thick with static electricity that it crackled. "Trust me on this one, man. Worry about the map that's *out* there, the *here there be dragons* part at the edge… The local stuff takes care of itself if you just steer in the right direction."

He covered his eyes again and settled down as if napping.

Sitting beside him in the blazing sun I pondered. What were my aspirations? What would I choose if I could choose, not from what was available, but from the whole universe of possibilities? I'd like to have a lot of sex, and a girlfriend, and I'd like to have a place to live and books to read and a way of feeding myself…a stereo…someday, a car…

Juvenile, prosaic, pathetic. But my strongest wants were negative ones—to be quit of my father, to be released from probation.

There had been a time when I had fantasized that my mother would return—not to put the family together again, but to rescue me from the man she had fled. To explain, in some flattering way, why she had left me behind, to praise me for my strength in enduring our separation, and carry me off to somewhere better. That dream had died, but by such gradual degrees I hadn't noticed its passing; it respired more shallowly day by day until its breaths became inaudible, and now, taking its pulse, I found that it was cold and gone.

What did I want? To be somebody, to be someone special, to accomplish something. Abstractions. Not the slightest idea what any of them meant.

"What do *you* want?" I asked. "What's your ideal, what's on the other side of your mountains?"

"I just want to be part of it all, part of the shift in consciousness that's coming. A standard-bearer."

I raised my eyebrows in skepticism. Pretty vague so far.

He grinned. "Pretty fuzzy, right? But I'm thinking the path from here to there may start with setting up a salon."

I had to laugh. "You mean a beauty parlor, or one of those cultural French affairs? Or maybe you mean *saloon*?" I laughed again, and the echoes in the canyon gave me such a creepy feeling that I shut my mouth tight and hugged myself.

Linc didn't seem to notice. "A little of the last two, salon and saloon. Picture this—a place where you'd live with a friend or two, and people would get together, loaded if they felt like it, and talk about what's really important. Be a center for what's emerging." Energized, he pulled his legs up and sat crosslegged on the boulder as he described his dream, a utopian community that didn't live together, but was knit together by a common interest in the massive transformation of society that was emerging. Everything was changing, the old power hierarchies dissolving, the old property-based rules of male-female relationships vanishing. The old boundaries were disappearing; people were traveling into space, and drugs like the one we were on at that very moment had opened up an equally large frontier inside the human mind... He moved his arms in broad gestures, but his fingers trembled as he did so, wired up on the acid and on his vision, and that vision was compelling, not through its originality or scope, but through his sheer conviction. "It'd be a house that would be what schools really ought to be. We could share books, go to the most important new movies and get together afterwards, or listen to the best in music. Encourage people to do their own stuff, their art or their writing or their music—"

The vision was so seductive to me that I felt I had to poke holes in it. "There a lot of artists around here?"

"Some. And there's musicians. And there's a lot of people who'd like to do something with their heads if they were just given a chance."

"Yeah, get fucked up, mostly."

"Come on. Look at Leslie, Randi, hell, look at you. Smart people, creative people…"

"Smart people looking for a way out of this town."

He stroked the sides of his jaw between thumb and fingers as if smoothing a nonexistent beard. "Why are you so down on this?"

"I'm just saying you ought to take it somewhere else. San Francisco, maybe."

"San Francisco doesn't need us."

I blinked. "Us?"

He waggled his shoulders, loosening them, and swallowed. "You asked what my ideal would be. Ideally, you'd be included. You're a natural, Rick. You're smart, you read—even if you don't read enough of the experimental stuff—"

"Hey, I'm catching up…"

"—but, most of all, you're a real head." He looked straight into my eyes. "If I could select any partner for this, it'd be you. That's the truth."

I was touched, flattered, and embarrassed, all at once, and I had to drop my eyes. "It sounds great, man. And, well, you're my best friend. I'd promise you if I could. But who knows where I'll be after high school?"

His hand touched my arm. "Look at me." I raised my head. "I'm not talking about after high school. I'm talking about now, as soon as possible."

I started giggling, gesturing weakly with my hands. "But how—I mean, we've got—I've got—"

"We've got everything we need except commitment." He stared at me and my giggles faded. "The idea. Are you committed to the idea?"

"Sure. I just have no clue how we start."

He scooted close and threw an arm over my shoulder, hugging me tight. "We'll find a way," he said. "The important thing is to set out."

9 | REWARD: LOST DOG

When I'd first taken the tab of acid with Linc, a thousand years ago, I lived in one world; six hours later, I lived in another.

Around five in the evening we staggered out of the canyon and into the dark green of the grove. I was exhausted from listening, seeing, smelling, perceiving; Linc seemed even more drained from talking.

We slumped up the hill of the boulevard, car after car roaring past, each one leaving a shockwave of desperation. Seventh Street was quieter, almost eerie after the muscular, sixty-mph rush of the boulevard, and when I stepped into the green sanctuary of the park it felt as if every tree, every bush, every blade of grass reached out to welcome me, exhaling the oxygen, but not yielding it up by the mechanics of brute nature; instead exhaling it as a friend, an ally, a guide swinging a censer, going on to cleanse the way before us.

At the drinking fountain I slurped down water like a camel just arrived at the oasis. We sat in the middle of the park, under the sheltering arms of a blue spruce, letting the place hold us, watching the insects dance through the air: tiger swallowtails, mourning cloaks, monarchs, trim blue mayflies, predatory dragonflies, and, this being Yucaipa, slow, fat buzzing bluebottles. The flies are still with us, but as California has been covered with houses, everything else has started to disappear. Who would have thought so many common insects would become rare; or that the grouchy horny toads, who squeezed droplets of blood from their eyes when you captured them, would be on the verge of extinction? I foresaw none of this, but that day the swirl of common invertebrate life in the air was a marvel to behold, and I felt the web of life stretching out across the continent, small swirling things filling the skies everywhere, while people blundered along, unaware that they lumbered through a vast, intricate dance.

Linc laid back and stared up into the tree. I decided I needed another drink of water, and told him where I was going. "Need me to come?" he asked.

"Nah."

"Don't wander off, then."

I drank again, and then stood, hands on hips, surveying the park. Having someone beside you and being alone are so different. I'd spent so much time by myself over the years that a whole day with someone overloaded my circuits; and on this, the longest day in my life, it felt as if I'd been breathing Linc's air for an eternity.

Being by myself also made me feel more stoned. Nothing to do but notice the complex motions of the leaves in the breeze, the baroque patterns of bark on the treetrunks.

A sign was tacked to one of the Chinese elms, turned at an angle where I couldn't see it. Curious, I wandered over.

REWARD LOST DOG
Tristan, brindel shepperd
Our families loving pet for more than eight years.
Last seen near Yucaipa Vally Park.

Please help us and find her. Cash reward no questions asked.

Without the slightest foreshock of emotion I began sobbing. Life's tragedies are everywhere, but my mind grasped this one in its entirety—the family, accusations, the children in tears, the poor dog lost and terrified, guilty and alone, cars roaring by, the night settling in, the dog in fear and maybe in pain, and every member of the family imagining what the lost dog might be enduring, its hip shattered by a car, dying alone in a ditch somewhere along the side of the road…

And the misspellings and questionable grammar on the sign made it even worse somehow. My legs folded and I sat on the grass, face in my hands, and cried, deep hard sobs that left me gasping for breath.

Lost Dog. But at least someone wanted him back.

Abandoned Dog. Hunted Dog.

Feeling Obnoxiously Sorry For Himself Dog.

All day long I'd been trying to be cool—to impress Linc, to be *a man* when dealing with Rob Motiff and Donnie Briscoe, to be a man when handling the powerful effects of the LSD. A woman is a woman just by virtue of her age and sex; being a man is something that apparently has to be worked at, something you have to fight every day to achieve. Come on, don't let them treat you like that, stand up for yourself; be a man. Come on, that doesn't hurt, don't cry; be a man. She's left you, they've turned on you, he's been cruel to you, you've lost your job your friend your chance your teddybear your faith your reason for continuing to breathe; get up and get going, Be A Man.

Next time around the Great Wheel, I thought I might try the whole woman thing.

"Rick?" A female voice. I looked up. It was Randi Mayfield.

She sat down beside me. "Are you okay?"

"Never better." I sniffed and wiped my hand across my eyes. "I'm shapeless," I said.

"Uh-huh." She studied me through eyes that saw everything. "Linc sent me to see if you were okay."

"Why didn't he come himself?"

"He's talking to Lisby. They're sort of fighting… You seem kind of messed up. Is this your first time?"

"On acid. Yeah." I realized I really must look like a disaster, and dried my nose and eyes a bit more carefully. "You ever done it before?"

"Oh, definitely." I snuck a glance at her as she talked. God, she was gorgeous, her whole body illuminated by her intelligence. I felt a familiar stirring in my pants. "It can be hard. Some people really get into it. Me, it's like a lot of freaky things in my life: glad I did 'em, glad I don't have to do 'em all the time."

"What are they fighting about?"

"The usual, with her. She wants to crawl inside his skin, he wants her to back off. She wishes he'd just hang out with her; he wishes she'd hang out with some other guys too. But it's not good timing, bad time for her to be hanging on him."

"'Cause…?"

"'Cause he's tripping, and he's one of those no-touchie boys."

I made a face to show that I didn't get it.

"Ah," she said, "first-timer. Well, acid makes some guys, like one in four, one in five, really horny—*if* they get around to thinking about it. But most guys, it's Soft-On City; they may get all cosmically lovey and stuff, but balling isn't part of it."

Involuntarily I stared at my lap, and then blushed when I realized she'd followed my gaze to the erection pushing inside my jeans. A moment of furious embarrassment, and then I laughed. "No big deal," I said. "Better to have a hard-on than not…except maybe in the locker room."

"Is that true?"

"About the locker room?"

"No. About better to have a hard-on. I've just had so many boys over the years give me that rap about, oh please, oh come on, if I don't get off it's a major medical emergency…"

I blew out a derisive puff of air. "Orgasms are overrated."

She gave me a sardonic look. "Do you really mean that, or do you just think it's something interesting to say?"

"I mean it. It's something you can do just as well by yourself, maybe even better. It's getting there that's the fun part, and the explosion just means the ride's over. If I had to give up sex or give up orgasms, it's orgasms that'd get the boot."

I suddenly felt idiotic, shooting my mouth off to this older girl, and my blush started to come back, but she didn't notice my discomfiture. Before I'd even finished, she was leaning forward, and said, "Exactly! It's not even the best part. And it's not really that specific—well, at least not for girls. I mean, there's gradations, and some of the things that are, like, excruciatingly pleasurable wouldn't be an orgasm in anybody's book. I mean, sure, sometimes the whole thing's like climbing a mountain, and the orgasm is what you get when you stand up on top and look around, the reward for that long slog, but other times sex is like eating, and you just do it until you're satiated, sometimes until you couldn't take another bite, and you don't really have an orgasm, you just kind of thrust back hard a few times to release the tension, kind of like stretching when you get out of a chair. But guys, they're always, Did you? Didn't you? How many? Scorekeeping. And it seems to me that—"

Pink crept into her cheeks beneath that olive skin, and she gave a flustered smile and sat back. "Jesus." She fiddled with her hair. "What's the story with you, anyway? You seem like this sort of puppydog guy, but every time I talk to you I find myself telling you all kinds of stuff, like you're some kind of confessor. Do you have this effect on people a lot?"

I thought back on Stacy's ramblings in the orange grove, Linc's recent speech. "Maybe. But I like hearing about you."

She gave me a look that clearly said, forget it, little boy, you don't have a chance. "So. Speaking of orgasms, I hear through the grapevine that you've been showing our JenBen a really good time."

I rubbed my ear. "I guess so."

"Did you have a good time too?"

"Oh, yeah."

"A word to the wise. Our Jen doesn't get too involved. Sleep with her if you want to, but if you try to spend a lot of time with her, you're headed for heartbreak."

"Uh-huh. She said something about a guy, Brad, or somebody…"

"Ah, yes, Brad, Brad, Brad. Don't we get an earful about *Brad*? But we almost never see *Brad*. I think sometimes that *Brad* is just Jenny's way of making sure she doesn't get too emotionally intimate with anybody. She doesn't really let anybody get inside."

This was true in a way Randi didn't know about. I asked, "So you only believe in sex with a serious relationship?"

This made her laugh. "I don't know what I believe. But I'm pretty sure that I don't want to rule anything out in advance. And I don't know why I'm knocking JenBen, either, I'm probably just jealous." I frowned, and she clarified it for me: "I think she's kinda cute too, you know." I tried to digest this, but she interrupted my thoughts by stretching her arms above her head, yawning. I tried to keep my stare unobvious. "We should get back to Linc and Lisby before they send out search parties."

We rose to our feet, Randi with lithe grace, me with all the poise of a dairy cow. We headed back toward the middle of the Park. "Are girls like that, too, with acid? I mean, some it turns on, some it turns off?"

"Girls aren't as simple as boys. We don't have that many Yes/No things going on. More like, Yes, but, or No, but…"

"God. What a weird town." I spread my hands to the sky. "It's like, it's like all this stuff is happening up here, even though it's *nowhere*."

"That's the deal, right there. There's nothing else to distract us out here but each other. Haven't even got a movie theater. We aren't LA, but you can see it from here; but this ain't Omaha, either." She glanced at me and I was so taken with her eyes that I stumbled. "Ever see this funky monster movie, *The Land That Time Forgot?* Yucaipa, Rick. The thing is, the Edge of Somewhere and the Edge of Nowhere—they're right on the same line."

Lincoln handled the car like he was straight, although the whole vehicle felt to me as if it were made of sloshing fluid encased in plastic. Every time we slowed for a stop-sign, the car heaved forward and then washed back; when we accelerated away, a ton of invisible goop rolled back past me.

"Girls," Linc said. "Isn't one in a hundred who can get beyond the meat phase of it all." He glanced over at me, and scanned me from hip to face. "Oops. Maybe I'm talking to a meat phase." He wheeled the car around a corner, and I marveled that he could coordinate it all—steering, braking, accelerating, talking. "No offense, my man. You're welcome to it. For me, though, acid is a kind of vacation…partly a vacation from having your consciousness slung around by the mere presence of pussy."

Back at the trailer we relaxed and smoked some more hash. This increased the visual effects of the acid, making complex patterns run across my field of vision like translucent wallpaper, but eased me down even further. I could even imagine sleeping, some day, some far-distant day, letting go of the roiling questions and insights and needs and fears, and just…sleeping.

Not for a long time yet, though.

"You want a fucking nutty piece of prophecy? By the end of this century, ten percent, twenty percent, fifty percent of the men in this country will be homosexual, just to get their power back. Power is the power to say no."

Most girls my age had said *no* about a thousand times. I'd been given maybe two opportunities to say that word, and had said *yes* instead. "Oh, come on, Linc," I said. "I mean, there's boys that want to do it with other boys, I know about that, but man, it's really really rare."

"Bullshit. And I *dig* women. But are you telling me that if all the women on the planet vanished tomorrow, that ninety-nine percent of us would just be sitting around jerking off to auto-parts calendars? Our meat is obsessed with sex, and we've got to do it with somebody. We can't say no. *They've got the power.* All of this shit around us, four-bedroom houses and dishwashers and flowered wallpaper and toy poodles—are you telling me that guys have all the power, and this is what they decided to do with it?"

"If women have so much power, why are there prostitutes?"

"Yeah, right. Tell you what, Ricky-boy: You head downtown and strut around, and see how many girls will pay *you* to fuck *them*."

I snorted. "That's ridiculous."

"Uh-huh. Why?" I didn't respond; it seemed obvious, and yet I couldn't explain it. He persisted. "So tell me again, who is it that has the power here…?"

He seemed wrong, but I couldn't refute him. Hell, in my experience, everybody had more power than I. The women held more of it, dispensing it with more etiquette than the men—my mother snuck away, Stacy let me down as easy as she could, while my dad just slugged me in the nose—but the women dealt it out anyway. "It's all about power, then? I don't believe it."

I couldn't believe it, or I'd lay down right there and die.

"No. That's the trick. Once we get past the power thing, there's a whole new world out there. The world is changing in ways that almost no one sees, and change is accelerating. My grandfather saw his first car when he was ten; he was born before airplanes. If a caveman could see where we are today—well, that's what it will be like for us, in twenty years. But it isn't all nuts and bolts; it's consciousness. And I'm not going to let Lisby hold me back, and I'm not going to hold her back, even if she wants me to."

He tossed a paperback onto my lap. "A little bedtime reading. If you're cool, I really need to go crash. I was up late last night."

I mumbled my farewells, unprepared for his abrupt departure.

The book was by Arthur C. Clarke.

Childhood's End.

Still stoned, I wasn't sure I could read.

I lay on the bed and masturbated, first JenBen and then Randi, with Stacy elbowing her way in every so often and my mind shoving her away, and I apologized to every one of them, it ought to be just for You, I Dedicate This Wasted Sperm To You, as if you fucking care, and finally it was only Jenny because she was real and somehow mine and I could smell her and me on the mattress, so hard to believe it was only last night—

A long dark tunnel filled with writhing traceries in green and purple.

Semen on my belly, on my hand.

God, what an orgasm.

And me all by myself.

Eternity passed, my cock softening in my hand, before I realized that I wasn't sleeping, and wasn't likely to sleep any time soon.

Childhood's End. Science fiction.

I doubted at first that I could focus my eyes.

I read it straight through.

I've never read it since, for fear of finding it less than I remember.

A time when the world is visited by an extraterrestrial race—a race with a very special characteristic, that I won't mention for fear you haven't read it—and they are here to prevent the planet from blowing itself up while we evolve, which is sudden…

Beginning in one year, all the children are born different, almost autistic, yet they can communicate with one another in some strange way, and in a few years they link hands and start this dance, this continent-spanning, incomprehensible dance, and many of them die, exposed to the elements or torn apart by natural hazards, but they dance on, and eventually turn into one massive organism that ascends into the cosmos…

…leaving us behind.

Everything we've done—our great art, our science, our cities: Meaningless. Irrelevant.

Forgotten.

It's all about something else, something unknown, something unanticipated.

I lay naked in the trailer, arms sprawled wide in the hot June night, utterly shattered by a 95-cent paperback.

Maybe everything I believed—everything—was wrong.

10 | FIRE AND WATER ISN'T ENOUGH

On any earlier day of my life, sitting around naked with twenty or thirty other high-schoolers would have had me near a state of nervous collapse. The boys were older than me, broad-shouldered and vigorous, and the girls…

But today everything was different.

Linc had awakened me about noon and dragged me from the sauna-like trailer, my brain still reeling from my first acid trip and the following six hours of *Childhood's End*. He stuffed me into my clothes, force-marched me into the McFaddens' kitchen to down scrambled eggs and toast, and finally loaded me into the car.

Four miles north of Yucaipa, Mill Creek cuts through the huge gates of the mountains. In beyond those narrow cliffs, the slopes gape wide to cradle a long boulder-strewn valley, the remnants of the channel of a mighty Ice Age river. A few tree-covered mesas rise from the midst of the boulders, and smaller, narrow valleys feed into the main canyon where smaller creeks have carved their own slots through the surrounding cliffs.

The breeze through the car window slapped my face, the air scented with waterplants and the aroma of buckbrush baking in the sun. Off of Highway 38, up Mountain Home Creek Road, Linc pulled to the side and parked. A dozen or more vehicles sat along the stretch of road, parked wherever there was enough pull-out to fit a car.

A quarter of a mile away, where the road narrowed, we'd stepped off the pavement and headed down a path into the trees.

It had been a stumbling, sliding climb, our feet skidding along on the loose rocks and dirt, the whole slope knitted together only by tree-roots. When the slope lessened we passed between head-high rock outcrops, and the trees thinned until we rounded a house-sized boulder and looked out across a wide expanse of granite, half a football field in extent, blinding white in the afternoon sun.

The creek had cut a deep, wide pool there, surrounded on all sides by smooth, massive chunks of stone, and in the water, and perched on the rocks, and lolling in the sun, were naked teenagers.

High-school boys and girls naked together, moving and positioning themselves with the artificial grace that is self-consciousness pretending to be uncontrived. It was a scene that would have been impossible even five years before.

I was sure that I was looking at the future.

Before I could take it all in, Linc said, "C'mon," and stripped off his clothes.

I did the same and then ran down just behind him and dove into the pool before I had time to think.

A good thing, too. Much of the water this early in the year was still snowmelt from only a few miles away, shockingly, numbingly cold even in the June heat, and if I'd tried to ease in I might have spent ten minutes, putting a toe in, taking it out, getting up to the ankles, then the knees…

All my sweat and fuzzyheadedness vanished into the frigid, clear water. Yesterday, and this morning in the sweltering trailer, I'd been through the fire, but now it was complete, and I was washed clean.

Or so I thought. We love the rebirth image, the cleansing, the baptism, but it's as fictitious as Virginity Regained. Everything is always there: you can run from it, you can climb on top of it, or you can carry it all on your shoulders, but fire and water isn't enough—even the alchemists knew that.

But for a while that day I was free, able to gaze around me without measuring myself, and so unattached that I could let my cock flop between my thighs without fear that the mere sight of a girl would launch it like a rocket.

Drying in the sun, I watched them all around me, naked happy children—posturing, it's true, but children aren't devoid of artifice, either. Slowly I recognized many of them; people appear so different without their uniforms. Cro-Magnon and Jilly dangling their legs in the water; Rob Motiff and Don Briscoe sitting atop a high boulder; a smattering of other people I'd met in the Park.

"I know you're thinking, *Eloi and Morlocks*," Lincoln said, "but it's not the case."

"Huh?" I'd been thinking no such thing.

He had to explain H.G. Wells' *The Time Machine* to me, the elven Eloi, joyous and simple, fed and then eaten in turn by the troglodytic Morlocks.

I decided not to pursue this, and instead asked him about *Childhood's End*. Did he believe Clarke's vision of human destiny was real, heading toward an obliteration of all we once held dear?

"Nah. And I doubt Clarke does, either. How would you work up the energy to write a book if you thought it was all going to become irrelevant?" He lay back on the warm rock and shut his eyes. "I think it's his way of saying that we're headed someplace new and unimaginable, and that the old ways that we all relate to are dying. Look how much things have changed in the last couple of years. And, hey, next month, they're supposed to land on the Moon, a human being setting foot on another planet."

"It isn't really a planet."

"The hell it isn't." He didn't bother to open his eyes. "*Planet* is Greek for *wanderer*, as opposed to the stars, which stay in the same relative position. The Moon wanders in the sky, and so does the Sun, so both of them, according to the Greeks, are planets, and it's their goddamn word and they thought of it all first, so the fact that some Johnny-come-lately modern astronomers want to redefine the term doesn't impress me at all." He covered his eyes with a forearm. "Cold water, hot sun…naptime."

I walked back down to the swimming hole and dove in, pulling myself deep toward the stony bottom. I opened my eyes as I frog-kicked my way toward the other side, and glittering minnows skittered out of my way.

I burst to the surface at the other edge, clinging to a rock as I sucked in air. My eyeballs ached from the cold.

Cro-Magnon and Jilly sat a few feet away. He had his legs in the water up to mid-shin, but she'd pulled hers up against her breasts. He acknowledged me with a jerk of his big head, and Jilly gave me a wide, dopey smile and let her head fall clumsily to his shoulder. Stoned on downers again, no doubt. Cro shrugged with his free shoulder and raised his eyebrows, as if apologizing.

Upstream, at the far end of the pool, a loud whoop, and Rob Motiff plunged into the water, diving deep. I watched the white of his body shoot along the bottom a dozen feet down, the ripples on the surface distorting him into mad wobbles.

To my surprise, he surfaced beside me, spouting water from his mouth, and then shook the water from his blond curls. Poseidon goes Nordic. "Rick!" he said, as if he'd been seeking me for days.

"Hey, Rob."

"Wow. Good to see you. Long time."

"Yeah, haven't seen you since yesterday."

He laughed, showing teeth. "Yeah, but, it's been a long time since yesterday, man, like *years*." He took a big mouthful of water and shot it to the middle of the pool from between his teeth, a thin stream that must have arced across fifteen feet.

His ebullience, good looks, and sheer size made me feel like I was shrinking. "How long did you have to practice that?" I asked, with as much sarcasm as I was willing to risk.

He laughed again. "Hours and hours, man, in my uncle's pool. Talk about a wasted youth." Then he chuckled. "Wasted youth—guess that's us, huh? I'm sure wasted." He let his voice drop a bit. "Rick, did you take any of that Blue Flash stuff Linc gave me?"

"Flats. Blue Flats."

Muscular shoulders shrugged, a happy Humpty-Dumpty disregard for words.

"Yeah," I said, "I was coming on while you guys were with us in the Park yesterday."

"Whoa. Me and Donnie did the stuff late last night, up in Big Bear. Man, I had no idea, you know? The most amazing thing. I thought it just made you see fairies and stuff, but it's not like anything I've ever done before. I mean"—he waited, searching for the right phrase—"I mean, I spent the whole night just *thinking*, man. I didn't know you could spend that much time just in your head. If you give it a chance, man, it's like Disneyland in there."

"How did Don like it?"

His face turned a little grim. "He didn't dig it much, actually. He's still real bummed. And sometimes last night it was like I could see what was going on in his head, and he wasn't liking being alone in there." He gave a lopsided smile and pointed at his temple. "But it wasn't all posies and popcorn in here, either. I've really been kind of fucked up, you know? Fucked up when I thought I was being cool. So some of the time I was really sad and pissed at myself, but later on it felt like I'd cleared a bunch of shit out of my brain, you know what I mean?"

"I know exactly what you mean, Rob."

"Linc bugged me for years to do acid with him. I wish now I had...so, maybe the three of us can take some together sometime."

"Years? How long has Linc been doing L?"

"Forever, man. Like since he was thirteen or fourteen. Before he had hair on his balls, probably." He took a deep breath and sank down beneath the water feet-first, then erupted from the surface shaking his head.

"Hey!" Cro yelled from behind Rob. "That's cold, dude."

Rob levered himself around. "Mr. Magnon! Hey, man, you got a few Reds I can borrow?"

"Probably. You into downers again, or you going on a date?"

"Donnie. We were up all night on acid, haven't gone to bed yet, and I don't think he's ever gonna sleep unless he goes to Seconal City. And I need to crash, but I'm kinda worried about doing it until he gets down, you know?"

"Okay." Cro pulled his feet up into a squat, the perfect ancestral man, and stood. He walked back from the water to where his clothes lay and pawed through the pockets of his pants.

Rob braced his hands on the rock ledge and then shot himself out of the water onto his feet, as neatly as a competition swimmer. "Later, Rick. Let's get together some time." He began shaking his right hand side-to-side, loose-wristed, and I realized he was trying to dry it before touching gelatin capsules.

Jilly moaned and lay back on the hot stone, arms above her head, legs flopped apart. Between my legs, my friend and constant companion woke suddenly—and after behaving so well all afternoon. I ducked under and swam away; one second more of Jilly and I'd have to stay in the water until it got dark.

But for the hammering heat of the daylight hours, which drove me from my bed before I'd had enough sleep, the next few days were like a fantasy of what life ought to be. I'd shower off the sweat in the mornings, running only the cold tap; read over breakfast, and keep reading until Linc dropped by. We'd drive up into the cool of the mountains and sit in the shade, smoking hash, talking, or just lounging. Evenings, we'd drive to the Park and work the crowd.

I now had three sets of clothes, all borrowed from Linc and all slightly too small, but more stylish than anything I'd owned. The Park was a big floating party on those warm nights, up to a hundred kids drinking and getting stoned. Only rarely did the sheriffs bother to come up onto the slope, since it was near impossible to catch anyone inside the Park; instead they cruised the surrounding streets, waiting for an excuse to pull over departing cars, like Great Whites patrolling just offshore a colony of seals. And like the seals, the Park crowd knew it was best to hit the streets in bunches, since one patrol car couldn't pull over everyone at once.

I was welcomed into most of the circles beneath the trees, even without Linc, especially since I usually had a gram or two of his hash in my pocket. I got no further than chatting with the girls I met, though JenBen hung on my arm for a few hours one night; but Melissa, Randi, and Lisby all accepted me as one of their crowd now, and we were comfortable together, talking and lounging on the grass. I discovered that I wanted this—simple acceptance and companionship—as much as I wanted sex.

Well, almost as much.

Linc, on the other hand, apparently got laid whenever he liked. I wasn't sure what he had, but I wished some of it were mine. Lisby was available to him at any time, but he had a whole string of girls—like the pink pages of a baby-name book, Amanda through Zoe—who gladly disappeared with him for an hour, or two, or a whole night. I suppose he was good-looking in a dark, bomb-throwing-Bolshevik sort of way, but he wasn't movie-star handsome, and he wasn't tall, or unusually muscular, or superhumanly endowed; yet they came, and more important, came back again and again.

I'm not sure where he disappeared to on many of those nights, though on a few occasions when I arrived back at the trailer it was clear that something hot and heavy had happened on my mattress.

Leslie Andrews disdained everything about Yucaipa, so it was a surprise when I looked up one evening from a conversation with JenBen to find her standing there, in the Park, like a plebian. "*Les-lie*," I said, rolling the words in my mouth, "sit down." JenBen snuggled up next to me, marking me as hers as surely as a dog hiking its leg on a pole, but Leslie didn't notice.

"Is Linc around?"

"Disappeared with Beth Townes, I think. Why?"

"I'm going to a party in Riverside tonight. I promised I'd try to score some grass—it's totally dry over there."

"Dry here, too. Will hash do?" I patted the ground, and Leslie slid down to sit Indian style. "Where've you been?"

"Hash would be better than nothing. And, to answer your second question, as far away from here as possible. I think I've sorted out a deal where I can just do college-level credits over at UC Riverside next year—I won't be admitted, technically, but I won't need to keep taking the high-school stuff over here."

"Congrats." I sensed JenBen studying Leslie, but she stayed silent. I passed Leslie two grams of hash and brushed off any thought of payment—generous with Linc's largesse, but willing to claim credit for it myself—and then took the opportunity to say I thought the ending of *French Lieutenant's Woman*, which she'd loaned me, was innovative, and that the intrusion of the author's voice, acknowledging that it was indeed a novel, actually enriched the whole thing. "It wouldn't have worked if he'd come down so hard sooner," I said, "but I thought it really added to the climax."

"You're a strange boy," she said, "but that's beside the point. I thought it was more like what one critic said about the Chorale in Beethoven's Ninth—*a plaster head on a marble statue of Venus.*"

"Do you feel that way about the Ninth?"

"No. I think the Chorale's great."

I spread my palms open, displaying my point. "Well, then… maybe you just need to give Fowles some time."

"Okay. So, to use a Beethoven metric, what, a century-and-a-half?"

I smiled. "Fair enough. Check in with you early in the twenty-second century." I paused, and when she didn't say anything, I asked, "How am I strange?"

"Are you going to college?" I must have looked blank. "Are you even thinking about it?" She held up her hands as if I'd proved her point. "See? You read all these books, but you're not *doing* anything with it."

"What's to do? They're stories. My mom read to me a lot, and liked for me to read…and we didn't have much money, but I could always go to the library. And when things got bad, books were always a place to go."

"Uh-huh. Strange. Speaking of going, I need to get to that party." She stood.

"How should I get the book back to you?"

"Keep it, or pass it on to somebody."

"Aren't you going to reread it?"

She smiled. "Sure, but you gave me a hundred and fifty years. I'm bound to get to the library between now and then." She wiggled her fingers goodbye. "'Night, Rick. Jenny. Good to see you."

I watched her silhouette as she disappeared.

"*Are you going to college?*" JenBen mimicked, her face still slumped on my shoulder. "*But!… To use a BAY-TOVVEN metric…*"

"Jeez, Jen, cut her some slack. So she thinks she's better than all this. Big deal. Aren't we all? Let her."

"Uh-uh." JenBen sat up. "She doesn't think she's better than all this. She's afraid that this is what she's all about."

"Hey, it's just like Randi—she just wants to go somewhere and be something…"

"It's not like Randi. Randi knows who she is." She chewed her lip, and, my attention being drawn there, I decided it would be a good time to kiss her, but she pushed me away, without rancor, insistent on finishing her thoughts. "It's like—the rest of us know where we are, down here in White Trash Paradise, but we're looking *up*. Leslie, she's trying to pretend that she's already up, but she spends all her time looking *down*, worrying she's going to fall, and be like everybody else here, just some, some *person*, instead of the Egg Princess."

"Come on, that's a little extreme…"

"Hey, you just got here, okay? Plus you want to fuck her, and so you can't see straight."

I started to deny it, but there was no point. JenBen and I were faking some things for the rest of the world, but why fake it with each other? I shrugged.

She laughed. "So ball her. I don't care. Tell me the juicy details. But meanwhile…"—she waggled herself up next to me, pulled my face down and kissed me, a long, hungry kiss—"meanwhile, you want to go back to your trailer and mess around, even if it's only little old me?"

"Yeah," I said, my tongue thick.

"Same rules as last time?" she asked.

"Yeah," I answered. "Sure." I swallowed. "Fuck, yeah."

On Friday of that week, I dropped through the counseling office at the high school, where I usually met with my PO. It had been more than a week since I'd had any contact with my father, so I had no way of knowing if Leo had called our house, but I figured the office might know if there was any change planned in his once-a-month routine.

In the interim before the start of summer school the campus was nearly deserted. The counseling office was a modular building, the governmental equivalent of a mobile home, plunked down outside the main rectangle of the school. I half-expected it to be closed during the break, but the wail of the window-mounted air conditioner—the Yucaipa equivalent of the Neanderthal's campfire—said that humans were gathered there.

I opened the flimsy door and presented myself to Mrs. Murrelson, the secretary whose desk dominated the main room. "Rick Leibnitz?" I said, as if suddenly unsure of my name. "Wanted to see if Leo Malheur had set up any kind of schedule for his interviews over the summer, or had left any messages for me…"

I noticed smoke drifting out of an open drawer beside her and stood on tiptoe to peer in. A cigarette burned in an ashtray in the otherwise-empty drawer. She frowned at me and slammed it shut. "Haven't heard from him, haven't heard anything about you. Far as I know, he'll be here once a month, like always."

A man cleared his throat. Mr. Kraft, one of the counselors, stood in the doorway to one of the tiny private offices. A heavy-set man who wore a dark suit and tie every school day, it unsettled me to see him in civilian clothes, his potbelly encased in a powder-blue polo shirt. "You're Rick Leibnitz?"

I nodded.

He crossed over to me with his hand out. "I'm Al Kraft," he said, pumping my hand. I knew this, of course, so I just smiled. "Can I talk to you for a minute?"

This sounded like bad news to me. I imagine that it would have been within my rights to say, *No, school's not in session, and I'd rather not*, but I shrugged and said, "Sure." Mrs. Murrelson opened her drawer again as I followed him away.

It was cramped in his office, and he filled most of the space. "I was just on the phone to your probation officer yesterday," he said. "We had a very interesting talk about you."

Oh Christ. I said, "Uh-huh?" as casually as I could manage, but my voice sounded squeaky.

"We got your test results back on Wednesday."

I was baffled. "Test results?"

"Statewide aptitudes? The fill-in-the-bubble jobs? All computerized, so the turn-around is almost immediate. Of course, most of the results don't get sent back for another month or so, because they tabulate the stats down at County schools first, but anything out of the ordinary, they shoot over to us right away."

Was screwing up a test a violation of probation? I sighed. "You know, I was kind of distracted that day—didn't have much sleep—" I recalled that I'd actually spent about half the test time staring at Melissa and Leslie, but that didn't seem to be a very good defense. "I've been having some problems, and didn't really try as hard as usual…"

His eyebrows went up. "Really? Maybe that explains it. But I don't think you're understanding me. Your test scores were way above average—at the gifted level, in fact."

My mouth opened and closed a few times before I managed to say, "Then why am I in trouble?"

"You're not in trouble. At least not with me." He shook his head in that patronizing, aren't-kids-just-a-bundle-of-surprises way.

"Then why'd you call Leo?"

"Look, when your test scores came in, I had no idea who you were. So I checked with Records, and found you'd just transferred in. I called down to Redlands Unified, and made sure that you were the same person… Your test scores are thirty, forty points above the other times you've taken the exam. You were High Normal before, but you're way out in Mensa territory now." He leaned forward and clasped his hands, his forearms resting on his fat thighs. "Frankly, there was initially some suspicion of cheating—that you'd copied from another student. So we checked with County on the whole cohort that was in the room that day, and—I'm not supposed to tell you this, but your scores were higher than any in the room. So there was nobody to copy from."

"I still don't see why you called my PO."

"Oh. Well, checking up on you, I found out you were on probation. To tell the truth, we don't end up with many gifted students on probation—though there's more of them nowadays than there were. Sounded like you were a special case. So I called Leo and we had a little chat about you. You've been through a lot, and it's clear to me that the school system down in Redlands failed you in a number of ways. You should have had enrichment courses, and a college-prep track, and a—well, many things you didn't have. And now it's my job to make sure we don't make the same mistakes up here."

We talked about my family history, and it was clear that Leo had already given him extensive background. At one point he leaned forward and put a beefy hand on my knee. "It's got to be tough to have your mother take off like that."

I shrugged as if it didn't matter. His touch made me uncomfortable, and I stayed tense until he removed his hand and sat back in his chair. "Do you find you have a lot of hostility toward women?"

"What?" I asked, astonished.

"Women, girls: do you find you have a lot of anger towards them?"

"Well, no," I said, baffled. "I like girls, a lot, probably more than most guys." I thought about it for a moment. "It's more the other way around."

"You know, Rick, you shouldn't read too much into the fact that she took your brother and sister. They were so young, I'm sure she believed she had no choice but to take them. I'm not making excuses for your mother, not at all, but you shouldn't take it as a rejection of you in particular. It's just that you were older."

I knew the real reason she'd left me behind, but I saw no reason to tell him. "Can we talk about something else?"

He asked me about my interests, and when he found out how much I read, he asked what authors I liked best. My mind was a blank, and then I started to list writers I'd read, in no particular order. "Fowles. Kafka. Walter Tevis, and Hemingway, and Twain and Conrad, of course…and, oh yeah, John Barth, and Steinbeck, and Raymond Chandler, and I don't know, some real trash, too, like Ian Fleming. Oh, and D. H. Lawrence, and Camus… I don't know. Lots of stuff."

He laughed. "You're probably better-read than anybody on the faculty here. So why are your grades in English so…unremarkable?"

"I like reading. That doesn't mean I like diagramming sentences. Or doing book reports."

"Hmm." He thought about this, and then changed tone. "I called your father this morning, by the way. Leo gave me his number."

I tensed. "And?"

"And I asked if he could have you get in touch with me. He said you were staying with relatives. So I talked to him about your test scores, and told him that, in my view, the military-school option that Leo mentioned was a very bad idea."

Good for you, Al. "What did he say to that?"

"He told me, and I quote, to *mind my own goddamn business*. I pointed out to him that this was exactly my business, my job, in fact." Kraft smiled. "He told me that if I called him again he'd contact the school board and I wouldn't have a job anymore. He apparently doesn't understand about tenure. And then he said some very nasty things, and hung up."

"Sounds like Dad, alright."

"Leo and I have agreed to work on him about this military school issue, although Leo isn't sure it's such a bad idea, your going away to school. By the way, are you and Leo having some kind of a problem?"

I sat upright in alarm. "Why?"

"Nothing specific. He just seemed…troubled. And it felt like there was something he wasn't telling me." He waved it away. "Probably nothing. Now, have you considered summer school? We have several special programs coming up…"

I told him, lying, that I really wished I could afford to attend summer session, but I needed to find a full-time summer job. "To help pay for military school," I added, with a smirk I hoped was both eloquent yet subtle.

He stood and ushered me out. "We'll work on that issue." He clapped a hand to my shoulder. "I know it's hard. The door here is always open." He squeezed his hand in a little vibrating motion that was intended to be reassuring.

Linc's Impala sat in the McFadden driveway when I arrived after the long, hot walk from the school. I found him shirtless in a lawn chair, tilted back against the trunk of the umbrella tree; one hand held a beer, the other a library copy of Barth's *Lost in the Funhouse* which I'd urged him to read. "Some of this is pretty good stuff. Especially *Night-Swim*—sperm pondering the purpose of their lives."

He pushed off the trunk by thrusting a shoulder back, and put his feet on the ground. He had a crooked little smile on his lips. With his odd skin color—dark hiding beneath pale—and his unruly black hair, he looked like a satyr straight off a Greek vase.

"Sit down," he said, "but not too close."

"Why?" I sat in one of the other lawn chairs.

"Because I don't want you jumping up and kissing me when I give you this news."

I waited.

"Yesterday I went to see Sue Andrews at her place and told her that if she didn't get your dad to leave you alone and keep his mouth shut, that I was going to tell her husband all about the two of them."

"Oh fuck." Vicious and stubborn was what my father was all about. "Linc, that's just going to make him worse. And she might leave Andrews and go live with him."

"No way. She likes the money, likes being the richest lady in town. No way she wants a divorce."

"If she got half of what Andrews has, she'd still be the richest lady in town."

"She won't get half if the cause for divorce is adultery. She won't get shit."

"Our word against hers."

"I'm sure Leslie'd say whatever we want, too."

"Oh, Linc…I wish you'd told me about this first. This is *such* a bad idea. My dad would rather—"

"Hear me out, slick. There's a couple of things you don't know. First off, the Andrews family basically owns your dad. He started borrowing money from Andrews Ranches against his own ranch, long, long ago. He's been running in the red for years, and when his place went under, Andrews got the deed. The second thing you don't know is that our little Susie was also banging Rob Motiff's older brother a few years back. So we *own* her ass…and she, in turn, owns your father's ass. Sort of this long evolutionary line of ass-ownership—"

"Linc, you don't get what a self-destructive jerk he can be—"

He silenced me with a raised palm. "No. Already settled. Sue will do anything to stay on in her role as Mrs. Andrews, so I gave her the terms yesterday. I went and saw her again today." He leaned forward, confiding. "We got it all."

"All what?"

"Your dad agreed to everything. He'll leave you alone. He'll lie to your PO, tell him you're still at home and doing great. If your PO calls and wants to see you, he'll take a message and pass it to Sue, who will get in touch with my mom. The bad news is, you're stuck in Yucaipa: no military school after all. The good news is, he wants you out of the house and doesn't want to see you again. We're going to pick up your stuff tonight after he leaves for work; he told Sue if it's still there tomorrow, he'll burn it all."

I sat in stunned silence, and when I spoke, the best I could manage was, "I don't believe it."

"Believe, and ye shall be saved."

"Oh, you're Jesus now, too? Takes more than one miracle, Linc."

"More like Buddha, I figure. You couldn't have made this happen. It matters too much to you, you care too much. Me, I could do it with no lust of result. And our friend Susie—well, she was willing to do *any*thing, and I'm sure she was very persuasive."

I tried to absorb it all, and realized with horror that tears were leaking from my eyes.

"Hey, man, that wasn't the reaction I was looking for…"

"…*sorry*…" I whispered. The last thing in the world I wanted to do was cry in front of Linc, but there I went, The Waterworks Kid. "It's just…oh, *shit*…"

He knelt beside me and put his arm around me. "Hey, man, it's okay. It's okay. It's gonna be great now." He hugged me, and my weeping cranked down a notch.

I gulped, gulped again, and tried to explain. "It's like thinking you've got this, this disease, and you're going to die, and then they tell you you're going to live…" I sniffed and sniveled a little more, and then said, "Thank you, man."

"Uh-huh. You can kiss me now if you really want to. No tongue, though."

"Fuck you, Linc," I said, laughing.

"So—I figure we need to waste at least five more hours before he leaves for work. Let's go swimming." He stood up. "And now you've got no excuse for not getting a place with me and starting our little salon."

"Except that I'm broke."

"There's solutions to that, too. Would that all problems were that simple to solve. So get out of the goddamn chair."

I did, and followed Lincoln around the house to his car.

11 | THE MOTHER LODE

I felt ridiculous riding a horse, but Lincoln sat his own mount as if he'd been born on a cattle drive. Except for his daypack, he could have been a cowboy, or, given his dark looks, a vaquero. The stable owner had greeted him as a regular customer, and apologized that Linc's favorite horse had already been rented for the afternoon.

The stables were in Calimesa, Yucaipa's sister city, divided from Yucaipa by a deep, broad wash, but by little else. We rode north from Fremont Street onto an old Jeep trail that, judging from the road-apples, was a favorite riding trail. It led toward Kehl Canyon, and into the system of twisting arroyos that ran through the hills between Calimesa and Cherry Valley.

The night before, we'd gone to retrieve my things from my father's house. Since I'd never unpacked, it should have been an easy job, just a matter of carrying the boxes out to the Impala. But at some point—probably after Sue had laid down the law—Dad had dumped everything onto the floor and done as much destruction as he could. Some of my shirts were torn, but what hurt most is that all of my paperbacks had been ripped apart, right down their fragile spines. "Let's just get the clothes," I'd said. "To hell with the rest of it."

My horse sped up for no apparent reason, and in defiance of my tug on the reins. "Where are we going?" I asked again.

"The Mother Lode. I'm going to show you something." He looked over at me. "I'm trusting you here, Rick. Don't fuck me over."

He was the best friend I'd ever had, and now was the closest thing I had to family. "I'd never do anything to hurt you, Linc. No matter what."

Thirty minutes into the ride, he steered us down into a dry creekbed filled with sycamores. We tied the horses in the shade, and he tightened the shoulders of his daypack. "A little hike."

The hike was no more than a half-mile, but it crossed three brushy hills where there was no shelter from the noon sun. "Wish I had a beer," I said, "or better yet, a rum and Coke."

"Later. What we do here now, we do one hundred percent straight."

We headed down the north side of a steep hill, into blessed shade. Toward the bottom a few massive live oaks grew on the slope, their shiny, holly-like leaves quivering in the slight breeze.

We stopped beside the biggest of them. Many of its roots were exposed, reaching out around granite outcroppings until they could find a gap of soil, then plunging deep. "The Mother Lode," he said. "Keep scanning the area. We can't let anybody see us."

Linc dropped the saddlebag and then scrambled ten feet up the slope between the massive roots. He lifted a head-sized rock and set it carefully down, using a root like a shelf. He pulled out three more and set them down, and then, leveraging with all the strength in his back, rolled a tall, flattish boulder to the side.

There was an excavation behind the rocks—a short, dark tunnel about three feet high and three feet wide.

He crouched down and pulled a large metal canister from the tunnel. It was about the size of a five-gallon bucket, and had probably once held industrial quantities of lard in some restaurant kitchen.

He worked his way down the short slope to the dry streambed and lowered the canister to the sand. Then he returned to the excavation and lifted out a lidded plastic bucket. From the way he rocked side to side as he picked his way back down to level ground, I could tell the bucket was filled with sloshing liquid. He sat it down carefully, as though it were loaded with nitroglycerin.

He pried open the lid of the metal canister and lifted out a plastic garbage bag. He undid the tie and reached inside. "Keep looking around," he said.

Slabs of hash the size of a thick hardback, each wrapped in clear plastic. He selected four and set them aside. He then produced a pair of jars, one with what must have been a hundred hits of Blue Flats, the other full of red gelatin capsules. "You sell Reds?" I asked in surprise.

"No. I only sell hash. LSD I give away to anybody who needs some. The Reds—well, I've just had so many people bug me for them over the years that I keep some around, the way people who don't smoke have ashtrays for their friends who do."

He dumped some Reds into one baggie, and a small handful of Blue Flats into another. He replaced the jars, and then lifted out a fist-sized cloth bag and replaced it with a similar one he'd brought in the daypack. "Desiccant," he said. "Keeps it all dry." To my puzzlement, he carried the plastic bucket back uphill and replaced it without ever opening the lid. He sealed up the canister, carted it back up to its hiding place, and then spent at least fifteen minutes replacing the rocks, and scattering handfuls of dried leaves.

Once he was satisfied his hidey-hole was camouflaged, he stuffed the hash and baggies of drugs into the daypack, shouldered it, and set off the way we'd come.

"All right," I said, after we'd marched in silence for ten minutes, "you're just waiting for me to ask, aren't you? What's the deal with the bucket full of liquid?"

"Half-full of concentrated sulfuric acid. There's another in the car. If it looks like we're going to get rousted, everything goes into the acid. So, we're pretty safe when we're at the Mother Lode, pretty safe once we're in the car. The risky part is right now, getting from the stash to the car...but, having lugged a couple gallons of H_2SO_4 up here on foot and horseback once, I'm willing to take the risk for an hour or so rather than cope with trying to move the acid with the goods."

"Does that work? The sulfuric acid, I mean?"

"Did a couple of experiments." He held out his arms for balance as he skied down a steep section of leaf-covered slope. "I've wiped out hits of acid, Reds, marijuana. Hash doesn't go so fast, it's kind of oily, but it gets eaten up in time."

"So with these big blocks of stuff you've got…"

"Half-pounds. Yeah, they'd take a while to get chewed up. But"—he looked back at me and gestured at the air—"I figure nobody who's searching us would be real eager to stick their hands in there to fish 'em out."

I thought about this. "They could use something to hook them out. Or just pour the whole thing out on the ground."

He shrugged. "Sure. Nothing's foolproof. But while you negotiated, the sulfuric might eat everything. And then when you told the cops it was a jar of sulfuric acid, that might make them stop and think even longer…and how do they know what pouring it out on the ground might do? Not foolproof, but a hell of a lot better than just driving dope from place to place with your fingers crossed."

"Why keep it out here, though? Wouldn't it be enough just to carry it in the car?"

"Maybe. But suppose someone followed us? Or suppose the cops came swooping in with helicopters…? Even if somebody comes after us when we're riding along, we can make a run in either direction, car or stash, and have a place to dump it at either end."

We reached the spot where the horses were tied, and he undid the knots and handed me my reins. We mounted up, Linc swinging into the saddle like Gene Autry, me hopping along with one foot in a stirrup as the horse moved. He wheeled his steed around in the direction of the stables with a slight, confident toss of the reins, and my horse followed without any urging on my part. "Do other dealers do the acid thing?" I asked.

"As far as I know, I invented it. But a long time ago—well, come to think of it, it was only a little over a year, but it was back before I could even drive—I was helping a guy run stuff up from the border. I'd strip the stuff and get it ready—"

"What do you mean, *strip the stuff?*"

"I'll show you some day. Anyhow, he'd come down and pick me up in the afternoon. Always drove a car with this super aircon, always arrived colder than hell. We'd hide the stuff under the backseat, and he'd pick up this tied pillowcase from the floor and lay it on the seat. Then we'd go get dinner in this Mexican restaurant, and by the time we got back it was pretty warm in the car."

I made a puzzled face at this apparently pointless story.

He raised a finger. "Punchline coming. One night we did get pulled over, just outside Palm Springs. Cop is doing the usual cop stuff, shining the light in our eyes, looking all around the car. *What's in the bag?* the cop asks. *Rattlesnakes*, my friend says. Cop gives us this, yeah, right, expression, opens the door and pokes the bag with his flashlight, and all hell breaks loose. You know how a rattler sounds when it's pissed." I nodded. "Picture five of them going off at once, inside a car. I mean, I knew it was coming, and I still jumped so hard my head almost hit the roof."

He looked back over his shoulder and scanned our trail before continuing. "So, the cop leaps back so fast he almost falls on his butt, and then says, *Jesus Christ, what the hell is wrong with you people?* My friend says, *It's our job, we catch 'em and then sell them to this place that milks them to make antivenin.* The cop shakes his head, says, *Man, you guys are nuts*, and lets us go."

"Where'd he get the rattlesnakes?"

"Caught 'em, and then kept them in aquariums—excuse me, aquaria—around his house. Real conversation pieces. Easy to handle as long as you cooled them down first, let them go torpid and dopey. When we'd finish the run, we'd let the car sit in the driveway with the aircon blasting for an hour or more, and then he'd lift the pillowcase out and put his babies away; I'd undo the seat and unload the goodies."

"So this is your version of a bag of venomous snakes?"

"The snake thing makes a good story, and it got me thinking. This isn't perfect, but it's the best I've been able to come up with so far. The suggestion box is wide open, if you come up with a better approach."

I rode in silence for a while. "So that's two pounds of hash in the pack there. That's worth a fortune."

"Depends on who you ask. A pound is four hundred fifty-four grams. Street value, which is how the cops always report everything, because it makes their numbers sound bigger, is anywhere from eight to twelve bucks a gram. But I don't deal in grams—may give them away, but I don't sell them. At, say, ten bucks a gram, each of those half-pounds is worth, say, two thousand three hundred. But I sell them for less than half of that, about a thousand bucks per half-pound. So, to me, this is around four thousand dollars. I buy it in Mexico for a third of that, depending, so that's, what, a thousand to fifteen hundred dollars profit on the deal." He gave me a wry look. "But I guarantee you, if I got busted with it, the cops would say it's worth fifteen or twenty thousand dollars."

I rubbed my forehead, staggered by the sums. Inland in California, you could rent a decent house in those days for a hundred dollars a month; you could live well on four hundred a month, and salaries above ten thousand a years were considered good incomes; twenty thousand meant you probably belonged to a country club. "How could you dump that much money into a pot of sulfuric acid?"

"How much would you pay to stay out of YA? Number one consideration: I am *not* going to jail. Ever. For anything. I keep enough money stashed away that I can dump a whole run's worth of material and still start again. I'm not greedy. I don't flash my money around, I drive a beat-up Impala. I keep enough for clothes and good times, I pay for the groceries at my house, I try to be halfway generous."

The way Linc gave away acid, or tossed friends grams of hash; the way he'd left me twenty dollars when I'd moved into the trailer—it all fit now. "You're more than halfway generous."

"About some things. About some others…well, I'm running a business. Here's my five rules." He held up a fist, and ticked them off by raising fingers. "First, sell only to a few people, people you know and trust, and give them better prices than they could get anywhere else. Second, if the buyer gets arrested for anything—even taken in for questioning—no more business with them, no matter how much you think you trust them. Third, find a really great place to hide your personal stash, preferably outside the house, even if it makes it a pain in the butt to get. Fourth, try not to go anywhere with more stuff than you can eat. Fifth, when you have to move more stuff than you can eat, take a jar of concentrated sulfuric." He looked at his widespread fingers and considered. "Damn. Make that six rules. Sixth, never do business loaded. Oh, and hide your money away from your house."

After we dismounted in the stableyard, Linc handed me some money to pay the owner. When I returned to the car, he was already behind the wheel. I opened the passenger-side door and saw that a lidded plastic bucket sat on the floor in front of my seat. I climbed in, straddling it carefully, and Linc handed me the daypack. "Keep the lid on tight," he said, "but if I say dump it, you peel the lid back and feed everything in there. Try not to splash, but don't hesitate. If we get pulled over, that stuff isn't money, it's a one-way ticket to jail till we're eighteen."

He drove us up Wildwood Canyon Road and across the gap into Cherry Valley. "The risky part is the actual sale. If the cops have a setup going, or a stakeout, that's when it's going to get triggered—and the buyer's involved, so responses aren't all under your control." He glanced my way. "I can drop you off some place for twenty minutes, pick you up on the way back…?"

"I'll come," I said.

We pulled up a gravel driveway to a ranch-style house right out of a TV sitcom. Linc jumped out, came around to my side, opened the door, and picked up the stash and the jar of sulfuric from the floor. "Wait here. Anything goes weird, feel free to start the car and split."

"I don't know how to drive. I'll just come in with you."

He snorted. "I don't think they'd like that much, man."

He slammed the door.

I waited. I should have been nervous, but Linc seemed to have it all figured out.

It took no more than ten minutes. "That was fast," I said, while the engine roared back to life.

"Doesn't take much time if you don't sit around getting loaded with the customers. What's to talk about? Here's drugs, there's money. Bye-bye." He tossed the baggies of Reds and Blue Flats down by my feet, where he'd put the jar of sulfuric. "Remember, we're still carrying. But the hard part's over. Sulfuric'll cut through that stuff in no time."

He drove without talking until we reached Wildwood Canyon again, his eyes flicking to the rearview mirror every few seconds. For some reason, he relaxed once we were driving down the canyon road, as if the canopy of live oaks that overhung the road might hide us from predators. "The question you need to think about is this: do you know any dealers in Redlands who can move, say, a pound a month? And of those, are there any of them that you'd trust? If you can really answer yes to those questions, then we'll expand the business a little. We go get the stuff together, we sell it on to the street dealers; we split the profits. Cool?"

"Yeah…" I searched for words. "Why me, Linc? Why me?"

"You need it. You deserve it. How sure are you of these guys?"

"They're Mexicans, man. Machismo, honor, the whole bit. They'd let guys pull their nails out before they'd give me up."

"It's settled, then. I'll start looking for a place for us to live. You decide who you're going to deal to. This is gonna be good."

We drove a little farther before he asked, "Are you afraid of getting busted?"

"Yeah," I admitted.

"Good," he said. "Stay that way."

We didn't intend for the party that evening to get so large, but that was Yucaipa—once word got out that a party was happening, everyone in town considered themselves invited.

Plus, it was Saturday.

Lincoln called it my Emancipation Party, pleasing himself with the pun on his name, and baffling the guests, since he didn't give out details; but there was a vague understanding that it was somehow in my honor, and so most of the pre-sundown arrivals treated me like the birthday boy.

Rob Motiff was the first to arrive, carrying a keg over one shoulder, trailed by Donnie Briscoe, who struggled along carrying a second keg in his arms, like a bridegroom crossing the threshold with his beloved. We set these up in tubs of ice under the umbrella tree.

Anticipating what was likely to come, I ran inside the McFaddens' house and shut the doors to the bedrooms, taping up hasty *Keep Out* signs, as well as a few with arrows that read *Bathroom*.

By the time I got out back, there were two dozen people in the yard, and someone had set up a stereo, plugged into an outlet in what

I thought of as *my* trailer. Cream's "Strange Brew," from the *Disraeli Gears* album, drifted into the reddening sky. People lifted their waxy paper cups of beer on high as I passed through, congratulating me on they knew not what.

Randi and Melissa were both there, sitting near the speakers, but with guys I didn't recognize, older guys. Randi pulled on my arm and shouted over the music, "What's this party about? Linc said you were celebrating."

"Long story," I yelled.

"Want to tell it to me?"

"Not unless you want to go somewhere quieter!"

She looked at her friends, and then put her mouth to my ear and said, "Maybe later, or some other time, or something."

I nodded. Whatever you say, Randi.

Linc had appointed himself official greeter and stood by the rear corner of the house, Beth Townes hanging on him. I saw him pointing at me and talking, apparently telling people that I needed congratulations.

No Jenny.

I wandered through the crowd, insinuating myself into the clusters long enough to hear part of the stories being told, then disengaged myself and moved on.

Disengaged. The exact word. I was accepted as one of them now, but still felt like an outsider.

"Rick!" Leslie waved at me from across the crowd, hopping up onto her tiptoes to see. I wound my way in her direction, pleased but puzzled; she was the last person I expected at a Yucaipa party.

An older guy, probably a college student from the UC, had his arm around her. Jealousy surged through me, made worse by the fact that he was big, and handsome by any standards. Red mustaches swept around his mouth and down to his chin, giving him the look of a Viking lord. She introduced us. I let him crush my hand, but refused to register the name.

"And this," Leslie continued, "is the infamous Casey Carroll." She gestured. In my envy of Nordic-boy, I hadn't noticed the girl standing beside her.

"So," Casey said, not offering her hand, "this is your local Cyril Connolly?"

"The same. Slimmer, though, I'd think. We're going to go *mingle*. Shout when you've had enough; this was *your* idea, remember."

Who the hell was Cyril Connolly? Leslie and her boyfriend meandered off, leaving Casey and I to study one another. She was pale and slender, with a nervous, Victorian air of delicacy about her, as if she might be prone to fainting spells or hysteria. "Is there someplace we can sit down?" she asked. "You have anything to smoke?"

I assured her that the answer to both of these questions was yes, but had to scan the area for anything to sit upon other than the ground; chairs and lounges were already filled, and wooden crates and old tubs had been pressed into service all over the yard. I spied the old bench outside the back-porch entrance, and led her over there, her long Indian muslin skirt swishing through the dry weeds.

I started setting up a pipeful of hashish. "What did Leslie mean, *this was your idea*?"

"She's always bitching about this horrible town she's from, telling unbelievable stories, and I keep saying I want to see the place. So"—she gestured, displaying the crowd to me—"my wish is granted."

"And what do you think so far?"

"It looks like the offspring of a bunch of Steinbeck's Okies."

"Makes sense. That's pretty much exactly what it is. But these would be the grandkids." I torched the pipe, took a long hit, and passed it to her. I exhaled, and waited for her to blow out her own lungful before I asked, "So where are you from?"

"Santa Monica. But I'm in my freshman year at UC Riverside, which is where I met Leslie. She hangs out there a lot."

"Studying?"

"Double major in English Lit and Botany."

"Interesting."

"Not really."

That was a conversation stopper for me, so I decided to outwait her. I relit the hash, took my hit, slipped the hot pipe into her elegant fingers.

When she exhaled, she said through the smoke, "My father isn't that crazy about girls going to college in the first place. He says if he's going to pay for it all, then I'd damn well better major in something practical—either education, or one of the sciences. The English lit is for me."

"Why botany, though?"

"Of the sciences, it requires the least math. I'm not big on math."

I asked her about her Lit classes. I genuinely had no idea what college literature courses might be, but I assumed that it involved something more than longer book reports.

She talked about theory—deconstructionism, metafiction, text analysis—and about books they'd read and analyzed. The abstractions were entertaining enough, but whenever we came to specific authors or works that we'd both read, we disagreed. Punctuated by puffs of hash, we argued, and none-too-pleasantly, about authors that ranged from Hemingway to Vonnegut. She disliked Hemingway in general, and I mentioned that I hated the ending of *A Farewell to Arms*. Naturally, she found it to be one of the only authentically moving moments in all of his writing; I thought it was cheating. "What happens isn't a result of anything the characters do," I said, "or of what happens in the story up until then. Until then, it's a great book. But at the end, things are going well, he's happy, and Hemingway says *time for a tragedy*, and so he just invents one."

"Oh, come on, Rick. It's not like he has her get hit by a bus. It's *child*birth. He loses her and the child both."

"But why? What does it have to do with the story, or anything anybody did? What's the point, Sex Kills?"

"Don't be asinine. The point is that tragedies do happen. It doesn't all have to make sense. Life doesn't."

"Life doesn't have to, but isn't that why we have novels?"

"No. We have novels to *reflect* life. And the modern novel knows that there aren't neat lessons. Grow up, Rick."

We argued our way through half a dozen others until we arrived at Vonnegut, who she contended was a weak author because his characters weren't deep or *round* enough. I countered that the nature of satire required that characters not become too deep, or the comic edge starts to slide into pathos, and that the best comic novels had characters that were little more than two-dimensional, citing *Catch-22* in support of my point.

She either didn't have a good answer to this or was bored, because she changed the subject. "So what do you write, or what do you hope to write?" she asked.

"Write? I don't write anything. I just read."

"Oh, come on. All avid readers secretly want to be writers."

"That's ridiculous."

"But true."

"It doesn't follow at all. That's like saying that everybody who likes girls wants to be a lesbian."

"Now who's being ridiculous?"

The conversation, such as it was, came to a halt. I tried once more. "Is Casey short for something?"

"Cassandra. I hate Cass and Cassie, so…"

"Cassandra. So, do you find you have a hard time getting people to believe what you say?"

"Ha ha." She stood. "I think it's time to go 'mingle.' Later." She walked off, a little unsteadily, into the crowd.

An annoying woman, but she had kept my attention; I hadn't noticed that twilight had turned to night.

I needed to clear my head of the smoke and noise. I made a wide circle around the clusters of people and headed out toward the deserted back acres of the property.

The half-moon bled down enough light for me to see that it wasn't as deserted as I'd assumed; off the path, in the knee-high weeds, a few resourceful couples had laid out blankets, and naked skin moved in the moonlight. At the edge of the field, I could even make out one blanket that seemed to have three occupants, though I couldn't tell the genders from that distance.

At the fence surrounding the collapsed stables I leaned back with my elbows on the toprail and stared back at the party. Music—Hendrix, now—laughter, and chattering voices, all of them drifted across the field distorted, as though I were under water, and I thought that maybe this was where I really belonged, out at the margin, not on the inside.

I heard a board creak and looked to my left. A figure perched atop the fence, smoking a cigarette. I walked that direction with tentative steps, curious but not wanting to intrude.

"Hey, Rick." Lisby's voice.

"Hi, Lisby." I climbed up beside her. "You okay?"

"Not really." She smelled of beer and cigarettes and gardenias.

"Anything I can do?"

"No." She waited, rocking forward and back, and then said, "Yes. Tell me why Linc doesn't want me."

"Did he say that? Because he tells me—"

"What?"

"That you're really, well, exciting, and…"

She flicked her cigarette butt onto the ground, stepped down and ground it out with the toe of her diminutive boot, and climbed back up. "He says we need to stop seeing each other so much. Once a week, now, he says. And I guess I already used up my slot." She lit another cigarette, and in the flare of the match I saw dark circles under her eyes. "I love him, Rick." Her voice faltered, full of the unfairness of it all. "Why doesn't he love me?"

I opened my mouth to say one thing, and then another, but I finally settled on, "I'm sure he does love you, Lisby. He loves a lot of people. I just don't think he wants to get all tied up in anything. He's only sixteen."

"I'm only sixteen, too."

"Yeah, and you should be having a good time, having experiences, not trying to…settle down. You should see other guys."

"I've seen other guys. I've been with lots of other guys. And I'm done with that."

"Except you seem to want a different him than who he is."

She threw me a hard glance and then looked down. "Will you talk to him for me? Will you tell him how much I love him?"

"I'm sure he knows all that."

"Will you do it anyway? As a favor?"

"Sure. But you can't expect to be with him all the time, at least not now."

"Easy for you to say. He told me you and he are going to live together. Your little *salon*."

I sighed. "Lisby…I'm not in competition with you."

"No. Ten million other girls are, though."

I clasped and unclasped my hands. I knew exactly what Lincoln wanted—freedom, a chance to live and experiment, and to let relationships evolve into some new, better pattern. Lisby essentially wanted to marry him, even if she didn't put it that way. Were I in Linc's position, I'm not sure I could have resisted her. She was beautiful in a doll-like way; she was relentlessly in love; and, from the things I'd overheard when they were balling in the living room of the trailer, she was an all-out, no-limits, sexual dynamo. If she'd aimed herself at me like that, I might have concluded that Lisby was more than enough, and just buried myself in her.

I patted her hand on the toprail, and she clasped mine and squeezed before letting go. "Let's go back to the party," I said.

"I want to be by myself a little longer, okay? Have another cigarette, then maybe come over, drink a beer, and drive home."

I persisted a little longer, urging her to come with me, or volunteering to stay there with her, until she said, "Rick. I'm fine. I just want to be alone for a while."

I headed back toward the house, a little depressed. I kept my gaze down on the dust of the path, ignoring the moans and gasps from the blankets in the weeds.

Randi and Melissa stood with their escorts, Melissa draped on hers. With delight I saw that a figure with her back to me was JenBen—I could recognize her shape from any angle. I eased up alongside her and hugged her. "Hey, Rick…" she said, and then addressed Randi in an exasperated tone. "But I thought I was going to stay at your house tonight."

Randi laughed. "Well, you can. It's just that *I* might not be there."

Jenny whispered in my ear, "We're having sort of a problem. Can I catch up with you later?"

I smiled and patted her affirmatively before I moved on.

Someone had found a broken-down sofa somewhere, probably in one of the outbuildings, and hauled it up next to the trailer. A couple of girls sat at one end with their bottoms on the edge of the cushion, as if they feared contamination.

At the other end of the couch, Rob leaned back, apparently fending off a sexual assault from a black-haired girl. She was hugged up beside him, his arm trapped. She kissed and nuzzled his neck, and he, laughing in a way that didn't sound entirely amused, attempted to ease her away with his free hand, a task complicated by the cupful of beer he held. The girl slung her leg over his thigh, and her tight miniskirt rode up around her waist as she ground her panty-clad pelvis against him. His eyes widened, and then fixed on me, and he cried, "Rick! Man, been waiting for you all night!" He waggled himself onto his feet, practically dumping the girl onto the couch. She glowered at me as if it were my fault.

He clapped me on the shoulder and turned me around. "Needed to talk to you," he said, his voice booming. He threw his arm around me. "Let's take a walk!"

I looked over my shoulder as he marched me away, where the girl tugged her skirt back down. I marveled that he could walk away from her: she was hot in every sense of the word.

"What did we need to talk about?" I asked.

"Nothing," he whispered, still steering me through the crowd. "Not that I don't want to talk to you. Just needed to get away from Alicia... She's gonna make somebody a very happy guy tonight, but not me."

"What's wrong with her?"

"Shhh. Just wait a minute, okay?"

It took some time to get beyond the throng. Multitudes had arrived while I was talking to Lisby, and there must have been a hundred people in the yard, maybe more. We stopped to let a guy with a fresh keg pass by.

When we got beyond the fringe of the horde, Rob just kept walking me, crashing through the weeds, until he sighed and dropped his arm from my shoulder. "Whoa. Man. Shit. What a relief." He stretched his arms and yawned. "Wow. Look at that moon."

"What's up, Rob?"

"Me." He laughed. "And *not* me, too, if you see what I mean."

I didn't, so I raised my eyebrows and waited.

"I took some more of that stuff, that Blue Flash."

"Flats. Tonight? You mean, you're on acid right now?"

"Yeah! A party is just—you just see so much of what's really going on. It's like the best movie I've ever seen." His pupils were dilated to the max. "Thing is, though, Alicia starts coming on to me, and sex is the last thing I want, you know? I mean, it's Uncle Wiggly time. I couldn't get stiff if they froze me." He frowned, and lowered his voice. "Is that normal?"

Not for me, but that was none of his business. "Pretty common, I guess."

"Ah." He nodded. "Cool, then. You aren't on acid, are you?"

I shook my head.

"Hey, then, you should go grab Alicia before she drags somebody else under the trailer."

Appealing in principle, but I couldn't picture it in practice. *Hi, Alicia? You don't know me, but I couldn't help noticing that…* I chuckled. "I don't think so."

He shrugged. "Your loss. Man, I wish there was someplace I could sit down for a while by myself. Just sort of relax, without all this… input."

I thought. "In the house. The bedrooms are all closed up…"

"Cool."

We walked to the back porch, avoiding as much of the press of bodies as possible.

At the bench, Casey was easing herself away from a groping Don Briscoe. "Rick," she said, "tell 'iss twerp to leave me alone." She stood, unsteady on her feet.

Donnie's look challenged me to tell him anything at all.

"Leave her alone, twerp," Rob said, and laughed.

Don smiled—all a big joke, anyway, right?—but shot me an ugly look before he slunk away.

Casey hung onto my arm. "Hey, who's your friend?" Her speech slurred.

"This is Rob, and he's blasted on acid right now. Come on."

I led the way into the house, Casey still clinging to me. A few people stood in the kitchen, smoking cigarettes and drinking beer.

Despite the signs we'd posted, the bedrooms were both occupied, locked from the inside. To my surprise, the living room was dark and deserted, though it was clear from the crumpled beer cans that the party had rolled through there as well. "This good?" I asked.

"Perfect, man, perfect." Rob lay down on a sofa. "Just a little time in the dark and quiet…"

I walked Casey back through the kitchen. "We should find Leslie," I said. "I think maybe you need to head home."

"No no no. Just sit down with me. For a while. Someplace with a li'l *priv*acy… 'Sides, we never finished our *talk*."

I considered. Dragging her through the crowd looking for Leslie in her state would be a chore, maybe impossible. "Trailer," I said, and headed us that way.

The living room of the trailer was empty, but I heard noises from behind my bedroom door. To hell with them. I helped her up the two steps, and sat her down on the couch. I pulled the door shut and sat down. "I think you should lay down a minute—"

"C'mere, c'mere, c'mere." She grabbed my upper arms and pulled herself against me, and patchouli and sweat sought my nose.

"Casey, you've had too much to drink."

"Didn't touch a drop. Not all night."

"I don't believe it."

The bedroom door came open and a couple I'd never seen before clambered off the high mattress and hurried out the front door. "Sorry, man," the guy said, and shut the door behind him.

"It's true. But that guy…the one who was bugging me…he gave me some Rainbows." She giggled. "Bet he thought I was gonna ball him. But I'm gonna ball *you*." She kissed me and dragged my hand to her breast, braless under thin muslin.

I pulled my face away, but she kept my hand pinned to her, a stiff nipple poking in the center of my palm. "Casey, this isn't a good idea. I mean, you're turning me on, but I don't want to make love to you just because you got stoned." And if I did, what would Leslie think of me?

"You arrogant little shit," she said, overenunciating like a drunk. "You're just a kid. You think I don't know what I'm doing? What the hell you think I took those for, huh?" She snuggled closer. "Whassa matter, you a virgin?" She rubbed my hard cock through my pants. "I can tell you want it. You want it, don't you?"

"Yes," I said, my tongue thick in my mouth.

She grabbed my ear and jerked my face close to hers. "*Then put me on that bed and fuck me.*"

I rose and locked the front door, and when I turned back to her she was standing on one foot tugging down her panties, her skirt already a ring on the floor like a wilted blossom. She staggered. "Shit." She stumbled to the open door that shut my bed away from the rest of the trailer, sat down heavily on the mattress, and peeled her panties off there instead. "C'mon, little boy." She pulled her blouse over her head and then dragged herself all the way up onto the mattress. "Get naked."

I did, and then crawled onto the bed beside her. Her body was so pale that even in the dimness I saw the blue of veins beneath her skin. A narrow-waisted body, curvaceous yet hard and angular at the same time, it looked as if her soft little breasts had been added on as an afterthought.

Outside, the music stopped, and the cacophony of voices came through the little windows. I hesitated, puzzled, and then the music started up again. Iron Butterfly, "In-A-Gadda-Da-Vida."

I lay beside her on one elbow and leaned down and kissed her. She kissed back for a moment, and then pushed my face away. "This isn't a romance novel. Skip the kissy-kissy."

Fine. I rolled away and clambered down the mattress and put my face between her legs. She lifted her legs. Her hipbones jutted out like sharp fins to either side of her belly, and I reached under her legs and grabbed them for leverage as I rubbed my tongue back and forth, hard. Her juices were thick, sticky, muskier than her Victorian delicacy suggested. Her hands settled on my head. "Thass more like it, thass more like it, boy…"

She patted me. "C'mere. C'mon up here, now."

I climbed atop her and eased myself in. She moaned, but I actually cried out with the pleasure of it. I moved slow, a little deeper each time.

"Whass wrong with you?" she gasped. "Why you going so slow?"

"I don't want to hurt you."

She blew a dismissive puff of air from her lips. "Shit. Go ahead and try. C'mon, boy, make me *feel* it."

From the sounds she made, I succeeded, but not for long. I slammed myself into her, but I could feel the explosion building…

"Don't come in me," she said, panting, "take it out—!"

I pulled out at the last moment and her fist closed around me as I pumped semen onto her belly.

I groaned and rolled onto my side.

Using the edge of her palm, she squeegeed my come off her skin and wiped it on the mattress.

"Aren't you using…protection?" I asked.

"I'm on the pill, yeah. Want to stay tight, though. Don't wanna get all sloppy in there." He voice took on an edge. "I mean, we're not *done*, are we?"

"No, no…" My chest still heaved. "Just give me a few minutes."

That dismissive puff of air again. "No, I don't *think* so…" She rolled drunkenly onto hands and knees and took my softening length into her mouth.

Through the wall I heard the end of Ron Bushy's drum solo, which ought to establish how long our first session took.

I'd never had sex devoid of affection before, and I wasn't sure if I cared for it. Exciting, yes, and for one as naïve as I, educational as well. She ran me through all of the basic positions, many of them more than once, and slurred out commands. Do this. Do that. Grab that. Squeeze. Harder. Slower. Faster.

As it went on longer I began to get angry with her—I'm not sure why, just something about it, the whole situation—and the anger fed through my body into the sex.

That seemed to be just what she wanted.

She only kissed me once while we fucked, at a moment when I think she must have orgasmed. She got all melty and pulled my lips to hers and kept me there, holding my hips still and moving hers ever so slightly. When she finished she released my hips and my lips at the same moment, and then made me change positions.

A long time later, when I'd gotten off for the third time and sprawled back on the mattress, she said, "I'm done, if you are."

"I'm good," I gasped.

She patted me. "That was fun."

I'd almost fallen asleep when the music stopped.

The crackle of a police bullhorn. "Awright, folks, time to break it up! Too late, too loud, and too many minors here, so let's take it all home now, okay?" Grumbles and moans from the crowd. "Move it out, or we'll come in and break it up for you."

A few shouted jeers and challenges, but I sensed the crowd starting to move.

Casey had fallen asleep.

A rap on the window, and Leslie's voice. "Casey? Are you in there?"

I crawled to the window on hands and knees. "She's in here, but she's asleep."

"Rick? Hunh." A pause. "Is she, uh, dressed?"

"Not exactly."

"Well, well, well. Aren't you the Casanova? Wake her up and tell her we need to head back to Riverside."

"Okay. This may take a minute, though."

"Doesn't matter. The whole street's jammed with cars right now anyway."

I managed to shake Casey awake and made her sit up, and by the time she was dressed she was no less sober than your average Elks convention, which is to say she could weave unaided.

I helped her out of the trailer. Leslie gave me a strange look, at once searching and bemused, and her Viking winked. At this point, Casey gave me a long, deep kiss, apparently for the audience. Baffling.

"Can I come see you?" I whispered, even though I wasn't sure I wanted to do so.

"Dunno. Let me think about it." She kissed me again and left with Leslie.

I leaned back against the trailer. Twenty or thirty people remained scattered around the yard, some still drinking beer, some too wasted to leave. I shut my eyes. I felt good—confident, wrung out, initiated. I felt bad—empty, sad, abandoned. I didn't know how I felt.

"Hey, Rick," JenBen said from beside me.

"Hi. I thought you were going somewhere with Randi."

She shrugged. "She's going off with that Troy guy, and they were trying to talk me into doing a threesome with them."

I looked at her, but she stood beside me staring straight forward. "Randi's cute, for a girl. But she doesn't know that—"

"Yeah."

"You have a good time in there tonight?" Her voice carried a strange timbre.

"Are you jealous?" I asked, surprised.

"No." She met my eyes, a sad little smile on her lips. "It's just—I mean, now that you're getting the real thing, I guess we won't be... having our little game anymore."

"Oh, Jen—" I put my arms around her. "Any time, any time, any time at all." She hugged back, and I said, "Stay here tonight. Sleep with me. We don't have to mess around if you don't want, but sleep with me."

She thought for a long time. "You have to take a shower first."

12 | IF YOU CAN STILL SAY "PURPLE DOUBLE-DOME..."

A hard rapping on the door of the trailer woke me in the morning heat. "Just a minute," I yelled. I rubbed my eyes, patted around the mattress until I found my jeans. There was something authoritative about that knock, and my first thought was that the McFaddens were home a week early.

I opened the door, half-expecting an angry Mr. McFadden, who, never having met the man, I swelled in my imagination to gargantuan proportions.

Leo.

"Hi, Rick." He waited, his expression unreadable, and then gestured beyond me. "Can I come in?"

"Uh…I don't think you really want to. It's like an oven."

He saw the sheen of sweat on my shirtless torso and nodded. "Under the tree, then?"

We pulled up chairs.

The only remaining sign of the big party was that half of the weedy field had been trampled flat, and that, if anything, was an improvement in the looks of the place; I'd had four days to clean up, but I still scanned the ground as if there might be an empty keg or a baggie of drugs lying about.

Leo put his hands behind his head, and I saw that he was dressed, not in his invariable suit and tie, but in jeans and a light cotton shirt. "So, what's up?"

"Nothing, really." I stood on dangerous ground here, and decided not to volunteer anything. "I didn't expect you for more than a week. They told me at the counseling office that—"

"A little surprise visit. There've been a lot of surprises lately."

I folded my hands and waited.

"I called your father yesterday to try to set up a special appointment, but he said you were gone for a couple of days camping. But I had to meet with Don Briscoe this morning, and he told me how to find you."

Donnie. The little fink.

"Nice campground," he said. "Cracker heaven. Mind telling me what you're doing here?"

I explained about catching my father with his boss's wife, and my subsequent beating and banishment. I said that a friend's family had offered to let me stay in the trailer. Linc's smooth blackmailing of Sue Andrews didn't seem like something Leo needed to hear, but I added that I thought I might have a job soon…which had a slight element of truth to it.

He leaned forward and clasped his hands between his knees. "There's a few people out there rooting for you, Rick. The teachers I talked to said you did fine for the short period that school ran. Al Kraft has high hopes for you. And I haven't heard anything about any kind of trouble you might be up to—but the PO almost never finds out until the cops have his client in custody again." He chewed his lower lip. "Are you handling this? Can you live like this without getting your ass in a sling again?"

"Sure. I'm not doing anything wrong."

"I doubt that very seriously, given that just living on your own at fifteen is practically a crime itself. But that's not my point. My question is, are you discreet enough? Do you have the maturity not to be the impulsive little jerk you used to be down in Redlands?"

I thought about it. "I sure hope so."

"Then maybe we should think about emancipation."

I rubbed my face. It was too early in my day for this. "What?" Linc had used the same term when my father capitulated to our list of demands, but I had no idea what Leo could mean by it.

"You've never heard of the Emancipated Minors program?" I shook my head. "Section 7120 of the California Family Code. If you're over fourteen, living apart from your parents or guardians with their consent, and can prove that you're self-supporting from some legal activity, you can petition a court to order your emancipation, which means that you are legally entitled to live by yourself, sign contracts, make your own medical decisions, move from place to place...all legal. Of course, the courts don't look too kindly on petitioners who are on probation—though statements in support of the petition from the minor's *former* probation officer almost always makes a judge look favorably on the petition." He leaned back and crossed his legs, gesturing in the air with elegant fingers. "The big problem is the declaration required in accordance with Section 1285.50 of the California Rules of Court, which is a detailed income and expenses statement that convinces a judge you can take care of yourself." He smiled at my astonished look. "Don't look so amazed. I'm in law school nights."

"I wasn't—" I stopped and reorganized myself. "I wasn't amazed at the legal codes you were spouting. I just—how come I've never heard of this stuff before?"

"Because it doesn't come up very often. Point is, if you keep your ass out of a sling for a few months, and figure out how to support yourself in a way that's legal, mind you, *legal*, Section 7121 even says that specifically...then I might consider letting you off probation and help you petition the courts."

"I'm—" I swallowed and started over. "That'd be great."

"If you make it happen, yes, that would be great. But I'm not all that optimistic, given that you left your father's house and didn't bother to call me." I started to protest, but he raised a silencing palm. "I know. Point is, I'm on your side, within the limits of what I can do... but unless I see you trusting me a little, it's kind of hard for *me* to trust *you*. Message received?" I nodded. "Okay. Here's how I'm trusting you. Officially, I'm going to be unaware of the fact that you're not living at home. You're going to stay low to the ground for a few months, stay the hell out of trouble, and show me money in the bank from a legitimate source. Can you do that?"

"Sure. And I'm sorry I didn't tell you about all this, but—"

"But I'm The Man. I know. It's weird for me, being the Cop all the time." He stood. "Better hurry and get yourself sorted out. They're trying to rescind my deferment and draft me."

I stood. "Jesus."

"Yeah, well, I'm practically a lawyer, and lawyering is ninety percent about knowing how to stall when you want to." I started to follow as he headed out to his car, but he said, "Don't bother, I know the way." At the corner of the house he stopped, and looked around, hands on his hips, surveying I know not what—the property, Yucaipa, or the whole of the Southland—and shook his head. "You want my advice, get emancipated, and then clear the hell out of here."

Clearing the hell out of Yucaipa was the last thing in the world I wanted to do. My feelings about my new life were mixed, but instead of a broth of good and bad, they were a mixture of good and even better. Preventing my ebullience from spilling over was the hard part, because for a time everything went right.

Selling hashish into the Redlands market that summer was like being granted the ice-water concession for the Sahara. The grass famine had hit the town hard, and anything smokable commanded premium prices. I looked up only a single acquaintance, Alberto Gutierrez.

Alberto was a tough guy, probably twenty-five, with a scarred face. We weren't friends by any stretch of the imagination, but he had a rep as a solid, reliable dealer, and he knew me through a lot of my pachuco buddies. He greeted me suspiciously at first, aware that I'd been busted not two months previously; but when I explained that I was looking to sell, not score, he offered to take a pound as soon as we could deliver. With a little more lead time, he added, he could take whatever quantities we could offer.

Not only was I living on my own, I'd learned a trade.

Linc found us a house for eighty dollars a month in Mountain Home Village, no more than six miles from the center of Yucaipa… if Yucaipa could be said to have a center. This enabled me to leave Giles McFadden's house five days before the family returned from their vacation; after I used six dollars of my new-found wealth to buy new sheets for his parents' bed, there was no evidence of my Emancipation Party other than the trampled weeds behind the house.

Money, freedom, and no commitments other than the duty to feed my head.

Concerts. We drove to LA to see Zeppelin at the Inglewood Forum, Robert Plant's thin, frightening voice slicing through the dope-laden air even when, in the middle of "Dazed and Confused," his microphone shorted out. Hendrix played Swing Auditorium, leaning against his own amp for most of the concert, clearly smacked out, the heroin-induced slowing of time letting him wander the strings, varying his patterns in a way that must have had Bach *pater* smiling down from heaven. The Doors at Kaiser Dome, Morrison feral-eyed on acid and chugging beers, stalking the stage, spinning his mike by its wire like a lasso, whipping it just inches above the heads of the audience.

John, Jimi, and Jimmy. Dead men.

For the first time in my life, there was too much to do: concerts, movies, books, records, parties.

And acid.

As time went on, I became a true head, a freak, a psychedelic baby. At least once a week, sometimes twice—more often than that, and LSD stops having much effect—I would drop a tab or even two, sometimes with Linc, just as often on my own. Blue Flats at first, of course, but eventually Orange Sunshine came to town, succeeded by Orange Barrel, Clearlight, and, finally, Purple Double-Dome ("if you can still say *Purple Double-Dome* two hours later, then it wasn't Purple Double-Dome"). I'd hike, go to parties, read, stand on my head, attend movies, make the scene at concerts, make love—there wasn't anything I wouldn't do on acid, and this, more than anything, gained me the respect of everyone in town who mattered. I could *maintain*, man, *Main Tain*, ride with the flow and keep some level of sanity no matter how distorted the world became, no matter how bizarre the circumstances, no matter how the glowing phosphene patterns crowded into my vision—I could handle it.

Most of the cool crowd had taken acid at least a few times—enough to admire and fear it—but only a handful did it repeatedly, and Linc and I were held in some degree of awe, like highwire artists who worked without nets. Real heads, man.

Genuine freaks.

Stupid, I know: respected because you could keep at least one skinny string tied to rational consciousness while the world dissolved; but it made me a star, a gunslinger, a stud, and God forgive me if my walk took on just the slightest swagger.

Easier for me than most. The occultist Dion Fortune advises those who dare venture through inner space to avoid drugs because they "unloose the girders of the mind;" but I'd been born yesterday. My girders hadn't even been delivered, much less riveted into a structure. Make me forty years old, give me a job, home, family, and regrets, what Zorba called "the full catastrophe," and then launch me on my first acid trip. How much of a stud would I be then?

I have a friend, a big guy, who in junior high school grew ten inches in a single year. We usually see our growth only in retrospect, but my changes were so rapid I could watch myself alter day by day.

Mountain Home Village sits at little more than three thousand feet, but its climate is montane rather than valley. Huge trees weave their branches across the tiny one-lane streets, and the blue feathers and crest of Steller's Jay flash muted colors in the shadows.

Our house sat toward the bottom of Coulter Pine Drive. A few steps south and a path led into the stony reach of Mill Creek wash, and a hundred yards away, the Gateway Ridge soared up a thousand feet, bristling with pine and oak.

The house itself must have been a product of the forties, what ought to have been a Craftsman-style bungalow perched on a high foundation against the possibility of floods. The two bedrooms were small, but the living room was spacious, and there was a sleeping porch out back that we used as a guest room. The front porch gave the impression of being a balcony, supported on a river-rock foundation ten feet above the tree-shaded lawn.

Linc and I weren't together as much as I'd expected. At parties, we'd usually split up, and even at home, one or the other of us was often locked in a bedroom with a girl—much more often in Linc's case than in mine. Linc also spent time helping Martha with work at the nursery. I was technically on the staff there, too—we'd decided that having me carried on the books as an employee was a good way to satisfy Section twelve-hundred-whatever-it-was and explain my growing bank account. On days where he helped out at the nursery, he'd offer to drop me in town, but I often stayed at our house, enjoying the solitude, or crossing Highway 38 and hiking up to the swimming hole.

That morning I had Blue Flats for my late breakfast, with a cup of tea.

I listened to records, smoked a little hash to calm the prelaunch heebie-jeebies, read Tolkien. I'd scoffed at Linc's pleasure in what I thought of as "fairy stories" until I read them; but Tolkien had a deep effect on me, giving me a window into the deep magic of the natural world, the numinous power that united rock and tree into the mystery of place.

I peaked in the early afternoon, listening to an album of Scarlatti harpsichord sonatas, a snowstorm of swirling notes that carried me to a high and barren place within, a hard and rocky place where the mathematics of matter were made manifest.

When I could see again, when I could walk again, it was midafternoon.

I passed through the shady lanes and into the blazing sun of the highway, dashed across, and then hiked up the side road to the swimming hole. An hour before my legs had been wobbly; now, nimble as any woodland elf, I stepped light from tree-root to tree-root on the steep path, dashing down nature's own staircase.

Sunbathers waved to me when the slope gave way to the stony clearing. I waved in reply, but headed straight for the water, shedding clothes as I went, my whole body eager for the coolness of the stream.

I plunged deep and clung to a rock at the bottom. All around me the pool carried the sounds of the stream, my right ear listening to the water pour in upstream, my left hearing its retreat as it tumbled out over the rocky falls. Complex, rich sound, and the longer you listened, the more there was to hear…

I shot to the surface and gulped air, the bright sun now a friend.

Six hours alone on acid is like several days alone, and I was hungry for human companionship. I worked my way through the groups and couples, chatting for a while with each, my joy in the day and in creation itself so evident that, even though they exchanged looks amongst themselves—wow, what a stoner this guy is—they also were pulled along by my mood, my silly exalted grin slowly infecting every face I met.

I'd seen Randi sitting on a long rock shelf at the lower edge of the long pool, but I'd saved her for last. I was no fool, though; I pulled on my jeans first.

She sat crosslegged on her ledge like a yogi, palms face-up on her knees. As I made my way over the boulders, she turned her head my way without moving any other muscle. Her skin verged on olive. There must have been Mediterranean blood in her family, despite the Mayfield surname, and when I saw her long face in half-profile, I was reminded once again of some aristocratic, high-bred hound, a Borzoi or Afghan. I knew she was large-breasted, but free of blouse and bra, her breasts somehow echoed her face, long, smooth and slender, as if she had been put together by a sculptor who thought in thematic terms.

There was, I decided, no safe or graceful way to tell a girl she looked like a dog, no matter how I couched it, and no matter how appealing I found the look.

When I got a few feet away, I saw that she wasn't alone. A white body lay just beyond her, face-down on a beach towel. "Melissa," Randi said, in answer to my glance.

I leaned an elbow on the rock shelf. "You looked like a yogi sitting here," I said, "like there were waves of something coming off of you."

She peered at me. "You're totally blasted, aren't you? …*Yogini*, I believe is the word applied to females. And I actually can do some." She reached her left arm around behind her back and twisted that direction until she had ahold of her right hipbone, and used this to turn her torso backwards in a way that seemed impossible.

She released, and her breasts slung back into view, the visual impact nearly knocking me flat. "Wow. I'm impressed." I looked at the dog-eared paperback laying on the stone beside her. Kierkegaard, *The Sickness Unto Death*. "Is that any good?"

"Tell the truth, it's pretty hard to take seriously on a day like today."

"What's he on about?"

"Oh, sort of a Christian existentialism—with some pretty sharp critiques of the whole Hegelian approach to finding truth. And, speaking of truth, to tell some, I'm pretty bored with this book. But he's one of those people you're supposed to read. One too many Northern European winters, that's his problem. Ignore me, I'm coming down."

"From?"

"Mushrooms."

"What's that like?"

"Sort of like acid. But an easier ride, and shorter, too; six, eight hours. I'm going to need to go crash soon."

I nodded at Melissa. "Her too? That why she's so zonked?"

Randi snorted. "We were up at this all-night party in the mountains. We drove back this morning with a couple of guys, and I decided to do these mushrooms while the sun was coming up, but Lissa here stayed in the backseat making out with this guy, drinking beer, and, before we got home, doing half a roll of Reds. Then she went off with the guy into a bedroom and he fucked her brains out, leaving me sitting around the living room stoned on psychedelics with this other guy, who I didn't even want to be with. Talk about a mindfuck of a situation. Play some records, try to make small talk with this drunk guy, try to ignore all the noises squeaky-toy here is making in the bedroom. Gah!" She threw her hair up into the air with both hands, presumably simulating her head exploding. "So when I felt like I could drive, I dragged her to my car, made her sit up in a coffee shop long enough to eat something, and then we drove up here. I think he really did fuck her brains out, literally; she's been a moron all day."

"What is it with downers around here? I mean, I've done Reds, Rainbows too; all they do is make me feel drunk and kinda mean."

"Yeah? You get mean? Hard to picture."

Once again I felt like a kid talking to a woman, and I realized that was probably what it looked like, too.

Randi's psychedelicized senses read distress in my expression. "No, I just mean you seem sort of sweet." *Sweet* wasn't my aspiration, but it beat *dorky*. I was about to say something just to keep the conversation going when Randi went back on topic. "The thing with Reds seems to be different with boys and girls. You're right, with boys it's drunk and mean. With girls—well, it loosens you up, sort of like alcohol but more so, and it kind of…" Her eyes looked up and to the side while she searched for an explanation. "Okay, you know how when your whole leg goes to sleep, before all the pins and needles start, there's that time when it's just numb?" I nodded. "Well, when its like that, do you ever want to sort of slug it, just punch it, to make it feel?" She demonstrated by slugging herself lightly in the thigh.

"Yeah, I know *exactly* what you mean," I said, amazed, "but I didn't know other people felt that thing too."

"I haven't done a survey, but I bet a lot of people do. Anyhow, that sort of numb thing, downers make girls feel like that. Especially, you know, up inside? So you kind of want this"—she thrust her fist forward—"this whole sort of *punching* thing, and…" She'd been so intent on making me understand that it was a moment before she realized what she'd said, and then she added, "Jesus, there I go again. I can't believe I just told you that."

Neither could I, but I liked her for it.

"Is it you," she asked, "or is it me?"

"Huh?"

"Am I just stoned and therefore like excessively honest? Or is it your puppydog-priest thing happening again?"

I shrugged. "So are you into this downers and sex thing?"

"Pressing your luck, aren't you?" she asked with a mock-critical frown. "Yeah. I tried it. It was fun. Not my thing though. I'll *try* lots of things. You know the quote from Voltaire?"

"You mean *Candide* Voltaire?"

"No, Bob Voltaire. Are there others?" She raised her eyebrows. "I *can* read, you know, without even moving my lips."

"Sorry. Just caught me off-guard."

"It was a little test for you, too, I guess. Anyway, you know what quote I'm talking about?"

I shook my head.

"One of Voltaire's friends took him to this bordello that catered to rather, they say, specialized tastes—though I've never read what, exactly. He had a great time, so the friend invited him again. Voltaire declined. The friend said, *But you had a great time*, and Voltaire replied, *Once is philosophy, Twice is perversion*. I figure you should experiment while you're young." Her mouth tightened. "My mom decided to start experimenting after she had a family, and things have been pretty shitty around my house ever since."

"Sorry."

"Yeah. Everybody's got a sob story."

The tone of her voice, tinged with psychedelic intensity, made me uncomfortable, so I glanced away. I noticed that Melissa was getting pink. "Do you think you should tell her to turn over? She's getting burned."

Randi looked. "No kidding." She pushed her. "Hey, Lissa. Roll over."

Melissa mumbled something.

Randi shook her harder. "C'mon, party-toy, time to do the other side."

Melissa said something incoherent that clearly translated as *leave me alone*.

"Crap. Help me roll her over."

I climbed up on the rock shelf. We rolled Melissa onto the rock beside the towel, ignoring her doped-up protests, and then I lifted her shoulders and Randi lifted her feet and we put her on the towel again.

"Isn't she adorable when she drools?" Randi sat back on her own folded towel, and I dropped down beside her. "How come you have pants on?" she asked.

"Because I was coming over here."

"You didn't want to offend us with your nudity? Didn't want us to check out your equipment?"

I may have had a way of making Randi spill intimate details, but she had a way of making me blush. "No. It's just that…I'm not sure I could…you know, keep it down."

"You figured you'd get a hard-on just from talking to me? I'm a better conversationalist than I thought."

"You forgot the part about you being naked. Maybe I could keep it under control, maybe I couldn't. But I can tell you I made the right decision. No chance at all, if you're going to do naked yoga in front of me."

She laughed. "I see why girls tell you stuff. You're so…"

"Honest? Harmless?" I could have added several more, successively less self-flattering.

"Those, sure, but I think *ingenuous* is the word I was searching for. I can see you checking me out, I could even see you checking out Sleeping Beauty there when we picked her up. You're scheming on me, but it isn't really scheming, you haven't got any lines. You haven't even got an angle. You're just hanging out hoping."

"You make it sound like I'm the family dog, watching everybody at the dinner table."

"Yeah, it looks kinda like that. I'm not putting you down."

"It's okay. I like dogs." And you look like one, a gorgeous one, but I'm not under any circumstances going to try to tell you that.

"It isn't going to happen, you know, you and me. I like you, but you're, what, fifteen?" Randi rubbed her face with both hands and sighed. "We wouldn't be having this weird conversation if I weren't loaded." She thought about it, and added, "But we also wouldn't be having this conversation if you weren't loaded, and being the way you always are anyway. So I blame both of us." She glanced over at Melissa. "How the hell am I ever going to get her ass back up the hill?"

In the end, we decided that a good dunk in the water would bring her back to something like waking consciousness. Through a combination of cajoling and brute force, we got her down off the ledge and walked her down to the swimming hole, her arms draped over our shoulders. At the shallowest spot we sat her down on a smooth rock and put her legs in the water. "Uh-uh," she said.

"*Uh-huh*," Randi corrected, and dragged her into the water.

"Oh shit!" Melissa staggered, waist-deep in the frigid pool, then slipped and went completely under. Randi pulled her to the surface. "You bissh," Lissa slurred, water running from her mouth.

"Wake up and clean up, Lissa." Randi climbed out of the pool. "Time to head home."

"Want to sleep some more."

"Your butt is already burned bright pink. We need to go back to my place."

"Shit." Melissa weaved a little, and then seemed to come around, splashing water on her face. Then she stopped and whispered, "—*sick*—" and turned away, bent forward with her hands over her mouth, stumbling deeper into the pool.

I jumped in just as she fell and dragged her ten feet downstream, where the creek came out of the pool and tumbled down a series of boulders. There, in water no more than four inches deep, I got her on hands and knees and kept my arms around her as she vomited, undigested remnants of eggs, hashbrowns, god knows what else hitting the fast clear water and zipping away downstream. Not just breakfast, but parts of what must have been dinner, and a few beers, and when she'd gotten rid of all that she had the dry heaves, choking uselessly, her whole body convulsing in my arms.

When it was over she rolled onto her side, but I pulled her back into water deep enough for us to sit and washed her face and rinsed her hair, made her swish water in her mouth and spit. At last she sighed and sort of curled up against my chest, floating on my lap. "I'm never gonna do that again," she said.

"Do what?"

"Anything."

I let her rest there for a while, and then walked her back upstream to where Randi waited. Having purged, she was weak but more competent than before, and it was easy for us to help her out of the water.

Melissa sat on a rock, gathering her wits, and Randi smiled at me with an expression I couldn't read.

"What?" I asked.

She nodded at the crotch of my soggy jeans. "Good call on the pants," she said.

I hadn't noticed, but I wasn't surprised.

I helped Randi work Melissa back up the path toward their car, and ran into JenBen coming down. "Just who I was looking for," she said, and gave me a long, possessive kiss. The three of us got Melissa into Randi's car, and Jen and I watched as they drove off. "Want to come back to my place?" I asked in my most suggestive, lounge-lizard voice.

Jen looked into my eyes. "You're tripping, aren't you?" I smiled. "You sure you want to?" I smiled even wider. "Okay. But a swim first."

13 | ONE IN FIVE, MY FRIENDS, ONE IN FIVE

The landlord had rented the place to us unfurnished, but told us we were welcome to whatever furniture was there, a hodgepodge of mismatched pieces, some probably left by the original occupants, others left behind by a few years of renters. I'd inherited a low dresser topped by a massive mirror, its silver oxidized black in places, and that day the late-afternoon sun came through the window, filtered through tree and leaf, touched the mirror, and scattered around the room in bright, moving dapples. JenBen stalked in from the bathroom, already naked, and let me watch the leopard-like effect crawl across her skin as she headed for the double bed.

She lay back on the bed, raised her eyebrows when her hip sagged into a low region of the mattress. I just stared, stoned, mesmerized by her body, paralyzed by my own good fortune.

She swallowed. "The way you're looking at me…"

"I know." My eyes felt wide as dinner plates, my head dominated by those twin orbs like those improbable nocturnal primates that hunt insects in the rainforest canopies.

She lifted her legs wide and held them there with her hands, looking out from between her knees to watch my face. What she saw there made her mouth widen in a sexy, lazy smile, and she luxuriated in a gratuitous exercise of her power, writhing her body just slightly, each deliberate move causing an audible catch in my breath, each catch in my breath widening that smile.

My clothes hit the floor, and I knelt on the bed and kissed my way around her labia in a wide but tightening spiral, up one lifted thigh, across the belly, down the other thigh, over all those subtle landscapings that have no names, and wherever the smoothness of skin gave way to something new, at her navel, at her anus, at the mole on her thigh, I paused to lick and nuzzle, until the course of my narrowing ellipse passed through pubic hair all the way around, and then I kissed her vagina, a long, passionate, deep kiss, as if it were her mouth.

For the next hour I wasn't Rick anymore. I was a conduit for an ethereal fluid flowing into my spine and out through my fingers and lips and tongue. There was no ego, no posturing in the face of this power, for I was barely there. Behind my closed eyelids male and female energies intertwined, dark green and blackish-purple snakes of force twisting and coalescing and then releasing only to come together again, a jungle of tangled lianas where no one tree, no one vine, could stand or fall alone.

Even in the midst of closed-eye visions, though, everything Jen felt seemed to pass into me, and I moved in two places at once, on that plane of biological force and somewhere inside JenBen's skin. When at last I slid my fingers inside her I sensed her own hand sliding toward her clitoris, ready for release. I gently intercepted it and moved it away, wanting to prolong everything, and she moaned in affirmation, letting me go on and on, kissing, licking, probing, until much later she came off unexpectedly, grinding her mons into my face.

The girl never did understand just how hard her pubic bone was.

My cock had been forgotten through all of this, and I was surprised to find it still hard and straining. It felt numb from its long lonely vigil, but when she slid it into her mouth full feeling flooded back.

My orgasm shattered me and left me in a dark distant place, a featureless twilit desert, where a low horn called out like the sound of a ferryboat far across a bay.

When I came back to awareness, years later, JenBen stood at the dresser, studying her face in the mirror. She straightened, put one hand on her naked hip, and turned to the side and frowned, as if considering the way an unfamiliar gown rode on her shoulder. She noticed me watching, and said, "I wish sometimes I had tits."

"You do."

"No. I mean, like"—she gestured with both hands upturned in front of her chest as if hefting—"I mean, *real* tits."

I rolled up to one elbow. "I love your tits."

She sat on the bed by my upturned hip. "I see you checking out Randi sometimes. Her boobs are great."

"They are."

"Well, then...?"

"Well, what?"

"Well, you can't have it both ways. Either you like them big, or you don't, right? One of us is your type, and the other doesn't quite make it."

I groaned at the ignorance of this. "That's like saying—" An endless sea of similes confronted me, none of them adequate. "That's just stupid." I waved a hand in exasperation. "And I don't have a type."

"I thought boys all had types."

"I feel sorry for anyone who does. That's like living in a prison and being proud of it."

"You're still stoned."

"So?"

She leaned so the small of her back rested on my hipbone. "Brad thinks..." She sensed, correctly, that I didn't much care what Brad thought, so she stopped. After a while, she said, "They have these operations they can do now, you know, they put in this stuff that makes your breasts bigger. I've seen pictures, there's girls who are built like me, and then, *voom*, they're like out here." *Here*, according to her hands, was ridiculously far from her chest.

"Oh, Jen, don't do something like that." I shuddered at the images that rose in my mind. "The idea of someone using a scalpel on those..."

"But suppose we could just do it, by magic. Suppose you could just wave your hands, and, *bing*, my tits would be bigger. You'd do it then, wouldn't you?"

I exhaled. "If I could change one thing about your body, I'd change it so it stopped changing. Stopped right here, just like this forever. It's perfect right now." I started to get a little irritated. I nearly started a diatribe that began, *Jesus, I spend hours all over you with my tongue and fingers even though you won't let me fuck you, how much evidence do you need that you've got everything in the right proportions?*, but it seemed likely she'd focus on the wrong aspect of the message. "Look, is there a single square millimeter of your body that I haven't admired to death? Kissed, licked, panted over?"

She looked at me and then rolled her eyes up, pretending to search her memory. "Yeah." She bent her wrist against the side of her neck and lifted her elbow toward the ceiling. She pointed at her underarm. "There, I think."

The speed of my lunge caught her off guard, and my face was buried in her armpit before she could avoid me. She shrieked with laughter and fought to escape, but I encircled her torso with both arms and held her captive, licking and smooching at that soft skin. "You idiot," she gasped, "that tickles!" She hammered at my shoulders with her trapped arm and struggled with her whole body, curling into a ball, but my grip was too good and she was too weak with laughter. I decided that I liked it under there, velvety and salty and smelling of girl-sweat, so I kissed her pit with more passion and she screamed, slapping the top of my head until I let loose.

She fell back on the bed, panting, laughter still leaking from her. "You *moron*," she said. "You are just *so*…oh, what an idiot."

"Let me do the other one."

"Oh god…oh, that tickles so bad…"

"Let me. Let me. What's the problem, you saving your left armpit until you're married?"

"You jerk," she said, amiably. "Are you making fun of my…policy?"

"No, no, never…just seeing if your policy extends to your underarms."

I reached a hand toward her and she flinched away, but I used it to caress back and forth across her breasts. They were indeed little more than soft places surrounding her nipples.

And I'd told the truth when I'd said that they were perfect.

"You listen to me, Jenny Benedict," I said, with mock gravity. "The next time I hear you complain about any part of your body, or say anything about surgery on those tits, or just anything at all that pisses me off…I'm going to tie you down with your arms over your head… and have my way with your armpits."

She rolled her eyes at my relentless and willful stupidity, giggling, and pulled her arms tight against the sides of her body. I let my hand stray down from her breasts onto her belly, and she shot a glance at my crotch. "Uh-uh…" She pushed me away and rolled to her feet, still amused. "No way. Maybe later tonight, but still too soon." She picked up her folded clothes from beneath the mirror. "Plus it sounds like you have guests."

I'd noticed sounds from the living room, but I'd been too busy to care. I got into my jeans and stepped through the door.

Lisby sat on one couch, her knees pulled up in front of her face. Linc stood at the living-room window, staring out into the yard. Randi sat in an old armchair, her face turned aside.

"Happy scene, guys," I said trying to get some oxygen into the room. "Who died?"

They all looked at me then. Linc's expression was grim, Randi's eyes were red-rimmed, and Lisby was ravaged, her eyes puffed, her whole face wet with tears.

Randi sniffled and answered, "Jilly Kramer."

I stood open-mouthed. I hadn't heard JenBen follow me, but from beside me now she asked, "When? How?"

"Last night. OD'd on Reds."

"Jesus." Jen crossed the room and sat on the arm of Randi's chair, hugging her.

"I knew it was coming," Lisby whispered. "It's my fault." She rocked, hugging her own knees.

Jenny's eyes were full of tears, but she managed to keep her voice even and say, "Lisby, that's not true."

"It *is*. I could tell it was only a matter of time, and she wasn't happy, she *wasn't*, and I knew it was coming and I didn't do anything, and… well…*now*—" She hid her face behind her knees again and sobbed.

JenBen rose and ran to her, crying, and hugged her, rocking with her, whispering to her.

My own eyes were wet, too, though I barely knew Jilly.

Linc cleared his throat and spoke to me above Lisby's keening and Jenny's litany of comfort. "Cro found her when he came home, drove her to the ER. They asked what she'd taken. He told them." He paused. "He also admitted that he'd bought them for her."

Randi wiped her wrist across her eyes. "They'll probably lower it to manslaughter, but they're charging Cro with murder."

I waited there in the middle of the room, trying to absorb it all, stoned and awkward and useless.

JenBen looked up at me, tears pouring down her beautiful cheeks, and I staggered over and sat down on the other side of Lisby and gathered both of them in my arms, and then, in turn, Randi and Linc came and knelt in front of us and hugged themselves into our mass of flesh, huddled there. Suddenly I felt frightened and clutched harder, using the solidity of Jen and Lisby to fortify me against a world that in an instant had turned so fragile.

By an hour into the discussion, the salon had The Communist on the run.

In private, Linc had called them Active Tuesdays: discussion groups that met to discuss selected books every two weeks, and gathered to hear an eclectic group of speakers on the alternating weeks.

When Linc first invited Rob, Rob laughed. "Why the hell do you want me in your little sewing circle?" Despite his initial scorn, Rob showed up for quite a few of them, and after a few weeks, everyone called the gathering *The Sewing Circle*. The name itself kept the riff-raff out; it wasn't the sort of designation that drew the party people.

The complement of Active Tuesdays, at least in Linc's view, was the institution of Passive Thursdays—soon dubbed *Out-Of-Town Nights*, since the evenings commenced with car caravans to LA or Riverside. Movies, concerts, even an occasional play—anything that, as Leslie pointed out, McLuhan would have classified as a "hot" medium—all were targeted for Out-Of-Towns, and afterwards we'd all gather in Mountain Home for what started as a discussion but usually turned into a party.

Out-Of-Towns drew a larger crowd than Sewing Circles.

There was no pretense of democracy. Linc accepted suggestions on what should be read, or seen, or lectured on, accepted them gravely and gracefully; but total control over the schedule of events delighted him, like a chef designing a multi-course meal. And like the master chef, he was autocratic but well-intentioned, seeking the fullest possible experience for the diners, cajoling the conservative into trying the unfamiliar while urging those with jaded palates to re-examine basic pleasures.

In the discussions, Linc displayed a new side of himself, managing the groups with such consummate skill that no one realized he was leading them. My attention was always divided between the discussion itself and watching Lincoln work. He affected a casual air, sitting crosslegged on cushions, but his whole body trembled with birddog alertness, sniffing the air, sensing the quarry behind the words long before it was flushed. When he listened, especially to the shy or inarticulate, his intensity made the speaker feel as though he'd captured Linc's full attention; thus emboldened, the timid surprised everyone, not least themselves, with the force of their opinions. Yet he could equally well insinuate himself into any harangue that threatened the flow of the discussion, and disguising his verbal judo as spontaneous musings, send the disruptive energy hurtling off in a better direction.

The moments I remember best, though, were when the discussion flagged. Linc would lean in and begin speaking, calm and quiet at the outset, touching on points raised earlier and giving credit to those who had raised them; and then his voice would rise, and he'd let his energy pour into his words, the merest trickle at first, but then in an accelerating flow, his body swelling along with his expansive tone, his gestures broadening, his eyes making contact with everyone in the room, assuring them that he spoke to everyone, but especially to you, to you in particular.

Genuine mesmerism. Always there was a period where everyone sat silent, in a trance, letting his energy wash across them; but then some phrase or question or idea that Linc spouted would make someone else catch fire, and Linc would find his oration interrupted, and the discussion would rocket ahead once more. Linc would sit back, forgotten for the moment, and give me just the hint of a smile.

I wasn't immune to his manner if he turned his full powers of persuasion on me, but living with him gave me some degree of resistance. One night I tried to keep notes on what he said during one long oratory riff. Examined later, these scribbles assured me that the power wasn't in the words or the ideas, which were trivial, or platitudinous, or even self-contradictory; the power was in the sheer energy of the presentation, like an evangelical preacher high on the Lord.

On the night of The Communist, though—everyone forgot his name within a few days—Linc entered the discussion only once.

Our guests in previous weeks had been an expert on the Tarot, followed by a member of Leary's *League for Spiritual Discovery*. Lincoln had pressured Leslie into finding an anti-war speaker from UC Riverside, and she'd obliged at last.

She'd warned we wouldn't care for him.

Leslie naturally didn't attend our little soirees, but she came that night, joining Linc, Lisby, Joel, Rob, Randi, Melissa, and me. We'd formed a wide circle of cushions on the floor and were sitting and chatting when The Communist arrived.

Clad in a Mao jacket despite the warm night, he whisked into the room trailed by a young black woman. Her hair had been pumped into a frothy Afro, but The Communist's hair was clipped short, as if the Revolution might turn military at any moment. He jerked his head at Leslie in what must have been intended as a greeting. With hands on his narrow hips he turned about, as if searching for a podium, and Linc waved to a trio of cushions at one edge of our seated circle.

He nodded to himself. "Fine. Fine." He lowered himself to the cushions and gestured impatiently for his companion to join him. "The War. Fine. But to understand the imperatives that drive the War, there's a great deal you must first know."

With that, he launched into a long introduction to the principles of Marxism. We paid dutiful attention for about fifteen minutes before the fidgeting started. Lisby leaned onto Linc's shoulder, and he gently but firmly elbowed her away. Rob studied the black woman with frank admiration. Joel Krippner, who I hardly knew, stared at the palm of his own hand as if attempting divination.

Leslie watched with a grim smile.

It wasn't long before it became clear that our speaker wasn't really Anti-War so much as Pro-North-Vietnam. He spoke of Ho Chi Minh with the reverence Catholics reserve for the Virgin, and then launched into an anti-America diatribe that revealed to us that the USA was the most corrupt empire that had ever existed, because it had gone the furthest in institutionalizing private property as a structural element of government. "That's how we arrive at what is seen in America today," he said, "a nation where ignorant sports figures earn hundreds of thousands of dollars, while scholars starve on the street corners."

Linc made his one contribution of the evening. "I agree it's silly when the most popular figures in a country are grown men who spend all day trying to keep the ball away from other grown men, but you keep talking about The People, and that happens to be what The People admire. Twenty years from now, sports will probably be dead, but some other heroes will emerge. People want heroes. It's a matter of evolution in consciousness what kinds of heroes they choose."

"Close." The Communist pointed at Linc and waved his index finger up and down. "Close, very close. But consciousness cannot evolve when it is held in the shackles of private ownership. The power elite control the media, the schools, the smallest details of everything we consume—"

"Except the dope," Rob said.

"No no no! They *want* you to have drugs! They want you to waste all your revolutionary energy chasing them, they want an excuse to arrest you, and they want your willpower sapped by staying doped up. Part of the system, part of the plan!"

He went on to explain that when all property was held in common that all forms of crime would vanish, as all crimes resulted from one of two things, either the maldistribution of wealth or miseducation, and some, like prostitution, were both, the need for money combined with the idea that women's bodies were themselves property.

"And how will sex happen in this Worker's Paradise?" Randi asked. "Will The People decide who bangs whom?"

"In a free and classless society," he said, "I am sure that any Sister would offer herself freely to any Comrade who was in need of relief."

Groans from all the girls, and even his companion threw him a glance. Leslie caught my eye and gave me an evil told-you-so smile.

"*Need of relief*," Randi muttered.

"This is sounding better," Rob said.

"This is total bullshit," Lisby said. "Bodies *are* property. We own our bodies. And other—"

"What you have to understand—" he began.

"Shut up. I get to talk, too. Look, we own our bodies. We own ourselves. And other people own us, too, other people have rights to us, and we have rights to them—to their bodies, their time. That's what love is, when you get down to it—I have rights to the person I love, and that person has rights to me."

The Communist held up a placating hand. "I need to clarify... um, what was your name?"

"Lisby. And I'm not finished. Everything you're talking about is stupid. I care most in the world about Linc, here, and then after him about all these people, my friends and family. And I can *say* that I care about somebody way across the country, I can even *say* I care about starving kids in Africa, but that's all just a theory, an idea, and any system that expects everyone to care about everyone equally is stupid." She sat back. "Doomed, too."

Before he could answer, Leslie said, "She's right. The problem with Marx is that he didn't know enough anthropology. We're tribal. It's how we're made."

"Yes, *made*, made by a corrupt society," he said. "And most anthropological studies show the kinds of results expected by the powermongers who foot the bill. If—"

"Wait." It was Joel. "I have a question for you. Suppose there's a homosexual man in your worker's paradise. Or even one in our society today. If he's *in need of relief*, would you offer yourself to him?"

Everyone burst into laughter except for Joel, who only smiled, and The Communist, who attempted to talk over the hubbub. Even the girl in the Afro chuckled.

The Communist had his palms up, waving, and the room quieted enough to hear him. "A modern, Freudian interpretation of Marxism shows quite clearly that perversions like homosexuality are themselves products of capitalism. There's ample—"

"Hey, *fuck you*, you little fascist," Joel said. He got to his feet. "This country tells homosexuals that they're criminals. The country that you want will tell them they're sick. Well, fuck off. Lisby's right. We own our bodies. You want a revolution?" Joel looked around the group. "Last month at a place called Stonewall, homosexual men—gay men—stood up for their rights for the first time in history. *There's* your fucking revolution. Just wait and see." He swallowed. "One in five, my friends, one in five."

He looked back to The Communist, added, "I'm not listening to any more of this shit," and then left, slamming the door behind himself.

The Communist stood too. "This is pointless. There are stages in education, and everyone in this room is too indoctrinated to hear the truth. Your day will come. For now, stay here, smoke your marijuana cigarettes—"

"Got any?" Rob asked.

"—and lower your consciousness and play your social games. Talk to me when you grow up." He strode from the room, but didn't slam the door, pulling it shut carefully instead.

His companion sat blinking, and then climbed to her feet.

"I'll walk you out," Rob said, and opened the door for her.

"One in five?" Melissa asked.

"Twenty percent," Randi said. "According to some people, that's how many guys would rather be balling other guys."

"Can't be," I said. "Not *that* many…"

Rob stomped back into the room and sat down beside me. "Not bad," he whispered to me, "got her phone number."

"So, does that mean that Joel's…?" Melissa asked.

"Oh, hell yes," Rob said. "I mean, I always thought he was a little flitty, but a couple weeks ago, up at the lake, I walked past his car and he had his face in some guy's lap." He shrugged. "Used to be I'd beat up queers, but now I figure, who cares? All the more girls for me."

Leslie stared at the ceiling. "How very evolved of you."

"Yeah. I always knew you'd see the good side of me sooner or later."

"So who says," Linc asked, "that Tuesdays aren't as much fun as Thursdays? And now, since we don't have any *marijuana cigarettes* with which to lower our consciousness, shall we break out some hashish?"

Linc and Lisby began dragging snacks out of the kitchen, and the meeting broke up into a casual party. I smoked hash until my brain began to grow fur, watching Leslie and Randi from across the room, and trying to work up the courage to insinuate myself into their conversation. I probably would have failed anyway—they were scary enough individually—but Rob clamped a big hand down on my shoulder and tried to persuade me that we ought to drop acid together sometime, maybe overnight at his brother's cabin at the river…

I eventually extricated myself to use the bathroom, but found Randi forming a line of one outside the door. From inside came the sounds of retching. I raised my eyebrows. "Leslie," she said.

"She's sick?"

Randi tilted her head with a tired expression. "Does this all the time. Her little diet plan, I guess."

I headed into the darkness of the front yard and watered the lilacs, breathing in the night air to clear my head. When the mists parted, I crossed the grass and ran up the steps.

In a shadowed corner of the porch Lisby stood enfolded in another girl's arms. Both turned their faces to me. "Sorry," I said, feeling I'd invaded an intimate moment, and slunk toward the doorway.

Beth Townes' voice said, "No big deal. I was just going in anyway." She released Lisby from her embrace and started for the door.

"Think about it, okay?" Lisby asked.

"Not up to me, hon." Beth stepped around me, patting my arm as she passed.

I put both palms on the front rail and stared out into the dark yard, the trees hissing softly in a light breeze.

Lisby stood in an unconscious imitation of my posture. "So what about that guy?" Lisby asked. "We don't own our bodies, and even if we did, the government ought to own any place we could set them down. As if the politicians don't have enough power already…"

"I think he's figuring we'd have a different kind of politician under his system."

"Fat chance. Hey, it looks like Joel is finally making it official. I mean I always knew…but good for him."

"You always knew?" I thought perhaps there was some marker or sign I'd never learned. "How?"

She gave me a laugh. "He was my first real boyfriend—the first one I ever messed around with, anyhow. And he dug it when I touched him, and he sort of touched back, but…you know, when I finally let another boy get as far as trying to undress me, it was a whole different thing—like my panties were the door to a warm house, and the guy was freezing out in the snow. Joel just never wanted in that bad."

"His one-in-five thing—is that true?"

"Who knows? It's not like they keep stats. With girls, it's probably even higher than that, but girls aren't so single-minded. They're more likely to go back and forth."

"It doesn't seem like they'd—" I fumbled for the words. "I mean, girls can't really do it together, can they?"

She snorted. "Grow up, Rick. Haven't you shown a girl a good time without getting your cock in the middle of things?"

I'd been doing nothing else with JenBen for almost two months. "Oh. Yeah."

A long silence fell between us, though the sounds of the party drifted through the open windows.

"Lincoln thinks I should fuck you," she said.

I shook my head to knock the marbles out of my ears. "What?"

She smiled. "You heard me. And don't worry, I'm not going to."

"But…" What the hell did that mean? "I don't exactly… I mean, why?"

"Why does he think that, or why am I not going to do it?"

"Both, I guess."

"There's a lot of reasons he might suggest it." Her voice stayed casual, but a bitter tone trickled beneath it. "Bring the two of you closer together, sort of like blood brothers. Maybe create some new kind of living arrangement, his effing marriage-form of the twenty-first century, a whole bunch of us in some semi-committed thing, close, but not too close, loving but not really in love. But most of all, to push me away. I'm too 'close.' I sit too close, I spend too much time with him, I understand him too well, I *love* him too much, though he doesn't like that word. Or, rather, he likes that word a lot, but likes it in the namby-pamby, peace-and-love way." She looked into my eyes, tilting her face to the side and up. "You ever been in love, Rick?"

"Yeah," I said, remembering Stacy, "I think so. Thought so."

"Then you know how it feels, and you probably know something about how *I* feel, all the time. And it's actually how Linc feels, too, but he won't let himself really feel it, because—I don't know, he doesn't want to get too dependent, or he thinks it'll derail his plans, or he thinks it will hold him back from experiencing things. As if I ever held him back from anything. It's just that I want to be there too, I want to be in the picture. It's not his life and my life, it's our life, too."

"Lisby…" I tried to express what I thought Linc felt, but realized I didn't understand. "When he talks to me about you, it's obvious he loves you. He just thinks that you want too much. He thinks you'd move in here if you could."

"And I would."

"What would your parents say?"

"Parent. I forget you're not from around here. Everybody in town knows my dad. Or, everybody thinks they know him. Lamont Seeger. Mister Baptist. The Lord's Own Anointed. After Mom died, he started fucking Janelle, my older sister. Or so she says." She rolled her neck a few times as if it were stiff. "Probably true. I remember him touching me in the bathtub when I was, oh, ten or so."

"Jesus, Lisby…"

She laughed. "*Jesus* is right. When Janelle left home, she told him that if she ever even thought he was laying a hand on me, she'd tell all, or maybe get a shotgun and send him straight to hell. I think he's more worried about having his congregation hear about it than he is about the eternal fires."

"Well, why the hell doesn't she tell everybody? They'd put him away."

"And me in foster care, probably."

"Still it seems like you could do *something*..." That's me, always quick to give advice I couldn't implement in my own life.

She breathed in the night air. "You can smell the creek sometimes from here, can't you?" She turned and hoisted her butt up to sit on the railing. "Janelle lives in Phoenix now, claims she's going to blow the whistle on him when I leave home, but I doubt it. Either way, Daddy leaves me alone."

"So that's why you can spend so much time hanging out..."

"Did you hear how you put that?" A sad little chuckle. "*Spend time*. When you spend money, you can go earn some more, but time—we start out with a fixed amount, and we never get any more."

"That's a depressing viewpoint. Look, that would say that we shouldn't be wasting our time here talking."

"No. I'm choosing to spend my time right now with you. I could be watching TV or ironing clothes. I could be sleeping, or shooting junk, or training for the Olympics. This is what I'm choosing, and that means that I'm not choosing a million other things, and that's the nature of life. If you want *this*"—she held out one hand like a platter, and then raised the other into a mirrored position—"you can't have *that*."

What she said sounded true, and I didn't want to accept it. "But there's time to have plenty of different things. Even if you can't have them all at once."

"Uh-huh. You've been spending too much time with Linc. He thinks we're all going to live forever."

"Who knows? We might."

"Sure, Rick. Ask Jilly about that."

She pressed her hand down on mine, and then hopped down off the railing and moved as if to go.

"You didn't answer the other question," I said.

"Hmm?" She paused, thinking. "Oh. Why I'm not going to ball you?" She smiled. "Does it matter?"

"*You* brought it up."

"Do you want to?"

I almost answered *Of course*, but stopped and thought about it. "I don't know."

"Smarter answer than I expected. The reasons I don't ball you are the same reasons that he wants me to. It's designed to push me away, when my whole point is to stay in the picture." She looked up at me. "If he'd said, how about you and me and Rick, all three of us at once, I might have gone for it." A sly smile stole onto her lips as she watched me try to process this. "Yeah. Now there's something I bet you hadn't thought about before." She reached up and touched my cheek. "Later, Rick."

Everyone was older than me, and everyone was weird. Linc wanted his main girlfriend to have sex with me. Fine with her, but only if Linc came along for the ride. I tried to keep my mind open on all matters sexual, but this idea made me uneasy, and I wasn't sure why.

14 | THE ELMER FUDD EFFECT

We'd vacuumed Linc's car as though we were FBI agents searching for trace evidence. Every inch of the interior had been sucked, swept, and where possible, scrubbed. The drive across the desert had taken most of the night, and we crashed in a truly crummy motel in Calexico until the 11 a.m. checkout.

Breakfast at noon, and a late-afternoon crossing into Mexicali. We purchased the token Mexican auto insurance, and then drove through the back streets. Linc followed the route with the ease of someone who'd covered it many times.

We stopped at a little bodega and spent nine dollars to purchase a trio of gallon jugs of tequila. Linc had me help leverage up the base of the backseat, and he stowed the jugs there and hammered the seat back into place with his fists.

Our next stop was A. Alverez and Sons, Import-Export. Handicrafts and Native Items. Linc was expected, but the two Mexicans who came out to greet him eyed me warily.

Linc passed over a roll of bills, beer-can thick, and the apparent owner clapped him on the shoulder and gestured to a mélange of tourist souvenirs piled at the side of their quonset-hut office.

Serapes, sombreros. Wooden chests the size of milk crates. Big plaster casts, blinding in the sun, of utterly worthless crap: burros wearing saddlebags, Mexican peasants sleeping with their backs against saguaro cacti, fake Aztec stone calendars, and one HydroCal cactus so large it barely fit in the backseat. We loaded it all, filling the trunk and the backseat, pushing the doors closed firmly by leaning in with our hips, levering the garbage out of the way.

"It's in there somewhere, then?" I asked, once we headed back toward the border.

"Must be," Linc said.

"The chests," I said. "Got to be."

"Uh-huh," he answered, "could be."

"Come on, Linc, let me in on it."

"It's easier to *be* ignorant than to *act* ignorant, Rick."

"Fuck you, Linc."

"Talking sexy will get you nowhere."

The US Customs guard took one look at us and waved our car into the pullout. "Shit," I said.

"Been across a dozen times," Linc said, wheeling us to the curb in the inspection bay. "Been searched a dozen times. It's four-thirty. These guys have been here all day. Go off-shift soon. Cool it." He killed the motor. "On second thought, don't cool it. Act nervous and guilty as hell."

Those last words were enough to make me relax.

Officer Bardon, inscrutable behind mirrored sunglasses, directed two others as they searched the car. First they pried off the hubcaps; then popped the hood and fooled around in the engine well.

When they found nothing, they methodically unloaded all the kitschy trash from the trunk and backseat, lining it up on the asphalt as if they might execute it. "What's all this crap for?" Bardon demanded.

"Sell it at garage sales upstate," Linc answered. "You wouldn't believe what people will pay for this shit." He gave the man a knowing smile, and almost winked. "I mean down here, crap is crap, but people up north…"

Bardon nodded, and suddenly they were co-conspirators, preying on the ignorance of those Up North, a civilization so ignorant it deserved whatever exploitation could be visited upon it. "Yeah, I believe it. You wouldn't believe the garbage people bring back through here, smiling like they'd just hit the jackpot at Vegas."

"Jack." One of the inspectors summoned Bardon. "Think we have false bottoms here." One of the chests stood with its lid open, and the inspector rapped at the floor of the trunk, giving forth a hollow sound. My stomach sank. The inspector groped inside, looking for a release.

Linc stepped over. "Yeah, you're right, here, I'll show you." He reached inside, and, with hands thrust into the chest, leaned back so Bardon and his colleague could see how it was done, and lifted out the false bottom. They all stared inside, and then Linc put the floor back, and I heard a snick as it snapped into place.

"Cute," Bardon said.

"Yeah, they eat this shit up. You ever see those 'poison rings,' where the gem flips open and there's a little place inside? I run down to TJ for those a lot—buy 'em for a dollar a pop, sell 'em for ten."

Bardon laughed. "Maybe I'm in the wrong racket."

"Could be. I come through every couple months. Snag me next time, and maybe we'll start our own company."

"Uh-oh." Another inspector had laid the giant plaster saguaro on its side. "Got a hidey-hole." The base of the huge cactus had a wide rubber stopper inserted, and the guard tried to leverage the plug free with a penknife.

"Whoa, hey, don't do that!" Linc said.

The inspector freed the black rubber disk, and sand poured out onto the pavement. "What the hell?" the inspector said. He lifted the plaster form higher, and more sand rushed out, forming a giant anthill.

"It's hollow, 'cause it's so big," Linc said. "They load sand in the base as ballast."

"Sorry," the inspector said.

"No big deal. Sand's cheap."

"Hey, boss." Another inspector had pulled the backseat out. "Got something here." He held up a jug of tequila like a trophy.

"Huh." Bardon looked at us. "So, one of you guys twenty-one?"

Linc hooked a thumb in my direction. "He is."

Bardon snorted. "Oh? Got some ID?"

"He doesn't drive. Seventh-Day Adventist or something. But he's twenty-five."

Bardon laughed. "Right. And I'm Dick Nixon." He leaned into the backseat and pulled out the other two gallon jugs, sat them on the ground to either side of his feet. "You seem like a smart kid. Why even try a stunt like this? I ought to fill out a report on you and confiscate things, but…well, you lose the booze. You got a problem with that?"

Lincoln had his hands out, palms up, warding off any further pursuit of this issue. "No problem at all."

Bardon hoisted the two jugs. "Then load it up and move it out." He lowered his voice. "Stay on the right side of the law, kid, 'n you might make something of yourself."

Back in Mountain Home we waited until after midnight, and then staggered out into the middle of the wash, our arms burdened with burros and sleeping Mexicans. After smashing the statuary against the rocks, we chipped away the last bits of plaster with hammers, freeing up sixteen pounds of hashish, each slab wrapped in aluminum foil.

We got rid of the plaster fragments that night. The next day, the bucket of sulfuric acid on the floor between my legs, we drove to Calimesa, mounted our trusty steeds, and rode and then hiked through the canyons until we reached the Mother Lode.

As the summer wore on, the world got crazier.

The War had sparked such opposition that the coming of a revolution was taken for granted, but there seemed to be little agreement about what the Revolution would do. In the cities many adopted Marxist icons, from Lenin to Trotsky to Mao to Che, but Black Power and Brown Power and Gay Power and Women's Lib activists all had to invent new models. The Human Potential movement, centered around Esalen, thought that the revolution would come from different ways of living together, with encounter groups spreading viruslike across the nation, appearing just as often in the suburbs as in the communes.

And our theory? Inchoate, really, though we could yammer about it for hours. But the essence was that any revolution that mattered would be in the nature of the Copernican Revolution; that, just as Copernicus and Bruno had shifted the center of the solar system from the Earth to the Sun, the coming revolution would shift the center of human focus from the outer to the inner. Nothing new there: Buddha and Jesus had both preached this, centuries before.

Long time coming, though.

As the days of August gathered us into their sweaty arms, we learned that LSD, like hang-gliding or sword-swallowing, wasn't for everybody. For the naturally introspective, it was rocket fuel for a journey already underway, but for those who'd never stopped to reflect, it could be terrifying: a thousand years alone with their own insistent, runaway thoughts. Linc and I became the area's unofficial babysitters, called over at parties to gentle someone through their bummer, even fetched from our house and driven somewhere else to talk someone down. An easy enough job when you were straight, but harrowing if you yourself happened to be on acid when you were summoned—and we often were.

A lot of burned hands from LSD that summer, but no permanent damage. But if 1967 was the Summer of Love, then 1969 was the Summer of Sex. The Pill was available to almost anyone, the more virulent strains of syph and gonorrhea hadn't made their way over from 'Nam yet, chlamydia was known only to biology grad students, and herpes was the thing that gave you cold sores, not genital sores. AIDS wasn't even a shadow on the horizon. Yet as time went on, I began to see that for many people, sex was a territory as risky as acid. In the try-anything sexual atmosphere, boys and girls alike did things that hurt themselves. Bad sex that undermined self-confidence. Sex designed to hurt someone—sometimes the partner, sometimes Mom or Dad or a boyfriend or girlfriend or someone else not present; sometimes sex apparently designed to hurt oneself. Sex with inappropriate partners, sex that one might not have had but for peer pressure or drink or drugs or just a random impulse in an ambiance where impulsiveness could be acted on.

And people did get hurt, many times that summer. Yet I'm still not sure it wasn't for the best, that they weren't all better adults for having been through it. If you're going to need to pursue a dozen sex partners just to satisfy yourself that you haven't missed anything, isn't it better to do it young than wait until you have a family to sacrifice on the altar of your curiosity? If you're going to get drunk and have sex you regret with an inappropriate partner, isn't it better to get through that when you're Sweet Sixteen than to end up banging the boss's spouse at an office Christmas party?

I know I'm in a tiny minority here. And the main answer, particularly from the Christian Right, is that the choices I've posed are false ones: the solution is abstinence, and monogamy, both in youth and in adulthood. I'd take this idea more seriously if so many of the leaders proposing this solution didn't end up being caught with their pants around their ankles and a hooker's legs around their waist.

And, hell, by the time Romeo and Juliet were the age I was that summer, they'd already been dead for a year.

Sex for me that summer was good. A wondrous weekend with Christine, one of two female hitchhikers someone dropped off at our house as a convenient crash pad. Several nights with Phyllis, down from Seattle for a month visiting her cousin. A couple of one-night stands after parties. And, the constant drumbeat of my sexual life back then, the visits from JenBen, our weird, constrained, almost ritualized sex all the more exciting for not being complete, for not being unlimited.

The ancients claimed that Aphrodite, the quintessence of desire, regained her maidenhood every morning upon arising. Though there is a part of me that wants to say, ouch, bad idea, Jenny made me see deeper into the meaning of the myth. That was her in those days, gloriously young, overflowing with lust and sexual greed, and yet through it all, still a virgin. My Aphrodite, with her little blonde bob.

After some point I admitted to myself that I was, somehow or another, in love with her, though I didn't mention it to her for fear of spoiling things. Our non-sex sex life bound us into a secretive little world even more intimate than that shared by newlyweds headed for their honeymoon. Nobody knew, nobody knew but us. And I would have liked more of her, I lusted to know her better, ached to be in love rather than only her bed partner…but I'd take what I could get, and if I had to wait through years of this before she opened her heart to me… well, I was having a hell of a good time waiting.

With the exception of my unconfessed love, though, I was expected to open up for her. When we lay in bed together after sex, or between sessions, she wanted everything from me, not least of all the details about other girls. There was never a note of jealousy, though I sometimes sensed a lingering fear that I might abandon her for someone who allowed penetration—which, of course, included everyone else. No, she wanted a full, voyeuristic portrait of what had happened, run through the filter of my brain, as if she wanted to be there inside my skull as I fucked these other women, and there was never any pretense that this was idle or intellectual interest. This was sexual, and it was for the purpose of turning her on. Did I do *this*? Did she let me do *that*? What were her nipples like, what sounds did she make, how did she smell, what was her skin like, a barrage of questions that exceeded my powers of description, and her hand would drift south and she'd touch herself as she interrogated me, and that, invariably, was like a gut-punch for me, leaving me breathless at her frankness for that instant before the blood in my forebrain all flooded toward my groin.

Phyllis, the Seattle girl, had revealed to me by demonstration—and to my considerable amazement—that anal penetration wasn't only desired by homosexual boys in lieu of a more serviceable orifice, but something certain girls enjoyed too, if sufficiently aroused; in her case, in fact, it was the grand finale of the whole process, the denouement, the signal for the final curtain, after which there was nothing left but to receive the wild applause of the audience.

All news to me.

Probably not news to JenBen. Girls are fond of pretending to a naivete they don't possess; I believe they are born knowing more than we do. Not news, but violently arousing, possibly because as, at her insistence, I described it all, she saw a way around her weird, self-imposed prohibition and leapt for it like an attorney spotting a loophole in the law, pausing like a predator until we were intertwined and panting over one another before she whispered, "We could try that..."

No we couldn't. I don't know how I had the resolve—and she slugged me hard a couple of times when I doggedly kept to our usual routine—but I knew that the spirit of her law, if not the letter, specified no penetration other than oral, and I'd be damned if I were going to risk everything we had for a moment that might turn out to be awkward and painful, probably abortive, and, above all, would violate the contract between us. Let her punch me; it didn't hurt much at the time, and I knew I had Right on my side.

As well as tactics. Frustration and arousal fed each other, and when she came she jerked her pelvis up so hard that I had to discreetly sniff back the blood of a minor nosebleed. One of those little indignities that boys don't mention to girls.

She fell asleep there in my arms, something she usually resisted; and when she came around and pulled herself up in preparation to head home, she whispered, "I'm really only ever myself with you…"

"Then stay," I said, not knowing what I meant. Now. Tonight. Forever. Any of the above.

She sat on the edge of the bed and pulled on her blouse, then rolled back and kissed me. "You know I can't."

What if, our first time in the trailer together, when she'd said, Please, c'mon, just fuck me…suppose I had? What if, that afternoon, when she'd whispered, *We could try that*…should I have? Was it all a contract that she intended for me to break, the breaking binding her to me in some deep way?

Or did I do exactly what she wanted, my observance of her boundaries letting her be free in a way she couldn't if she'd had to monitor her own limits? Did I blow it? Or did I keep it alive, give it a place to live?

I ponder it, because not a day goes by that I don't think of her. And sometimes I wonder: Does she ever think of me?

Summer rolled on. The Sewing Circle worked its way through *Slaughterhouse-Five*, *Catch-22*, and *Giles Goat-Boy*. Passive Thursdays took in *2001*, still in circulation a year after its release, *8½*, finally making the circuit in America, and *I Am Curious (Yellow)*, when the Supreme Court finally released the impounded prints, as well as concerts that included Zappa, Pulse, and Buffalo Springfield. Of all of these, *I Am Curious (Yellow)* provoked the biggest response.

In one of her rare appearances, Leslie Andrews showed up for *I Am*, and rode with us to an "art" cinema in Riverside. The theater was a run-down porno hall, the mainstream theaters refusing to show it. Leslie sat beside me and seemed ready to climb onto my lap, an event most fervently anticipated by yours truly, but she was drawn there not by my appeal, but by her reluctance to sit her wonderful round miniskirt-clad butt down on that cracked vinyl seat.

Innies and outies, like belly-buttons; sometimes I think the bulk of gender psychology boils down to that. A lot of what is *icky* to the female is based on some intuition that this, this, this *stuff* might somehow insinuate itself up inside them. Show me a guy who worries about sitting down on a ratty sofa or a stained mattress, and I will show you a very gay boy—one who recognizes *innie* potential in himself. Girls? Hey, I'm not putting my hips down there; I don't care how many layers of clothes I have on—germs have got legs.

I had to grant that the theater was indeed disgusting. Dark, with as little air conditioning as the weather allowed, the atmosphere smelled ammoniacal, as if semen droplets floated on the breeze. The seats weren't sticky, but the floor was, and the context suggested something other than a few decades of spilt Dr. Pepper.

The movie wasn't what anyone expected. Some patrons stormed back to the office, having expected a porn flick. Others groaned at the direction the movie took, anticipation and a long series of court hearings having made them expect something politically explosive.

A comedy, really, and something too ambiguous for the revolutionary mindset. Not really political, not really porn, and the scene that caused the most controversy is one where the supposedly political woman, after her lover's infidelity, trashes the house, especially the political tracts and impedimenta they have accumulated.

Back in Mountain Home, Rob was certain what this meant. "It's about sex, man. She's pretending to think about that other stuff. But it says what girls really care about."

Groans from all the females in the room, and several of the boys. Randi leaned in. "Right. Like boys have any idea what girls like. As if somebody gave you an operator's manual. You guys don't know shit."

Rob, unimpressed, waved his hands. "We know. We know by how you act."

"Yeah," Leslie said, "that's the key word: *Act*. A lot of the time, we're *act*ing."

A hubbub of voices, and then Lisby. "You're all making it too simple. If it were something you could have an argument about, they would have just written a letter to the editor. It's about being owned by your body, or vice versa…and I don't think there's a single person in this room who can say for sure how that really works. It's stupid to talk about, you know." She threw up her arms. "*That's why they made the film.*"

The discussion raged on, but I found myself nodding across the circle to Lisby, realizing she was right. It was why they made the film, this ambiguous, vague, unfocused film, it was because their message was incoherent, vague, uncontained…

We smiled at each other.

***

Active Tuesdays and Passive Thursdays, they rolled on, bankrolled to some extent by the hash Linc and I sold. We were rich; not Kennedy-Rockefeller rich, but genuinely rich, richer than I've ever been before or since. There was nothing I wanted that I couldn't afford; but, then, I didn't want all that much. Booze, drugs, gasoline, food, plus enough cash left over to treat others to what they might not be willing to afford from their own pockets, be it a movie or a concert or a hit of acid… sheer luxury, the fat of the land. If I wanted a book, I bought it; if I wanted a record, I bought it; and if a friend wanted something, I often bought that as well. Yet the money piled up.

In my memory those days are a glorious miasma of sex and drugs, movies and books and music, but there was a structure. Tuesdays and Thursdays were sacrosanct for Linc and me, no matter how faithful or faithless others might be. The weekends, Friday and Saturday nights, we'd usually cruise the parties. Mondays and Wednesdays tended to be sex days for partners who'd lasted beyond the party nights: JenBen and

Phyllis for me, Lisby and Beth and Jessica and Katrina and a host of others for Lincoln.

Most Sundays we'd drop acid together. Since LSD interfered with Linc's erections—as opposed to mine, which it enhanced—he dropped a lot less than I did. Of course, I was making up for lost time; he was a hundred trips ahead of me. So I slammed it down when he wouldn't: when I knew sex was in the near future, when we'd be in groups that required clear, coherent focus, when basic motor skills were required. I couldn't drive anyway: who cared if the whole world went paisley in front of my eyes? They're always talking about the fabric of the universe, maybe that fabric is mostly paisley; how the hell else did they come up with that design?

The party scene reeled out of control. August was the time that so many parents decided to bolt, to take time together and shore up their tottering marriages. Dire threats on the way out the door were never sufficient; a parentless house meant a party, damn the consequences. Only the wisest of their children had the foresight to hide breakable items in safe places, and only the richest of their children had the resources to repair or replace the damaged goods. *Uh, Marge? Is this the same coffee table we've always had?*

The party of the year was at Larry Palitzer's house, out past the end of Wildwood Canyon. Palitzer's dad was a Lockheed engineer with such a passion for horses that he bought forty acres in Yucaipa and suffered the long weekday commute to Pasadena.

No neighbors to complain. A huge house and grounds, so that new arrivals could be accommodated without crowding anyone out. Linc and I arrived late, after eleven. When we pulled onto the Palitzers' quarter-mile driveway, the blast of music and voices sounded like a rock concert.

Cars lined the asphalt drive on both sides, two wheels pulled off into the weeds. We parked near the bottom of the hill and trudged toward the party. The moon was just past full, bright enough that it threw our shadows onto the parked cars as we walked, our distorted shapes laying flat between cars and then springing up again in stages, trunk, door, roof, before rolling down onto the hood. I'd taken half a hit of Purple Double-Dome a few hours previously, nowadays a negligible dose for me, but I was stoned enough that the dancing shadows seemed to be escorting up the hill to where some primal rite was already underway.

A giant ranch-style house. Giant but unimaginative; the usual suburban house on a grander scale, equipped with more rooms, and every room oversized. Lights had been dimmed for the party, or in some places replaced with colored bulbs, red or blue or blacklight. Linc and I edged our way into the living room. He shouted something.

"*What?*" Though I yelled, I could hardly hear my own voice.

He grinned, and did it by pointing: You-me go apart. Together later.

I smiled and nodded, and he eased off around a couple drunkenly slow-dancing, despite the fact that the stereo blasted out "Subterranean Homesick Blues."

I worked my way through the crowd. People yelled what I took for friendly greetings in my ear, slapped me on the shoulder, or pumped my hand, but I saw no one I knew well, and in many cases I didn't even recognize the people who seemed so happy to see me.

Pleasant and alienating at the same time.

I wandered the house. Navigating got easier once I was past the living room, and the stereo volume was lower as well.

What I took for Mr. Palitzer's study seemed dark and deserted at first, but a couple I didn't recognize had just finished making use of his naugahyde sofa. They smiled at me as they pulled their clothes back into place, both of them sweaty and pleased and slightly embarrassed, and then stumbled past me toward the door. The girl paused and then dashed back, snatched up her panties from the floor and wadded them into her fist.

Palitzer had a huge cherrywood bookcase behind his desk. I stepped over and scanned the titles by the light from the hallway, my acid-enhanced pupils ranging across the spines. All engineering texts, as far as I could tell, a festival of improbable titles. *Elementary Metal Fatigue. Cavitation: Prediction and Simulation. Understanding Drag and Lift.*

I pulled out a thick tome entitled *Fluid Dynamic Principles in Optimum Airfoil Design* and thumped it down on the table, the volume as hefty and self-important as a Gutenberg Bible. My fingers fumbled for the switch on the desk lamp, and I winced at the brightness when I found it.

Fascinating. Diagrams and formulas, vectors and nomographs. None of it, not a single scribble, made the slightest bit of sense, but when I stared at the diagrams, stark black lines on brilliant white paper, I could intuit that there was knowledge hidden inside them, that these things spoke to someone the way the pages of a novel spoke to me. I paged through the book and gazed, frowning, willing them to make themselves known.

How long did I stand there? Hours, it seemed. A laughing knot of kids burst into the room, and one said, "Oh, sorry man…didn't know anybody was here."

I shook my head. "No big deal." The kids took me at my word and spread out onto the couch and floor. I closed the book and placed it back on the shelf, feeling as if I'd spent hours poring over the original of *Leonardo's Diary*, or the *Egyptian Book of the Dead*.

"Hey, Rick," one of them said, "you wanta smoke some with us?"

I stared at the speaker, trying to place him. Never seen him before. "No, man, thanks," I said, and ventured out into the hallway.

The first bathroom I tried was locked, giggles coming from behind the door. The second was vacant. I gasped with pleasure as I emptied my bladder, the splash of my urine on the surface of the water ringing like windchimes.

I opened the door and someone almost smashed into me. "Whoa, hey, Rick!" It was Phil, a guy I recognized from a few of our Thursdays. "Hey, man, somebody's pulling a train down in the master bedroom." He hooked his thumb down the hallway. "You should go grab a piece of it."

"Did you?"

He shrugged and weaved around me, eager to get to the toilet. "Nah. Becky's here, she'd kill me." He pulled the door shut and I heard the snick of the lock.

Nowadays it would be called a gangbang, but train was the preferred term—the image derived, I suppose, from the single and singular female pulling along a long line of more-or-less interchangeable males. As time went on, the term morphed in the mouths of some boys, who found the image of the girl as the engine to grant the female too much power; the phrase sometimes migrated from *she pulled a train* to *we pulled a train on her*, as if it were a prank or practical joke.

I'd never been involved in one, though I'd heard about at least ten that had already gone down that summer. By all accounts no less than three of them had been pulled by Vicki Perry, good-girl cheerleader gone bad, and I figured that this might be her fourth performance.

The master bedroom was far at the rear of the house, distant from the blare of the music, and it took me a moment to verify that I was in the right place. I don't know what I'd expected—probably a loud ring of boys, drinking and laughing, piling onto a half-buried girl, urging her through a sequence of increasingly kinky acts.

The master bedroom was huge. To the left of the bed, sliding-glass doors stood open to the patio. A light breeze drifted in. The lights had been dimmed by the expedient of draping someone's shirt over the lamp on the nightstand, and, clustered there on the right side of the bed were a dozen boys in various stages of dress; a few had their pants off, a few had their shirts off, and a few were fully clad, but no one was naked. I recognized Rob, Donnie, Giles, and a few others.

Quiet as a chapel. The boys did talk amongst themselves, sipping their beers, and talking in library whispers, but their eyes were all on the bed, where, from my vantage, all I could see was a boy going at it, his jeans down on his thighs, the presence of a girl indicated only by the feminine feet reaching around his hips, and the tiny moans that accompanied every thrust.

A subdued, ritualistic atmosphere, made even stranger by two other groups in the room. Just inside the door were a few others like me, mostly boys but at least one couple, who stared but hadn't joined the train; and outside the open patio doors, as if held back by an invisible barrier, stood a half-dozen girls, silent, watching, still as a row of marble caryatids. I had the sensation of looking at some ancient jury gathered in judgment, their arms crossed as they studied the accused, until I realized that the tight-wrapped arms showed tension. One of them undid her arms and let her hands touch her hips, briefly, and I saw with surprise that it was Randi, Melissa standing by her side. None of them knew what to do with their hands, and Randi soon crossed her arms over her breasts again, stuffing her hands under her armpits.

On the bed, Giles clambered up by the girl's unseen head, offering his half-hard penis. The timbre of her rhythmic sounds shifted as she took him into her mouth. A couple I didn't recognize edged behind me and stood by the doorframe, watching from as far away as possible.

The boy riding her sped up for a few frantic thrusts, slapping his pelvis against hers, and then groaned, fighting not to make noises that were too loud or too peculiar. He lay for a moment, and then hoisted himself up and rolled to the edge of the bed, fighting to pull up his pants. Giles backed away too, and his erection sprang from the girl's mouth, fully revived.

It was Leslie Andrews.

She moved her body in a long writhe, arching her back, and her breasts rolled like waves, heavy slow swells. She seemed dazed, unfocused, and I had a sudden fear that this wasn't her idea at all, that this was a kind of rape; that I ought to do something.

Then Giles climbed between her legs, and she lifted them wide, and when her hands snaked around and grabbed his buttocks to pull him in, any thought that she didn't want this vanished.

Astounded, I watched Giles pound away at her, obviously going full-bore, but the sounds he evoked were nothing more than the steady, quiet, moan-per-thrust she'd allowed the previous boy.

I wasn't surprised by the act itself: who knew what Leslie liked, or what her fantasies were? The shock was that she'd do it here, in this town, with this particular squad of boys…assuming, that is, that, in her trance, she had any idea who she was doing it with.

I glanced over at the girls watching from the patio. They'd been joined by Alicia, whom I recognized from my Emancipation Party, and she'd failed to adopt the crossed-arm pattern, but she, too, seemed unsure of what to do with her hands, and kept hers stuffed deep into her pants pockets.

I glanced at Randi to find she was already staring at me, and we looked away, back to the bed, both embarrassed by this strange intimacy.

Linc had appeared by my side. He craned far to the right to see who had elected themselves Little Engine That Could, and came back with raised eyebrows. "I'll be out back," he whispered into my ear.

Giles hammered away and then made a sound like a dying beast, pushing and grinding the last few times, but Leslie refused to grant him any sign she was impressed. When he leveraged himself off her and tried to knee-walk off the bed, he fell, and there was a brief commotion when the other boys caught him and stood him upright.

Semen glazed Leslie's thighs and buttocks, clear and shiny on her skin, but bright white where it smeared across her dark pubic hair. Whatever trance she inhabited dissolved for a moment, for she stared right into my eyes, her pupils wide, and then tilted her head in a come-here gesture; and when I didn't move, she made the tiniest of hand movements, urging me over there by cupping her fingers back in a little wave, one-two-three...and then she was hidden from me as Rob blundered his way between her legs.

As discreetly as possible, I fled.

In the first unoccupied bathroom I locked the door, and, standing, jerked off. After only a half-dozen strokes I emptied myself. No lust, no joy, no wondrous images in my head, just the need to expel this feeling from my body, a sensation closer to vomiting than to orgasm. Masturbation for me was as natural as breathing, but as I cleaned up the countertop my face flushed with an unaccustomed shame.

I found Linc out beyond the patio holding court in a circle of five on the steps that led up to the Palitzers' stables. He retrieved one of the two hash pipes in circulation and came down the steps to meet me.

He handed me the pipe. "So?"

I sucked gratefully. "So what?" I asked, inhaling slightly to preserve the smoke.

"Did you caboose yourself onto the train?"

"No."

We sat on a concrete bench at the edge of the back lawn. Lights, loud rock music, the roar of a party...and all around us, acres of brush and low trees, woven together like burlap in the moonlight. I wondered what the wild animals made of all this.

"Have you ever?" I asked.

"Nah."

"'Cause...?"

"Lots of reasons. Not worth two weeks of celibacy and tetracycline, for starters. That many people, and somebody's got to have the clap." He nursed the pipe, decided it was dead, and torched it, the lighter flame glittering in his dark eyes. "Plus I'm selfish. If I'm going to bother, I want it to be more than, *Let's see, so you must have been number seventeen, then...?*"

"Hmm." I'd felt strange about leaving, especially when Leslie herself had summoned me; Linc made me feel better.

"Really makes you envious, though, doesn't it?"

I tried to make enough sense of this to answer, and realized I didn't know what he meant. "Of...?"

"Girls. There's no equivalent, is there? It's not like a boy can just lay back, the object of lust, and exhaust twenty or thirty eager girls, is it? And even if you could, how're you going to keep it stiff the whole time? Give in to what's happening, and, plink, you're out of the game... A girl, if she wants to, can devour this whole line of boys, grind 'em up and spit 'em out. Scary. Probably the reason most societies have repressing female sexuality as their first agenda item."

I gazed at the moon, silver light trickling down my optic nerves like a cool stream. "They *can* do it, I guess, but most of them don't."

He laughed. "That's the bizarre thing about the universe, isn't it? Male/female, yin/yang, proton, electron. Everybody wants them to be opposed but equivalent, like two football teams. But everything is asymmetric. Protons are huge, electrons are tiny, only their charges are equal but opposed. Guys would like to line up fifty women and mow them all down in one marathon, but we can't; women *can* line up fifty guys and demolish them, but they don't want to." He flipped his hair back from his forehead and it fell down exactly as it had been before the adjustment. "I'm not complaining. Lots of advantages to being a boy. Though, other than pissing standing up, none come to mind right this second."

"It was weird in there," I said, "not like what I pictured. Plus all the people hanging out and watching...surprised me when Melissa and Randi were at the patio door, just glued to the whole thing."

My words grabbed his attention. "Oh? They still there?"

"Probably. Didn't look like they were leaving anytime soon."

"We've got to go ambush 'em. Sacred duty. Girls get into that kind of thing, they'll do anything."

"What's that mean?" My mind drifted back to Stacy in the orange grove, telling me to nibble on the tendon in her neck, whispering, *Just keep that up, just that, and I'll let you do anything.* "What's *anything*?"

"Huh? It's whatever you like."

"When a girl says that to you..."

"Oh. Oh. When a *girl* tells you *I'll do anything*, that's completely different. That means, *I've got something nasty I'm embarrassed to ask for, so your job is to read my mind.* The theory being that whatever she happens to be obsessed with must be universal—yet not so universal that she can admit to it."

"Man, that's convoluted."

"That's chicks." He stood. "Randi still on your number-one list of hot things?"

"Yeah."

"Come on, then. Tonight's your big night."

"I don't get it." I stood anyway.

"Believe me, believe me. They'll be leaking out of their panties by now. The fact that they sort of like us, well, that sews it up. They'll be going home with *somebody* tonight, so let's make it us." He tugged on my wrist, pulling me toward the patio. "C'mon, c'mon, front of the line, time's a'wastin'. *Carpe noctem*, my man."

<hr>

We stood behind them for a while before Lincoln slipped an arm around Melissa's waist and said, "Are you going to watch the floor show all night, or do you ladies want to come up to our place and get loaded?"

That was all it took.

The hash pipe stayed overloaded on the hike down to our car, expensive excess smoke trailing through the night air. Melissa and Linc walked in front, already touching, a done deal. Randi and I followed.

After her first hit on the pipe she let the smoke out with a long groan. "Better," she said. "I did some crosstops earlier, and I'm wound too tight." I found this hard to believe; my supposedly covert glances showed her hips easy and loose under her skimpy sundress. She caught me every time.

In the backseat of the car she gave me one slow, sardonic smile, and said, "Well? Isn't this what you've been scheming on?"

There wasn't much point in denying it, so I took a deep breath and leaned over to risk a kiss. She pulled me to her and accelerated to full speed, as if we'd been making love for an hour.

If the drive had taken a minute longer, we would have been fucking in the backseat. I didn't flatter myself that it was me, but I didn't complain either.

We stumbled to my bedroom, tossed aside my pants and her panties, and then fucked, hard and fast, Randi pulling furiously on my hips. Too much, too much; I came too soon.

She took a quick bathroom break, and then we started again.

I'd dreamed of this, but in my fantasies Randi had been less formidable. Even though her waist was slender, she probably outweighed me, and whereas most of my weight was bone, hers was lush female flesh. I was a child climbing atop a woman, and she was so wet and open and deep that I wondered if she felt me at all.

If she'd given the slightest hint of disappointment or disapproval I would have wilted away then and there, never to go erect again in this lifetime, but Randi said not a word, showing me what she wanted by moving me. She fucked with urgent concentration, pulling on my hips and slamming herself back at me, her eyes closed to slits and focused on something within her. Unlike most busty women she made no attempt to protect her breasts, as if she'd warned them before we started that they were on their own; when they flounced too hard, she winced, but her hands were too busy steering me to be bothered with coddling a pair of wayward tits. Her ruthlessness with her own body scared me.

And it could have been passionate yet cold, like it had been with Casey; but without warning Randi would open her eyes and laugh, a glittering laugh that showed her teeth white in the dimness of the room. Her passion was a sea she plunged us into, but at any moment she could break the surface long enough to laugh, her gaze asking, Isn't this fun? Isn't this a little silly? Aren't we carried away? and then, just as suddenly, she would dive down again, dragging me back under her dark waters. Even when she went onto hands and knees she kept it up, turning her head back to look up at me, her laughter intimate and triumphant.

It sounds all wrong, as if she were interrupting our sex, distancing herself.

It was the opposite. My cock was already buried in her, but the laughs were moments where she let me even deeper inside, opening her consciousness and pulling me in there, too, reminding me that there was this smart, wry girl inhabiting that body, and that she was fucking me with full intellectual awareness of exactly what she was doing.

A turn-off for some people, I suppose. For me, the erotic charge verged on lethality; every laugh from Randi made me gasp, as though she'd pierced me.

It went on and on, and with an edge of LSD still roiling through my synapses, I stayed right with her until she whispered the only word she'd said since we'd begun, "Come."

I did.

We both sprawled on the bed, panting, letting the night air cool us.

"Randi..." I murmured.

"What?"

"Nothing. Just like saying your name."

"Aggh. I hate my name."

"Why?"

"It's lame. Plus being British for 'horny'... And it's not a diminutive, it's a whole name that sounds like a diminutive." She rolled toward me, and I heard the faintest echo of the crosstops accelerating her speech. "When I'm famous, a professor or something, I guarantee you, it'll be R.G. Mayfield on everything I write."

"What's the *G*?"

"Galanos. Mother's maiden name. So, are you all done?"

"Yeah," I said. I was out of breath and found myself slightly alarmed at the prospect of a third round. "Aren't you?"

"Definitely. I'm wiped. But I didn't want to assume…"

"Done as I've ever been." My mind scanned my body. "You know in the cartoons, where Elmer Fudd is trying to shoot Daffy or Bugs or whoever, and they stick their fingers in the shotgun, and it blows up on Elmer, the barrel sort of peels open like a banana and sits there smoking?"

"Yeah…?"

"My dick feels like that shotgun. I mean"—I reached down and slapped its softening length—"it's like ten thousand volts went through it. It's like it's not even there."

"Poor baby. I had fun, too."

I snuggled over next to her, caressed her cheek with my fingertips. "I really like you," I said.

"Ohhh-kayyy," she said. "We're not thinking this is the start of a major romance, here, are we?"

My spirit sagged, but I answered, "No, I'm just saying I really like you."

"That's good. I really like you, too, but I've worried that if we did this, you might start sitting outside my bedroom window and howling." She scooted her butt off the wet spot accumulated on the mattress. "You were just lying in the weeds waiting for me tonight, weren't you?"

"Guilty."

"Nobody to blame but yourself, then, is there?"

"Am I giving you the impression I'm sorry? 'Cause I'm not."

"Can't believe I just balled a fifteen-year-old kid. You realize that in a month that'll be statutory rape?"

"So we can keep going right up to your birthday?"

"Ha ha." She lifted her head and pulled her hair from beneath her shoulders, splaying it back across the pillow. "I ask you a question?"

"Sure."

"Why didn't you join in tonight? When all the other guys were doing Leslie, I mean. I saw you in there…and I always thought you had the hots for her."

"I do. Did. But…" I rubbed my temple. "I don't know. The whole thing just felt weird, you know?"

"It didn't turn you on?"

"Of course it did. Sort of. But it was—I don't know. And it's not just about getting to fuck somebody, you know."

"Really? So if I'd come over here tonight and passed out drunk, you wouldn't have fucked me?"

"Well, no," I said, appalled. "You wouldn't even be there for it, you wouldn't be *want*ing me..."

"I had a guy do that," she said, matter-of-factly.

"Ugh. What'd you do about it?"

"Do? Nothing. Avoided him after that. Thought he was pathetic." She sensed my revulsion and touched my arm. "Even when you're conscious, a lot of guys are just jerking themselves off with your body."

"Not me."

She rolled onto her side and stroked my forehead. "No, not you. Any outsider would probably say *I* used *you* tonight, little boy. But it's still your own fault."

"Because I waited until you were so turned on?"

"Yep."

"Have you ever done that?"

"What?"

"Pulled a train. Fucked a whole bunch of guys at once."

She made a small sound of incredulity. "No."

"But it turns you on?"

"Oh, you noticed? Hey, wait a second, fuck you, Rick, you're doing it again. That priest-in-puppydog-clothes thing."

"It's just a question."

"Okay. I'll answer your embarrassing, personal questions. But you first. Embarrass yourself."

Truth be told, I felt inadequate and maladroit a lot of the time, but nothing special came to mind. I fished around in my head, deliberately dragging my shiny lures through the places we don't like to look, and suddenly I had not one fish strike at my line, but a whole school. "The first girl I ever had sex with, I thought she'd had this awesome experience, and I thought we were in love, and when I went back to see her she couldn't be bothered with me—didn't want to ball me again, didn't even want to have me around...and just now, when I was inside you, I just felt so small, I wasn't even sure you could feel me, I mean, I could feel you and it was great, but I was sure I wasn't long enough or thick enough or hard enough, or something, and I was so scared I was disappointing you…and, let's see, tonight after I left the room where Leslie was doing her thing with all those guys, I ran to the bathroom and jerked off, which was good because otherwise I would have come all over you before we got out of the car, but it was weird and I felt kind of bad about it, and—"

She put her fingers over my mouth. "Okay, already, you've convinced me." She took her hand away. "And you're a fine size, if that's something you're worried about. I was just really, really, hot. And I have to tell you, being able to just have it whip in and out when you're so wet you don't have to constantly fidget and adjust yourself…it's a really nice place to be. I mean, why do guys assume that we want it to be right on the edge of hurting all of the time? Or past the edge?" She rolled onto her side, pulled her shoulders back, thrust out her chest, and waggled herself in a prone imitation of a macho swagger—though this, given her build, had little of the masculine in it—and lowering her voice into a Randi version of Elvis, said, "Yeah, baby, I'm 'a gonna make you *feel* it." She rolled onto her back, and added, "What the hell is wrong with you people, anyway? It's like, hey, she liked a maraschino cherry on top of that ice cream sundae—maybe she wants one on this cake. In this glass of milk. On her pizza. Bowls of them for breakfast. Maraschino cherries everywhere, the complete food, the whole fucking food pyramid right here in my trousers if only it's big enough hard enough fast enough. She didn't like it? Hasn't figured out yet that she really digs maraschino cherries, 'cause they all really do, man. Still doesn't like it? Not enough maraschino cherries, I guess. Still doesn't effing like it? What the hell is wrong with this lesbo bitch?"

I stared, having lost the thread of her metaphor, and she looked at me and laughed that laugh and I shuddered as I felt myself slip into her head.

"What?" she asked.

"Nothing. Just…nothing."

"Oh. Where were we, before I lost my mind?"

"I asked you if the idea of fucking a whole roomful of guys turned you on."

"And since it wasn't easy to deny it, given present circumstances, I think I said yes. Or, *duh*, or something."

"So, why don't you, then? Christ, Randi, everybody wants you, all you'd have to do is snap your fingers…"

She laughed and hugged me, those strange slender breasts soft against me. "God, I love how simple-minded you are sometimes… Look, think about one of your favorite sexual fantasies. Got one? Now suppose somebody gave you the chance to act it out. Would you do it?"

"We just did."

"Yeah, yeah, real sweet, but you already fucked me, so you can stop pandering now." My expression made her stop. "I'm sorry. You meant that, didn't you? Don't mind me, I've got a mean mouth sometimes. But your fantasy—I mean something more extreme, something kind of kinky. You don't have to tell me what it is, and it doesn't even need to be possible. Got it?"

Randi and JenBen in bed together, with me somewhere in there with them, I didn't much care where. "Okay."

"If you had a chance to make it happen, would you do it?" She watched my face.

"Of course. Isn't that what a fantasy is, something you want to have happen but can't get?"

"No, that's what *boys'* fantasies are." She touched two fingers to my forehead as if blessing me. "Keep this to yourself, 'cause the International Chick Council will take away my secret decoder ring if they find out I told you. *Girls fantasize about things they would never want to happen in real life.* Some of the hottest ones are things you wouldn't want anyone to know you even thought about. I mean"—she rolled her eyes, on the verge of embarrassment—"do you think I'd be telling you that the idea of letting a roomful of guys ball me is a turn-on, if you hadn't already sort of caught me with my hand in the cookie jar?"

"I don't get it. If it turns you on…"

"Jesus. Are you actually curious about this, or is this some freaky way of messing with me?"

"No. I love the way you are inside."

"Okay." She nodded to herself, and looked up at the ceiling, as if she could read what to say up there. "The fantasy. I'm the girl, the complete and utter center of attention of this whole pile of guys. Everybody wants me—me, not just pussy, not just my body, me—and I'm not even sure who the hell they are, because they're only there to serve me, this endless line of Eveready cocks, and I can take everything they throw at me and more, and I have orgasm after orgasm, for just as long as I want, because I'm this amazing goddess, this slut-goddess, and it takes me places I've never been before, I'm out of control, but even though I have no control it still all happens exactly the way I want, they do things to me I didn't even know I wanted, nasty, unbelievable things, but I want them, and it's perfect, and like Goldilocks, if it's too this or too that for a minute, that's because it's all just a prelude to being *just right*." She thought for a moment, and added, "Oh, and there's no consequences afterwards—no awkwardness, no pressures I don't want...hell, as it turns out, I don't even need a shower."

I ran my hands over her breasts as she talked, cupping and hefting.

She frowned. "Are you getting turned on again?"

"Maybe. Aren't you?"

"Fuck you, Rick." She held my hand to a breast, pinning it there. "Now, reality. The guys are sloppy, and hey, some of them smell funny. People you don't like show up, and if you think it's just automatically wonderful having things shoved into your pussy I wish I could loan you one and let you check it out. And, not everybody seems to realize you're a goddess. You get excited, but everybody's timing is so shitty you don't get off, and they really don't much care if you do, but if you manage to, they probably laugh about it and congratulate themselves on what a bunch of studs they are, and you're a little bit out of control alright, but amazingly things don't happen exactly the way you want them to and when you want them to, and things you may not even enjoy happen, and afterwards it's uncomfortable whenever you meet the guys, if you can even recognize them all, and a lot of them joke about you behind your back, and some of them assume they can now have you any time they want, and three days later you discover that you have the clap, and a strange itch, and crab lice, and a raging bladder infection that makes you think you need to run to the toilet every thirty seconds even though nothing happens when you get there." She took a deep breath. "Hey, I admire Leslie for putting herself out there like that. Gutsy. Would *I* do it?" A snort. "Not anyplace but in my head."

I worked my hand loose from hers and sent it sliding down her belly, but she caught me and set it palm-down on the mattress. "I thought we were done," she said, "but no matter what, I have to pee."

The bathroom break is usually an excuse for girls to do something more than urinate. Freshen themselves, call former lovers on the phone, masturbate enough to be aroused when they come back to bed, re-lube themselves after wiping away all that good accumulated goop, fill out loan applications, write free verse—I don't know what happens in there, though I've often wished I did. That night, though, Randi was fast. Crawling back onto the mattress she stopped and smiled at my erection. "Elmer Fudd rides again."

"Cartoon characters recuperate fast." I pulled her down against me.

"My little fantasy turned you on too, huh?"

"No. But thinking about you thinking about it sure does."

"Mmm." She kissed me. "Maybe you're not as simple-minded as I thought." She kissed me again, and then pulled her tongue from my mouth, licking across the side of my face, and my image of her as a high-bred canine came back. "Why are you grinning like that?"

"No reason." I rolled onto my side, spilling her onto her back. "Let's pretend I'm ten guys, then."

"Hah," she said, but opened her legs for me. "This'll have to be a hell of a performance, then."

I knelt between her thighs. "I didn't say I was going to impersonate ten guys, I said you were going to *pretend*."

"Oh. Well, if I'm the one who has to do all the work, why don't I make it twenty?"

I answered by fitting myself to her and sliding all the way in. She gave a satisfying gasp—satisfying to me, at least—and laughed that laugh again before giving herself up to whatever visions danced behind those slitted eyes.

15 | THE RED-LIMBED CHORUS

People hear the term *drug dealer* and get an immediate image—maybe a gangbanger riding crosstown with an Uzi on his lap, maybe some creep in a trenchcoat hanging out beneath a streetlamp, maybe a Columbian with thick gold chains dangling in his chest hair as he slices open a package to taste the goods—but I bet most of them picture somebody who is busy, well, *dealing drugs*.

Fact is, we spent at most five or six hours a month at it, and when Linc pulled over on a side street in the Lugonia district of Redlands, I expected it to take fifteen minutes, max: around the corner to Alberto's, pass the goods into his waiting hands, take the cash, make nice for a couple of minutes, and then jump back in the car. Linc was in a hurry in any case; we were headed over to the UC Riverside library to look up details on his latest passion, traditional shamanic psychedelics.

I opened the car door and lifted my leg carefully over the lidded bucket of sulfuric acid. I grabbed the bag—two pounds of hash in half-pound slabs—and climbed out of the car into the afternoon heat. "Catch you in a second," I said. Linc nodded, already absorbed in a paperback, and I slammed the door.

His obsession with not getting caught, his buckets of acid, had struck me as melodramatic when he'd first revealed them, but after a few trips I'd come to count on them. As I turned the corner to Alberto's street, walking farther and farther from those comforting gallons of concentrated sulfuric, my palms grew damp. If there was a problem, it would be at the drop, the farthest point from safe disposal. If the cops leapt from the bushes, what would I do? Make a dash for the sulfuric? No, that'd lead them right to Linc. Run? Yeah, past experience showed how well that worked…

Standing on the front porch of the cottage I shook off the fear. 'Berto wasn't a friend, but he was a hard case in the classic pachuco sense, and that made me feel safe.

At my knock he swung the door wide and ushered me in, a heavy hand on my shoulder as he steered me into the comparative darkness of his living room. "Eh, *vato*, how you doin'?"

I sat on the couch as he pulled the slabs from the bag and glanced at them. He pursed his lips, slid them back into the bag, and tossed it onto an armchair in the corner. "Don't want to weigh 'em?" I asked.

"No, no, man, I trust you. Howabout a beer?"

I shook my head. "Just the money. I need to get somewhere."

"Sure, man, sure." He pulled a rubber-banded roll of bills from his pocket and tossed it to me. I fumbled the catch, picked it up from my lap, and slid it into my own pants pocket. "You don't wanta count it?" he asked, mocking my tone in a friendly way. "See, dude, we're on the same team here. Though I gotta say, Ricky, I could move more—three, four pounds, this time. The city, she has her legs spread wide for anything right now; dry, dry, dry…"

The door to the bedroom creaked open and a white guy stepped out. Jeans and white tee-shirt, probably thirty years old or even more, he had those hard, stringy muscles guys get from pumping weights behind bars. "Hey, Rick," he said, "I'm Chase."

"*C-s*, 'Berto…" I warned, *con safos*, don't mess with me. "*Que onda?*" *What's your deal?* Pretty much the outer limits of my pachuquismos.

"*Firme*, Ricky. Chase is cool. You guys just need to meet."

Chase came over to the couch, his walk a little too sedate for a swagger, a little too macho for a slink. "Alberto says you're the man these days." His eyes flicked across me, and I thought I saw amusement there that I might be considered any kind of a man, but the rest of his face showed nothing. "Maybe we can do some business." He sat down beside me with unnecessary heaviness, put a hard hand on my knee. He talked to my face, but I kept staring at 'Berto. "I operate out of Berdoo. Run stuff there, Colton, Fontana, up over the Cajon. Not personally, you know. Got dudes. Thing is, we need sources, and you seem wired in. So, a little proposition for you. Knock the price down a little, just a little, say twenty percent, and we can move as much as you want." He squeezed my knee and I glanced at his face, uncomfortably close to mine. He smiled in what he probably imagined was a comforting way. "I mean that, as much as you want. You make me rich, I make you rich, everybody goes home happy. Okay?" I studied his blue eyes, and his pupils kept widening and contracting again. "Okay?" he asked again, and I dropped my gaze. He patted my knee. "Good. You think about it. Get back to us."

I stood. "I'll think about it. Right now, I'm in a hurry." I stepped around the coffee table, away from Chase, and headed across the room.

'Berto opened the door and waited there. Like most of my Hispanic friends, he could do the impassive *Indio* look whenever he wanted, but I tried to read his face as I passed, and imagined that I saw something beneath the surface. Amusement? Concern? "*Ay te miro,*" he said, *see you later*.

Fumbling through the scrambled mental index cards of my years as a pachuco-ito, I came up with, "*Ay te watcho, ese.*" Another way of saying, *See you later, dude*…but, literally, *Watch yourself.*

I turned down the street the opposite way I had come, and turned down the first dirt alley that presented itself. Once hidden from view of Alberto's cottage, I ran, jumped a low fence, cut across an empty lot, and then walked more calmly back to Linc's Impala. He looked up when I opened the passenger door, and started to get out to open the trunk so he could wedge the bucket of sulfuric between cinder blocks. "Later," I said, and slid onto the seat, swinging my legs over the bucket and then slamming the door. "Just go."

"We being chased?"

"No. But go." Sitting still, the sweat from my run broke from every pore at once, and I fought to get the window down as Linc's boat of a car started rolling forward.

Once we hit I-10, I stammered out an explanation of what had happened. Linc was concerned, but not alarmed. "Not good," he said, "but just break the connection. Let it lay for a while, and then you can hook up with somebody else in a couple of months."

"A couple of *months?*"

"Yeah. Let it cool down." He looked at me and frowned. "You need the money for something urgent?"

"No." I had seven hundred dollars in a bank account, more than a thousand stashed in a coffee can across the wash…and my share of what was in my pocket was between two and three thousand dollars. I was living large, by my standards like a 1920s millionaire waving fistfuls of cash, but even with rent and utilities and drugs my extravagance was running me perhaps three hundred bucks per month. Math was never my strong point, but I could easily work out that I already had enough to live like this for more than a year. "He did say he could make us rich, though…"

"Don't think that way," Linc said, moving to the slow lane, "not even for a minute." He revolved his shoulders, letting it go, and changed the subject. "You know, this yage they drink down in the Amazon, this ayahuasca—"

"This aya-*what*-ska?"

"Well, that's the question. It has various components to it, but none of them appear to be psychoactive on their own. It's pure synergy, like some alchemical transformation…"

I slid down in my seat and reflected on the fact, which Linc had pointed out to me many times, that no matter what problems I thought I had, I was wildly, improbably blessed.

Sure, I knew at the time I was one of the luckiest boys who'd ever wandered the planet, but I didn't appreciate the depth and breadth of my luck. Fortunate, yes, to be having sex, so much sex, with so many wonderful girls—six of them in a few months following my fifteenth birthday. What I failed to appreciate as providential at the time was that all of them were older than me, experienced girls who knew what they wanted and could find their way around their own bodies. Girls who told me, by hints or urgings or just outright commands, what they wanted me to do next.

Looking back I see how different it could have been, how different it must have been for most boys. I could have been coaxing virgins down some path I didn't myself understand, or trying to excite girls who had never even touched themselves *down there*, in that ominous term that so many women apply to everything from navel to thigh. Worse, I could have ended up with girls whose expectations were based on romance novels, waiting for me to sweep them up in my muscular arms and *take* them, my steely gray eyes knowing their innermost desires, crushing their rosebud mouths to my cruel yet sensual lips...

Hard to live up to when the girl's chest is wider than yours, when you can't even locate your swash, much less buckle it.

So many guys I've met—even the Don Juans...no, especially the Don Juans—can't open their mouths about women without dripping casual venom. *Can't live with 'em, can't live without 'em. She's only yours until a bigger dick comes along. You fuck them a few hours a week, they fuck you your whole life. Woman: the life support system for a cunt. They're all the same in the dark.*

The fact that both men and women use the phrase *I got fucked* shows how deep this problem runs; in response to that assertion, does anyone ever respond, *Hey, that's great?* If I'd felt like I was on stage every time I kissed a girl, if I'd had to struggle my way through a girl's resistance and inexperience and was still expected to deliver some earth-shattering experience, if I'd felt hostility and judgment every time I touched a girl, maybe I'd be saying those things too.

But anyone who claims *they're all the same in the dark* just isn't paying much attention.

My luck was my misfortune as well, because three months after Stacy had broken my heart, I was in love again.

In love with JenBen.

In love with Randi.

And though I couldn't imagine life without them in it, I knew there was no future. Randi would head off for UC Santa Cruz in a matter of a couple of weeks; and I dared not press too hard on Jenny, because in the background I knew there always stood, as Randi called him, Brad Brad Brad.

A strange dance indeed. Randi wanted to have sex with JenBen and me—or, at any rate, JenBen and a boy, though Randi had the good grace to cast me in the male role when she talked about it. Jen wasn't averse to the idea of sex with Randi, but couldn't do it without exposing her clandestine virginity. So it went, through the closing days of summer: in bed with Randi, while she described all the things she imagined I and JenBen doing with her; then in bed with Jen, while I detailed everything about fucking Randi, including Randi's fantasies about Jen. An erotic hall of mirrors, but only I could see all of the reflections.

With Randi it wasn't just sex. She could talk about books and ideas just as energetically as Lincoln; but unlike Linc, her take was often cynical, a pessimistic view of human behavior that she could back up with ample historical data. As time went on, her womanly body intimidated me less, but her intellect made our age gap seem even wider, and it frightened me.

And for you armchair psychiatrists out there, you Monday-morning quarterbacks of the intellectual set, who are all muttering, well, of *course*, it's something related to a*ban*donment by his *mo*ther, I say: Mommy? Uh-uh. We're talking the Devouring Mother, here, the Great Goddess Kali, *vagina dentata*, soft and yielding but with teeth, and at any moment, had Randi chosen to do so, she could have stripped the flesh from my bones like some ancient god out of Lovecraft. That she didn't is why I loved her.

That and her belly. And her calves. And her breasts, yeah, sure, her breasts, every time I appeared with her in public everyone's eyes, male and female, were on how those bosoms filled her blouse, glory come anew in our diminished days, but tits are overrated and, really, it was freaky how they echoed the thin curve of her nose… I mean, JenBen's tits, now you're on to something, no extra flesh but all yearning nipple. Hell, slap Randi's knockers onto someone else's body and they'd just be weird, and if I had to choose I would have traded both of hers for the curve at the low of her back, where the muscles gathered beneath the curve and then vaulted skyward, like a Brancusi sculpture at his most weightless, a small glide for the hand of a man, but a great leap for womankind, a leap so bold that when my fingertips traced it I flew off from her coccyx, an Olympic ski-jumper, legs bent and braced for that moment when gravity would crush me down again.

You think this is just a child speaking, a horny child, besotted with an overripe teen? Randi could have worn any body—I repeat, any body, Eleanor Roosevelt to Marilyn Monroe—and that laugh would still have done it, left me gutted and staked out, drying in the sun but aching for more.

We said goodbye in my bed the evening before she left for college. I stayed affectionate and calm, keeping up the tone of two good friends who would get together again. We fucked, hard. We kissed. We snuggled.

We were so, so adult.

The next day found me too restless to read, too distracted to want to get loaded. In the afternoon I hiked across the wash and found my way up the ridge to a head-high grove of manzanita I knew from earlier hikes. Their vermilion branches spread wide, smooth woody muscles like those anatomical drawings that show men with their skin flayed. Surrounded by this red-limbed chorus, I sat and hugged my knees to my chest, calming my breath, and then toppled sideways onto the crackling leaves and tried to weep. Years of trying to keep back the tears at critical moments, years of trying to be a man, and now, with no witnesses but these twisted trees, nothing came but snot and phlegm and noises of frustration.

I crawled across the leaves, each round and hard as a coin, and slammed my forehead into a thick red root, and when nothing came but little maggoty lights behind my eyelids, slammed my head again and again...and then, as the pain in my head swelled to fill the world, the tears came at last, but they were cheap, headachey tears of frustration, not the tears I needed to shed.

Back at the house I shut myself in the bathroom, grateful Linc wasn't home, and splashed water onto my face, over and over, as if the feelings might wash away with the tearstains and the swelling knot on my forehead. After I turned off the faucet I leaned on the sink and stared into the mirror, with the sudden conviction I was no longer in my body, but rather on the other side of the glass watching myself, only an observer as I picked up the scissors, opened them, and pushed the point into the soft flesh of my forearm, just below my elbow. A ruby jewel rose around the steel tip.

Like a master calligrapher I drew the metal down my forearm in a long, easy curve, not too deep, just opening the skin, letting the gorgeous red wine bloom out on my pale skin, so pretty so fine, because, hey, I'm beautiful inside, and then I brought the silvery blade back to the bunched muscles in the thickest part of my arm and pushed the tip in hard, wagging it a little to slide it in deep, millimeter after millimeter, and the demanding alarm of this pain yanked me out of the mirror and back into my body.

I dropped the scissors into the sink. I started crying again. "What's *wrong* with me," I whimpered, unsure who I expected to listen, "what's *wrong?*"

The sound of the front door opening, and Linc's voice raised in anger. "Yeah. True... And when you get a life of your own, maybe it'll happen."

Lisby, tearful. "Do you just want to kill it? Don't you even, don't you even...*shit.*"

They weren't headed for the bedroom, and the longer I waited the more uncomfortable this discussion would become. I wiped my eyes with a handtowel and then wrapped it tight around my arm.

I opened the bathroom door. "Sorry," I said.

They both stared. Lisby had been crying for some time, eyes puffy, nose red, somehow more beautiful because of it. Linc's eyes looked hunted. Neither seemed to notice my arm.

"We just need a break from each other, just a break," he said to her. "Jesus, Rick, tell her—this isn't the fifties, we're not going to settle down, we're not going to *settle* for anything at all."

"*You* know how much I love him." Lisby reached out her hands to me. "*You* understand, *you* love him too. God, Rick"—a quick sob—"it hurts so much to be pushed away..."

Linc tightened his fists and then opened them. "And it suffocates me," he said, his tone even. "There's no *air* in here right now."

Lisby started, "Rick, can't you—"

"*Fuck* you people," I said. "Goddammit, Lisby, if you love him so goddamned much, can't you just be content with what you have? And, Christ, Linc"—my voice cracked—"can't you see what you've got here? Nobody's ever loved me like that. Nobody ever will. And you just treat it like, like, like—" I was going to say it, the perfect, pointed phrase that would tell him how lucky he was, how lucky they both were, but it didn't come, and instead I said, "Oh, shit, just fuck you both." I covered my face and stumbled off toward my room.

"Rick," Lisby asked in a startled voice, "are you *bleeding?*"

"Leave me alone," I said, and fumbled the door shut behind me.

I sprawled facedown on the bed and heard their voices, indistinct, far beyond the door.

Later, a knocking. I grunted something unfriendly, but the door opened anyway, and then closed behind someone. From the weight of the tread and the little sounds, it had to be Lisby, and the scent when she sat beside me on the bed, baby-skin and musk, confirmed it. She stroked the back of my head. "Randi," she asked, "or JenBen?"

"Both," I said into the pillow, my face turned away.

"What is it?"

I breathed, the sound of my respiration loud in my own ears. "I love them," I said, and then lifted my head and turned it on the pillow so I faced her, my eyes still shut. "They don't love me, but I love them."

She touched my cheek, and, even though I found Lisby among the sexiest of God's creatures, for a moment it was nothing more than mother and child. "Have you told them?"

"No." A long pause, as if the story might explain itself, and then I tried. "Jen already belongs to Brad Brad Brad, we agreed on that from the start, and Randi, Randi's made it clear that this just isn't *that kind of thing*."

"But it is, isn't it?"

"For me."

"Then tell them."

"They'll—" I swallowed what felt like a tennis ball, big and rough going down my throat. "They'll go away."

"Maybe. But you should tell the truth."

"A lot of good it's done you."

Her knuckles hesitated on my cheek for just a moment, and then resumed their slow caress. "How they react doesn't change how you really feel, does it? They can't say 'no' if you don't tell them how you feel, but they can't ever say 'yes' either."

"Maybe I don't want to know."

"Are you unhappy?"

"Yes."

"Well, at least you'd know what you were unhappy about. Right now, you're just unhappy because you're a coward."

"That's not it…"

"What's this, then?" He fingers tapped at the soaking red towel wrapped around my left forearm. "What the hell else is that, Rick?"

My eyes opened. "What the fuck do you know about it, huh?" I pushed myself up and jerked my mutilated arm away from her as if she'd tried to steal it, cradling it against my belly, the sopping crimson cloth wet against my shirt.

She reached out her arms, palms up. "Look." A spiderweb of tiny white lines covered each forearm, some fainter, some deeper, and the more I stared the more I saw, until it seemed that there was no natural skin on her arms, only scar over scar. "Here," she said, lifting her wrists higher and giving them a little shake, as if beseeching me to remove shackles, "check it out." Across the wrists, thick white slashes, pink around the edges, ever-so-slightly raised. "You been there yet? Because that's where you're headed." She stood up. "We'll show 'em all, won't we? Then they'll be sorry, won't they?"

She turned and left the room, but eventually came back with a bowl of water, towels, and Band-Aids. She wordlessly cleaned me up and put me back together. Mean-spirited to the end, I said, "So I guess you have it all figured out, then?"

She held a Band-Aid up to her mouth and peeled the backing away with her teeth, her other hand busy holding one of my deeper cuts together. She spat the wax paper out as she spoke. "Ultimately we're both equally screwed, probably." She pasted one sticky end on my arm, squinched my skin in tight, and used the other end to bridge the slit in my flesh and hold it shut. "And I don't know what works. But when I tell you something *doesn't* work, believe me."

Telling JenBen the truth was hard, because I had to do it in person, and had no excuse to put it off while I composed the perfect letter. I started when she came over the next day, before we got hot and heavy, while we were still necking on the bed.

I explained that I cared about her far more than I'd let on, probably even loved her, whatever that meant, that I missed her whenever she wasn't there, that I pined for her in the lonely hours of the morning; that I'd memorized and cherished subtle little curves of her body that she'd never even seen, unless she had contortionist skills that she'd never shown me; that I loved her and Randi both, and that I'd be torn apart between the two of them but for the fact that neither of them laid claim to me; that I had nothing to offer her, didn't even have some sort of plan or goal; and that I treasured what we had already, and hadn't said a word about how I felt because I was afraid I'd screw everything up, but I thought that now I had to tell her.

She rolled over and faced away from me, and I let my hand stroke gently down the curve of her waist and then on to the sudden upheaval of her hip, her sheer green panties clinging there like a carpet of ferns on a ridge, the grade steeper and more unexpected than the most violent landform, yet smooth and soft.

"Suppose," she asked without turning back to me, "suppose I wanted…" Her voice trembled. "Suppose I told you that what I really wanted was for everything between us to stay just the way it was?"

"I'd say, okay," I said, "and be grateful." I swallowed. "But I wanted you to know how I feel."

She turned back to me and her eyes were wet. "No new rules? No questions?"

"Maybe a question."

She studied me, wary. "What?"

"Can we take the panties off now?"

"You dipshit!" She slugged me in the shoulder, pretty much as hard as she could; but she wriggled out of them and tossed them to the floor.

Much later, before she went home, she kissed me and said, "Me, too."

"Me, too, *what?*"

She bent down and kissed me lightly again, and left without answering.

Did I know what JenBen was all about? Nary a clue, nary a clue. I was relieved to have told her, but had no idea whether she'd be back.

16 | THE SLUT'S COMPLETE GUIDE TO ETIQUETTE

The start of the school year changed things. The Salon's Tuesdays and Thursdays continued, though they were less well-attended than in the summer. Lisby still came to every session, but she and Linc were in what he called "breathing space," and each time Lisby arrived she ostentatiously chose a seat opposite him in our circle. Some of the former attendees vanished for college, a fact I was reminded of every time Randi's ghost took its place in the room.

The long, accommodating vacation days disappeared, and my tripping scaled back to weekends only. Even I, the Kid Who Could Maintain, wasn't willing to deal with high school on acid.

Al Kraft had been as good as his word. My new schedule had me in college-prep classes, following in the footsteps, I soon found, of Randi, Leslie, and, to my surprise, Lincoln Ellard. The English class was fun, focused on literature rather than diagramming sentences, but the new math class was over my head, and I dropped back to one of the remedial classes. I half-expected to find Linc there, but he had met with Mr. Prafter and argued his way into Intro Calculus, where he pulled his light from beneath Ubelovsky's bushel and proceeded to slash his way to the head of the class.

Linc's enthusiasm for shamanic potions hadn't abated, and we still headed over to the UCR library at least once a week. "It's just phenomenal," he said, one hand on the steering wheel, the other drawing in the air. "There's DMT, right, a psychedelic"—he pointed at a notation on his imaginary chalkboard—"but if you take it orally this enzyme, MAO"—he pointed farther right—"monoamine oxidase, chews it up as soon as it gets absorbed into the bloodstream. But these Amazonian Indians, these so-called primitives, found this other plant, this liana they call the Vine of the Souls, and it acts as a monoamine oxidase inhibitor. So you brew up the Vine of the Souls plus a DMT plant—it turns out there's lots of them—and you end up with this psychedelic tea. It's this amazing technology, this advanced pharmacology developed by these people who live in huts. And nobody's ever even thought about this stuff in North America—I mean, if you had this MAO inhibitor, there might be hundreds of plants growing all around us that turn out to be psychedelic!"

"What's the big deal? Acid's cheap, reliable, easy to get…"

"Don't you see, though?" He wheeled us into a parking space behind the library and cut the motor. "There's a whole world of other psychedelics out there. I thought LSD"—he pulled the brake handle out with a loud ratcheting sound—"was something completely new, but it's just the latest in this hidden tradition that stretches back thousands of years. It changes the whole meaning of history. I mean, all the crazy visions in the Bible, all the witches thinking they could fly, India and the sacred soma that let them talk to the gods…we're just rediscovering this ancient thing."

As if wanting to deepen the rift between the sciences and the humanities, UCR had hived off the sciences from the main library. Linc might be in the BioAg library, or in the Physical Sciences Annex—the Qs and Ts were split between them—but I'd definitely be wandering the stacks of the main building, the Rivera, so when he was finished he'd come fetch me from the Ps on the second floor.

My first time in the university library, I'd expected to be accosted by authority—by demands for college ID, perhaps, or just for an explanation of what I thought I was doing. But the same code prevailed there as in the public library back in Redlands: keep quiet and mind your own business, and you'll never be questioned. Next to the elevators a cracked naugahyde sofa, once wheat-colored but now turning yellow at the seams, was invariably occupied by a sleeping student, napping being well within the code of behavior.

I had no borrowing privileges, of course, so I spent my time dragging piles of promising texts back to student carrels for perusal, scribbling down notes of authors and titles I wanted to search for elsewhere. I had my nose in a puzzling novel entitled *Omensetter's Luck* when a female voice said, "Looking for me, I suppose?"

Casey Carroll leaned against the shelves, a notebook clutched to her chest. Despite the air-conditioned chill of the library, she wore a sleeveless blouse and a miniskirt, showing as much of her blue-veined, goosebumpy skin as possible. Her mouth wore what she might have intended as a seductive, knowing smile. To my eyes it was a smirk, and I had the urge to slap it off her face; better yet, fuck it off her face. Perhaps that was the effect she wanted, because she smiled a little wider as she watched my reaction.

"I thought about calling you a couple of times," she said, "but it turns out you don't have a phone." True enough; Linc had toyed with listing us as The Mountain High Salon, but in the end we decided that a telephone, like a television, was a distraction we didn't want.

She put her notebook on my desk, topped by a paperback copy of Lawrence's *The Fox*, and ripped out a page of ruled paper. "I've got to run to a seminar," she said, "but call me the next time you're around." I smelled her beside me, more intimate than a touch, as she scribbled out her name, number, and address. "It's only a little ways off campus." She patted the back of my shoulders, solid open-palm pats, as though I were a good, robust dog, and then gathered up her things.

A few feet away, she turned back to me. "What's up with Leslie these days, anyhow?"

"Why?" I asked, the first word I'd uttered since she'd arrived.

"She showed up for classes when the semester started, but she hasn't been here in, oh, at least a week and a half." She raised her eyebrows and gave that smug little smile again before she spun and walked away, her hips tossing hard side-to-side for what I assumed was my benefit.

I ignored the signals coming from my crotch. I took the notepaper with her address and crumpled it into a tight, hard ball, feeling giddily empowered, as if I'd made the first real choice in my life.

The next afternoon I begged a ride to the Andrews' place. "Sure you don't want me to come in?" Linc asked. "I could entertain Susie The Stepmom…" I gave a long-suffering sigh and climbed out of the car. "Want me to wait? What if Leslie isn't home?" I slammed the door and headed up the long flagstone walk.

Sue Andrews answered the bell, peering around the half-opened door. She frowned in puzzlement, probably not recognizing me with hair, and finally said, "Oh, Rick!" She put on a hostess smile, but it wavered as we looked at each other and pretended we had no shared secrets. She opened the door a little wider in an instinctive welcoming motion, and then just as quickly moved it back again. "What…can I do for you?"

"Leslie home?"

She relaxed her grip on the doorknob, and then let loose, her hands reaching down to smooth her skirt. "Yes. She is, but she hasn't been feeling well. I'm not sure she's up to seeing anyone." Her eyes kept scanning my face and then dropping, avoiding eye contact.

"Could you check, please? Some of her friends at the university asked me to look her up."

The tip of her tongue worked at her lips, and she made a decision. "I'm sorry, what am I thinking? Come in." I followed her into the kitchen. "Have a seat, and I'll go see." She paused, and then, deciding to play it as Mom, she added, "Can I get you anything? A drink, or maybe a sandwich?"

I sat down at a counter; the kitchen, though huge, had no table. "No thank you, Mrs. Andrews." The title seemed to reassure her, and she clicked away in her pumps with a more confident manner.

A corkboard at the end of the counter had a list of instructions push-pinned down, and I was scanning them—instructions to a maid and to a cook, it seemed—when Sue Andrews bustled back in. "She's feeling a little better, I guess. She'll be out in a minute or two." She squeezed one of her hands with the other. "I don't mean to be inhospitable, but I was just on my way out, so if you don't mind waiting alone…?"

I assured her I didn't, though judging from her lack of makeup I sincerely doubted that she had been on her way anywhere at the time I arrived.

Ten minutes after Sue Andrews shut the front door behind her, Leslie peered into the kitchen from the living room. Dressed in jeans and a white tee-shirt, her dark hair pulled back into a tight ponytail, she looked not like herself, but like a relative—her own younger, smaller sister, perhaps. "What do you want?" she asked.

"Just to talk." She stared. "Casey said you hadn't been to your classes, and I haven't seen you…"

She nodded, expressionless, and gestured for me to follow her.

She sat on the shelf in front of their stone fireplace. The nearest chair was a dozen feet away, so I sat crosslegged on the thick hearthrug. Her face was pale, with just a touch of darkness beneath the eyes.

"I think Casey is worried about you…" I began.

"Casey." Her voice was dismissive, but without enthusiasm.

"Okay, *I* was worried about you. Not because we haven't seen you. We expected we wouldn't see much of you once you were at UCR…"

"Figured I'd be ashamed to show my face in these parts again."

"No. I just thought you were happy to be done with this town."

She crossed her arms over her knees and rested her chin on her forearm. "Nice going-away present I gave myself, huh? Slut-of-the-Year award." Her voice was too passionless to be bitter.

"Not even close." I waited a moment, and added, "You made the Top Ten, maybe…"

A weak sniff of amusement. "So what do they say about me? Around town, I mean."

"Not as much as you probably think. The usual, after something like that. *Did you hear?* and *Did you get any?* This place has a short memory. Plus everybody's always talking about Vicki Perry's latest. I hear her stuff is acrobatic."

"Every time I make eye contact with a guy in this town, I get to wonder…" She laid her cheek on her arm and regarded me with a face that, despite her words, was amused. "I don't remember them, but they all remember me…so it seems like I'd be the important one." She lifted her head. "Doesn't feel like it, though."

"You really don't remember…?"

An acidic laugh. "Oh, I remember some of them. Wish I could forget. And I remember you…" She sat up straight, looked at me, then looked aside. "You really surprised me. I gave you the come-hither and you just split." She looked down and poked her index finger into her denimed thigh as though she were testing a cake for doneness. "Guess I was pretty repellent by then."

"No." I touched her arm and she started. "No, you've got that part all wrong." In truth I'd been repulsed somehow, but not by her, and I didn't understand what I had felt well enough to risk an explanation. "No, you were…amazing." I chewed my upper lip, wiggling my jaw back and forth as though sawing, searching for words that would be true and also make her feel better. "I guess I didn't want to be in there with all those other guys. Doesn't affect your appeal though." I wasn't sure if I was telling the truth or not.

"Even after…that?" She held up fingers in warning. "That's not an invitation. I'm celibate for a while. Maybe forever."

"Leslie. If you think what you did changes you from being gorgeous to being ugly, your mind is really fucked up about this whole thing."

"Rick…my mind *is* really fucked up about this whole thing." She swallowed, wet her lips. "And sometimes I think about, about who I did it with and when—what was I trying to do? I despise them, and at the same time I'm letting them degrade me…?"

"That's kind of confused, Leslie."

"Duh."

"No, I mean—look, it's one way or the other." I was on dangerous terrain here, picking my way through the swamp of whatever damaged brooding she'd done since I'd seen her last. "Either you're wrong about this place, and the people in it, in which case there's nothing *degrading* about it. Or you're right about this place, in which case, who gives a shit what they think? But you seem to want the worst of both worlds, thinking that everybody's beneath contempt and also worrying about them judging you. That's…well, that's nuts."

"I think I *am* nuts," she said, and her voice started to crack.

"Listen. I have to tell you something else, too. There were girls standing on the patio watching you."

"I noticed, but couldn't really get a fix on it. I was…busy."

"Randi Mayfield was one of them. And she told me how much she admired you for doing it. Said that it turned her on, but she didn't have the guts."

"Randi said that?" Leslie searched my face for signs of truth. "When?"

I exhaled a nervous laugh. "That's a little personal, but what the hell. She told me that night, that same night. She was one of the people watching, and she was so excited that she came back to my place and fucked me senseless."

"I don't believe it."

"What, that Randi fucked me? I didn't believe it either, at first."

"No. That she was…like that."

"Leslie, I've got to tell you. All the girls who were watching were so hyped up that they'd have gone home with anybody who had a dick. Or even something shaped like one. I got there first, thanks to Linc, and he took Melissa home, and she's been fucking him ever since. So I owe you big time. No way Randi would have ever bothered with me, if not for that night. No way. But after that, we sort of became a thing, until she went off to college." We'd been discussing a gangfuck, but I was suddenly shy when I added, "I think we're sort of…something."

Leslie laughed; still not a happy sound, but at least closer to her old cynical self. "I need a drink." She stood and crossed the room to the wet bar. As she clinked bottles and glasses, she said over her shoulder, "I know you're twisting all the facts to make me feel better, but it makes me feel better anyway."

"I'm not twisting anything." Omitting, perhaps. "And if you don't believe me, why don't you write Randi a letter and ask what she thinks? I've got her address." She returned and sat down, passing me one of a pair of glasses. I sipped. Gin and tonic, no lemon, no ice. "I'm just sorry that you seem to feel bad when you shouldn't. And I'm really sorry that you took a big risk but didn't have a good time."

"Yeah. Well." She rubbed her forehead. "I'm twisting the facts, too. I really did like it, at first. For a while, it was the most exciting thing I'd ever done. And then it got kind of weird, along about the time you were there…just weird, and that's part of why I wanted you to… well. Fuck it. And then later, after you left, it got a little bit out of hand, a little rougher than I would have liked…"

"Oh."

A dismissive sound. "Good thing, really. It was getting sort of… boring, if you want to know the truth. A whole bunch of hard cocks, you'd think there'd be some level of, of *enthusiasm*, but if there was it didn't get across to me. So having things get out of hand at least woke me up. Got me motivated to disengage. Turns out you can't just stop all of a sudden and say, thank you all very much for coming to my little party tonight…but you don't think about that part of it when you start."

I was certain that Randi had thought about this, but Randi seemed to have worked all the details through in her mind. Which, of course, is why I was sitting here comforting Leslie rather than comforting Randi; R.G. Mayfield knew a bad bet when she saw one. "Maybe you should write to Emily Post."

"Yeah. Or write a book of my own, The Slut's Complete Guide to Etiquette."

"Oh, stop with the slut stuff already. I'm a slut, Linc's a slut, Rob's a slut, every guy I know is, by any definition of the word I've ever heard, a slut. We're just not very successful at it."

"Failed sluts. Wow."

"Why do you think guys are so pissed off all the time? We set our sights low, and we still don't make it."

"You're okay, Rick." She tousled my hair, which made me feel I was about ten. "You really think it would be okay to write to Randi about all this?"

"I'm sure of it." We drank quietly for a while. "No one's down on you, Leslie."

"There's quite a few people who think I'm a stuck-up bitch."

"Nobody in our crowd." Not quite true, but…

She raised her eyebrows. "I appreciate your including me in 'our crowd.' But aren't we kind of the damaged bunch?" I must have looked puzzled. "Have you done the stats? Look at your family. Look at mine." A gesture at the room. "Or Lincoln, no dad, crazy mother, literally. Lisby, no mom, religious child-molester dad. Randi—her parents are still together, but her mom's in the same deceptive bitch league as Susan. JenBen, a couple of hopeless alkies for parents—"

"So we aren't from Disney families. So we grow up faster than other kids." I took a big swallow of my drink and winced at the gin content. "The people you despise the most around here aren't even on the list you just went through."

"You're right." She sat there for a moment before she started laughing, and tears spilled out of her eyes. "The ones I fucked." She laughed harder and her drink sloshed in her hand. "The ones I fucked, they're just *fine*!" I watched, not sure if I should hold her, or laugh with her, or do that movie thing where you slap the person and they thank you afterwards. I did nothing, and she slowed, and set down her drink, and wiped her eyes. "God," she said, "I'm such a fucking moron. I mean, they matter, or they don't, right?"

"They don't. They don't matter. You're smart and you're beautiful, and you're richer than most people around here, so people are jealous. Hell, *I'm* jealous."

"But why did I do what I did?"

"Who cares? You did it *once*. Something you do once doesn't change the pattern of your life, unless maybe you kill somebody, but we aren't killing anybody here. As Randi says, quoting Voltaire, *Once is philosophy…*"

"So if I do it twice, I'm lost?"

"Nah. Do it a bunch of times and call it all 'one period.'"

She chewed on the inside of her cheek for a while. "You need a ride home? Before my dad gets here, I mean?"

Outside she looked at the sun heading down into the LA smog and threw her arms back, stretching. She let out a long breath. "I haven't been outdoors in a week."

In her Mustang, on the way to Mountain Home, she said, "You're the only one who came by, you know. Or even called."

"Nobody knew. Anybody in our bunch would have been here."

She nodded to herself as if wondering whether to say what came next. "You know, Rick, all these people—our bunch, as you call them—aren't as smart or attractive or edgy as you seem to think they are."

"And maybe you're so busy looking down your nose at this place, you don't see what people are really about." My tone was shorter than I'd intended, and I tried to crank down the intensity. "These people—you people—are the closest thing to real family I've got."

She turned this over in her mind, and decided to change the subject. "You and Randi, huh? I thought you and JenBen were a thing."

"I like JenBen. Hell, I love her. I guess. But it isn't what it looks like."

"But the Randi thing works?"

I almost said, sure, it's great; but instead, I found myself saying, "I thought so, but I never really… She said we weren't supposed to get too romantic, and…" I sighed. "And I don't think she feels the same way. We haven't talked about it."

The sun was behind Crafton Hills, and she pulled on the headlights as we entered shadow.

"I just wish," I said, "that somebody'd tell me what to do. I know I'm too young for her, and I don't want to fuck up what I've got by trying to get more, you know what I mean? But I'm not sure she knows. But probably she knows and just doesn't want to tell me she really doesn't feel that way about me. Or maybe—"

"Have you told her any of this? Or is she supposed to read your mind?"

"It just seems like she'd be able to tell."

"So you *do* think she should read your mind."

"Don't be mean."

"I'm not. But you have to give her a chance, you know. Plus…"

"Plus what?"

"Nothing."

"What?"

"It's just—how are you so sure you know what love is?"

It seemed self-evident, until I thought about it. How did I know? "When you want to be around somebody, and you can't stop thinking about them, and, I don't know, your throat gets all tight and—" I frowned, angry, but unsure whether I was angry at her or at my own lack of insight. "What do *you* think love is?"

She laughed, incredulous. "Me? What the fuck do I know about anything? Jesus, Rick, I'm not instructing you on something, I'm the last person in the world who knows anything. You just sound so certain. So I asked a question."

A question I couldn't answer; a question both important and yet unfair. I chewed on it all the way to Mountain Home.

Leslie let me coax her into coming inside and smoking a bowl of hash. Linc, to his great credit, sat down with us and treated her with casual familiarity, as if she'd been gone for a while but her return was no great surprise, either—a comfortable, friendly attitude that suggested nothing extraordinary had happened in her life since we'd last sat together. And it could be that he thought nothing of what Leslie had been going through—thought the act itself was of little consequence, and her brooding upon it was of none whatsoever. But I doubted it. For all his didactic airs, for all his fuck-you bluster, beneath it all, Linc was sensitive as a cat, and could tread as unobtrusively as one when needed.

The weather stayed warm enough that the park was still crowded on weekend nights, but already some of the magic was beginning to fade. People were getting busted—none of our close associates, but people woven into our web. *Who's The Narc?* became the new game, everyone certain that there was a Judas in our midst. People started to be wary of old friends; a few of the bigger dealers let it be known they'd started carrying pistols in their gloveboxes. Nearly getting busted became worse than actually being arrested and charged—being picked up and released, or even pulled over, put you under a cloud of suspicion. Why did *he* get off? Did he give somebody up? Has he been working for the Man all along?

The busts coincided neatly with a wave of crosstop whites from Mexico, rolls of Benzedrine that fueled speedfreak paranoia. And unlike the combo of acid and smoking dope that had prevailed during the summer, the classic biker combination of speed and beer that started to spread through the community made people impulsive and mean. Threats, fistfights, and two rapes—the latter splitting people into factions, not along gender lines, but along the gulf of *she was asking for it* versus *only literally asking for is asking for it*. It frightened me to discover how many people, how many apparently sane people, thought that certain behaviors on the part of the victim justified the use of force in sex.

It frightened me even more to find how many of those people were girls. Yeah, well, look at how drunk she got, look at how she was dressed, look at how she was hanging on everybody, what the hell would I expect if I were acting like that? *She was asking for it.*

Scary.

But there was something even more menacing in the air of those early fall nights, something that roiled up from the Tate-LaBianca murders down in LA. Hippie cult killers? Plenty of people denied it, and the stupidity and savagery of the slaughters supported them: Hey, man, there's something hinky here, this has got to be a right-wing frame-up. But underneath it all, we knew, our hearts knew; and there was mounting evidence from the murders in the Black Power community, and in the violence from the Weathermen and the SLA and a dozen other nasty little ideological gangs. The Manson Family wouldn't be identified and charged for months yet, but we knew: There were sick people among us, just as in any other generation, and hair and clothes and attitudes and drugs for them were nothing more than disguises they had donned.

What had been glorious craziness in the summer looked more like actual madness in the fall.

And the Lisby-Linc feud continued.

They'd established a trial separation, but she made sure that she wasn't forgotten. At the salon she was more outspoken than ever. When the days were still warm enough she showed up at the swimming hole, and it seemed that every time we went to the Park, she happened to pass through. For the first week or two, she'd wave gaily as she passed by with friends; she'd make a point of stopping to talk to me while ignoring Linc.

It didn't stay so happy. By late September she'd stumble through the Park, ostentatiously hanging onto someone's arm, girl or boy, it didn't matter. Linc would mutter that it was good she was starting to play the field, but his words were forced.

I think they managed to stay apart for three weeks. One night when Linc and I sat under a tree, Lisby rode into the parking lot hanging off the back of Glen Corbett's motorcycle. They parked it, and he patted her butt before he sauntered over to talk to a circle of his biker pals.

She scanned the Park, spotted us, and headed in our direction, staggering slightly. For a moment I thought that she'd ridden in after a sex marathon, but the loose toss of her hips as she walked wasn't postcoital relaxation, but a drunken, fuck-me abandon, ready to go.

"Hey, Rick." Her words slurred just a bit, and she crossed her arms. Not booze, I thought. Reds.

"Lisby." I patted the ground. "Sit down. You okay?"

"Oh, yeah. Never better." She squinted at the place I'd patted, but didn't sit. "Caught a ride to the Park on a chopper. Ride far enough on one of those, you don't need to fuck. 'Course, he wants to fuck me anyway, not just ride me around on his bike. I don't like him, but maybe I should let him fuck me, huh? Whaddya you think, Rick, think I should let Corbett fuck me?"

"C'mon, Lisby, sit down."

"Maybe you wanta fuck me instead? Huh? Understand you been fucking everybody in town lately, Lincoln's got you right on track, yeah? You can, you know, if you're not too busy, you're officially approved." She wavered. "Right, Linc? He's ideal, right?"

Linc tightened his mouth as if resisting speech, but the words came anyway. "Jesus, Lisby, show a little respect for yourself."

"Why should I? You don't." She sat down, hard, more like a controlled fall, and made a sound as if she'd been punched in the belly. "How 'bout it, Linc? Think I should fuck Corbett, maybe some of his friends, huh? Show 'em how it's really done—"

"Liz, just—"

"—'cause I know all the tricks, don't I, Linc, you taught me everything, I could show 'em all how I can—"

"Goddamit, Lisby, shut up!" Linc jumped to his feet. "Will you just shut up?" He towered over her where she sat. "What the hell do you want from me?"

She looked down at the grass, refusing to answer. I thought she'd fallen into some Seconal trance when at last she said, "Don't make me live like this."

He stood there breathing through flared nostrils, and when he reached down for her I was so worried I almost blocked his hands, but he gripped her under the arms and hoisted her to her feet. "Okay," he said, his voice even, "you win. Let's go home."

I watched them as he walked her down to the parking lot, his arm supporting her wobbly gait. When he helped her into his car, there was an explosion of laughter from the biker crowd, though I wasn't sure if it were directed at Linc and Lisby, or was only some random outburst.

17 | JUST TELL THE TRUTH

On his scheduled Wednesdays, Leo usually saw us at the close of school, a little after three; but that day he'd called ahead to let Al Kraft know that he wouldn't be there until well after four. In fact, he hadn't arrived until after five o'clock. Donnie had spent the hours fuming and staring at the floor; I'd spent the time immersed in a book.

I wasn't angry, but I was anxious; I'd arranged to meet JenBen back at the house at five. Leo called Donnie into the office first, and whatever he had to say took nearly thirty minutes. When Donnie walked out of their interview, he was pale, and it looked as if he might have been crying earlier.

Leo glowered at me as I took a chair. "What a little jerk," he said to me in a stage whisper. Then he smiled, and I let out a sigh of relief that his former expression wasn't connected to me. "I hope you have better news."

I did. I showed him the bank-book for my savings account—modest weekly deposits, courtesy of the Ellard nursery, and even more modest withdrawals, showing an accumulating cash balance that would have done a Puritan proud. I talked about my classes, not exaggerating my performance, but making sure he knew I was taking school seriously; and he nodded his way through my description as if it squared with whatever Kraft had been telling him.

"Anything you aren't telling me?" he asked, fixing me with a stare that made me deeply uncomfortable. Abruptly he laughed. "Of course there is. There always is. I just hope for your sake it isn't anything significant." He opened a manila folder on the desk, pulled out a pamphlet, and passed it to me: *California Emancipated Minors Law Q&A*, published by the California Legal Aid Society.

"You'll find that ninety percent of that doesn't apply to you," he said, "but read it all anyway." He started gathering his papers. "The courts are more reluctant to grant these things before you're sixteen—it helps if you're old enough to drive. But that's probably too far off in your case. I think we should aim for the end of the semester." He stood, and in that little office he seemed to be twenty feet tall.

"Is there anything I need to do?"

"Of course. Do keep the job. Do keep the bank balance rising. Do keep performing in your classes. But the don'ts are more important: Don't get busted, don't hang out with known felons, don't get anybody pregnant, and in general just don't fuck anything up. The courts aren't crazy about granting minors adult rights, so you need to wow them with all the new leaves you've turned over." He clapped me on the shoulder and then went to the door. "You staying here?" he asked. Only then did I realize that the building was deserted except for the two of us.

It was after six. I hurried down to the Park to cadge a ride, but the afterschool crowd had disappeared, and it was too early for the evening bunch to arrive. The floodlights were already on over the athletic fields, and the empty, shadowed Park had the feel of a movie set waiting for the cast and crew to return.

As if everything were in conspiracy against my evening with Jen, my outstretched thumb was ignored by everyone on the boulevard. On any other night, it wouldn't have been more than fifteen minutes before someone recognized me, but that evening I might as well have been in a strange town; when someone finally stopped, it was an old man on his way to Forest Falls, and he lectured me all the way to Mountain Home about the dangers of hitchhiking.

I walked the shadowy streets from the highway toward our house, half-expecting everyone to have left for the park, but the lights blazed from our house, a welcoming yellowish glow spilling through the windows. With pleasure I saw JenBen's VW parked on the street, right behind Linc's Impala.

I pushed open the front door, holding the *Emancipation* pamphlet up like a trophy. "Sorry I'm so late, guys, but—"

A sharp pain in the shins, a vicious shove from behind. My legs flew back behind me, and for one long moment I lay face-down three feet in the air, so astonished that I did nothing to break my fall. I slammed onto the hardwood floor with a force that drove all of the air from my chest.

It had been years since I'd had the wind knocked out of me, but the sensation embraced me like a familiar, despised relative. Booted feet moved to either side of me, but I was busy fighting for breath, begging my stunned diaphragm to move. I felt my arms being pulled across the floor until they were stretched out above my head, as though I were diving into a pool.

At last I pulled in a long sob of a breath, painful but welcome. Something was being done to my wrists, but I sucked air for a while before I lifted my head and looked forward.

'Berto squatted there, holding the short length of chain between the handcuffs on my wrists. "Stay cool, *vato*," he said, "there's a gun pointed at the back of your head."

A boot toed me in the side. "Up. On your knees."

"—*can't*—" I managed to gasp. The boot toed me harder.

"Chill a sec," 'Berto said to whoever was standing over me. "Let him get it together."

I lay the side of my face back down on the cool floor, and then winced at the pain. They let me breathe for a minute, and then 'Berto said, "You good now? Come on, then, up on your knees."

They helped me up, 'Berto keeping his grip on the cuffs so that I ended on my knees with my arms stretched out before me like a cartoon sleepwalker.

Chase stepped from my side to stand next to 'Berto. A gun dangled casually in his hand, one of those snubnosed, fat revolvers popular in old detective movies. "You kept us waiting a long time. Let's just take it real easy and go over with your friends." He turned and headed across the long living room, apparently confident that 'Berto had me under control.

'Berto jerked on the cuffs. "Just stay on your knees, walk with me." He reached his free hand into the back pocket of his jeans and produced a switchblade, flicking it open with a *snick*. "Come on."

Walking on your knees isn't easy, especially with someone urging you on by tugging on your cuffed hands. I tottered forward, one knee, then the other. "'Berto," I whispered, "whatever this is, don't."

"Sorry, *ese*. No choice. Business." He continued walking backwards, a step to every two or three of my knee-shuffles. "And remember, you left me dry."

He stepped a little to the side to turn and glance at Chase, and I saw across the room. JenBen lay on the couch, her arms behind her, a swath of duct tape across her mouth. Near the couch, Linc had been tied into a wooden chair, his forearms bound to the armrests, ankles secured to the chair legs.

"Lay on a little more speed, dudes," Chase said.

We stopped a half-dozen feet away from Linc's chair. A little more than an armsreach away, JenBen's eyes sought mine. She looked panicked, but unhurt.

The same couldn't be said for Linc. The usual darkness that lurked beneath his skin had fled, his face pale beneath his black curls. He'd been knocked around; an eye showed early signs of a bruise, and blood showed in a red line on his split lower lip.

He gave me a groggy look, and then glanced down at his left hand. It had been bound up tightly in duct tape, and a scrap of bloody washcloth protruded from the binding. I shuddered, not so much at the sight of his bandaged hand, but at his listless, pallid manner.

"Guys," I said, trying to keep my voice from trembling, "this is no good. We can come to an arrangement. But you can't fuck with us too much"—Chase started at these words, as if ready to bend down and smack me—"I mean, you can't really get away with much. If something happens, if we…" I swallowed, then managed the words. "If we go missing, they're going to know you're tied up in it—too many people know we're connected."

'Berto clucked his tongue. "Sorry. But I never told nobody. Nobody but Chase."

"But people around here know…" I said.

A small laugh, entirely through his nose. "I don't think so. You're too careful for that."

"We been fuckin' around too long," Chase said.

'Berto jerked hard on my cuffs and I fell outstretched on the floor. He placed one booted foot in the center of the chain, pinning my hands there, and then squatted. "This *pinche coñito* of yours told us some fucking stupid story about where you keep your stash, where you keep your money. Lookit this." He grabbed my hair and turned my head to the side. Chase leaned down and held out something pinkish, and it took a moment for me to recognize it as a severed finger. I recoiled instinctively, and struggled, and 'Berto, still gripping my hair, jerked my face up to look into his. "You just tell us the truth. The stash. The money." He released my hair and my head dropped from its painful arch, but in the next moment he had the edge of his switchblade pressed against the pinky finger of my left hand, right above the bottom knuckle.

"Tell them the truth," Linc said, his voice weak but raspy.

"Yeah," Chase's voice said, off to my right, "truth. Doesn't agree with his story, then *somebody*, somebody gets fucked up. We been waiting on the chick, I guess she's your"—I'd never heard the term used with such contempt—"your *girlfriend*. Bet we could teach her a few things. Already had to tape her mouth shut to keep it off my dick. And, hey, she's got ten little fingers, too…so far."

"No *respisas*," 'Berto said, quiet and hunkered down near me, "but a nice ass…" His voice dropped even further, into a tone that at least tried to sound sympathetic. "Make this easy, *ese*. Make it easy for everybody."

What had Linc told them? Hell, he'd told me to tell the truth. I took a deep breath. "The stash is buried. Way up a canyon, over in Calimesa. We take horses to get there. My money is in a coffee can, way out in the wash behind this place. I don't know where Linc keeps his. Probably hidden down at the family nursery business somewhere."

"Fuck." Chase exhaled a tremorous breath, and I realized he was probably wired. "Fuck, *fuck*." I heard his feet as he stomped on the floor, seemingly turning in little circles. I felt the pressure of 'Berto's blade ease up on my finger, but then Chase kicked me in the ribs so hard that I yelped. "You stupid motherfuckers! Why would you put it in the middle of fuckin' nowhere?"

I curled my body to the side, instinctively coiling around the pain, but the boot on the cuffs kept me from rolling into a ball. "Your money's around here?" 'Berto asked. "Where?"

"I already told you. Out in the wash."

"Get him up," Chase said. They pulled me to my feet. "You and me, we're gonna take a walk."

I shot a glance at JenBen. Her eyes were eloquent, but fluent in a language I didn't speak.

The gravid moon spilled her light into the wash. Too much moonlight can be as bad as too little; the shadows of the boulders against the bright sands were sharp, and the contrast hid rocks and potholes. By comparison with Chase, though, I was surefooted. He stumbled along behind me, cursing under his breath, each blunder pumping adrenaline into a bloodstream already overloaded with amphetamines.

I should have lied about my hidey-hole. As soon as he had my money, he wouldn't need me anymore.

I'd been cherishing the belief that they'd strip us of our cash and goods and then leave, but now, listening to his under-the-breath monologue I knew with utter conviction that they were going to kill all three of us. To a mind like Chase's, letting us go would be no more than an opportunity for us to come after him.

On the far side of the wash, hundreds of yards from the house, I scrambled up the little path to the ridge and knelt by the pear-shaped boulder.

Chase stood behind me, breathing hard, and I imagined I heard his whole body vibrating. I rolled aside the first of the fist-sized rocks, and he said, "Here? Just, out here? Why? You stupid motherfucker. Why?"

I lifted out the last rock and eased the coffee can from its hole. I heard a metallic click, probably Chase doing something with the gun, and I knew I was going to die, and in that moment the strangest thing happened: I felt calm pour across me like a soothing lotion, and I exhaled and then drew in a deep, satisfying breath. For the first time in my life, I gave up, surrendered, and was at peace.

"What?" Chase asked, sensing the change in me.

I took another long breath.

"What the fuck?" he asked.

Smiling, not looking at him, I said, "It *is* a stupid place. Folks come out here every day, all over this section of the wash. Run their dogs. Fool around. The path we came up is there because some people start the day by hiking up this ridge." I opened the coffee can, pulled out the roll of bills, and held it over my shoulder.

A long pause before he took the cash, and then he said, "Let's go. Gonna be a long night."

The Kehl Canyon riding trail was easy to navigate in the moonlight. For the first twenty minutes JenBen and I had flanked Linc, keeping him from weaving, but finally the crosstops he'd demanded kicked in, and his body and gait both stiffened, grim and purposeful.

"How fuckin' far is this?" 'Berto asked from behind us.

"Forty-five minutes more, maybe an hour," Linc said, his voice flat. "I don't know. We only come out here on horses."

"Stupid," Chase said, "just goddamn stupid."

Before we set out from the car, Chase had wanted to cuff us with our hands behind our backs, but Linc had explained that the last leg of the hike would be over hills and ridges, off the trail, and that we'd need our hands to open the hidey-hole in any case. Chase hadn't liked it, studying us through narrowed, speed-freak eyes, but the argument was unanswerable: We each ended up with our hands cuffed in front of us, walking abreast in front of our captors.

"My hand's bleeding again," Linc said in a quiet tone. He nodded down, and I saw a drop, black in moonlight, fall from his bandage to the dust of the road.

"What'd you say?" Chase demanded.

"I said I'm bleeding again."

"*Firme*, dude," 'Berto said, "do your stuff good and then we get you to a doctor, eh?"

"Yeah, right," Linc muttered under his breath.

"Stop talking!" Chase said. "You want to talk, you talk to me."

On and on, weary prisoners staggering down a moonlit road to nowhere, like a fever dream inspired by Beckett. At last Linc halted in a grove of sycamores, their limbs like polished bone in the silvery light. "Here's where we head cross-country." He sank down onto a granite outcrop and hung his head.

I half-expected Chase to yell for him to stand up and move, but 'Berto and Chase both found rocks of their own. JenBen and I sat down beside each other, not speaking, not even making eye contact, but with my right thigh against her left.

Chase was tired, but too fidgety to stay put. After only a few minutes he jumped up and began pacing, then sat again, and finally ordered us to start moving.

We pulled ourselves to our feet and started up the first hill. It was rough going in the dark, the ground covered with old leaves and duff that slid away beneath our feet. Chase had the worst time of all, skating back and nearly losing his balance several times. After the first hill I could hear his breathing every moment, shaky and strained.

My peace and resignation had evaporated, replaced by a mounting concern for JenBen. It wasn't my fault she was here, not really; it was Chase's fault, 'Berto's fault. But I felt responsible nonetheless, and the guilt sat uneasily atop the fear that already filled my belly.

The final downslope. I wouldn't have recognized the route, but once Linc set off for the ancient live-oak, I knew we were there.

He stopped in the wash below the tree and sat down on a rock.

"When the fuck we getting there?" Chase asked in a reedy voice.

"We're here."

"Well?"

"Let me catch my breath." Linc tilted his head back, stretching his neck. "No point in waiting, I suppose."

He scrambled up the slope toward the tree. Chase followed only as far as the edge of the sand, his gun poised in a shaky grip.

Linc pushed away leaves, rolled away rocks, and then came halfway back down the slope. "There it is," he said. "Help yourselves."

Chase took a step, then paused. "How's it stored?"

"Three big containers, stuffed into that tunnel."

"And?"

"And, nothing. They're just sitting there."

I heard Chase's breathing accelerate. "Fuck this. I ain't stickin' my hand in there. You bring 'em down here."

"My hand's fucked up!"

"'Berto. Go get the goods."

"Get it your own self, *cabron*."

Chase waved the revolver at Linc. "Just do it!"

Linc exhaled a weary breath and clambered back up the slope. He worked the big tin out of the tunnel, and then turned and carried it down to the wash, gripping it with his right hand, but using only the heel of his left. He stumbled once, and winced. He stepped off of the little shelf at the base of the slope and eased the tin down onto the ground. Without pause, he turned and headed up again, saying over his shoulder, "Have at it."

Chase and 'Berto looked down at the tin and exchanged a glance. Chase pointed to me with the gun. "You do it."

"I—I'm not sure I know how," I lied.

"Just fucking do it!"

'Berto backed out of the way and edged over to where JenBen sat, a dozen feet to my right. Chase moved a few feet back from the tin.

I knelt and started prying the lid open, willing myself not to look upslope despite the sounds—a dragging sound, a little fall of leaves and soil. I glanced up. Chase was looking up at Linc. "Shit," I said, tugging at the lid.

"What?" Chase asked, and backed away another foot.

The lid came up with a hollow pop, and I picked it up and gently poured the contents onto the sand.

At that moment Linc charged down the slope. Chase turned, gun raised, but Linc made a sound between a roar and a sob, and heaved the contents of the bucket right into Chase's face.

Chase screamed, and both hands went to his eyes, but then the gun hand came away, blindly pointed. He squeezed off a wild shot.

I hefted a smooth oblong stone in both hands and slammed it into the back of his head as hard as I could, and he crumpled to the ground.

Linc hit the sand still running and snatched up the revolver.

'Berto turned and ran, and to my surprise, JenBen threw her body off the rock and in front of his legs. He tripped over her, fell hard, but scrambled back onto his feet.

Linc aimed the gun and fired. 'Berto's leg collapsed under him and he went down.

He started crawling, whimpering, but Linc ran after him. "Linc, don't—" I began.

Linc caught up to him, leaned down, and shot him in the back of the head.

I went over to where Chase lay on his back. His face and hands looked as if he'd been in a fire, and blackish blood leaked from where I'd shattered his skull.

JenBen came up beside me. "Is he dead?"

My ears echoed from the gunshots. "I don't know."

Linc pushed between us. "Let's make sure." He pressed the gun to Chase's acid-burned forehead and blasted a dark crater in it.

18 | WHAT THEY NEVER SHOW YOU IN THE MOVIES

We never see the aftermath, do we? In the closing scene, the hero emerges from the smoking rubble and embraces the heroine; or the alien spacecraft gets zapped and crashes into the base of Mount Rushmore while the good guys cheer; or the serial killer gets shot, eviscerated, and finally, after lurching up from the floor for the second time, gets soaked in gasoline and plunges through the plate glass of a high-rise window, engulfed in flames—and all I can ever wonder, as the credits scroll, is, how are they going to explain all this tomorrow, and, more important, who on earth is going to clean up this mess?

We rolled the bodies out of the open and made our way back over the hills and down the night-clad road, arriving back at 'Berto's jacked-up Malibu well before midnight.

I sat on the rim of the plant bed outside the Redlands ER, thinking about taking up smoking; it would be nice to have something to do at such moments. The automatic doors whooshed open, and JenBen sat down beside me and interlaced her fingers with mine.

After a long silence, she said, "They seemed to buy his story—power saw, fall from the roof after he cut himself. They told him he should have brought the finger, they might have been able to reattach it."

I squeezed her hand. "You okay?"

"Yes and no. You?"

"I haven't figured it out yet. I killed somebody. Seems like I should feel different."

"I don't care that we killed them," she said. "I saw them cut off his finger. Fuck 'em, I'm glad they're dead." She sniffed. "But that it happened at all...I don't know."

"Me either."

We sat together until Linc staggered out of the hospital, professionally bandaged, blasted on painkillers but still upright from the bennies.

I thought I might never sleep again, but Linc woke me at seven the next morning. "Up," he said. "Work to do."

In the Impala I couldn't keep from staring at his gauze-wrapped hand on the steering wheel. He caught me at it and gave me a bleak smile. "Serpents in the Garden. There's always at least one."

"I don't know how I feel about all this—" I began.

"Later." He pulled into an Ace Hardware store.

We bought canvas tarps and rope, and drove out to Calimesa, where we rented horses and headed up the canyon.

It was filthy, nauseating work. Alberto's body was untouched except for his gunshot wounds, but the acid-scarred flesh of Chase's head continued to weep fluid even in death, and this had drawn a swarm of ants. We rolled him into a tarp, looped rope around the package, and then tied ropes to the grommets so we could haul him across the hills. At first I tried to be gentle, as if even a dead body could feel jolts and drops, but in the end the recalcitrance of his weight made me angry, and I was gratified when our burden thwomped down over a boulder or bashed into a treetrunk.

We hid him under a glossy-leafed laurel sumac, took a brief rest, and then headed back for Alberto.

With the two bodies strapped over our saddlehorns we must have looked like psychedelic bounty hunters riding in from the plains. How many times had I seen that on television—the wrapped body thrown over the horse? Watching it on the screen, you say, oh, look, he's bringing in a body...but in real life you keep glancing down, saying to yourself, it's a body, an actual body, a dead guy for chrissakes—! I wanted to talk to Linc about this, about all of this, but something in him had changed. He'd always been so easy to talk to, but now I was afraid to say anything.

We dumped the bodies a couple hundred yards up the trail, and Linc managed to force the Impala that far up the track. We loaded the bodies in the trunk, returned the horses, and drove to Mountain Home.

We arrived around noon, and JenBen was already there. I hugged her, and she hugged back; but there had been a long hesitation before her arms came around me.

At the side of the house, hidden by the trees, we moved the bodies from Linc's trunk into the trunk of 'Berto's Chevy.

I rode with Linc in the Chevy until we got to Palm Springs. After my third attempt to get a conversation going, he suggested that JenBen, following in her VW, probably needed company.

"How you holding up?" I asked, as we pulled up the long slope out of Morongo Valley.

She shrugged. "I'm okay."

"I can't get it out of my head. But I don't feel as bad as I think I should."

"I don't feel bad at all." She downshifted with a vicious movement. "Not about them."

We crested the grade and drove in silence through the town of Yucca Valley.

"I'll tell you, though," she said, "I don't want to live like this anymore."

"What do you mean by 'this?'"

"This. All of it. This, this chaos."

"And what happens to us?"

She glanced at me, then back at the road, but the eyes I'd seen were shuttered. She stroked my thigh with her hand. "Rick…*baby*…it isn't a good time to talk about things."

We flew through the playas and dustbowls surrounding Amboy, and turned off toward Cadiz—towns that barely warranted names. The only vegetation other than the occasional creosote bush was the long line of sad ironwoods that flanked the rail line.

Despite the shelter of the ironwoods, the rails were laid on a high berm here, a dozen feet above the grade as a defense against drifting dunes. The slopes of the berm were covered with rip-rap, crushed stone, to slow erosion.

Linc crossed the tracks and eased his car onto a dirt road that paralleled the rails. He climbed out, had JenBen park her car near the tracks, and then the three of us drove the Malibu a mile down the unmaintained dirt road, my throat tight every time the tires spun in the loose sand.

Linc stopped alongside a trio of blackened ironwoods, scorched by some inscrutable fire. We buried the bodies in a largely vanished ditch at the base of the berm, climbing high on the slope and starting little rip-rap avalanches to pour stones down onto the canvas bundles. Such a little-kid thing to do, and in service of such a macabre task. It almost made me laugh.

Almost.

We ditched the Malibu along a crowded street in Indio, certain that such a jacked-up pachuchomobile would be stolen in a matter of days, if not hours; not as quickly as a low-rider, but fast enough to solve our problems.

Once the Chevy was parked, Linc climbed into the rear of JenBen's Bug. "We won't tell anyone," he said. "Not anyone, right?" After JenBen and I nodded, he curled up on the backseat and collapsed into a slumber that approached coma. When I thought about it, it wasn't surprising: he'd orchestrated everything, from the moment they'd marched us to the Mother Lode to the time we'd parked their car, needing every move to be perfect.

I wondered if he hadn't worked through some aspects of this scenario before.

I sat down on the corner of Linc's bed. He lay there on his stomach, reading, and he waited to finish a paragraph before he inserted a bookmark and closed the book—Clarke's *Profile of the Future*. He rolled over and sat up. "Well?"

"Just wanted to talk. You haven't been to school in days. I don't care if you go or not, but I'm getting sick of riding the bus." He rewarded me with a weak smile. "Seriously. You don't talk. A taciturn Lincoln Ellard is a contradiction in terms."

He shifted himself on the bed so his shoulders leaned against the flimsy headboard; it creaked back until it rested on the wall. "I'm okay," he said. "Just thinking."

"But you don't do anything. Just shuffle around."

"I'm still getting laid."

That was true enough; he still disappeared into his bedroom with Lisby or Beth or Melissa. But to me it looked like a matter of habit rather than desire. I took a deep breath. "Linc…I want you know how sorry I am. It's my fault, I know. I chose Alberto. And then—well, I just fucked up everything. I'd do anything to take it all back, I'd—"

He didn't look up from the bedspread, but he was shaking his head before I was half finished. His voice when he interrupted me was mild. "No. Not your fault. I see now that this was inevitable. If it hadn't been them, it would have been someone else." I started to object, but he raised his palm, just a little, in the attitude of Buddha calming the waters. "My whole approach to…all of this, it's been naïve. Dangerously naïve. Human consciousness doesn't evolve just because it's given the opportunity. Oh, some people want to take the next step. But for most people, a more charitable environment is just an opportunity for greed and powermongering."

This wasn't the talk that I'd needed to have with him. "Doesn't it bother you? That we…killed them, I mean?"

He tilted his head to the side as if watching something crawl across the bed. "Not really. That was their fault, wasn't it? What bothers me is that something like this was bound to happen. Serpents in the Garden, there are always Serpents in the Garden. You're different, I'm different, but people in general don't change their consciousness unless the environment forces them to. The Ice Age. Agriculture. Urbanization.

So the real question is, how do we shape the next step?" He finally met my eyes. "It isn't about how to turn people on. It's about how to change their environment, and the tools they bring to bear on that environment." His gaze drifted down to the cover of the book.

"I don't understand." I didn't really care, but I wanted to keep him talking.

"Neither do I. Not yet. But something's getting ready to emerge. Communications, media, computers…McLuhan's Global Village. Don't know. Don't see it yet."

"Linc. I'm worried about you."

He looked up and smiled at me, a calm, sad smile. "I'll be okay. I'll be okay, and you'll be okay, too." He picked up the book and opened it on his lap.

Perhaps Lincoln Ellard would be fine, but I wasn't. At unexpected moments my mind flew into the air, over the mountains, and far out across the desert playas, zooming in on the berm supporting the railway, focusing on the endless strip of grey-black rip-rap with the objectivity of a movie camera, and then, when I remembered what lay beneath those rocks, my stomach would drop, guilt and fear and doubt mixing me a vertiginous cocktail.

JenBen was no more forthcoming than Lincoln. I saw her at school, and we even spent time together during breaks, but she was mostly silent. She hadn't come up to Mountain Home since she dropped us off after our drive to the desert, and now I pressed her to come see me.

In my bedroom, I reached for her, but she shrugged me away. "Not now," she said.

"Okay. Do you want to talk about it?"

"Truthfully? No."

"Jen…I keep thinking about it—"

"My advice is don't."

I pulled her to me and kissed her, but she broke it off. "I don't want to. Not now."

"You don't want to talk, you don't want to mess around. What did you come over for, then?"

"I was wondering that myself." She stood.

"Jen—I didn't mean that the way it came out—" I jumped up from the bed.

She backed off a few paces. "I know." She started to say something, but the words didn't come. Standing there, she looked tiny, a child with weary eyes. "Rick. I'm not sure we should… Look, I just need to think, okay? Let's not get mean. Let's just leave it alone for a little while." I started to answer, but her expression stopped me: "Please?"

Is there a way to say no to that?

―――― ∽ ――――

Our Tuesday and Thursday gatherings evaporated. Folks still dropped through, willing to party even if nothing were scheduled, but the limp atmosphere in the house soon drove away all but the most determined. Smoking hash turned me inward in a scary way, dwelling on what had happened; I had the crazy urge to tell someone, as if fellow high-schoolers might have the power to shrive my soul. I soon gave up toking, and, though I toyed with the idea that a hit of acid might be cathartic, in my heart I knew it would be catabolic, causing a breakdown from which recovery would be like trying to unscramble an egg. My strongest urge was to get shitfaced drunk, but I feared what I might do or say.

With JenBen gone, at least for the moment, and Lincoln present yet absent, the two main props had been kicked from beneath my life, and I teetered, trying not to let anyone see me flailing my arms. Only a month before I'd been so cool, confident that I was riding the biggest wave of them all. Now I saw that Leslie had been right: None of us were as smart, attractive, or edgy as I'd believed. Well, edgy: we were edgy, all right, drugs and sex and a life unmoored from the daily concerns of the world around us; and, hell, now we'd killed some people. Edgy we could manage.

What did I do? Mostly school. I didn't know where else to put my energy and anxiety, so I studied. Laughable, really; with the exception of the fact that my job at the Ellard's nursery was bogus, I was everything that Leo could have desired: studious, chaste, clean, and sober. Through no desire of my own, I'd been transformed, for the moment, into a poster child for the rehabilitative power of the juvenile justice system.

Lisby was around the house many evenings, but she wasn't often with Linc except when they were actually fucking—Linc had manifested a new and astonishing ability to suck the air right out of a room without saying anything. Some nights she'd come out of his bedroom and sit on the couch, reading while I studied, and we seemed like some long-married couple on a winter night in the Great Plains—companionable but mostly silent, each sitting in their private pool of lamplight while night breezes creaked through the trees. But other nights she was wasted, despairing beyond the point of strong emotion, wobbling her way to the couch with a bloodstream-full of Seconal or booze. "When's he going to come back?" she'd ask, and I had no answer.

Her friend Karen Hillman lived a little over a mile away, in a well-known party house, and some nights Lisby would decide to stagger on over there. I'd usually tag along, to make sure she got there, and to keep anything disastrous from happening at the party. Oscar Wilde once said that he drank to make other people more interesting, and Karen's house taught me the truth of that; the crowd over there had no pretensions of doing anything other than getting wiped out, and it was unspeakably boring to watch when clean and sober. At the end of the night I'd get Lisby a ride to her home with a reliable party, or get her back to our place and bed her down: in Linc's bed if he didn't have another girl in it, or if he hadn't simply locked the door (which he had taken to doing), and under a pile of blankets in the guest room if Linc was unavailable.

After a few weeks of this, I decided perhaps this was what people meant when they talked about *maturity*: continuing to slog along, going through the motions, doing your job, even when there were no reasons to believe that things would ever improve.

I wrote Randi a dozen letters; wrote a dozen, and finally worked up the guts to send one off. I'm not sure if it was courage or resignation that finally urged me to the mailbox. The letter was as balanced as I could make it; I told her how much I missed her, how much I thought about her, but without making demands or exerting too much pressure—the furthest I went was to suggest that, if she weren't coming home over the Thanksgiving break, I might ride the bus or thumb up to see her.

Nearly a month had passed since violence had invaded our lives. Linc still hadn't returned to school. JenBen still hadn't returned to my bed.

I met with Leo for the second time since we'd buried 'Berto and Chase, my conscience clear except for the minor matter of having been involved in a double murder. I half-expected him to be accompanied by police detectives who would read me my rights, but instead he was alone and upbeat, pleased at my progress in school, and relieved that I hadn't drawn the attention of the authorities.

Meeting with Leo meant missing the bus. I wandered down to the Park to look for a ride. Slim pickings; the October time-change had taken effect, and twilight was already settling down, bringing with it a cold breeze that made me hug my jacket to my sides.

Two figures in thick coats sat huddled on a picnic bench, their bottoms on the tabletop and their shoes on the seat. I slanted downhill toward them, and recognized Melissa, and, to my surprise, Leslie.

They greeted me pleasantly enough, but I'd obviously interrupted a private discussion. "Just wanted to see if I could beg a ride off either of you—no big deal."

"Be happy to," Leslie said, "but we're in the middle of something. Can you come back in maybe half an hour?"

So I did. I spent the interim in a baseball dugout atop the slope, sitting backwards on the steps so there would be light enough to read the second volume of Asimov's *Foundation* trilogy. Linc had successfully expanded my reading tastes, and not in a direction approved by the *New York Times Review of Books*.

I came downslope; Melissa and Leslie hugged goodbye; and Leslie and I piled into her Mustang and turned on the heater.

Once we were on Oak Glen Road, once she'd cranked the heater down and we'd both struggled out of our coats, Leslie said, "I'd been hoping to run into you. Wanted to ask a question." She glanced my way, and I nodded. "Is there something between your dad and my stepmom?" I waited too long before answering, and she asked, "Is it none of my business?"

"No. I just—well, why do you ask?"

"Because my father and Sue have been fighting a lot the last few days. I can't hear them well enough to follow the conversations, but I keep hearing your dad's name come up."

"Do I have to answer?"

"No. But that seems like an answer itself."

It did. And if Leslie weighed in on the fight between her father and stepmother, it might screw up my precarious standoff with my father. "Leslie. Please. Please. If you say anything about this, it could ruin my life."

"Are you serious?"

"Very."

"Huh." She turned onto Bryant Street, the broad avenue that ran across the lap of the hills.

I decided to change the subject. "Have you written to Randi yet?"

"No. But you were right. I've talked to Melissa, talked to some other people." A sardonic smile, barely visible in the dark. "Nobody thinks I'm as big a deal as I do. Sad, I guess. A relief, too. Have you? Written to Randi, I mean?"

"Yeah." I leaned against the car door, feeling the cold glass on my cheek. "It's probably useless, though. It's so unfair. Just because I'm 'too young' for her."

Leslie laughed, a big, throaty laugh. "Ah, Rick, you make me feel like such an idiot. When you came over to my house, I must have sounded as stupid as you do now."

I failed to see any analogy, so I sputtered a little in response. "You don't understand. I'm, that is, I— She doesn't take me seriously. Because I'm just fifteen."

"You think it's really the age?"

"Yeah. Partly."

"You're probably right," she said, and drove on in silence.

"What is it?" I asked.

"Hmm? Nothing. I just said you were probably right."

"But you don't mean it."

She wheeled the car onto Highway 38, nearly deserted this time of day, and headed through the gates of the mountains into the dark of the narrow valley. "Leslie," I asked, "will you just tell me whatever it is?"

A nod of the head. She continued driving for a minute and then steered us into a pullout, turned off the lights, and cut the engine. She hiked her right leg up onto the seat, knee bent, so she could turn to face me. "I don't know how to say this without sounding mean…"

"It's about Randi, isn't it?"

"No." The headlights of an approaching car on the highway grew steadily brighter, and then sharp-edged shadows chased the light across her face. "It's not that you're young, it's that you *seem* young. Why do you think girls fall in love with boys? What do you think they want?"

"I don't know. Someone to love them back, mostly, I suppose."

"That'd be convenient, but no." She touched my arm, and I thought of a doctor breaking bad news. "Rick…look, you've got a lot going for you. You're good-looking…"—this had me blinking in surprise, since no one, of either sex, had ever suggested such a thing, and I had to jog mentally to catch up—"…and you're smart, and you listen, better than any boy I've met, and you're really good at letting girls know how much you like them. But you don't give people the sense that you're headed anywhere."

Somehow she had jabbed me in an injured place I didn't know I had, and I winced. "Are you telling me that's what it's about?" I asked. "What kind of job I'm going to get? How well I'll be able to support some little wifey?"

"Rick, calm down."

"I am calm."

"You're practically shouting." I wanted to dispute this, but I realized it was true, so I shut my mouth and waited for her to continue. "You're not understanding me. I'm not talking about money, I'm talking about a sense of purpose. You don't have anything that you really seem to care about."

Drugs and sex came to mind, but it didn't seem like these would help make my case. "Books," I said. "I read…and I'm part of Linc's whole thing, the salon, and…"

"You read. So what? Do you want to write, or study literature, or is it just like fancy TV for you?" That hurt, and I felt as if I were shrinking. "And Linc's whole thing—and I have my doubts about it—is just that, Linc's thing. Not yours."

"So nothing's important unless you can turn it into a job? Is that what you're saying?"

"Rick, you're not listening. I'm not saying girls are looking for someone with job prospects—though god knows, some of them are. But think of all the women who've fallen in love with painters or poets. I'm talking about a, a governing passion, a sense of purpose."

I didn't want to hear it. I folded my arms over my chest and sat there in the dark, trying to logic my way around what felt like emotional truth. At long last, I played the equity card, as if convincing this one female of something would change the way the world worked. "But that isn't fair. Boys don't look for that in girls. We don't demand some talent or goal, we just want someone who…" I tapered off as I realized I had no idea why I was drawn to anyone; or to any *thing*, for that matter.

"You're right," she said. She started the engine. "It isn't fair. It isn't sensible. Isn't even symmetrical. Look what a disaster I've been. Can you imagine a boy getting so messed up over fucking a bunch of girls?"

"So all I have to do is figure out what my life's all about?" My voice was half-serious, half-petulant. "Just get out there and discover my destiny, and women will fall at my feet?"

Leslie pulled on the headlights and eased the car back onto the empty highway. "They may not fall at your feet," she said, "but you'll seem less like a little kid."

That shut me up.

19 | A BONFIRE MIGHT FEEL GOOD

Lisby spent more and more nights stoned, and her arguments with Linc became louder and whinier—though only on her part. Linc was more soft-spoken by the day, quiet and remote, barely making contact. There were evenings where I held Lisby on the couch while she sobbed, and other nights, too many other nights, when I walked with her as she stumbled over to Karen's, where she proceeded to lay a couple of beers on top of whatever downers she'd ingested. I'd beg a ride and half-carry, half-drag her into our house, and put her to bed in her clothes.

Late one afternoon I came in to what I'd thought was an empty house, only to hear a noise from the sleeping porch. Lisby was back there, apparently sober, sitting crosslegged on the floor in a pair of shorts. I started to say hello, and then noticed the blood on the shiny hardwood, the razorblade in her fingers, the crimson, leaking lines traced down the inside of her calf. "Jesus, Lisby! What the fuck are you doing?"

She smiled, an indulgent, sloppy smile. "Just fooling around."

I ran to the bathroom, gathered up towels and Band-Aids, and ran back. I knelt, pried the blade from her fingers. "Jesus, Lisby," I whispered, over and over, "Jesus, Lisby, *why*?"

She let me move her around like a poseable doll, and I eventually pushed her onto her back and rolled her onto her side so I could deal with her right calf. None of the cuts were deep, but they were horrible:

long thin incisions in her perfect young skin. I had to wipe the welling blood away, stick down a Band-Aid, and then wipe again to do the next three inches. I trembled as I worked, fumbling to tear the Band-Aids from their crinkly wrappers and peel back the plastic non-stick strips, my body alert with fear and sick with feelings I couldn't even name.

"Why are you crying?" she asked, in a dazed, little-girl voice.

"I'm not," I said, through my swollen throat.

"But you *are*."

"Shut up, Lisby," I managed to say. "*Please*. Shut up."

When I had the bleeding stopped, I asked, "Why?"

She laughed without enthusiasm, still on her side looking across the polished floor, not at me. "Who knows? You're one to ask."

"But—" I almost said, *but you're a girl*. I almost said, *but look at your skin, your poor, perfect, beautiful skin—how* could *you?* What I said instead was, "It isn't worth it. He isn't worth it."

Her voice was distant, dreamy. "But Randi is? JenBen?"

"Lisby—" I tried to muster an argument, failed. So weary I could no longer sit upright, I slumped down onto my side on the floor and gathered her slashed, bandaged calf gently into my arms, bringing it to my chest and holding it as if it were the torso of a lover. I cradled it there and kissed her knee. "Lisby, please." It was painful to swallow, even more painful to speak. "No more. No more. Please."

She said nothing, but I felt her fingers stroke my hair.

My shirt soaked up Lisby's blood from the floorboards, warm at first, but then chilling against my flesh. Still I lay there, cherishing her injured limb in my arms, embracing it, and for a sad, luminescent moment, it was everything I'd wanted to hold but had lost, Stacy, JenBen, Randi; my brother, my sister, my mother.

<hr />

From Randi, the expected letter. She cared about me, she'd had fun with me, and maybe we'd even have fun some day again…but we were in different worlds right now, plus she'd warned me not to get too romantic; and Thanksgiving vacation? Sorry. She wasn't coming down, and, unfortunately, she'd agreed to go up the Sierras with some friends for the skiing.

Right. As if she knew how to ski.

You don't think, gee, I guess I'll go cut myself now. It's sort of a trance, but almost closer to absentmindedness. I'd only been in the bathroom to brush my teeth, but when I paid attention I saw that I'd started the tip of the scissors across my arm, leaving a trail of bright red, and then, remembering Lisby's leg, I threw them to the floor, clenched my fists, and, as if the energy had to go into some form of pain, slammed my forehead against the wall, right beside the mirrored medicine cabinet. Once. Then again.

Twice was enough. After the second time, my hands clutched the top of my head and I swore, dancing from foot to foot.

Cutting was entrancing, slow, and strange, with most of the pain delayed; somehow artistic, with the breathless wait as the skin opened like a theater curtain and the crimson bloomed forth.

Hammering your head against the wall, on the other hand, put self-injury in perspective: it hurt; it was stupid.

Yeah, boy, that'll show 'em.

I opened the bathroom door and Linc stood in the center of the living room, an armful of electronics texts under his arm and a puzzled expression on his face. I grinned, embarrassed, and he gave a perfunctory smile and headed for the front door. Off to the library, no doubt; he never went anywhere else these days unless he was giving a girlfriend a ride home.

I took some aspirin and settled down on the sofa with a book. When I heard a car pull up later, I assumed it was Linc returning, but instead there was a polite rap on the door, and then Leslie's head, peering in. "Come on," I said, waving her in.

She settled into the armchair beside me. Her expression was hard to decipher—a mixture of caution and something sly, possibly suppressed amusement. She searched my face, found it guileless, and then said, "Heard from your father since he left?"

My mind had gone in many directions—she'd heard something from Randi, she'd found out what had really gone on, or not gone on, with JenBen, she'd heard something from Casey, she wanted to talk more about her night at the Palitzers' party, even that she'd somehow learned about Alberto and Chase. News about my father hadn't been one of the possibilities. "Left? For where?"

The blank stupidity on my face made her laugh, a laugh she cut short. "Sorry. I haven't really thought this through. I guess I thought you'd be as much pleased as surprised."

"I'm...surprised."

"I said you would be." She responded to the question on my face. "My dad actually asked if I'd see if you knew anything about it." She made a face as if she'd just sucked a lemon. "As if I'd narc on you, anyway."

"What happened?"

"Your dad's been embezzling money from the company. And then he vanished."

I shook my head. "Not possible. I mean, he's the swing-shift supervisor—he doesn't have access to any money."

"Oh, but he does. Did. Pick-ups and deliveries go on all evening. Somebody has to be able to write checks after five. And the last couple of weeks, the accounting people started catching up with him."

Questions rushed through my mind like a flock of birds startled from their roost. Of all the queries that milled before me, I chose, absurdly, "How much did he take?"

"They're not sure yet. At least ten, maybe fifteen thousand. Maybe more. And he had almost ten from selling your house down in Redlands. They still haven't found all his bank accounts. But they're sure he left with at least twenty thousand dollars. Might even be thirty."

I sat back on the couch, and, to my own astonishment, began laughing. The sonofabitch. The evil sonofabitch. You had to admire him. In his view, Mal Andrews, and all the Mal Andrews of the world, had screwed him out of his business. And he'd spent the last two years fucking Mal's wife and stealing his money.

Style. Low-down, junkyard, trailer-park style, but style nonetheless.

What did this do to me? I had no idea. Perhaps it freed me. Or perhaps now, without a legal guardian, Leo would be forced to pull me back into Juvie and hold me there until I was either emancipated or placed in a foster home. In any case, an event beyond my control... and funny.

"Rick?" A pause. "Rick? Is this a problem? Are you okay?"

"I haven't had a drink in weeks. You want a drink?"

"Sure." She stared at me the way a cat might watch a bouncing balloon, fascinated by the motion, but also ready to flee. "I'm not sure I understand what's going on with you right now..."

"Me either."

I went to the kitchen, mixed two gin-tonics, and came back, my mind made up. "Got some time?" I asked. "Want to hear a story?"

I told her everything about my family. I told her about my mother's disappearance, the fact that she'd had children by someone other than my father, the fact that she'd taken them and left me behind. I told her about the collapse of the egg ranch, which my father attributed to machinations by rich owners like her own father. I told her about how I ended up in Juvie, how I ended up in Yucaipa, and about the day that I surprised my father and her stepmother on our living-room couch. I told her about the weird, slick blackmail Linc had imposed on Sue, pressuring her to pressure my father to leave me alone for once. And I told her about Leo, and the fact that I had been headed toward Emancipated Minor status, and that I had no idea what the hell this latest development meant.

"Amazing." She pondered a moment, and asked, "Can I tell my dad about Sue and your father?"

"He doesn't know? I thought you said they were arguing about him a while back."

"Yeah. But I think now that they were just fighting about the money he was stealing. Sue does some kind of stuff with the books." She sat upright. "Hey. You don't suppose she knew, or helped?"

I gave a whole-body shrug. "Who knows? But Leslie...?"

"Yeah?"

"If you can resist telling your dad about Sue...I'd appreciate it."

"What difference does it make?"

"I don't know. Maybe none. But I still feel like I owe her, sort of. It's hard to explain."

"I'll try to keep my mouth shut if that's what you really want. But she and your dad both seem like they deserve anything that might happen to them. They're hateful."

Sue had always been nice enough to me...but, then, there were people who thought my dad was a great guy, too. "I'm not sure I want everybody to get what they deserve. I'm not sure I want to get what *I* deserve. Let it lie, if you can." I took a long drink, and after weeks of abstinence the alcohol stormed the gates of my mind. "I don't know why he hated me so much, anyway. Makes no sense."

"Maybe he saw himself in you. Maybe he wanted to hurt himself."

I snorted. "Doubt it. I heard enough crap like that from school counselors when I was twelve. I don't think people decide to punish themselves."

"No? I've done things that are hard for me to explain without self-hurting being at least part of the picture. And you know what I mean."

"Seems like you'd be more sympathetic to Sue, then."

That stopped her for a moment. "Maybe I should be, then... My point is that people do things you can't explain except in terms of self-hurting." I made a wry face and started to respond, when she glanced at the Band-Aid on my forearm, and added, "I've even heard of people who cut themselves up. Try and explain that any other way."

In the long silence I sought for a reply, and found none. Eventually Leslie rescued me by saying, "The authorities have all your dad's stuff locked up right now, searching for—well, I don't know what, but searching his stuff. In a couple of weeks, though, they should be done, and my stepmonster says you can come take whatever you want."

"I don't need anything from him."

"Still, worth a look, don't you think? Maybe there's something of your mom's."

"I don't need anything from her either."

"Doesn't hurt to look, though."

"Might."

"And this is the brave knight who wants to sweep Randi Mayfield off her feet? C'mon, Rick." She couldn't know about the letter, but she could see from the way I stiffened that she'd hurt me. "Sorry. That was over the line. But, hell, think of it as cleaning up. Think of it as, as an exorcism. And anything you don't want…you can put it in a big pile and burn it all."

I nodded, mulling it over. A bonfire might feel good.

※

"You believe in reincarnation?" Lisby asked. The street leading to Karen's house lay beneath an arch of pines so tightly interlocked that not a scrap of moonlight made it to the ground; Lisby's face was hidden, but I could hear a Seconal slur creeping into her voice.

"I don't know." I hunched deeper into my coat and picked up my pace, hoping she'd match it. "Lisby, are you on downers again? Already?"

She continued to saunter as if it were a summer evening. "Little. Just a little."

"You should cool it."

"I know. 'n I don't care."

We heard Karen's cottage before we could see it. Set well to the east of other homes in Mountain View, it sat inside the edge of the wash as if challenging nature to wipe it away. Music—Zeppelin—pushed through the night air, muffled but not contained by the walls of the house.

We passed out of the trees and onto the ghostly sands, and followed the dirt drive toward the lights. "I care about you," I said, "even if you don't."

"'n I care 'bout you, too. But I don't tell you what to do, do I?"

A half-dozen cars, the usual assortment of bored dopers looking for something to do. We were greeted lackadaisically, and I slumped down on the sofa. Donnie Briscoe sat at the other end, and he gave me a sullen nod that, by his standards, was positively cordial. Lisby had grabbed a beer and seated herself at the dining room table with Karen and some of the other girls.

I dug out my paperback copy of Sappho's poems, the Mary Barnard translation, and tried to shut Robert Plant's screaming falsetto from my ears. I'd picked up the book on a lark, expecting and hoping for something more salacious. I was surprised to find her verses both beautiful and hard-edged; and from what I could tell from the poems themselves, the poetess had loved and celebrated men and women equally—indeed, in many of her verses the gender of her object of desire isn't apparent.

> I confess
> I love that
> which caresses me…

In those few words she impaled me on the point of her quill. My problem exactly: caress me and you had my heart, it seemed. A terrible way to live.

The front door sprang open with a rush of chill air, and Rob barged into the room, holding a Sears shopping bag over his head like a trophy. I put away my book; no chance of reading once Rob arrived on the scene.

I soon forgave him. He had two new albums, just released in October, and each turned out to be a musical landmark. The first was *Santana*, a riveting fusion of Latin and rock, bound together by one of the most distinctive guitar styles in history. Those of us who weren't wiped out on downers stopped talking, reading, smoking, captured by the music. A dead silence as he flipped the record over, the hiss as the needle found its track, and then, amazingly, a second side as good as the first.

Most of us clamored to hear it over again, right then, but Rob insisted he wanted to hear his other purchase first: *In the Court of the Crimson King, An Observation by King Crimson*.

What can I say? Parts of it today sound overblown, other parts a little bit precious, but the relentless power of edgy guitar and screaming saxophone coupled with the sweep of the symphonic structure… We were flattened, destroyed. When the album was over, there was a long silence, and then everyone began talking at once; everyone but me, that is. I slumped lower on the couch and stared at the ceiling, trying to absorb what I'd just experienced.

When I came out of my reverie, I noticed Lisby leaning on the wall near the front door with Donnie hovering over her. She was zonked, beer on top of Reds being a short and reliable ride to oblivion. Donnie wasn't much better off, wobbly on his feet, but edging up to her.

God knows why I'd appointed myself the guardian of Lisby's non-existent chastity, but the idea of Donnie luring her off somewhere and fucking her while she was in a barbiturate haze made me sick. I jumped up and strolled over, adopting a false casual tone. "What's up, guys?"

"*There* you warr..." Lisby said, as if I'd ever been more than twenty feet away from her. She leaned toward me and clung onto my arm, and Donnie's eyes narrowed. "Donnie says he can gimme a ride. Ride home. Or whatever. You too, I bet."

"Yeah," he said, "going down'a hill anyway." He was more stoned than I'd realized. In sexual terms, Lisby was probably safe with him; he'd be so limp that he wouldn't be able to penetrate a bowl of whipped cream. But she sure as hell wouldn't be safe riding back to town with him driving.

I patted Lisby's clinging arm. "Let's just walk on back to the house, okay?"

"No. Don't wanna walk. 's too far. Too cold."

After some slurred debate, I reluctantly agreed that Donnie could drive us back to the house, and Lisby promised to spend the night rather than heading back to Yucaipa.

If there had been another car on the road, Donnie would have hit it. He weaved down the narrow streets, drifting to one side and then overcorrecting by twisting the steering wheel in the other direction. We winged a mailbox, and dragged the passenger side along the front of a hedge. He pulled up at our house and accidentally parked by letting the clutch pop out, killing the engine.

I helped Lisby out of the car, and then, feeling a certain responsibility to innocent drivers—and, okay, maybe even to Donnie—I said, "Maybe you should come in and crash, too, man. As wasted as you are, you're going to get pulled over."

His face turned mean for a moment, clearly ready to tell me that he was in great shape to drive. Then he noticed Lisby hanging on my shoulder, slack and pliant against me, and changed his mind, hoping, I suppose, for another bite at the apple. "Yeah. Yeah, man, thanks."

Linc's bedroom door was closed, as usual these days, but it sounded occupied by more than him. Melissa or Beth, no doubt.

I left Donnie sitting on the couch while I put Lisby to bed out on the sleeping porch. I was uncomfortable having him there, and I felt as if I ought to stand guard outside Lisby's door to keep him from inviting himself in. By the time I had her tucked in and made it out to the living room, though, Donnie was face-down on the couch, drooling.

I tossed a blanket over him and went off to my own bed.

The yelling and pounding woke me, and my first reaction was that the police had raided us at last.

Then I recognized Lisby's voice.

I stepped into the hallway, wearing only boxers. Lisby hammered on Linc's door with the flat of her palm. "Come on," she sobbed, "come out here…"

The door swung away from her in a sudden jerk. Linc stared from the darkened room, his face expressionless, almost serene. "Lisby. You're a mess."

"I know. I know." She swayed. "I need to see you. I need it. I just…need it. Need to talk."

"Not now." His lips formed more words, but no sounds came. He took a long, smooth inhale through his nostrils. "Look at you. You can't talk now anyway." He shook his head, like a disappointed parent. "Not tonight. I'll see you tomorrow."

He shut the door and locked it. Lisby slapped her palm against the door, once, twice, three times. "Linc, please…I can't live without you!" She pressed her face to the wood, crying hard. "Please, please…" She slid down to the floor and lay against the doorframe, her words going incoherent beneath her tears.

I hoisted her to her feet, retrieved her purse from the floor, and led her to my bed. I sat beside her in the dark and petted her hair until the tears stopped. "Sorry, Rick," she said, words slurring.

I glanced at the clock. It was two in the morning; she shouldn't still be this loaded.

"It's okay. Lisby, did you do some more Reds?"

"Only a little." She sniffled. "Only two."

I pushed open her purse and saw the long roll of aluminum foil, Reds packed into it like bullets in an ammunition belt. A roll of twenty, with flat places where two were missing.

I patted her shoulder. "You should get some sleep. Let's get you back in your bed."

"No." She held onto my arm as if I might leap away. "Lemme stay here. Just lay down next to me." She tugged. "Don't wanna be alone."

I scooted her over and lay down beside her. She draped an arm across my chest and snuggled her wet face against my shoulder. The Seconal took full hold then, and she slept, boneless, barely breathing.

In the dream I was with Randi, but something about it was slightly askew, and I woke to find Lisby naked, kissing me.

"Lisby—" Still groggy, I managed to say, "No, no, this isn't a good idea…"

"Please, Rick. Please." She lifted herself onto an elbow, and her tears fell on my face. "Preten' I'm somebody else…"

"It isn't that. I just don't think—"

"*Please*. Do it 'cause you're my friend." She kissed me, and rolled me on top of her, and no matter what I thought about it, my body was more than ready.

I didn't know how it was for her. I hated it. I hated it even while it felt as good as it had ever been. She fucked me desperately, still crying, and every so often she said Linc's name, and I wasn't sure if she were calling for him, or blaming him, or pretending that she was with him, but her sobs sent little clenches down through her belly, seizing me like a skilled yet heartless masseuse, and then she came, a horrible, joyless orgasm, and wrapped her arms and legs around me, sobbing, and just clung there. My erection, still not discharged, slowly went soft inside her, but it wasn't until she slept again that I could ease out of her.

A full bladder woke me a little before four. Lisby was gone.

I padded to the bathroom, pissed, wandered into the living room. Donnie still snored on the couch.

Linc's door was open. Maybe he'd taken her home when he took Melissa or Beth down the hill. I peeked in. Lisby's purse lay on the bed.

A sheet of notebook paper lay on one of the pillows. Curious, I walked over, leaned down, and read a sloppy scrawl: *I told you I couldn't live without you.*

Blankness, and then a wave of fear. I dashed onto the sleeping porch. Nothing. I ran to the center of the living room and gaped side to side as if she might be hiding there.

I found her on the kitchen floor, slumped against the drawers. She'd dressed herself and brushed her hair.

Her fingertips were icy blue in the dimness. A dried line of vomit had drooled from her mouth and onto her blouse. I willed her to be breathing, but it seemed too much to hope for. I fell to my knees beside her, crying, and, when I seized her hand in mine she made a choking noise. I hugged her and I felt her slow heartbeat against my chest.

Alive. Alive, but dying there in my arms.

No phone. No Linc. I thought fast, and probably not well. Run to a neighboring house and call an ambulance. I pictured the ambulance racing up from Redlands, and then meandering for precious minutes through the tangle of Mountain Home lanes. I pictured the explanations, the police, the inevitable search of the house, the discovery that two minors were living there alone…

Donnie had to drive.

I ran to the living room and shook him, rolled him onto his back and sat him upright on the couch. "Wha…?" He was still groggy.

"We have to take Lisby to the hospital. Now! She's dying."

He slobbered something incoherent and tried to shove me away. I shook him hard and yelled.

He took a swing at my face, a clumsy punch that landed on my shoulder. There was no chance he'd be driving anywhere.

I jerked him off the couch and dumped him onto the floor. He struggled, but I sat backwards on his chest, my knees pinning his arms, and fished in his pants pockets until I snagged his keyring. I jumped to my feet and charged into the kitchen.

"You fugger—!" he said. He tried to rise to his feet, slipped, and fell, banging his head on the coffee table.

I lifted Lisby in my arms. So light, so light and so frail. I writhed my shoulder down so I could reach under her and open the front door, and then I hurried down the steps and out to Donnie's old Chevy, leaving the door open behind me spilling light and heat onto the dark porch. I lay Lisby on her side on the front seat and then climbed behind the wheel.

I wasn't a driver, but I knew the rudiments. My father had even tried to teach me to drive his pickup once, heckling me as I fumbled with the clutch and gearshift. I pushed the clutch to the floor, turned the ignition, pressed the gas. The car roared to life. I let out the clutch, let it out too fast, and the car lurched and died. I repeated the process, and this time the ignition cranked, a repetitive mocking whine. Was this what they meant by flooding an engine?

I stopped and waited a moment, my forehead resting against the top of the steering wheel. Stupid. Stupid. I should just run next door, now, damn the consequences, Lisby was dying while I screwed around trying to drive…

The car started. I eased the clutch out, pressed on the gas, and the car hopped forward like a gargantuan bunny, but this time I kept the accelerator down and the car actually moved down the street—slowly, with a lugging sensation as if we were dragging a load of logs. I released the handbrake, and the car sped forward, whining in protest at being confined to first gear.

I steered all the way to the highway in first, unwilling to try shifting on an upslope, and then held my breath and, without pausing at the stop sign, turned left and headed toward town.

Rolling along, I felt more confident, and shifted neatly into second. I ground the gears horribly searching for third, and then made it into fourth, leaning forward, scanning the dark road.

Lights. That was the problem. I felt for the knob to the left of the steering column, and suddenly I had headlights.

I pushed the gas, up to sixty, then seventy. We were alone on the highway. I'd stay there as long as I could, down through Mentone, down Lugonia Avenue, turning south to Redlands Community Hospital only at the last minute. I made up my mind not to stop, not for stop-signs, not for red lights; I'd slow and look, but I couldn't risk killing the engine again. If the police pulled me over, so much the better; now that we were away from the house, the police would be welcome.

I roared through the strip-town of Mentone at seventy-five, and then into the shadowy groves of eastern Redlands. No police. Not even another car. Driving was a matter of keeping the wheel pointed straight ahead.

Now that the car was under control, my whole body shook. I reached down and touched Lisby's hair. "Don't die," I whispered, barely able to get the words out. I put my hand over her face and felt the faint moisture of her breath on my palm. I took my hand back and put it on the wheel. "Don't die," I said, louder.

At Tennessee Street I executed a left turn while running a red light, but had to brake so hard that the engine lugged. I slammed in the clutch, fumbled with the shift, and ended up in a screaming second gear. I got into third and decided to stay there, the engine wailing except when I slowed for corners.

At the hospital I turned right and drove down the side street, then steered toward the covered entryway under the red lights spelling out *EMERGENCY*. I coasted the final twenty yards, clutch in, the other foot ready on the brake. I halted and, in my hurry to get out, opened the car door and took my foot off the clutch. The car jumped forward, crashed into one of the stucco pillars of the entryway, and then sputtered and died.

I climbed out and ran toward the entrance, but ER personnel were already rushing through the sliding glass doors.

20 SEE, HERE'S WILBUR THE PIG

I was prepared for many of the questions from the police, and had answers. Not good answers, but answers.

They were decent about it. Even though I had no rights in the matter, they left me alone until the doctors had pumped Lisby's stomach and forced a ventilator down her throat. I knew that tube was saving her life, but watching the machine make her breathe was wrenching: sad, freakish, and somehow immoral, a symbol of everything that had gone wrong with what I'd thought was my wonderful life.

Once the doctors had assured me that she'd live, the police took me into a consultation room. I stared at the poster on the door: *Know the Seven Warning Signs of Cancer.* The cops arranged their notebooks and cups of vending-machine coffee on a counter furnished with cotton swabs and latex gloves. The clock on the wall read 6:15; it was either very early or very late in their shifts.

They started with their questions. Had she been trying to kill herself? Yes, I thought so. Where had she done it? In the Park. Why didn't I call an ambulance? I'd panicked. The car wasn't registered to me; where did I get it? I took it without permission, just swiped a friend's keys.

They'd checked. I had a record down here in Redlands, and a call to the County showed I was on probation. Driving without a license, joy-riding, consorting with a user of illegal narcotics—did I know that these were actionable violations of probation? I did. Was I aware that I, and my family, were financially liable for the damage to the hospital entryway? I wasn't, but it didn't surprise me.

The younger of the two officers seemed wearied by the interrogation, and I had the impression that if it was in his power he would have walked away from the whole situation with no more than a *don't let it happen again*. "I'm gonna grab some more coffee. You want some, kid?"

I thanked him and said no.

The older officer had raccoon circles around both eyes, but tiredness must have been his normal state. "So," he said, as if we were finally getting down to it, "we found about three rolls of what appear to be Seconal in the glovebox of that car. Three rolls of Seconal, and what appears to be a bottle of Tuinal capsules. Do you know what those names mean?"

"Yes, sir."

"Would you like to tell me what those were doing in the car? Who the drugs belonged to?"

I buried my face in my hands, thinking about it. I heard the door open and close, a chair scooting. When I looked up, both of the police were watching me, waiting.

"Those were mine, sir. I put them there."

They exchanged glances. "Seems pretty dumb," the young guy said.

No kidding. "I forgot."

I could see that neither of them quite believed it, but that neither of them cared to pursue the truth.

The older one flipped open a manila folder. "Your sheet has you living with your father, Jonathon R. Leibnitz, no mother, here in town. Information has no listing under your father's name. How do we get ahold of your father?"

I burst out laughing, and they stared at me. "That's more complicated than you think. You'd better call the County sheriffs and ask them. And then, you'd probably better call my PO. Leo Malheur."

Since it was noon by the time they trucked me over to Juvie, I got my haircut, delousing, and scrubdown on intake. My sky-blue pajamas hadn't even lost their creases when Leo showed up in my cell. Instead of hovering in the entry, he kicked the door shut and came over and sat down beside me on the bed. He looked at me, eyebrows raised, inviting me to speak. I waited.

"You might have told me," he said at last, "that your father had disappeared with felony warrants out for his arrest. Makes me look sort of incompetent, not knowing that."

"I only just found out myself." His eyes were skeptical, and I felt bad about letting him down. "I mean it. He only disappeared a few days ago. And I guarantee you, he didn't bother letting me know first."

Leo grunted. "You really fucked up this time, didn't you?"

"Yes, sir. And I'm sorry."

"I'll bet you are."

"I don't mean that way. I mean, screwing up after you trusted me."

"Don't try to butter me up."

I looked him in the eyes. "I'm not. I'm just sorry."

"Hmph." He looked away and crossed one long leg over the other. "This whole thing stinks, you know."

"How do you mean?"

"I mean I don't buy it. Hell, the cops didn't buy it. Let me get this straight: You steal Donnie Briscoe's keys, load this dying girl into a car you can't hardly drive, stop to toss a bunch of downers in the glovebox, and then just happen to forget them? Plus, I called Donnie on the phone, and he says, sure, you stole his car, but not from the Park. From where you were living. Oh, and they got your blood and urine workups back from the lab, and you're clean as a newborn baby. This whole number you're running is horseshit."

I stared at the wall.

"So," he said, "you're protecting somebody. Could be the girl. She obviously had plenty of downers. Maybe she stuck 'em in the glovebox, maybe earlier that evening. But I figure it's Donnie's stash. I figure it's Donnie's stash and you didn't even know it was there."

I said nothing.

"You look at me, Rick." I did. "I'm betting you anything that if I call Donnie Briscoe in this afternoon and have them pull blood, the workup'll show he's dirty. Won't it?"

I tried to keep my face blank, but I felt like I was flinching under his eyes. I dropped my own gaze to my lap.

He blew out a long, exasperated breath. "You're a hard case, aren't you? They aren't going to let this one drop, you know. Not when you're already on probation. This is going to mean Chino, maybe for up to a year." He waited. "You sure you don't want to give me Donnie?" He waited. "Jesus, kid, you're going to go to jail to protect *Donnie Briscoe*?"

I was tempted, very tempted. I disliked Donnie about as much as I disliked anyone who wasn't a blood relative. But it had been my fuck-up. I'd taken the car by force. I'd driven it into a pillar. And I hadn't even been smart enough to search it and dump the goods. "They were my drugs," I said.

"Right. And I'm JFK's love child." He sighed and clambered to his feet. "Do you have anyone, anyone, to act *in loco parentis* at the hearing?"

"Huh?"

"Any kind of relative at all, or anyone who could even possibly be construed as a guardian?"

"You come closest, I guess."

"I'm really fucking touched, but no thanks. If there's one thing this job does for you, it decides you against having kids. Should I send the public defender through? You have the right to a lawyer at this one."

"Do I have to?"

"No."

"Then skip it."

He walked to the door. "Still time to change your mind."

I gave him a fake brave smile.

"See you in a few days, then," he said.

He opened the door, stepped outside, and shouted for someone to come lock me down.

I reached for the Bible. Since I wasn't pining for anyone, Song of Solomon didn't appeal to me.

I settled on Revelations.

I heard keys in the door, and then a hesitation.

It was Aaron, his concave face as familiar as if I'd seen it yesterday. "No haircut problems this time, I see."

"Not this time." I smiled. "It's good to see you, Aaron."

He shook his head. "Wish I could say the same. I was hopin' like mad I'd never see you again. This is no place for you, boy."

I lifted one palm, offering no argument.

"You listen, and wipe that stupid smile off your face. Second time around. This is your last chance. You come through those doors a third time, you'll be a lifer. Guaranteed." He frowned, and his misshapen face gave his words the consequence of the Delphic Oracle. "Three's magic. Bad magic. You know Robert Johnson, boy?"

Robert Johnson? Who the hell was that? I shook my head.

"Just as well, maybe. But you listen. This is the Crossroads and it's gettin' dark. You're young, you think you can undo any bad choice you make. You can't. It's getting dark, and it's time to choose."

"Choose? Choose what?"

He held up a finger and pointed it at me. "Don't know what your story is, boy. But I see you in here one more time, I'm gonna know for sure that it's your fault, nobody else's. Your fault."

He pulled the door shut and I heard the tumblers turning; then a pause, metallic sounds, and the door opened again. "I was wondering. You get anything to eat yet today?"

In the movies, you get this wood-paneled chamber, with guards and witness stands and jury boxes and flags, and chambers from which the judges emerge, black robes fluttering.

In the juvenile justice system as I met it, you get a linoleum-floored rectangle the size of an average living room, equipped with folding tables and wobbly steel chairs. You aren't sure who the judge is until someone calls him "Your Honor."

I'd thought that Leo was pissed at me, but you wouldn't have known it from his performance at my hearing. I'd pleaded guilty, so the trial phase was over in a half-hour. At the time of sentencing, though, Leo rolled out a speech on my behalf as if I'd hired a top-notch attorney, a publicist, a band of mourners, and a sympathetic Greek chorus. By the time he was done, I was ready to vote myself into any office in the land; the Devil's Advocate himself would have pressed for my beatification. According to Leo, I'd struggled against impossible odds, been deserted by my mother and saddled with an abusive, felonious father, and, despite all this, had managed to support myself by working thirty hours a week while excelling in a college-prep program at the local high school. He rolled out laudatory statements from Al Kraft and my teachers; he submitted a list of stunning "anticipatory grades" they'd expected to award me at the end of the semester.

Hell, some of it was even true.

Then he went on to the subject of the night I'd driven Lisby to the hospital. I'd saved her life. A statement from one of the ER doctors suggested that at the time she'd arrived, she'd had maybe fifteen minutes to live.

My bowels clenched. It had been that close? That close, and I'd worried about the cops busting our Mountain High house? That close, and I'd staked her life on my incompetent driving, my silly-assed grandstanding?

He talked about the fact that my blood chemistry had been clean when they pulled a sample, suggesting I'd had not even so much as a beer. He talked about loyalty, maturity, and the fact that, had I pointed the finger at someone else—there were at least two likely suspects, one who owed me her very life—had I pointed the finger at someone else, I could have walked away, a free man.

A wild exaggeration. Within the structure of the laws as I understood them, I had nowhere to walk to, since I had neither legal guardians nor emancipated standing; technically, it was a crime for me to exist anywhere outside the custody of the California juvenile justice system.

Nonetheless, by the time Leo Malheur had finished, there wasn't a dry eye on my side of the table.

The judge was less moved. He admitted the strength of Leo's arguments; admitted a grudging admiration for my pluck and spunk; admitted that I'd had an uphill battle in life. However...

However. Under no circumstances could he countenance the idea that claiming responsibility for a criminal act to shield others was laudable. Indeed, to reward such behavior would amount to endorsing obstruction of justice. The laws were considered and fair, and were, in any case, the laws. It wasn't up to individuals to decide for themselves; that's why we had courts of law; that's why we had a Constitution...

He sentenced me to a year in CYA Chino, with possibility of parole in four months.

It was as if the judge's ruling had crushed Leo. Sitting beside me, his six-foot-five frame seemed no larger than mine. He stacked his papers and folders, unstacked them, and piled them in another pattern.

"Sorry," he whispered.

"No," I said, "that was awe-inspiring. My god, you're going to be the best lawyer in the country some day."

He chuckled. "C'mon, kid. It boils down to results. We lost. You don't deserve this."

But Leo didn't know what I did; Leo's mind wasn't arcing high above the mountains, out across the desiccated Ice-Age lakes, to the rail line where two bodies lay buried under piles of crushed rock. "Don't be so sure," I said. "Maybe this is exactly what I deserve."

Einstein was right: there's something strange about time. An event that takes only a moment can take hours to explain; but sometimes months of your life can be summed up in moments.

YA wasn't what I'd imagined. Based on Juvie, I'd pictured endless cell blocks, just like the Hall but grimmer, with tighter security and nastier guards.

What I found was more like a demented summer camp, at least in my ward. We were housed four to a cell, two bunk beds per unit, but the cells were for sleeping. Everyone messed in a large cafeteria with formica tables and linoleum floors, and there was a large fenced rec field for those who wanted to play basketball. (Football was banned as too aggressive, and baseball...well, who'd trust these guys with a bat?)

The number-one focus, of course, was on keeping us inside and in order; but after that, the camp's priority was rehabilitation in the form of education. For most of the inmates, this meant vocational training, and there was a sizeable wood shop, metal shop, and, most popular of all, an automotive shop with a full garage. With all these tool shops available there was naturally a major trade in homemade weaponry, particularly knives; some of the craftsmanship I saw was breathtaking. Yet there were few fights—perhaps because so many of the kids were armed—and there were only three or four stabbings a year.

There was bullying, just like at any public high school. And there was reputedly a fair amount of rape, though this was discussed only in whispers, and never even mentioned by the authorities.

On my second day inside I'd made it through the cafeteria line without incident and found a chair near my new cellmates. They ignored me, talking among themselves, but suddenly their conversation stopped and they looked past me.

A huge pair of hands came down on my shoulders. "Gotcha!" I twisted my head and looked up.

Todd Carley.

"Hey hey hey," he said, thumping me on the back, "didn't think I'd see you in here." A kid to my right stared up at him wide-eyed, and Carley said, "Move, huh? You mind? Wanna talk to my old pal Rick, here." The kid stood up so fast that the rear of his knees made the chair shoot back; he took his tray and vanished, leaving behind his carton of milk from Brookside Dairy.

Todd wedged himself down into the chair. "Man, betcha weren't expecting me, were you? What the fuck you doing in here? Sucks, man. Thought you were gone. I mean, it doesn't suck, it's great, but it still sucks, you know?" He tossed a huge arm over my shoulder and tugged me a little closer. "You know what?" he asked, in a lower voice. "I met some other guy who'd read that *Cuckoo's Nest* book. And he said it didn't go the way you told it to me. Like, not at all. *He* said you were just making shit up."

I swallowed. "I…added some things. Things the writer didn't talk about."

"Hey, no problem!" His arm crushed my shoulders in what I hoped was an affectionate squeeze. "The way you told it was way better. The stuff he told me sucked."

It came as a relief when he let loose of me and folded his forearms on the table. "So you decided not to, umm, try to get into Ward B?" I asked.

"No. No, I got in there. And they cured me, and then sent me right back here."

"Cured you?" It didn't seem like there was a cure for what ailed Carley.

"Yeah, they have this pill I take every day, and I don't go all funny."

"A pill? What kind of pill?"

He frowned behind his hornrims. "It's like, Dilantrim?"

"Dilantin?" I asked, astonished.

"Yeah, that's it. Dilantin."

"They found out you're epileptic?"

This seemed to trouble him. "No. I mean, I don't fall down and thrash and stuff." He blushed, and lowered his voice even further, like an old woman discussing the regularity of her bowels. "But they say that I did have fits. Sort of. That, when I went sort of crazy, that it was kind of a fit. And the pills stopped that." He looked around at the other kids, all of whom had been listening without staring, and raised his voice. "I'm still a mean motherfucker, though. Nobody messes with me."

"Todd, that's so cool. The medication, that is."

He grumbled under his breath, and then said, "Yeah, maybe." He interlaced his fingers on the table, as if he might say grace. "Problem is, makes me 4F. And the Army'll take you from here while you're still seventeen, sometimes. Lots of the guys, they've got out. But I'm stuck here for a whole 'nother year till I'm eighteen."

"That's better than being stuck in 'Nam for the next four years, isn't it?"

"Don't know. The soldier thing might have been fun. Kinda."

I laughed. "You like people telling you what to do?"

"No."

"Then I don't think you'd like the Army much, Todd."

He was chewing on this when the bell rang, ending lunch and calling us off to classes. He slapped me on the back again as he stood. "Anybody tries to fuck with you, tell 'em you know me. And, hey, maybe you want to move to my hole? We gotta guy's getting out pretty soon. Month or so…"

Within hours I was known all over YA as Carley's kissy, Todd's little cunt. Did I care? Not me. I'd instantly been awarded my place in the pecking order, without having to endure all the threats, shoves, and dick-waving that usually went with the process. I wasn't respected, not in any tough-guy sense, but people stayed out of my way. For a while I had the experience—unique for a boy—of being Daddy's Little Princess.

Whatever works.

I had no idea why I'd been summoned to that cheerless, windowless little room—a cube with a table and four chairs—and they let me worry about it for ten minutes until Leo came through the door, tossed a pen and pad down on the table, and took a seat.

He steepled those long, elegant fingers in front of his chest, acknowledged my greetings with a nod, and said, "I'm in a big rush today, but we need to go over a few things. First, your suicidal friend—Elizabeth, is it?"

"Lisby."

"Right. She's confessed that the downers in the glovebox were hers, and that you had nothing to do with it." He snorted. "This is the first time I've seen everybody so eager to confess to a crime."

"They weren't hers."

"I didn't figure they were. Makes no sense. If she was really trying to kill herself, and had all those pills, why not swallow them, too?" He pulled the notepad closer, clicked the ballpoint pen, and doodled an infinity sign, looping round and round.

"What's going to happen to her? Are they going to charge her? Is she okay?"

"She's fine. She's in Ward B over at County. As far as they're concerned, this is just a suicide attempt. Mental health business, not a criminal issue. Of course, they asked where she got the pills, and she spewed the usual line about someone in a park who she'd never met before. They don't want to bust her. Fact is, nobody really cares. You're already in here. Case closed." He drew a box around the infinity sign and started scribbling, filling in the box. "Now I know and you know that it was Donnie's stuff. You can go ahead and come clean about that. I'm not going to do anything about it—if I wanted to pop the little jerk, I would have called him in for a blood test. I just want to understand. Why did you do it?"

I scratched my head, surprised as always that there was almost no hair on it. "Because it wasn't right. I stole his car. I crashed it. Nobody would have known anything about anything if I hadn't screwed up. I couldn't get him in trouble because of what I did."

"Fair enough. Now here's the problem." He tossed down the pen, folded his arms behind his head, and tilted the chair back onto two legs. "In principle, with Lisby confessing, we could ask for a second hearing. Takes time to arrange, and might not do any good anyway. Judges don't like to be lied to, even if you convince them you were doing it to protect some pathetic young damsel. I'm guessing it would take two or three months to get them to wipe the charges, and there's no guarantee it would work."

I started to say that it still seemed like my best bet, but he settled the chair down on the floor and stopped me with an upraised index finger. "Listen. The real problem here is, so what? If we get the charges dropped, you're still on probation. Whose custody are we going to release you into?" He blew out a long breath. "You don't have anybody in California? Not *any*body? No aunts, no uncles, no older cousins…? You don't have any idea at all where your mother is?"

I shook my head. "No relatives around here. And Mom just left, and I never heard a word."

Leo chewed his lip. "I've met some cold cold cases, but that's still hard to buy." He shook his cuff back and glanced at his watch. "Now listen. I'm going to suggest that we go straight to the regular County Court with an emancipation petition. Otherwise, even if they let you out of here, you'd just bounce back to Juvie while they try to place you in foster care."

"You can do that? Do the emancipation thing while you're on probation and in jail?"

"There's nothing in the law that says you can't. It'd be mighty rare for a judge to approve it, but with your father deserting you, no family, and the confession from Lisby, I think we can make a decent case."

"What do I have to do?"

"Eventually sign some papers, go stand up in court. Right now what you need to do is stay out of trouble."

"That's what you said before, back in the summer." I looked down at the tabletop. "I really screwed it up, didn't I?"

He laughed, an outburst of genuine amusement. "Kid, you have no fucking idea what really screwing up is all about. Your performance is topflight, USDA-approved compared to most of my so-called clients." His mood had shifted from harassed to happy, and it stayed there. "No, I think we can sell this to the courts. But it sure won't help if you get in trouble in here." He stood up, still grinning. "And dazzle your teachers. And, while you're at it, ask them about hopping onto a GED program. They'll be happy to help." He paused, his hand on the doorknob. "Sometimes I think I have a thankless job, but being a teacher in here? Now *that* would be enough to break your heart."

The letter from Lisby was huge, eight pages spilling out of an envelope that the authorities had already opened. I couldn't imagine what she had to say that would fill so much space, until I discovered that the letter was written in purple crayon.

> Dear Rick,
> This looks stupid writing in crayon but it's all they let us have. And maybe it's about right for me to be writing like a stupid little kid. I feel like such an idiot in so many ways. Waking up

in the hospital bed was like waking up from this bad dream that has been the last two years of my life.

I met people in here who had electroshock and it's like what they describe. You wake up and everything's different and you wonder how that person you remember could have been you. I can't believe I lived in that fog for so long. Or that I wasted so much time trying to make Linc be somebody he wasn't. I'm the one who should be in jail because it's a crime to waste your life, and I remember how I lectured you one night about <u>spending time</u> because we only had so much of it. I was such a little know it all, and look at what I was really doing. I'm embarrassed to even think about it.

And I'm so sorry that I messed everything up for you. You were such a good friend to me these last months, spending time with me while I moaned about Linc and following me around to places where you didn't even want to be at just to keep an eye on me, and keeping me safe. My only real friend all that time I guess. And then you saved my life and I didn't even think I wanted it but it turns out I did. I wanted to live. I am so grateful to be alive now, and I am so ashamed so ashamed and sorry about everything. I'll make it up to you if I can ever find a way.

Love, Your Friend, Lisby

A slow, regular life, not unlike what I imagine a monastery might provide. Leo had been right: the teachers loved me, and in addition to the required classes, they loaded me down with Programmed

Instruction texts. Read a chapter, take a multiple-choice test in the proctor room, hand in the results, and move on. In a month, all my required classes were out of the way, and I was on to electives. Art History, English Lit, even Astronomy, all in easy, bite-sized chunks. I took about four exams most weekdays, a pace that put me through each programmed class in a couple of weeks.

The speed wasn't the result of my brilliance, but more of a testament to my boredom. Plus, the work couldn't have been too challenging to anyone. It was obvious why the GED wasn't offered to normal students in high schools; if it were, they would all graduate by the end of the tenth grade, and what would we do with all those kids out on the streets? And what would we do with all those spare teachers?

In the midst of it all, a miracle. In the programmed Introduction to Biology text I came across a description of the details of photosynthesis; then, a little further on, a discussion of mitochondria, the powerhouses of the cell. A glimpse into the heart of a great mystery, the transformation of light into living matter, the conversion of matter into energy. Explanations of the simplest, most obvious things. How plants grow. How cells reproduce. Why we breathe, for the love of god—I'd always known we needed oxygen, but I'd had no idea why.

For weeks I was trembling, on fire, each new revelation about nature as profound and affecting as an acid trip. No one wanted to hear about it, of course, not even the teachers; but they gladly sought out more material for me, borrowing programmed instruction courses in biosciences from adult-ed schools in the area, and, when these were exhausted, bringing me textbooks from junior colleges.

I couldn't understand the biology without the chemistry, and chemistry turned out to be fascinating in its own right, pushing me at last to master the rudiments of algebra—math wasn't that hard if you actually cared about the answer.

It's the great secret of our times. They've dressed it up in lab coats and squeezed the life out of the language, but it lives on—the passion of the alchemists for arcane knowledge, the hidden truths that pervade all existence. The Quintessence. I was buried in it, possessed by it. Call it biochemistry if it makes them happy; I knew I was undertaking, at long last, *Ars Magna*, The Great Work.

When the opening came in Carley's cell, they moved me in. Jaco and Scott, the other residents, seemed to take to me, or at least pretended to for the sake of getting along with Carley.

I wasn't in the mood to play storyteller anymore, but I was happy to read aloud. Not the stories I would have chosen for myself, of course, but the ragtag collection of paperbacks in the CYA fiction library was more suited to the tastes of my audience anyway. Edgar Rice Burroughs—both the *Tarzan* books, and a smattering of *John Carter of Mars*. Mickey Spillane's *Mike Hammer* novels. *Doc Savage*, by a whole raft of writers hiding behind the same *nom de plume*. I tried them out on Ian Fleming, but James Bond appealed to them much more on the screen than in Fleming's relatively dry narratives. About the only point where our tastes coincided was on Poe: grisly, overwrought, and gorgeous.

YA expanded my literary experience, though I can't claim it enhanced it much. I read to them most nights, during the hour of settling down before lights out; and if much of the material made me think I ought to be holding up the book to show the class the illustrations—*see, here's Wilbur the Pig, and up in the corner, there's Charlotte*—it made me feel valuable, and kept me from thinking too hard.

Then lights out, and the inevitable flight of my mind out across the desert, by the blackened ironwoods, where two bodies lay buried. I dreamed it so many times that eventually it felt as though it never really happened.

And then the wet dreams. Hard to jerk off with three male roommates, but Mr. Happy took care of himself. Randi. JenBen. Stacy. Some disturbing elements. Casey, where I kept hurting her more and more and she kept encouraging it. Lisby, sad, weeping Lisby, my best friend's girlfriend. And there were nights when I awoke, my fingers clasped around myself and covered in semen, and wondered how much noise I had made, or if I'd gasped out someone's name in my sleep.

Eventually there was a letter from Lincoln Ellard. In a few spots, the censor's black marker had made deletions, as if the missing words couldn't be inferred:

> Dear Rick,
>
> It took me a while to piece together what happened that night, and why you did the things you did. I worked it out, though, and you called it exactly right. Pretty ▇▇▇▇▇ crazy, but exactly right.
>
> I really ▇▇▇▇▇ up, in so many ways. I didn't see where things were heading with Lisby. And I didn't see all the other ▇▇▇▇ that was bound to happen with the stuff we were doing.
>
> I'm leaving town. Don't look for me. Martha and Momma won't tell you. (Of course, maybe you don't want to see me anyway.) Don't look for the ▇▇▇▇ Lode either. I cleaned up everything.
>
> I paid out the lease through May, so you still have a place.
>
> Lisby is out of the hospital and seems good. Better than before. Better without me. (Big ▇▇▇▇▇ surprise.) Make sure you see her before you go anywhere or do anything.
>
> Other news from Yucaipa, ▇▇▇▇ of the world. Leslie says that Sue had your dad's stuff moved into the garage of the place you lived down in Dunlap. The new evening supervisor lives there now, and he's got a ▇▇▇▇▇▇▇▇ to get it all out of there, so you should check it out as soon as you can.

Your friend JenBen is dropping out of school and heading north to get married to what's-his-name. She sends her love and says hi, though bye would make more sense.

I'm really sorry about everything. I see the places now where I went wrong. And I finally see what the next step must be, but it doesn't involve people, not immediately. Technology is the engine of human evolution. Minds change only when they must. And I need skills to make that happen. Skills and a long apprenticeship.

I know I'll see you again, because I know in my heart that we are on the same path. We tried, but we tried in the wrong ways and at the wrong time. But I know I'll see you again.

Look for me when you see me coming,

Love, L.E.

21 | A BIG YELLOW SMILE ON THE ROCK

Leaving YA was almost sad. For the first time in years, my life had been ordered and my days had been routine. Out of bed at six every morning, under the blankets by ten at night. School every weekday—mostly programmed instruction, in my case, but school all the same. Weekends spent reading and studying. Over the period of almost four months, there were only three breaks in the routine: the first time in January, when they drove me to County Court to appear with Leo in my petition for Emancipation; the second time, in early February, when a board convened to consider my release; and the third time, in mid-February, when Leo picked me up and drove me back to Yucaipa.

I was so grateful to Leo that it was hard to even begin. I sat silent until we were well onto Interstate 10, and then I started to stammer out my thanks.

He shrugged it off. "It's my job. And I can't tell you how nice it is to beat the system, just once or twice."

"I know this sounds stupid, but if there's anything I can ever do for you—"

"There is. Get out there and prove that I was right."

He asked about my plans. I was only three classes short of my high-school diploma, and the teachers at YA had assured me I could complete the rest of it at any junior college. "I thought I might go to Valley JC. Or somewhere. Finish up the high school stuff I have left, maybe take some college classes." In truth, I was eager to jump into college, hungry for more biosciences; but it sounded lame to say so. "And, when I can, I'd like to get a learner's permit. But who has to sign for it? Do I sign for it myself?"

He laughed. "There you have me. That's a wrinkle in the law that hasn't come up before."

"Can you find out?"

"Can, but won't. That's one piece of legal research you're going to have to do yourself." His smile faded. "Rick," he asked, "are you going to be able to manage it this time?"

I thought about it. "I sure hope so."

"Me too. Because I'm cutting you loose."

I rubbed my face. "What?"

"I'm letting you off probation. I'm letting all my clients off probation, except for two evil jerks over in San Bernardino who are probably going to kill people someday."

My mouth hung open, and I closed it, but it dropped open again.

"My exemption got rescinded, Rick. They're drafting me."

"Shit." I swallowed. "I'm sorry, man."

"Yeah. Fuck 'em. I did everything the right way, their way, and now this. So, consider it my little farewell present."

"Can you do that? I mean, don't you have to get permission of some sort?"

"Nope. My call."

I pondered this, and, to be frank, worried more about its effect on me than on Leo; but an expression of solidarity seemed necessary. "Wow. That fuckhead Nixon."

Leo made a sound of exasperation. "I hear that all the time. At least he might get us out some day. It's Johnson that got us buried up to our necks over there."

"Yeah, but..." But Johnson passed all that progressive legislation, and everything, while Nixon... "I just thought..."

"Uh-huh, I get that all the time from guys I grew up with—*but, hey, bro, Johnson be on our side, he's the civil rights man*... Well, I think he's a racist warmongering prick, and I think he pushed through all the civil rights stuff as a gift to us, the way Massa on the plantation might finally give me my freedom, like my rights are something he owns and I'm supposed to kiss his ass for giving them to me. Fucking Texans." He sat up straighter in the seat, his hair grazing the roof. "Meanwhile he was murdering us every day—his cops in the streets, and his shitty little war. You know what percentage of the foot soldiers in 'Nam are black?"

"Uh…no."

A malicious, unhappy smile. "You're a smart kid. Go look it up sometime. And then compare it to the percentage of people in the country who are black." He flipped a palm up, and waved the subject away.

"Are you going to go?" I asked at last.

He glanced away from the freeway for a moment and looked me in the eye, and suddenly we weren't PO and probationer any more, we were just two guys talking. "I don't know. Just don't know. I might do something else: Canada, or join the Panthers. Right now I got no fucking idea."

This tall, polished, smart guy, sitting behind the wheel in his suit: hard to picture him joining the underground. But if the leaders in Washington were driving people like Leo into the Black Panthers, they'd better watch out.

I directed him up the hill to Mountain Home, and eventually we pulled up in front of the house. To my surprise, he killed the engine and walked with me up onto the porch.

The afternoon was fine, crisp but clear, and jays squawked in the trees. Leo took a long breath of the mountain air and stood with his hands on his hips, looking out through the trees. "Nice place," he said. "I could stand to live some place like this."

I unlocked the front door and pushed it open. I had no idea what to expect, and was concerned that something inside would make it look to Leo like he was turning me loose in a dope den; but everything was as clean and orderly as if a realtor planned on showing the place. Clean, orderly, and utterly deserted. Afternoon light glanced off the waxed wooden floors.

He looked over my shoulder into the house. "Nice place," he said again.

"It is."

He cleared his throat, and I turned back to face him. "Got to go give the good news to a lot of other kids," he said. He put a big hand on my shoulder. "This is your shot, man. Don't blow it, 'cause this time it's nobody's fault but your own." He clapped his hand down one last time, squeezed, and stepped away.

At the bottom of the steps he paused. "Nice as it is," he said, "I still think I'd get the hell out of here."

I waved as he drove off, and then found myself alone in our forsaken salon.

When I thought about it, the whole town seemed abandoned. Randi was off at school, JenBen was off in Oregon marrying Brad Brad Brad; Leslie still lived in town, as far as I knew, but spent her days in Riverside; and Linc had vanished for who-knows-where. Lisby was still around, I assumed, and folks like Rob and Donnie were bound to be in town, but it was as if most of the main actors had disappeared in the middle of the movie. My script didn't seem to make sense anymore.

I thumbed down the hill in the fading light and made it to Dunlap just after sunset. The supervisor's cottage, where I'd once lived with Dad for a matter of days, looked the same but felt different: light streamed out through the windows, and I heard the clink and slosh of dishes in a sink.

Mrs. Curtis, the new super's wife, was a plump, bustling woman, the aproned sort of figure that had been born for the benefit of her grandchildren. She led me out to the one-car, clapboard garage behind the house, talking the whole way. "Mrs. Andrews said you'd be coming by, but that was months ago. We'll be happy to have the space, I can tell you—can barely fit the car inside with all them boxes. Not that I'm complaining, mind you." She opened the door and flicked on the overhead light, a naked bulb. She looked at the oil-spotted floor with some distress. "Maybe I should fetch a chair for you. And, goodness, how are you going to take things with you? I tell you what—you just set aside anything you want, and when Vic gets up tomorrow morning we'll pack those all up and drive them over to your place."

"Thanks, Mrs. Curtis. I really appreciate the offer. But I doubt that I'm going to want more than I can carry."

She looked dubious. "Don't hesitate. It won't put us out. And if it wouldn't be trouble for you, maybe you could divide things into three piles—things you want to keep, things for Goodwill, and things to go to the dump."

I agreed, and she urged me to come on into the house if I needed warming up.

It didn't take long to deal with most of the boxes. Clothes. Dishes. Towels. A box of kitchen crap: a toaster, a hand-crank egg-beater, slotted spoons.

Box after box into the Goodwill stack.

Then boxes of papers. I don't know what I was looking for. Baby pictures, maybe, or pictures of Mom? I sat down on a toolbox and dug through them. Old utility bills. Invoices from the bankrupt egg ranch, many of them ripped in two. Bank statements. Copies of income-tax forms.

Mrs. Curtis brought me a mug of cocoa and a paper plate with half a dozen chocolate chip cookies. "Just a little something to keep off the chill." I wondered what it would have been like if she were my mother, if I'd been raised in a normal family. But I was going too far based on a momentary kindness; for all I knew, life inside that little cottage was a perfect hell. Maybe the walls around every family home were there to hide a snakepit.

Maybe, but I doubted it. And it was good cocoa.

At the bottom of the second box of papers were envelopes, five of them, addressed to me. In my mother's handwriting.

They'd been ripped open, and every one of them was empty.

No return addresses. The faint postmarks showed that three of them had been mailed in 1965, the year she'd left, and the other two in late 1966.

I studied the postmarks. The first four were from Tukwila, Washington. I'd never heard of the place. But the last one had been mailed from Renton, Washington, and I knew about Renton—Jimi Hendrix's hometown, a suburb of Seattle.

She must have gone to her sister, the one who had married a Muslim and changed her name.

She had written to me.

Why had Dad kept the envelopes? For the postmarks? Had he been searching for her?

On the back of one of them, he had written, <u>LIEING CUNT</u>!!!

I stuffed the envelopes into my shirt pocket and started digging through the box, picking up papers and then hurling them onto the cement floor, faster with each handful, until I realized I wasn't even seeing the words anymore, wasn't searching, was only flailing.

I calmed down, and spent the next hour picking up and examining every sheet of paper in all four of the boxes.

Nothing.

I piled the boxes of papers into one stack, used one of Mr. Curtis's grease pencils to label them TRASH, and stacked the remaining boxes on the opposite side of the garage.

I returned the mug to Mrs. Curtis and thanked her. "Did you find everything you needed?" she asked.

"No. But I found all I'm going to find." I explained the two stacks of boxes, refused her renewed offer of driving anything I needed "over to your place," thanked her once more, and headed out of her bright kitchen into the dark streets. When I reached Yucaipa Boulevard I stuck out my thumb.

The cars roared by, and the wind as they passed added to the winter chill. A few times I thought I recognized students from the high school, but with my Chino-issue haircut I must have looked like a stranger.

My mother's sister. Her "kike sister," according to my father, who was incapable or unwilling to distinguish between Islam and Judaism.

Her name had been Aunt Chrissie for the first eight or nine years of my life, and then she had changed it to…what? We'd made fun of it around the dinner table, one of the few times Mom and Dad and I all agreed. A ridiculous name—the fake-Arabic surname her husband had adopted, and a bizarre new first name.

What had it been? An animal name, I thought, or a job. Dad had always pretended to misremember it. What had he called her?

Newshound, I remembered, his voice saying to Mom, *How's your sister Newshound? Still married to that nigger?*

Newshound. That was almost it. Newsrat. *Nusrat.*

Nusrat al-Bakar, aka Chrissie Perkins.

Of course she would go to her sister. I could have worked it all out years before. But I hadn't cared, because I'd assumed she hadn't cared.

And maybe she hadn't, really. All I had were envelopes, envelopes from years before.

<hr />

It took me two rides, and it was after nine at night when a hippie couple headed for Forest Falls dropped me off at the edge of Mountain Home. I shivered as I trudged down the lanes, wondering how the hell the heating system in our house worked—I couldn't recall ever using it.

As I rounded the corner onto Coulter Pine Drive, I saw the lights were on in the living room of the house. Weird. I certainly hadn't left them on. Then, as I neared the yard, I saw Linc's Impala in the driveway.

I hustled up the stairs to the porch, opened the door, and Lisby looked up from her seat on the couch.

She tossed down her book, jumped up, and ran into my arms. "God, Rick..." she said, and hugged me tight. "It's so good to see you..."

I kicked the door shut. It was warm inside. She took my hand and led me to the couch.

"Where's Linc?" I asked.

"I don't know any more than you do."

"No, I mean, I saw the car..."

"Oh. Oh, he gave it to me before he left. Signed it over." She looked at my face, and then added, "Sorry to disappoint you."

"No," I said. "I was just confused... There's nobody I'd rather see right now than you." My voice gained conviction as I realized, with some surprise, that it was the truth. "Nobody."

She reached a hand up and stroked my cheek. "You look great."

"I look like a dork." The soft brush of knuckles on my cheek went right to my heart. *I confess/ I love that/ which caresses me...*

"No, I mean it. You look older. Bigger. You really look good."

"Probably all the jello. We must have eaten jello twenty times a week in there."

She folded her hands on her lap and stared down at them. "I'm so sorry…"

"Forget it. I mean it. In some ways, it's the best thing that ever happened to me." I told her about my new legal status, emancipated and freed from probation. "Plus, you're alive. You're alive, and you seem good."

She looked up, and the glow I'd seen before returned to her face. "I *am* good. And glad I'm alive. And I'm glad I'm done with…how I used to be."

I smiled, feeling good just to see her, and I realized, with a bit of a jolt, that for perhaps the first time in my life I was more concerned with how a girl felt than with how she felt about me. A strange sensation, but a good one.

Admittedly I had been, as the correctional industry puts it, *deprived of the society of women* for about four months, so my senses were quivering just from sitting beside her…but she was different. Before she had been beautiful, but in a cute, small, wounded way. The self-pity was gone from her eyes; the booze-and-barbiturate sallowness gone from her skin. She seemed radiant in the most literal sense, effulgent with life. "God, Lisby," I said, "you're the one who looks great. It's unbelievable. What happened to you?"

She paused and gave me a solemn, contrite look before answering. "I accepted Jesus Christ into my heart as my own personal Lord and Savior."

She watched my face, and then exploded with laughter, sputtering, barely able to speak. "Oh!—oh, oh, I'm sorry…it's just… Oh, I'm kidding! No, I'm not sorry!" She doubled over, sat up, wiped away tears. "Oh, man, if you'd seen the expression on your face…!" She doubled over again.

I sat there with a stupid grin on my face, being laughed at. This was a side of Lisby I hadn't seen before, a side I hadn't even imagined.

She grabbed my arm, pulled herself up against me, and brought her laughter under control, still sniffling. She was in my nostrils, her shampoo, the salt of her tears, her delicate sweat, the undertone of musk. My cock was at full attention in my jeans—probably had been since she'd run into my arms—but Mr. Happy could just fend for himself. I shifted my legs away from her as unobtrusively as I could manage.

"I'm sorry," she said, not as sorry as she ought to have been. "I'm like that nowadays. I'm goofy." She released my arm and sat up on her own. "Do you know how long I was soooooo serious about everything?"

"Not really." Everything was off-balance for me.

"Rick." She moved into a more serious mode, though she had to exhale even more of her hilarity first. "I'm glad you're back. I'd be gone now, except that I was waiting for you to show up."

"What do you mean?"

"There's nobody I care about here anymore. Everybody's gone. Except you."

"I know what you mean."

"There's still Melissa…but unless I want to get wiped on Reds and fuck strangers, there isn't much point… Oh, shit."

"What?"

She touched my knee, a deliberate, brief touch, and then took her hand back onto her lap. "Of the things I'm sorry about, fucking you that night is the one I'm sorriest for." I'm not sure what my face showed, but she hastened to clarify. "That came out all wrong. I mean it shouldn't have happened like that. I'd take it back if I could. It must have been so bad for you, and bad sex messes things up so much, hurts people…"

"No." I took her hand in mine. "It's different for guys. We both want it to be the same but it's different. It wasn't bad." I chewed the inside of my mouth, and decided to try to tell the truth. "No, that's wrong. It was bad. But it didn't hurt me. If I'd disappointed you in some way, that would have been awful. And I was jealous that you were thinking of him the whole time. And it was sad, really, really sad. But I was sad for you, not me." I frowned, trying to decide where to go with this. "The sex part, I mean, the physical part, was good. Except you didn't let me get off."

"You *didn't*?" She said this in a curious mixture of amusement and dismay, her tone rising almost to a gasp at the end, and for a moment I thought she would cry. Or laugh. Or something. Instead, she relaxed, chuckled, and said, "Well, now you know what it's like sometimes."

"Something else that's different with boys and girls, I guess."

For a long time there was nothing to say.

"What are you going to do now?" she asked.

"Leave, I think." And I told her about my mother and father, and my fucked-up little family, speeding up when I realized that, in light of her own damaged relatives, she'd be unimpressed, and then explained about the discoveries I'd made that very night, the envelopes and the postmarks…

"You're going to try to find your mother?"

"I think so."

"Rick." I sensed her trying to find the right words, trying not to offend me, tiptoeing through the minefield of my screwed-up emotions.

"I want to find my mother."

"Why? You think that's going to fix something?"

"No. But I— She wrote to me. And she must assume I got the letters and never wrote back…"

"And then what? So you find her. It's good, it's bad. Is that going to change anything?"

"Too late for that. But I just need to know."

"And then what?"

How to explain? I looked down at my knees. "When I was in YA," I began, "I read some books—"

"On topic. Keep on topic." She reached out and twisted my chin around as if tilting my head might keep me on track.

"I am. I learned so much…" I launched off into a brief but impassioned description of biology, biochemistry, the Krebs cycle, the RNA-DNA-protein central dogma, and she tolerated it for a while.

"Stop. You're starting to sound like Linc. What does it all mean?"

"I think it's what I want to do. Go to college, maybe. Learn about this stuff."

"And that's going to give you all the answers?"

"I doubt it. But it's what I want."

"Why?" she asked. My God, she was beautiful, sitting there on the sofa, staring into my face as if every word mattered.

I thought. "Because it's what I want."

A stupid answer, a child's answer. I want it because I want it.

"I know that's dumb," I added. "But it's how I feel."

She narrowed her eyes, appraising me as if this was the first smart thing I'd ever said. "We're just kids, aren't we?"

I nodded, a noncommittal gesture of acquiescence, my mind starting to wander.

She slapped me, a resounding crack across the face. I gasped. "Don't patronize me," she said. "I'm just back from the dead, remember?"

I blinked back tears, my fists clenching. "Jesus, Lisby…"

"From now on I'm going to be *seen*. No more fading into the background. Do you understand me? Do you see me?"

"Okay, I see you, already."

"Did I hurt you?" she asked.

"No."

"You're lying."

"A little."

"Do you want to hit me back?"

"No."

"'Cause you can, fair's fair…"

"I don't want to, alright?"

"Okay, then. Now that I've actually got your attention, I want you to listen to me." She folded her knees up under herself and faced me. "I've thought about you a lot since that night. I don't really know how I feel about you. I think I care about you. A lot. But maybe that's just some immature thing because you rescued me. And I have no idea how you feel about me…"

"I like you a lot, Lisby, and—"

"No. No, be quiet, this is complicated." She reached out and touched my face where she'd slapped it. "I really walloped you, didn't I? Sorry. Look, it would make sense if you thought that I was nuts. And after the way I was when we fucked that night, I'd understand if I gave you the creeps. And here's the complicated part, I'll do anything to make it all up to you, anything except that I'm not going to not be me, never again." She rolled her eyes. "Wow. That sounded intelligent. What I mean is that—"

"Lisby." I put my hand on her knee. "Can you listen for a second? And maybe not hit me?"

She moved her head in the slightest possible affirmation, and watched me, her expression solemn, as though I was pronouncing sentence on her.

"You don't owe me anything," I began, and pressed on her knee to cut off the protest I saw welling up. "And I don't know about us together, or anything else. But you don't owe me anything and you don't give me the creeps either. I really care about you. So say whatever you want to say, and cut all the backfill."

Her tongue came out and moistened her lips. "What I'm trying to say is that I wish I could see how we are together, but I don't want to push you into anything, and you can say no any time you want, and you've rescued me enough already… Jesus! What I'm trying to say is simple. You're going to Seattle. Would you like a ride?"

"I'd like that." I watched her face, and it seemed to glow brighter, and it made my chest swell to produce that effect. "I'd like that very much. But only if we can take a side-trip first."

※

She hadn't asked a single question about where we were going, but in the morning, over breakfast at a greasy spoon in Beaumont, she'd handed me a packet containing six thousand, eight hundred fifty-six dollars.

Or so she said. I didn't count it.

"It's what he sold the rest of the stash for," she said, "plus what you guys took back from the fuckers who tried to rip you off." She watched my face, and then smiled, her eyes wet. "Hey, things weren't perfect between me and Linc…but you think he'd kill some people without telling me?" She rolled her gaze up to the ceiling for a moment. "Truth is, he told me to apologize to you for telling me. He figured you and

JenBen wouldn't tell anyone, so he was the only fuckup." Her eyes queried me.

"I didn't," I said. And JenBen: I'm not sure she ever told anybody anything about anything.

"The boy was right again."

I forked hashbrowns, golden with spilled yolk, into my mouth, and chewed. Chewed harder than required.

"You're never going to forget him…are you?" It was a question, but the way I said it was an accusation.

The waitress jerked her head in our direction, sensing the tension from my side of the table, and the coffee sloshed in her upraised pot.

Lisby stopped with her forearm in midflight, a bit of omelet and potato poised on her fork. She was genuinely astonished. "Are *you*?" she asked, and led the bite into her superb, round mouth. The fact that I'd not noticed her perfection while she was attached to Linc distressed me.

"Am I going to forget him? No. Of course not." I thought back over what he'd done for me: rescuing me from bullies on my first day of school, introducing me to everyone who counted, finessing my problems with my father and Sue Andrews, making me a full member of his vision, cutting me in on his business…

Not blaming me when Chase and 'Berto came after us. Not blaming me when he ended up mutilated.

"I can't forget him," I said. "But that's different."

"Maybe. And why's it necessary to forget him, anyway?" She chewed. "Look. Am I correct that you're attracted to me, or is that just wishful thinking?"

I'm always tempted to respond before thinking, just to keep everyone happy. I stopped. Stacy had been this unattainable social butterfly, and JenBen was someone who'd never opened up for me physically or mentally or emotionally, and Randi was this awesome erotic accident, and the others, Phyllis and Christine and whatever the hell their names were, had been these freaky, wondrous, sticky little episodes…

Lisby. Of course I'd been attracted to her. It's just that she'd belonged to Linc.

As if someone could have owned her.

A stupid conversation to have over breakfast. "Of course I am," I said, and sipped my orange juice.

"Then here's my proposition," she said, in the most reasonable voice possible, in the tone of someone proposing a plan to resurface your patio. "For a year, or some other period of time to be negotiated, or until we decide we can't stand each other, I'll keep my legs spread and lifted high—"

I choked and snorted juice out of my nose.

"—or in whatever position you like, and you will do your best to bang him right out of my mind."

I continued to choke, and the concerned waitress brought me a handful of paper napkins. She glared at Lisby as if it might be her fault...which in fact it was.

I sniffed and wiped my nose. "Jeez, Lisby," I said. "You sure know how to inject a note of romance into things."

"You've got a big advantage," she said. My eyes fixated on her nipples where they suddenly pushed through her blouse, and she followed the direction of my gaze and then looked up, smiling. "You saved my life." She interlinked her fingers and held them clasped beside her cheek, feigning the role of heroine in a melodrama, and adopted the cliched, breathless voice appropriate to the part: "Ah jes' cain't imagine how ah ever might repay you..."

"Christ, Lisby, if there's one thing that ever put me off about you, it's the whole way you get so clingy..."

"Fuck." She stood up so abruptly that her water toppled. "You stupid little fucker. I tried to make it so easy for him. I tried to make it so easy for *you*. You think this is all I am? Shit!" She threw a five-spot down on the table and stormed out of the restaurant before I could respond.

She'd peeled out of the parking lot before I could get out there; but as I pondered how to get from Beaumont to anywhere in the known universe, the long, clunky blue Impala wheeled back into the lot and idled up beside me.

I climbed in the passenger door.

"Take it out on me later, alright?" She drove all the way to the freeway before she spoke again. "It's not your fault," she said. "But maybe it isn't mine either."

She drove down I-10 with grim determination until I reached over and petted her neck. "Can you pull off?" I asked.

She drove with a fixed expression until she reached a rest stop. She wheeled us into a parking slot and stared at me as if I'd issued some challenge.

"Lisby. I'm not him. And I don't expect anything from you. Don't you see that I"—I pushed my fingers back through what remained of my hair—"I like you fine without anything. Without anything at all. And you don't owe me. It's…"

I choked up, unable to say the stupid pathetic sexist things I felt, unable to tell her that it was enough for me that she was still there, still breathing. Women and children into the lifeboats first. What the hell do they think that's about, and why do they take it so for granted?

She started crying first, which allowed me to hold her and squelch back my own tears. And the hell of it is, comforting her while suppressing my own feelings seemed right. It felt good to hold her, almost too good, and gave me a feeling of superiority.

Yet I was certain, in the core of my acid-soaked soul, that women had identical moments, when they bit back their feelings and soothed ours…

That's why it never ends, the war between men and women. To both sides, it's always been unfair.

And always will be.

I'm not stupid. I couldn't drive, but I'd loaded the trunk of the Impala with scraps of carpet and chunks of two-by-fours—the key ingredients, I'm told, for pulling yourself out of the sand.

As it turned out, we didn't need them. Lisby wheeled the car down the track along the rail line passing Cadiz. The tires spun occasionally, but she handled it with aplomb, jerking the steering wheel side to side as we slalomed through potential catastrophes.

It was farther than I'd remembered, but the three fire-blackened ironwoods were unmistakable.

When she switched off the ignition, the silence of the desert settled down on us like a thick fluid.

"Remind me," she said, "why are you doing this?"

There weren't words for it. My mind had been drawn back here again and again, as if my thoughts were in some sense free, but also orbiting some cardinal essence. This spot, this point on the globe, had become the hideous central spheroid of some alternate solar system that had me enslaved. "I just need to see it," I answered, as if that made sense.

I pushed open the passenger-side door and wobbled around the rear of the car, staring at the rip-rap-covered berm as though it might turn luminescent.

Things weren't as I'd remembered them. The slope wasn't as steep, the ditch not as deep, the edges not as sharp.

Lisby sat on the hood of the car and watched as I toed and kicked at the rocks, and eventually kicked and flailed, digging at the crushed stones with my fingers, flinging them aside until my nails were ripped.

I'd been in strange places: isolation, acid trips in the country, fucked-up parties.

This was the first time I'd thought I might be losing my mind.

I was prepared for horror. The stench of death. Flesh peeled from bone. Even dismemberment by animals, or eyes glaring accusingly from decayed, rotted faces.

Nothing. No bodies. No signs of bodies.

I sat down on the steep berm, crushed stone digging into my hips, and stared about in bewilderment.

Lisby, to her credit, left me alone, and it wasn't until the sun began to sink in the west that she said, "Should we look some place farther along?"

I stood, shaking my head. "No. No. This was it." I stared at the blackened ironwoods, accusingly, as if it might be their fault.

I staggered around the rear of the car, staring at my torn cuticles and bleeding fingertips. Wouldn't it ever end? Had I been crazy?

And then, lit by the sinking sun, red behind the San Bernardino Mountains, the boulder to the right of the car was illumined. Some vandal—I thought I knew who—had used yellow paint to leave a message:

L. E.
1970
Hi there.

Beneath this was a large yellow smile with crosshatched teeth, idiotic against the somber desert varnish of the stone. I laughed, sat down on the sand, leaned back against the side of the car, and laughed even harder as Lisby came around to read the words.

It was cold and clear on the evening we left. The car climbed out of LA, heading north on Highway 99. When I looked back the lights of the city winked back madly at the stars of the night sky, as if sharing some hidden joke.

We'd been listening to the radio, but reception vanished as we entered the long pass through the San Gabriels. "How far will we get tonight?" I asked.

"I'll go as far as you want," Lisby said.

I laughed, happy with how she'd put it. "But you're driving."

"Yep. Driving. Not navigating, not planning. I'm done with all that for a while."

We sat in a comfortable silence as she steered us through miles of gently curving highway, the black bulk of the mountains looming to either side, their mass felt more than seen in the darkness. At last, the dramatic drop of the Grapevine spilled us down into the endless bowl of the Central Valley.

In the long emptiness that led to Bakersfield, the tule fog rolled in. Lisby dimmed her high beams and dropped our speed. It was an uneven fog, a sculptured thing, with lobes and limbs, and I found it frightening.

"I guess I'm running away from things again," I said. "Story of my life. I don't seem to be able to stop it."

"Oh?" she asked. "And here I thought we were running towards something."

We caught up to a truck and trailer and Lisby stayed right behind it. When we emerged from the fog bank, half an hour later, she roared around the truck, beeping the horn as she passed, and the driver flashed his lights.

There was a high overcast to the sky now, hiding the stars, blackness to all sides of us, nothing to see.

Linc had told me that the important thing was to have vision—to look beyond the existing maps, to find the edges, to see the shape of tomorrow. Perhaps that's what some people are made for, to lead their fellows on toward the frontiers.

Not me. I saw Lisby in the green glow from the dashboard dials, every feature of her perfect and smooth. Ahead in the darkness, though, I could only see as far as the reach of the car's headlights, but I realized, for the first time, that this might be enough.

I curled up on the seat and lay my head on her lap. She took a hand from the wheel and caressed my cheek. I embraced sleep like a familiar lover, fragments of Sappho drifting down with me like leaves settling in a pond.

THE END

David T. Isaak (1954-2021) was an American author of both fiction and nonfiction.

Dr. Isaak held a BA in Physics and MA and PhD degrees in resource systems. His professional work spanned the globe, taking him to over forty countries. He co-authored three technical, nonfiction books on oil and international politics, and wrote numerous papers, monographs, and multiclient studies.

David had an eclectic life. His first major in college was music, and he played piano and flute. He was a certified Bikram yoga instructor, an accomplished vegetarian cook, a creative mixologist, and an avid reader of fiction and nonfiction alike. He was driven by great characters and story, original voices, and especially by his love of the craft of writing, all of which are reflected in his own writing.

David passed away in April 2021. The five novels he left behind are as diverse as his life. These novels form **The Isaak Collection**.

Sign up here to stay in touch and receive regular updates about **The Isaak Collection**:

https://theisaakcollection.co/IWillFollowYou

Keep reading for the first chapter of book 3 in *The Isaak Collection*

THINGS UNSEEN

THE ISAAK COLLECTION
DAVID T. ISAAK

Copyright© 2022 David T. Isaak and Pamela L. Blake
All rights reserved

***

1.

When they took me in for the formal identification, my first impulse was to deny it was her; she looked different somehow. Yet it had to be Claire: the tiny diamond-shaped scar that just touched the left of her upper lip was unmistakable.

She'd carried the scar more than thirty years. Dad had been beating our older brother with a belt, and seven-year-old Claire tried to grab his arm. The backswing caught her on the lip with the beltbuckle. I'd like to be able to report that seeing blood oozing from his daughter's mouth made Dad remorseful; if so, he hid it well.

Over the years the pale diamond of skin matured into an ornament of sorts, a strange beauty mark that stood out against Claire's tanned skin. Or had before—with this pallor the contrast lessened, as if she were a fading photograph of herself. Her eyes hadn't been closed completely, and it looked as if she peered out through her eyelashes, glancing a little to the side.

The left cheek showed a florid bruise. Her neck was ringed with uneven purple marks, garish under the fluorescent lights; but beneath these wine-dark blotches was a black tone that seemed to go deep into her flesh.

Naked under nothing but a sheet—it was impossible to believe she didn't feel the cold.

After answering their questions, I sat in the row of hard plastic chairs lining the hospital hallway, the kind of chairs you find in bus stations. I stared at the floor. If you looked just right, there was some kind of pattern in the blotchy tiles. I pushed my glasses up my nose and squinted. If you just barely closed your eyes and peered through your eyelashes the way Claire had, you could almost see a design lurking in the linoleum.

The deputy sheriff had left after the formalities, taking pains to ensure I understood Detective Bolles wanted to see me later in the day. The orderly stayed behind. He stood there in the hall and watched me with what must have been concern, a burly, ponytailed man with a golden name tag. *Leo Janus—Pathology.* A bright tattoo started in the soft flesh between his thumb and knuckles and swirled up to cover the whole thickness of his left arm, the hallucinatory colors disappearing into the sleeve of his green scrubs. I wondered how far it continued and why he had done it. Doesn't life leave enough marks on its own?

I felt Leo lower his bulk into the seat to my right. We sat quiet together in the hall. The faint sound of riotous laughter came from a television far away.

* * *

They insisted on giving me a tranquilizer and driving me back to my hotel. In my room at the Yucca Valley Inn, I sat on the corner of the bed. What was I supposed to do next?

Mourn? I wasn't sure how. My parents would have prayed, loudly and ostentatiously, but I wasn't a believer. Claire probably wasn't either—at any rate, I was pretty sure she didn't believe in the austere Lutheran God of our mother and father. What would Claire do if our positions were reversed, and I was under a sheet in the morgue?

I had no idea.

I wasn't even sure what had happened. All I had learned over the phone was that she had been found two days ago, murdered—strangled—in her home. The sheriff's department was stingy with the details. Perhaps I didn't press them very hard.

I'd driven up from San Diego, checked in just before dawn, and then headed straight to the hospital. Everything was still in the suitcase. It seemed wrong to unpack, somehow disrespectful, but what else was there to do? I've always been a reasonable, methodical person: waiting to unpack wouldn't change anything.

I'd brought enough clothes for three days; I folded these neatly into the top two drawers of the dresser. Toothbrush, toothpaste, and unwaxed dental floss I lined up to the left of the sink, but then I realized with annoyance the only place to plug in my electric razor was also on the left, so I had to move all my dental items to the right. No matter how you clean an electric razor there are always little whisker fragments, and I tried to make sure they stayed out of my toothbrush. I hardly needed a razor in the first place: I only used it to keep my beard trimmed and to shave about three square inches on my cheeks.

I found myself standing at the foot of the bed and looking at the empty suitcase. I didn't know how long the authorities would want me to stay out here, so I had brought plenty of work—and I had a conference paper that had to be e-mailed off in three days.

I unzipped the computer satchel, unloaded the stacks of papers and reprints, and took out the laptop and opened it atop the small desk. Motels all have tiny little desks, as if travelers never write anything more ambitious than postcards.

No reason not to knock off a few paragraphs right now.

I booted the computer, started the word processor, and brought up the conference paper, "Unconformities in Tertiary Sediments of the Sheep Rock Wilderness: Evidence for Post-Erosional Volcanism." I scrolled to the bottom. 'Despite what Everson postulated in 1943, there is '

There is. There is *what*? I must have known what I meant at the time I wrote it.

I turned to the stack of reprints on my left. On top were my bionotes for the conference, with a poorly reproduced photo of me at the head of the page. Everything about the picture was gray.

L. Walker Clayborne, PhD, is Ashford Professor of Geology and Geophysics in the Earth Sciences Department of the University of California, San Diego, and is considered one of the leading authorities on volcanic landforms of the Southwest. Dr. Clayborne completed his undergraduate studies at the University of Arizona—inexplicably my vision was blurring as I read—and received both his MS and PhD at Stanford University. After postdoctoral studies at the Hawaii Institute of Geophysics—my throat tightened, and it became hard to swallow—he took a position with USGS to develop a new emergency preparedness program—I could hardly breathe, an eon of tears seemed dammed up inside me—for major seismic and volcanic events in the Western states—oh God Claire I'm sorry, I'm so sorry, I'm so sorry—

I lurched to my feet and the chair fell over behind me. Blind, I stumbled to the bed, my fingers fumbling at my glasses, and threw myself down. I couldn't remember the last time I had cried, it had been years and years, even when Elizabeth and I divorced there were no tears on my part…

There were no tears now, either. I trembled on the verge. My whole body shook with the force of it, and I had to fight for each shuddering breath. My eyes burned. Part of me watched from a distance and noted the tranquilizer must finally be kicking in.

My trembling gradually subsided and I lay on my side somewhere between waking and sleep. Over on the desk my laptop gave a few urgent beeps, signaling that the battery had run low. When no one came to plug in the transformer, it shut itself down with a long electronic sigh.

* * *

I woke just before three in the afternoon. I took the time for a quick shower and trimmed my beard; at forty-four, there was already more gray than brown. I pulled on fresh khaki Dockers and a pressed shirt, topped this off with my old tweed jacket, and stepped out of the room.

I searched the parking lot for my Jeep before I remembered it was still at the hospital. My room was at the back of the motel, so I walked around to the front office. It was a stunningly clear desert afternoon, almost too warm for a coat. The parking lot and the front of the motel were decked out in full Christmas attire, the giant metal snowflakes and prancing reindeer bizarre against the backdrop of bare rock and Joshua trees.

As always in California it took a long time for the cab to come, but it was good I'd taken a taxi—the driver bothered to look at the card the officer had left. I would have driven to the County building over in Joshua Tree rather than the new sheriff's annex in Yucca Valley. This turned out to be a low-slung, concrete-block building with no architectural pretensions. As with most county buildings in the high desert, it was clear the designer had been told to build it fast and build it cheap.

Someone once said you know you're getting old when the policemen start to look young: the officer behind the counter was preposterously adolescent and blond. I explained I was there to see Detective Bolles; he replied politely that Bolles was with someone, but would be out in a few minutes. Would I take a seat?

I would. The waiting room was big, perhaps thirty feet wide, mostly empty concrete floor. The whole room seemed to have been designed to be as unwelcoming as possible. Were they afraid if they put in halfway-comfortable chairs that people would decide to hang out there and drink coffee?

Police radios crackled behind the desk. About ten feet away, a teenaged couple sat together. The boy leaned back in his chair, his body stiff, his arms crossed tight with his hands locked under his armpits; the girl had both feet up on the seat of her chair, and her arms hugged her knees to her chest. In the corner a middle-aged Hispanic man in well-tailored clothes sat rocking slowly in his seat, his gaze fixed in midair. I desperately wished I had brought something to read.

We all looked up as the heavy door by the front counter opened and a figure stepped through. It was obvious immediately it wasn't a police officer. The first impression was of a girl, short, slight, and seemingly lost in her dark, floor-length coat. The narrow, almost pointed face that stared out angrily between cascades of straight ebony hair corrected the impression—this was a grown woman, probably in her mid-thirties.

She stopped with her hand still on the door and stared at me as if in recognition. She looked straight into my eyes; her own were so black they seemed to be nothing but pupil. For a moment it seemed she was going to say something; but if so, she changed her mind, and instead tried to slam the door behind her.

A hand blocked the door with an outthrust palm and shoved it back open. Despite the blue suit and bolo tie, the man who stood in the doorframe was clearly a cop. He had a big, tight smile on his face, and he pitched his voice high to carry across the room. "Drop through whenever you feel like telling the truth, Mandy."

"Screw you, Rick!" she shouted back over her shoulder. She straightarmed the front doors open with surprising strength, and disappeared into the parking lot, her coat flying behind her like a cape.

The blond desk officer caught my eye and nodded toward the man in the doorway. I stood and walked toward him.

"Can I help you?" the man asked, wary.

"Detective Bolles? I'm Walker Clayborne." I held out a tentative hand.

"Oh…oh, yeah." He reached out and shook my hand, a single hard clench and pump. "Rick Bolles. Sorry about that. Having a bit of a hissy fit in the back there." He consulted his watch, then drummed on its face with the fingers of his free hand. "Is there any chance you could come back in an hour or so?" He lowered his voice, as if confessing some character flaw. "With one thing and another, I haven't had anything to eat since about five-thirty this morning, and I have a meeting in a couple of hours that'll run right through dinner… Or, if you want, we could grab a bite to eat together…"

"Sure." I didn't care where we talked, and I suddenly realized I hadn't eaten all day either.

"Okay. You just hang here for a second, let me grab a couple of things, and we'll go."

* * *

He came armed with a thick manila folder and a notepad, and ushered me out a side door labeled *Emergency Exit Only—Alarm Will Sound*. The sensors on the doorframe had been silenced by duct tape.

On the way across the parking lot he said, "Let me just say how sorry I am about your loss. It isn't easy to lose somebody, and losing them to murder is as hard as it gets." I made some noncommittal noise. The words sounded rehearsed, and I wondered how many times he had said them before. He didn't seem insincere, but there was an incongruity between his sympathetic words and his hyperkinetic body language. Even though he was probably five foot six and slender, he seemed as if his skin could barely contain him. His dark-brown hair gleamed with some sort of gel or spray. "I want to let you know we'll do everything we can. Claire was a nice person."

I was surprised by this. "You knew her?" For me, police detectives were people in movies or newspapers, not people you knew personally.

Bolles looked over at me without breaking stride. "Sure. Well enough to say hello, at any rate."

I felt foolish without being sure why. More to make conversation than out of real interest, I asked, "What was that woman back there so angry about?"

"Interesting you should bring that up. Means I don't have to." We arrived at a car, unmarked, one of those nondescript, oversized V-8s. Bolles looked at me across the tan roof of the car. The tip of his tongue came out and batted the center of his upper lip as he considered me. "You aren't by any chance acquainted with that woman, are you?" he asked. "Or, maybe, you remember her from somewhere?"

"No," I said, "why would you think that?"

"I don't. Just a passing thought." He tossed the keys up and caught them, and opened the driver's door. I heard a clunk as the door on my side unlocked.

The glove box on the passenger side had a large sticker pasted on it: Smoking Prohibited in This Vehicle by Order of the San Bernardino County Sheriff.

"Buckle up," he said. He backed the car out of its parking place, shifted, and then pulled us out onto Highway 62, headed east. "'That woman' paid us a visit to offer us information about your sister's murder." Bolles had very blue eyes, and every so often he widened them to underline his words. This showed the whites all the way around the blue and made him look slightly manic. "Problem is, you see, she claims the 'information' she's got came from a dream." He swung the car over into the fast lane, powered on past a pickup truck. To my annoyance, he lit a cigarette.

"A dream?" I was baffled. "So it's some kind of prank?"

"No, nothing so simple. She does have some facts—facts she shouldn't by rights know. Now, I pretty much doubt she got it from a dream—"

"What kind of facts?" I discreetly cracked the window.

"Now, Dr. Clayborne, you gotta understand I can't really give you details. In a homicide investigation, we try to hold back a few things, things only someone involved would know. Our friend Mandy knows some of those things. For starters, she knows what the murder weapon was." He accelerated us back into the right lane and gave a chuckle of exasperation. "The number of people who are supposed to know what the murder weapon was can be counted on my fingers, and I'd still have my thumbs left over. So either she really knows something about who did it; or, more likely—Shit, hang on a second here."

He braked quickly, just short of making the car skid, and pulled us up behind a patrol car. Two sheriffs were on the sidewalk arguing with a gaunt, bearded man dressed in Army fatigues. Bolles jumped out, threw his cigarette to the ground, slammed the door, and hustled over. All three of the other men towered over him, but there was no doubt he was in charge. The voices were indistinct, but Bolles talked loud and fast, pointing back and forth between the men, gesturing back over his shoulder with an outstretched thumb. He threw his hands in the air as if beseeching the sky, and then pointed at the patrol car. He gave a terse order and then stalked back to our car. As Bolles slid back onto his seat, I saw the sheriffs ushering the man into the patrol car, but doing so courteously enough.

"Christ on crutches." Bolles turned the key and pushed the accelerator. The engine roared, and we moved back into traffic. "Arresting pedestrians for public drunkenness? I wish we could get all of the drunks out of the cars and *onto* the sidewalks."

"Where are they taking him?"

"Home, if they know what's good for them." He drove in silence for a few moments, driving skillfully but a little too fast. He blew out a hard breath, pursing his lips. "Okay. In any case, either Mandy knows something about what happened, or, more likely, somebody in my shop or in the coroner's office has been talking out of school." He snorted. "Of course, let's not forget the possibility God Almighty revealed it to her. Take *that* to the DA and see what it gets you."

"So are you going to arrest her?" I felt lighter already. Maybe this would all be resolved quickly. "If she knows so much, maybe she's the murderer."

"Whoa, slow down. For starters, I know Mandy; she's not a killer. A little strange, but we'd be in big trouble if that were a crime around here. On top of it, women don't strangle people to death. Just don't happen. Check the statistics." Bolles thumbed open a tin of mints on the car seat, tossed one into his mouth, and offered the tin to me. I shook my head. The detective sniffed, and snapped the tin shut. "Chances are she's banging some blabbermouth in the coroner's office. But if not, we can learn more by keeping an eye on her than by locking her up. And what are we gonna lock her up for? Obstruction of justice? A half-assed charge if I ever saw one, and it never sticks anyway. Look at Nixon. Look at Clinton."

We wheeled into the dirt-and-gravel parking lot of a small diner on 62. More dirt than gravel: the dust rose up and clouded the windows when we parked. "Hop out." He opened his door. "By the way, I don't take just anybody to such nice places."

Faux farm kitchen layered over with Asian knickknacks and several posters of American flags. Bolles behaved like a regular, grabbing menus from behind the cash register and leading us to a table before the waitress made it out from the kitchen.

I ordered breakfast, a safe bet anywhere. Bolles requested a health-plate lunch special that included cottage cheese and a soy patty. Our server, whose name tag read, *Ng*, flirted with him while she poured our coffee.

Bolles took a drink of scalding coffee and sighed with gratitude. "I appreciate your getting here on such short notice; I understand you were just leaving on vacation."

"Actually, I was just leaving on a sabbatical."

Bolles made a noise which could have meant he didn't know what a sabbatical was, or that he didn't see any significant difference between that and a vacation. "Well, let's start by getting some background."

"Of course," I said, "but I really don't think I know anything that will be useful to you."

"Well, you might be surprised. Despite what the TV has this country thinking about 'random violence,' ninety-nine times out of a hundred the murderer is somebody who knew the victim. Suppose you just start telling me about your family, about Claire's life—friends, acquaintances, boyfriends...especially boyfriends."

* * *

Ever try to summarize the history of your family to a stranger? The fact my audience was poised to take notes made it even harder.

We ate, and I told him what I could. Our childhood in the suburbs of Phoenix. Our parents, both dead now, conservative and religious. Three siblings: Edgar, the oldest, brilliant in every way; me, in the middle, not nearly as smart as Edgar; and Claire, the baby, the rebel.

Edgar had sailed through school in theoretical physics, first at Johns Hopkins, later at Berkeley; for the last fifteen years, he had been happily ensconced at Cambridge, and showed no signs of wanting to move back to the US. I, on the other hand, had more or less trudged through college, smart enough to get good grades and acquire a decent transcript, but never able to mimic Edgar's effortlessness. Intellectually, if Edgar was a figure skater, then I was a guy scrunching along in snowshoes.

Claire was another story entirely. Her interests were wide-ranging and seemingly erratic. Starting in junior high school, one week it would be anthropology, the next, Pythagorean philosophy. One day she was a committed communist; the next, an Ayn-Rand libertarian. In the early days, her enthusiasm was infectious; even if you thought her latest theories ranked with the belief that the moon was a wheel of brie, the force of her conviction was somehow thrilling.

As she reached her late teens, however, things turned ugly. Edgar and I were both closet atheists by the time we were in high school. (Well, actually Edgar calls himself an agnostic; he claims anything else is unscientific. After all, he says, atheism is a belief too.) But both of us kept our opinions pretty much to ourselves—is there anything more pointless than arguing with someone about religion?—and we even went through catechism and confirmation without a murmur of dissent. Claire just wasn't built to keep anything to herself, and she fought ferociously with my mother about religion and faith. Edgar and I were away at college for most of this, but we received constant telephone reports from the warring parties: my mother's tearful complaints and worries about Claire's soul, Claire's scornful accounts of our parents' hypocrisy.

I could agree with most of what Claire said about our parents' faith, at least in principle, but I might have been more sympathetic to her side of the story if she had not adopted weird beliefs of her own. At first I thought this was just to antagonize Mom—it was no doubt pretty aggravating to have a Hindu, a Scientologist, a Lord-Knows-What under one's roof. But as time went on, it became apparent to me that Claire had a genuine mystical bent she wasn't likely to outgrow.

She finished high school early, with a spotty transcript, and promptly stage-managed a fight that neatly resulted in her expulsion from our parents' house. She spent a thoroughly disagreeable—for both of us—week sleeping on the couch in my Tucson apartment, where she quarreled with me about everything from God to socialized medicine; and, although her intellect was undisciplined and scattered, I came to the uneasy realization that maybe *both* of my siblings were a lot brighter than I.

I saw her only occasionally over the next few years. Mom and Dad almost never saw her. She was in and out of colleges (all second-rate schools), and seldom stayed long in one place. I received cryptic postcards from the most unlikely of towns, ranging from Tulsa, Oklahoma, to Port Moresby, Papua New Guinea. I had a few flying visits from her, and she managed to drop in on Edgar a few times; eventually, of course, there was Mom's funeral. She didn't come to Dad's.

She laughed when I said I was getting married, and didn't come to the wedding, though she did send a carved Senegalese fertility charm; when Elizabeth left me two years later, Claire observed she was surprised it had lasted more than six months—the implication being, I think, that it was my fault. Claire's day-to-day life was vague to me; I had the impression of men, a lot of them, and probably drugs of some sort. Somewhere along the way, she buckled down and finished her BA, and eventually received some kind of graduate degree or license in social work, but she never seemed to find full-time work—or, if she did, she never stayed long at the same job. She often borrowed small sums from me, but seldom repaid them.

She had been in the Yucca Valley area for about six years—some sort of record for her, I imagine—and it seemed she might stay in the High Desert permanently. She once even steered a conversation around to the subject of loaning her money for a down payment on a house; I had quickly squelched this idea, and now I felt a little ashamed.

* * *

Bolles had listened quietly to my monologue, making a few notes, but toward the end I caught him glancing at his watch. "Can you fill me in on the rest on the way back to the station? I need to head out pretty soon here."

We each paid our own check, Bolles keeping up a steady stream of pleasantries with Ng.

Bolles had just popped the locks on the car when his eyes focused somewhere over my shoulder, and he froze like a bird-dog on point. "Do me a favor," he said in a conversational tone, eyes still staring past me, "get in the back seat and just play it cool."

"Cool?"

"Just— Oh, don't say anything, and act like a cop." He put his fingers in his teeth and whistled, a nasty, loud shriek. I started to look over my shoulder, but the slightest shake of his head told me not to do so. He pointed his index finger over my shoulder in a double thrust—*you, you*—and then jabbed it down at the passenger-side door—*there, there*.

Act like a cop? I opened the back door, slid in, and shut the door behind me. Out the window I saw a scruffy man in his mid-thirties, hesitating by the crosswalk that ran across Highway 62. The man shook his head, but some gesture Bolles made must have changed his attitude. His eyes searched the highway as his palms rubbed up and down the sides of his grubby jeans. He shot one last look across the road, and then ran to within a few yards of the car. His voice was shaky. "Hey, man, this is really fucked up."

Bolles opened the driver's-side door. "Get in the car, Jesse." Bolles climbed in and pulled the door closed.

Jesse hesitated, and then made a dash for the passenger-side door. He opened it, glanced side to side, then ducked in and slammed the door. He couldn't have been more obtrusive about the whole thing if he had been wearing bells and safety orange.

Jesse's eyes widened when he saw me in the back seat. "Who the hell is this?" Jesse demanded in a whisper. "I don't know this guy."

"Let me worry about who he is. This guy's got nothing to do with it."

Jesse continued to stare at me. Even from the front seat, he smelled of stale alcohol, the kind that sweats from the pores of heavy drinkers on the morning after. "What the hell you calling me off the street for? Can't we get in my car instead?"

"Oh, good idea Jesse. That wouldn't look suspicious at all. There's a dozen reasons I might have made you get in this car. How would you explain my being in your car?"

"Well, what the fuck is so important?"

"Gee, I don't know. Seems to me maybe you didn't show up the last two times you were supposed to see me—don't call—don't return my calls. Basically seems like you've been hiding from me."

Jesse hunched forward. "Look, man, Joop and his bunch keep talking about how somebody's gotta be giving you guys stuff. It's like they're saying it around me just to spook me and see if I'll say something. I'm scared pissless."

Bolles made a so-what gesture with his hands. "They probably *are* trying to spook you. They know something hinky is going on, so they're probably trying to spook *everybody*. Don't be so paranoid."

"You don't understand, man. I get these phone calls, and there's somebody there, but they don't say anything; they just breathe for a while and then hang up."

"Probably a secret admirer. Maybe you should get caller ID."

Jesse patted his jacket pockets, found a pack of Camel Lights, and tilted one out.

"Hey!" Bolles snapped. Jesse jumped. "I know you're not the shiniest ornament on the Christmas tree, but can't you read?" He pointed at the no-smoking decal above Jesse's knees. "No smoking in this car. It's the law."

Jesse stuffed the cigarette into a jacket pocket without bothering to find the pack again. "Listen, I'm scared of Joop, he's fuckin' nuts. I need to get out of this shit."

Bolles lifted his hands, and for just a moment I was sure he intended to shoot his arms out and grab Jesse by the throat. Instead, he leaned across the seat, as if telling a secret. He draped his arm across Jesse's shoulders; Jesse jumped at the contact. "Jesse. You're scared of Joop?" His voice became very quiet. "You should be a lot more scared of me, you little fuck. Those disability payments you're scamming off the State? You're gonna need 'em for real if you screw this up. You want your PO to violate you on something? You want to bounce back with half a dozen new charges on top of it?" He leaned in closer, widened his eyes, and smiled. "Try me," he whispered, "just try me."

Jesse started to say something, but Bolles used his comradely arm around the shoulder to pull him closer. "Nobody else is on your side, Jesse. Try to be a little more cooperative." His voice was calm, reasonable, like a school counselor who is a little disappointed. "Try and be a little more productive. And try not to piss me off. Above all, when I set a meet, we meet. Right?"

Jesse mumbled placating things, and he left in a hurry, tugging his jacket around him.

Bolles leaned back against the driver's-side door, apparently at ease. He lit a cigarette. "Children, dogs, and horses," he said. "You have to use language they understand. Sometimes I hate this pissheaded job." He gestured for me to come up into the front seat and then started up the engine.

I asked if he could drop me at the hospital so I could pick up the Jeep. On the way, he quizzed me about Claire's friends, lovers, involvement with drugs. I couldn't help much. Even though my field work brought me out to the area frequently, I didn't see much of Claire when I passed through.

Bolles' voice stayed even, but I imagined I could hear growing exasperation. "Did she mention any other men you can remember? Was she living with anyone?" He glanced over at me, and I shrugged my shoulders helplessly. "Was she involved with any kind of religious cults or groups?"

"If there were any out here, then the chances are pretty good she was involved with them," I said. "I don't know anything specific."

"Did she mention anything about anyone she might have had contact with at the prison?" Bolles asked.

My astonishment must have been plain. I tried to envision Claire as—as what, a prison guard? A prisoner?

Bolles pursed his lips. "You didn't know she worked part time as a counselor at Eagle Mountain?"

I shook my head. "No...she never said anything about it."

"Ohh-kayy, then." He braked, and I realized we were in the hospital parking lot. "Think things over; call me if anything comes to you that might be useful." His voice said he'd decided I was a dead end. He handed me two business cards, even though I already had one of his. "The other card there is Wilson, our evidence guy; he'll be in touch with you regarding your sister's personal effects and other arrangements."

I thanked him for the ride and opened the door, but before my feet hit the pavement he added, "Oh. Appreciate it if you could give me your brother's phone number in, England, was it? I'd like to give him a call."

And why not? There was every reason to suppose somebody who lived halfway around the world knew more about Claire than I did. "I'll have to look it up and phone you; I have it on my computer, I imagine." Close family. "Umm—maybe I should stay around for a few weeks in case I can help with the investigation or something…?"

"That won't be necessary," Bolles answered. "Fact of the matter is, I'd discourage it. Just make sure we have your numbers."

* * *

The winter sun had already dipped behind Mount San Jacinto by the time Bolles dropped me at my Jeep. The long shadows pointed east, and I followed them a dozen miles to the entry gate at Joshua Tree National Park. I needed to spend time somewhere familiar, to stand on firm ground.

About seventy million years ago, huge stretches of California experienced a massive episode of intrusive volcanism. Rocks were sucked down toward the hot fault lines, melted, and then pushed up to form gigantic bulges just beneath the surface. When the blanketing soils eroded away, they exposed giant blocks of white, grainy stone which can still be seen from the Sierra Nevadas down to Joshua Tree.

I pulled over to the edge of the road and stepped out. The sun was gone now, but the rising moon provided plenty of light against the bright rocks and gravels. It had turned chilly, and I pulled my arms in close to my body as I crunched across the sand.

Claire once remarked that when night fell in the desert, you could immediately feel the cold of outer space seeping in. I had pointed out that in reality the Earth was reradiating its stored heat into the clear sky; there was nothing above the atmosphere from which to "seep." Tonight, though, I could see her point; it did feel as if a chilled fluid were leaking down from the black sky.

At the first large jumble of rocks my feet picked their way up the easiest surfaces, avoiding any paths that would require me to remove my hands from my coat pockets. Sixty million years ago, these had been sharp cubes and towers, like gargantuan building blocks. When I was still working on my dissertation, Claire had visited me out here. She had been in awe of the weird beauty of the place, and had spoken passionately about the strange power that had sculpted the rocks around us.

I'd explained that everything she saw was the result of low temperature—rather ironic, I suppose, for a desert landscape. When night falls, the moisture in the air accumulates on the rocks, especially on any sharp edges, and hydrolyzes the rocks to a kaolinite clay. Clay expands when moist, and this chips away at the rocks, and removes the corners and edges first, forever rounding and softening the shapes, like an ice cube held under a running tap. The real sculptor here was the cold.

She laughed and told me I was describing the chisel, not the sculptor.

I knew so little about her, really. Maybe it's like that with relatives; because we grow up around them, we don't have to get to know them. With friends, there's a process of discovery, as we accumulate facts and insights; with family, it now seemed to me there were mostly assumptions and prejudices.

Atop a large boulder I stared out at the rising moon. All alone here in the darkness, but with the glow of Los Angeles in the sky over the mountains. No wife, no children, both parents gone, my brother on the other side of the Atlantic.

I suddenly needed to understand Claire, to know her; maybe in some strange way, to make it up to her. I needed to know what her life was about, how she lived, what drew her to this place. I knew the contours of the High Desert better than I knew the curves of my own face; but, for the very first time, I wanted to see them through someone else's eyes.

And I wanted to know what had really happened to her.

CPSIA information can be obtained
at www.ICGtesting.com
Printed in the USA
LVHW042145210723
753026LV00003B/643

9 781958 840054